Joan
of
Arc

Joan
of
Arc

Edited and Introduced by
Imogen Corrigan

General Editor: Jake Jackson

FLAME TREE
PUBLISHING

This is a FLAME TREE Book

FLAME TREE PUBLISHING
6 Melbray Mews
Fulham, London SW6 3NS
United Kingdom
www.flametreepublishing.com

First published 2024
Copyright © 2024 Flame Tree Publishing Ltd

24 26 28 27 25
1 3 5 7 9 10 8 6 4 2

ISBN: 978-1-80417-717-4
Ebook ISBN: 978-1-80417-962-8

Cover image created by Flame Tree Studio based on elements from a bronze medal
depicting Joan of Arc, by Pierre Roche (pseudonym of Fernand Massignon), 1918.

All other inside images courtesy of Shutterstock.com and the following: Morphart Creation,
zizi_mentos, artform.

This book is an edited and abridged version, with a new introduction, of *The Life of Joan
of Arc* by Anatole France, translated by Winifred Stephens, in Two Vols, published by
John Lane, 1909.

Designed and created in the UK | Printed and bound in China

Contents

Series Foreword

STRETCHING BACK to the oral traditions of thousands of years ago, tales of heroes and disaster, creation and conquest have been told by many different civilizations in many different ways. Their impact sits deep within our culture even though the detail in the tales themselves are a loose mix of historical record, transformed narrative and the distortions of hundreds of storytellers.

Today the language of mythology lives with us: our mood is jovial, our countenance is saturnine, we are narcissistic and our modern life is hermetically sealed from others. The nuances of myths and legends form part of our daily routines and help us navigate the world around us, with its half truths and biased reported facts.

The nature of a myth is that its story is already known by most of those who hear it, or read it. Every generation brings a new emphasis, but the fundamentals remain the same: a desire to understand and describe the events and relationships of the world. Many of the great stories are archetypes that help us find our own place, equipping us with tools for self-understanding, both individually and as part of a broader culture.

For Western societies it is Greek mythology that speaks to us most clearly. It greatly influenced the mythological heritage of the ancient Roman civilization and is the lens through which we still see the Celts, the Norse and many of the other great peoples and religions. The Greeks themselves learned much from their neighbours, the Egyptians, an older culture that became weak with age and incestuous leadership.

It is important to understand that what we perceive now as mythology had its own origins in perceptions of the divine and the rituals of the sacred. The earliest civilizations, in the crucible of the Middle East, in the Sumer of the third millennium BC, are the source to which many of the mythic archetypes can be traced. As humankind collected together in cities for the first time, developed writing and industrial-scale agriculture, started to irrigate the rivers and attempted to control rather than be at the mercy of its environment, humanity began to write down its tentative explanations of natural events, of floods and plagues, of disease.

Early stories tell of Gods (or god-like animals in the case of tribal societies such as African, Native American or Aboriginal cultures) who are crafty and use their wits to survive, and it is reasonable to suggest that these were the first rulers of the gathering peoples of the earth, later elevated to god-like status with the distance of time. Such tales became more political as cities vied with each other for supremacy, creating new Gods, new hierarchies for their pantheons. The older Gods took on primordial roles and became the preserve of creation and destruction, leaving the new gods to deal with more current, everyday affairs. Empires rose and fell, with Babylon assuming the mantle from Sumeria in the 1800s BC, then in turn to be swept away by the Assyrians of the 1200s BC; then the Assyrians and the Egyptians were subjugated by the Greeks, the Greeks by the Romans, and so on, leading to the spread and assimilation of common themes, ideas and stories throughout the world.

The survival of history is dependent on the telling of good tales, but each one must have the 'feeling' of truth, otherwise it will be ignored. Around the firesides, or embedded in a book or a computer, the myths and legends of the past are still the living materials of retold myth, not restricted to an exploration of origins. Now we have devices and global communications that give us unparalleled access to a diversity of traditions. We can find out about Indigenous American, Indian, Chinese and tribal African mythology in a way that was denied to our ancestors; we can find connections, match the archaeology, religion and the mythologies of the world to build a comprehensive image of the human adventure.

The great leaders of history and heroes of literature have also adopted the mantle of mythic experience, because the stories of historical figures – Cyrus the Great, Alexander, Genghis Khan – and mytho-poetic warriors such as Beowulf achieve a cultural significance that transcends their moment in the chronicles of humankind. Myth, history and literature have become powerful, intwined instruments of perception, with echoes of reported fact and symbolic truths that convey the sweep of human experience. In this series of books we are glad to share with you the wonderful traditions of the past.

Jake Jackson
General Editor

Introduction to Joan of Arc

J EANNE D'ARC (known in Britain as Joan of Arc) is one of the most famous names in medieval history, remarkably so since she was neither royal nor noble, she was active for a relatively short time and she was female. That is not the usual profile for someone who became so well-known later. Endless myths swirl around her character, but the facts are that she was not a low-born peasant, nor was she given command of an army when she was a teenager with no military experience; but she did inspire many. It could be said that she was used by the French for as long as she was useful and then largely dropped. There has been much discussion as well about her hearing voices that she believed were sent by God; many have tried to diagnose her condition, but at the time that was not relevant. Her story is heroic and romantic, but it is also a story of gruelling travel, horrific warfare, scorn and high courage.

Anatole France's seminal work on Jeanne d'Arc was published in French in two volumes in 1907 and is presented here very much abridged. The full text is highly recommended to anyone interested in Joan of Arc and the background to her remarkable mission; what follows here is hoped to act as an appetizer. France's work has been reduced to about one third of the original length, but without (it is hoped) losing any sense of the story.

The Original Sources

France's account of Joan of Arc, the Maid of Orléans, is based firmly in the reference books and manuscripts available to him in 1907. Naturally he uses her 'Trial of Condemnation' account a great deal, a gift to any student of this period. In fact, the trial document is not a verbatim transcript and probably was not formally written down until 1435 at the earliest, Joan having been burned at the stake on

30 May 1431. At least five copies of the trial document were made, three of which are extant and are held in Paris. Minutes were taken during the trial and must have been done with some care, which may have been because of Joan herself. She had an acute mind; it seems that if she was asked a question twice or if old ground was being re-covered, she would simply turn to the notary to ask him to read out whatever she had said before. This might have seemed cocksure, pedantic or even infuriating, but the clerks will have realized that they would look incompetent if they could not do this. Perhaps they thought she was making fools of them.

Whenever the minutes were written up, they were useful at her 'Rehabilitation Trial' a quarter of a century after her death. Because Joan was questioned minutely on when she first heard the voices, whether or not she had eaten that day, what she was doing (farmwork or sewing) and especially about why she dressed as a man, we know many small details about her life and something of her character. The dramatic story aside, this is one of the reasons why Joan gripped public imagination much later on as it is rare to have such insight into how an ordinary person lived (although she was not a typical village girl!).

The other main documents that France used were Jean Chartier's *Chroniques de Charles VII* (written 1479–83, revised in 1858) and Vallet de Viriville's 1859 edition of the *Chronique de la Pucelle* (first published in 1661; 'la Pucelle' meaning 'the Maiden'). The original *Chronique de la Pucelle* document was written by Guillaume Cosinot in the fifteenth century and is an important contemporary source for the period. Lastly, the *Journal du siège d'Orléans (1428–29)* was written during the English siege of Orléans as a day-to-day diary from the French perspective. It was re-edited in 1896 by Paul Charpentier and Charles Cuissard. France makes in-depth reference to these documents and many others; his narrative is based on as much truth as the hype around Joan allowed.

Joan of Arc's Story Resurrected

France was a poet, novelist, playwright and journalist, winning the Nobel Prize for Literature in 1921 in recognition 'of his brilliant literary achievements, characterized as they are by a nobility of style, a profound human sympathy, grace, and a true Gallic temperament'. In all his prodigious works, *The Life of Joan of Arc* was his only foray into historical biography, and it is worth considering why he might have done so.

Although Joan is presented as a symbol of France today, and one of its patron saints, she was not canonized until 1920 (it is noticeable that Anatole France frequently refers to her as a saint even though she was not declared one for over a decade). Many images were made of her in her lifetime, especially on medals used both as souvenirs as well as spiritual totems. It seems that none have survived, although it may be that they have yet to be identified since they would have shown an apparently male figure, probably wearing armour. There is one thumbnail drawing of her in the margin of the condemnation trial transcript, but we have no way of telling how accurate it was (let us hope not completely accurate since it was little more than a doodle). There are thousands of statues and images of her in France today, but extremely few that pre-date the end of the nineteenth century. A poster made by Georges de Feure in 1896 is one of the earliest images of Joan and indicates that interest in her story was being rekindled.

It is not known if France wrote the biography of his own volition or if he was requested to do so. Either way, he did a phenomenal amount of research, although he also assumes a high level of knowledge by the reader. The fact of this brilliant, engaging writer producing such a great work certainly helped to bring Joan back to the public's attention.

After the Great War, the French population needed a boost. They had just had a major war fought largely on their land and their losses were greater than those of Britain. They had truly lost a generation, which impacts their demographics to this day. They wanted someone heroic, romantic, patriotic and Catholic to admire, someone who would catch the imagination – and it did not hurt that she had been burned at the stake by the English. George Bernard Shaw wrote his play, *Saint Joan*, in 1923, presumably on the back of what was then recent publicity about her.

French delay in appreciating Joan of Arc's talents, and the combined corrosive effects of climate and warfare on the land, means that it is rarely possible to see the ground or buildings as she saw them 600 years ago. Her house in Domrémy (today called Domrémy-la-Pucelle in her honour) still stands – a stone house, not a peasant's shack. Reims Cathedral still stands, albeit almost brought to its knees by warfare. If you go to Orléans, even the house Joan of Arc rented in 1429 is not only a reproduction, but a two-thirds scale model set some 600 metres from where the real building was (the original was demolished to make way for a new road before the Second World War). At Vaucouleurs, where her military 'mission' began, only an archway remains, and most of the numerous places of Joan's activities are marked simply by a statue of her either standing or on a horse. We must rely on contemporary writings where they exist, and this is where Joan's story stands out: the last two years of her life were remarkably well documented, especially for someone of her social standing.

Love Her or Hate Her – Joan's Reputation

In modern parlance, Joan of Arc is something of a Marmite subject. Readers of this book may be divided into those who love her and others who find her immensely annoying but possibly cannot quite say why. It was the same during her lifetime, but it is hard not to be intrigued by anyone who *allegedly* persuaded a prince to give them command of an army at the age of 17. When that person is a young woman living in the male-dominated period of the fifteenth century, then the story becomes fascinating. There is no evidence – and nor does Anatole France claim that there is – that she commanded an army: that is her myth. She did inspire many individuals in the army, which is something that France explores in depth. It is also accepted that before Joan arrived at Chinon, it was basically understood that English and Burgundian forces would beat the French forces: it was just a matter of time.

The crown of France was in dispute at the time between the Dauphin Charles, son and heir of the Valois King Charles VI (the Mad) and supporters of the English King Henry VI, who was still a child. His regent in English-owned French lands was his oldest uncle, John, Duke of Bedford. The Dauphin Charles had been born in 1403 and was therefore about nine years older than Joan. He was the eleventh child of the mad King Charles VI, and sounds to have been a thoroughly spoiled brat, but he did survive to adulthood, which many of the others plainly did not. Henry VI of

England's armies were in alliance with those of Philip the Good, Duke of Burgundy (whose father John the Fearless had been assassinated in 1419 by partisans of the Dauphin). Henry's army was occupying much of the northern part of France, not least the area in which Joan lived, so she was brought up against a background of raids and sudden alarms.

The Dauphin's cause seemed hopeless largely because of the simple fact that, five years after his father's death, he still had not been crowned (he was only 14 when his father died, but could still legally have been crowned). Reims was the traditional place for the investiture of French kings, and that was well within territory held by his enemies. As long as the Dauphin remained unanointed, the rightfulness of his claim to be king of France was open to challenge.

Domrémy was then on the frontier between the France of the Anglo-Burgundians and that of the Dauphin, so Joan, along with her fellow villagers, had already evacuated their homes because of Burgundian threats more than once; she was brought up fully in the knowledge of the tussle between the Dauphin and the English/Burgundians. Anatole France paints a romantic picture of Joan's life as a poor peasant girl, but we can see that this was not the case. Indeed, her father is said to have partnered together with other Domrémians to buy a disused château that was up for auction, simply to have somewhere safe to take refuge if necessary. It is likely that he contributed the lion's share of the funds needed. Her father was Jacques d'Arc, described in a document of 1423 as sergeant of the village; he therefore took rank between the mayor and the provost, and was in charge of collecting the taxes, among other things. Joan's family were not peasants, but neither were they nobility as other writers have occasionally claimed. The family had a strong local accent, which we know from amendments made in the margins of the transcript of her trial: the scribe has noted that he mistook the pronunciation of some words and letters that would tie in with the way French was pronounced around Domrémy.

We also know that Joan was strong-willed, even before the voices of Saint Michael, Saint Catherine and Saint Margaret told her to go to the Dauphin (the latter two saints' voices would remain with her throughout her journey to the pyre). There is the curious case of her being sued for breach of promise when she was about 16. This happened in 1428, when it seems her parents had promised her in marriage, with which she refused to comply. It may be they hoped that if she married, she might be distracted from what must have seemed to be wild and dangerous ideas. When Joan was accused, she had to go to Toul, 20 miles away, to defend her case in court. She said that she had been betrothed without her consent and therefore could not stand in breach of promise, and she won. This single incident shows us much of her character and confidence at a time when most young women would have found themselves obliged to go into a possibly loveless marriage. Later, this was held as evidence that she had always been wilful – perhaps not without reason.

Voices from God

Joan would have been much bolstered by the voices and guiding messages from God that began when she was 13. Interestingly, she was asked at her trial if she had eaten that day the voices first appeared, and one can see where the questioners were going with the query since it was not unusual in those days for people to starve themselves in the hope of gaining greater spirituality. Light-headedness could result in hallucinations, which might in turn lead to hearing voices or seeing visions. The voices were an important and sustaining factor for the rest of her life. They appear to have instructed her, but not always advised her, when she most needed it. It is impossible to know how genuine the voices were; could she have heard them once, but then continued to use them? Were they with her at all times? We cannot say, although it does seem that they were so much part of her everyday life that she spoke to them regularly, almost mundanely, as though they were part of some routine. It is interesting that no contemporary account denies that she could have heard them in the first place, nor do they ever ask why they also cannot hear them; it is how people reacted to Joan's voices that was relevant. In the same spirit, Anatole France presents the voices as being viable and certainly real to Joan.

Joan was not the only person who heard voices in medieval times. There are comparisons to be made with Margery Kempe of King's Lynn who lived contemporaneously, and who also had a parallel life going on in her head that was completely real and instructive to her, as well as Angela of Foligno (born c. 1250 near Assisi) who had similar experiences. These are but two of many. Some people feared these women lest they were witches, some found them utterly exasperating, but many – possibly the majority – held them in great respect. In each case, sceptical men in authority were won over by women seeing visions. What sets Joan apart is what she did in practical terms and how she used the voices as a distinct authority in all her actions.

Her initial mission was to drive the English out of France and to get the Dauphin anointed at Reims. Later, the voices added that she must raise the siege of Orléans. For this she needed permission and assistance; the road to Chinon and the Dauphin was some 300 miles, much of it through enemy territory. This she sought from Robert de Baudricourt who was captain of the nearest large town of Vaucouleurs. He did not agree instantly – she had to make at least two applications to him.

Eventually, Joan left Vaucouleurs on 13 February 1429 dressed in men's clothes for her own safety (and because it was practical). Later, and indeed, throughout her venture, her wardrobe was a serious issue and something that was repeatedly addressed during her trial. It is difficult for us today to understand why and how so much hinged on whether or not she should dress as a woman. At one point in her trial, she did revert to wearing a dress and covering her hair, but then insisted on wearing trousers again, which most certainly did not help her case, even if it did cause her to be described by George Bernard Shaw as the 'pioneer of rational dressing for women'.

It was held to be a heresy if a woman dressed in men's clothing and vice versa. Doctrinally speaking, she was safe to disguise herself as a page during a journey through enemy territory and she was safe to wear armour during battle. The *Chronique de la Pucelle* states that it deterred molestation while she was in the field, although that might not have been likely considering the very high esteem and/or fear in which she was held. Joan herself pointed out, when she was cross-examined at Poitiers at the start of her mission, that the clergy there agreed that if she had a mission to do a man's work, it was fitting that she should dress the part. France cites Deuteronomy xxii, 5: 'The woman shall not wear that which pertaineth unto a man, neither shall a man put on a woman's garment: for all that do so are abomination unto the Lord thy God.' He also points out instances going back into ancient history in which women were anathematized if they dressed as men and cut their hair short. As her story progressed, it is hard not to wonder at Joan's obstinacy in refusing to stop wearing men's clothes, especially towards the end when she knew that she was facing death.

On the way to Chinon, she dictated letters to be sent to the Dauphin so that he was not caught off-guard but, even so, it is impressive that she managed to gain access to him within a few days. There is a story that he hid in plain sight from her to see if she could recognize him, possibly without ever having seen a picture of him. This she achieved, which is why some have claimed that the two were in some way related. They were not. Joan impressed the Dauphin, but there was always a concern about heresies and whether this maid was some sort of sorceress. They would also have been cautious lest the Dauphin was being made into a figure of ridicule, so it was decided to send Joan to Poitiers, which was the temporary centre of the Dauphin's administration. She was thoroughly examined by theologians, academics and respectable women (Joan's virginity was an important factor in her credibility). After several weeks, the churchmen suggested that in view of the desperate situation of Orléans, which had been under English siege for months, any straw should be clutched at – obviously it was not phrased like that. It was at this time that Joan famously said, 'I shall last one year, hardly more'. In fact, she lasted almost 15 months and then spent a year in captivity before being burned at the stake.

Joan in Battle

At last Joan arrived at Orléans, which had been under siege for 200 days. Nine days later, on 8 May 1429, the siege was lifted. Many of her prophecies came true around this time, including that she would be wounded (perhaps not such a difficult one to foresee) but all of these things combined to make her an immediate heroine to the people. Others were less convinced, notably the so-called Bastard of Orléans, Duke John, whose name does not imply his temperament but his illegitimacy. It was not considered an insult at the time. He did not believe in Joan's spirituality and most certainly neither expected nor required her to be involved in military matters, but he did see that she could be useful as a morale booster and rallying point. He routinely failed to include her in planning meetings and did not bother to brief her on decisions made, not, I suspect, to undermine her, but it simply would not have crossed his mind that such a young, inexperienced girl should or could offer anything useful. Likewise, the soldiery would not have been willing to be under her command. Her presence was fine, even uplifting, but her military authority was not.

That said, Joan was present at various battles, for instance Jargeau, Meung-sur-Loire, Patay and Beaugency. Several more swift victories led to Charles VII's coronation at Reims on 17 July 1429 and thus settled the disputed succession to the throne, so she delivered her promise to him. He was crowned with Joan by his side. What is not clear is why she continued with her quest rather than simply returning to her village. She had achieved her main aim, but perhaps she did not want to go back to life in Domrémy. She had had status, months of intense drama and travelled hundreds of miles which would have been hard to give up. It is likely that at this point, she starts being a thorn in the newly crowned king's side. How much would he want a constant reminder that a possibly unstable, female teenager had achieved what he had not?

More battles being achieved, Joan was captured by the Burgundians at Compiègne on 23 May 1430 and subsequently sold to the English for 10,000 francs, that being the practice of the day. It is noticeable that even though there was an element of public hysteria about her being taken, no one – not even the Dauphin – tried to buy her back. She was taken to Rouen, the centre of the English occupational government, where she was held prisoner. Physically courageous as ever, she tried to escape by leaping from a 70-foot-high tower, which she survived.

Tried – and Re-tried – for Heresy

Joan was tried for heresy, although it was politically motivated. The Duke of Bedford claimed the throne of France for his nephew Henry VI. Joan had been responsible for the rival coronation, so to condemn her was to undermine her king's legitimacy, especially if it could be shown that she was a heretic and/or a witch.

Legal proceedings began on 9 January 1431, continuing until the end of May, a long and exhausting time for all and a frightening time for Joan who had no one to speak for her but herself. That said, she acquitted herself well and remained unafraid of the authority of the daunting array of academic and theological minds facing her; all ultimately seeking her death. For example, we see that when she was told to take the oath that she had taken the day before, and to swear to speak the truth, she repeatedly replied that she had taken an oath yesterday, and that should suffice. Trials throughout history have begun with the accused taking an oath to speak the truth; Joan was right that, once given, it should not legally or morally have to be repeated. The trial record also demonstrates her remarkable intellect. The transcript's most famous exchange is an exercise in subtlety. When Joan was asked if she knew she was in God's grace, she answered: 'If I am not, may God put me there; and if I am, may God so keep me.' The question was a scholarly trap and hardly a fair one to put to an uneducated person, but Joan knew that Church doctrine held that no one could be certain of being in God's grace. If she had answered yes, then she would have convicted herself of heresy. If she had answered no, then she would have confessed her own guilt. The notary Guillaume Colles de Boisguillaume would later say that when the court heard this reply, they were astounded.

Joan was found guilty of heresy and witchcraft and burned at the stake that same day. The trial was a travesty. She had been thoroughly examined at Poitiers by the French, but at no point did the court ask to see a transcript of the findings even though Joan asked for them to be produced. Perhaps this need not surprise us, but even then it was a gross breach of justice. The distressing scene of her burning in Rouen's marketplace is best glossed over. After she died, her ashes were raked over, reburnt and thrown into the Seine – the normal procedure after burning a 'witch'. There is no possibility that Joan survived, as was claimed by a fraudulent Maid of Orléans a few years later. It seems that this person was encouraged and abetted by Joan's two brothers, arguably hoping to turn a quick coin.

Almost a quarter of a century later, Charles VII called for the trial to be reopened. Ostensibly it was pushed for by Joan's mother, Isabelle Romée, another strong-minded woman. It was Charles VII's wish that this should happen since he was still anxious that the trial undermined his own coronation, which had been brought about by a person who had been deemed to be a witch. At the rehabilitation hearing on 16 June 1455, the sentence of 1431 was declared unjust, unfounded and iniquitous. It was nullified and pronounced invalid.

The Historical Joan of Arc

It is apparent that although Joan was not an educated woman, she had charismatic leadership qualities. She made a strong and lasting impression on all whom she met, whether churchmen, lawyers or royalty, and she continues to imprint herself on the public imagination even today. It has been said that she was executed not so much for crimes that are no longer capital offences, but for being unwomanly and insufferably presumptuous. She patronized her own king and at one time summoned the English king to do repentance and to obey her commands. At times she tried to overrule the plans of generals; but she did inspire their troops to victory. She had an unbounded and unconcealed contempt for official opinion and authority. As George Bernard Shaw has said, there were only two opinions about her: one, that she was miraculous, the other, that she was unbearable. In his play, *Saint Joan*, Shaw had Charles VII say 'if only she would keep quiet or go home' after his coronation. He may well have said that and must surely have thought it.

Joan of Arc has remained an important figure in Western culture and beyond. In her native land, from Napoleon to the present, French politicians of all leanings have invoked her memory. Worldwide, dozens of writers, artists and composers have created works that stand as a testimony to her endurance. Whatever you think, you have to admit that she was brave, capable and a natural leader.

Imogen Corrigan (BA, MPhil, FRHistS, FRSA) is a specialist in Anglo-Saxon and medieval history. After spending over 19 years in the army, she retired in the rank of major at the end of 1994. Subsequently she went to the University of Kent to study Anglo-Saxon and medieval history, graduating with first class honours, and later gained an MPhil from the University of Birmingham. She is an accredited Arts Society speaker who works as a freelance lecturer and runs study tours for specialist travel companies. Corrigan's first book was published in 2019 (*Stone on Stone: The Men Who Built the Cathedrals*, The Crowood Press). She has the Freedom of the City of London being a Freeman of the Company of Communicators.

The Life of Joan of Arc
Volume I

The d'Arc family lived in Domrémy which is now in the Vosges (department) in north-eastern France. During Joan's life in the fifteenth century, the area was held by Burgundian/English forces whose boundaries regularly changed. Joan's childhood was full of alarms and raids, so she had a good idea of how dangerous the situation could be but, buoyed up by the voices of saints that she first heard when she was a young teenager, she determined to bring victory to France. That said, it took about four years for her to persuade the authorities to allow her to travel to the Dauphin at Chinon, by which time Orléans was under siege.

She persuaded the Dauphin that she could do three things: raise the siege, get him anointed king and drive the English out of France. The war (today known as The Hundred Years' War) had dragged on for so long that it is possible that he thought anything was worth a try; this young woman being expendable after all, if she failed. Joan was examined physically, morally and spiritually for six weeks at Poitiers before being given permission to join the fight. The siege lasted 209 days, being raised nine days after Joan arrived. This paved the way for the Dauphin to be anointed at Reims with the 'Maid of Orléans' at his side.

The war was not over. The perception was that France now had victory after victory, seemingly under Joan's command – but was this true or was it part of Joan's myth? Once crowned, the king largely ignored her, but wild stories about her leadership and deeds flourished with almost no basis in fact.

Chapter I
Childhood

✠

IN THE LITTLE VILLAGE OF DOMREMY, situated at least 12 kilometres (seven and a half miles) further down the river than Neufchâteau and 12½ above Vaucouleurs, there was born, about the year 1410 or 1412, a girl who was destined to live a remarkable life. She was born poor. Her father, Jacques d'Arc, a native of the village of Ceffonds in Champagne, was a small farmer. His wife came from Vouthon, a village nearly six and a half kilometres (four miles) northwest of Domrémy, beyond the woods of Greux. Her name being Isabelle, she received the surname of Romée. That name was given to those who had been to Rome or on some other important pilgrimage.

She had already borne her husband three children: Jacques, Catherine and Jean. Her fourth child was named Jeannette. That was the name by which she was known in the village. Later, in France, she was called Jeanne.

As soon as she was old enough she laboured in the fields, weeding, digging, and, like the Lorraine maidens of today, doing the work of a man, but she would rather do housework or sew or spin; and she was pious.

In 1429 King Charles' council was uncertain as to whether Jacques d'Arc was a freeman or a serf. And Jacques d'Arc himself doubtless was no better informed.

Lying at the extreme south of the castellany of Vaucouleurs, the village of Domremy was between Bar and Champagne on the east, and Lorraine on the west. They were terrible neighbours, always warring against each other.

At Domremy there was a castle built in the meadow at the angle of an island formed by two arms of the river, one of which, the eastern arm, has long since been filled up. Belonging to this castle was a chapel of Our Lady, a courtyard provided with means of defence, and a large garden surrounded by a moat wide and deep. This castle, once the dwelling of the Lords of Bourlémont, was commonly called the Fortress of the Island.

The village folk decided to rent it and to put their tools and their cattle therein out of reach of the plunderers. The renting was put up to auction, a certain Jean Biget of Domremy and Jacques d'Arc, Jeanne's father, being the highest bidders. The precaution proved to be useful. In that very year, 1419, Robert de Saarbruck and his company met the men of the brothers Didier and Durand at the village of Maxey, the thatched roofs of which were to be seen opposite Greux, on the other bank of the Meuse, along the foot of wooded hills. The two sides here engaged in a battle, in which the victorious Damoiseau took 35 prisoners, whom he afterwards liberated after having exacted a high ransom, as was his wont. From one of the hills of her village, Jeanne, who was then seven or a little older, could see the battle in which her godmother's husband was taken prisoner.

Meanwhile matters grew worse and worse in the kingdom of France. This was well known at Domremy, situated as it was on the highroad, and hearing the news brought by wayfarers. Thus it was that the villagers heard of the murder of Duke John of Burgundy on the Bridge at Montereau, when the Dauphin's councillors made him pay the price of the blood he had shed in the Rue Barbette. There followed the war between the Armagnacs and the Burgundians. From this war the English, the obstinate enemies of the kingdom, who for 200 years had held Guyenne and carried on a prosperous trade there, sucked no small advantage. But Guyenne was far away, and perhaps no one at Domremy knew that it had once been a part of the domain of the kings of France. On the other hand, everyone was aware that during the recent trouble the English had recrossed the sea and had been welcomed by my Lord Philip, son of the late Duke John. They occupied Normandy, Maine, Picardy, l'Île-de-France and Paris the great city. Now in France the English were bitterly hated and greatly feared on account of their reputation for cruelty. There was mourning in many a French household when Queen Ysabeau delivered the kingdom of France to the *coués*, making of the noble French lilies a litter for the leopard. Since then, only a few days apart, King Henry V of Lancaster and King Charles VI of Valois, the victorious king and the mad king, had departed to present themselves before God, the Judge of the good and the evil, the just and the unjust, the weak and the powerful. The castellany of Vaucouleurs was French.

In 1420 the English occupied the bailiwick of Chaumont and garrisoned several fortresses in Bassigny. Messire Robert, Lord of Baudricourt and Blaise, son of the late Messire Liébault de Baudricourt, was then captain of Vaucouleurs and bailie of Chaumont for the Dauphin Charles. He might be reckoned a great plunderer, even in Lorraine. In the spring of this year, 1420, the Duke of Burgundy having sent an embassy to the Lord Bishop of Verdun, as the ambassadors were returning they were taken prisoners by Sire Robert in league with the Damoiseau of Commercy. To avenge this offence the Duke of Burgundy declared war on the Captain of Vaucouleurs, and the castellany was ravaged by bands of English and Burgundians.

Jacques d'Arc was then the elder (*doyen*) of the community. It was for him to summon the mayor and the aldermen to the council meetings, to cry the decrees, to command the watch day and night, to guard the prisoners. It was for him also to collect taxes, rents and feudal dues, an ungrateful office in a ruined country.

Under pretence of safeguarding and protecting them, Robert de Saarbruck, Damoiseau of Commercy, who for the moment was Armagnac, was plundering and ransoming the villages belonging to Bar, on the left bank of the Meuse. On the 7th of October, 1423, Jacques d'Arc, as elder, signed below the mayor and sheriff the act by which the Squire extorted from these poor people the annual payment of two *gros* from each complete household and one from each widow's household, a tax which amounted to no less than 220 golden crowns, which the elder was charged to collect before the winter feast of Saint-Martin.

The following year was bad for the Dauphin Charles, for the French and Scottish horsemen of his party met with the worst possible treatment at Verneuil. At the same time Robert, Sire de Baudricourt, was fighting with Jean de Vergy, lord of Saint-Dizier, Seneschal of Burgundy. It was a fine war. On both sides the combatants laid hands on bread, wine, money, silver plate, clothes, cattle big and little and what could not be carried off was burnt. Men, women and children were put to ransom. In most of the villages of Bassigny agriculture was suspended, nearly all the mills were destroyed.

Ten, 20, 30 bands of Burgundians were ravaging the castellany of Vaucouleurs, laying it waste with fire and sword. At Domremy life was one perpetual alarm. All day and all night there was a watchman stationed on the square tower of the monastery. At the approach of men-at-arms the watchman would ring a noisy peal of those bells, which in turn celebrated births, mourned for the dead, summoned the people to prayer, dispelled storms of thunder and lightning, and warned of danger.

At that time Jeanne was 13 or 14. War everywhere around her, even in the children's play; the husband of one of her godmothers taken and ransomed by men-at-arms; the husband of her cousin-german Mengette killed by a mortar; her native land overrun by marauders, burnt, pillaged, laid waste, all the cattle carried off; nights of terror, dreams of horror – such were the surroundings of her childhood.

Chapter II
Jeanne's Voices

✟

NOW, WHEN SHE WAS about 13, it befell one summer day, at noon, that while she was in her father's garden she heard a voice that filled her with a great fear. It came from the right, from towards the church, and at the same time in the same direction there appeared a light. The voice said: 'I come from God to help thee to live a good and holy life. Be good, Jeannette, and God will aid thee.'

It is well known that fasting conduces to the seeing of visions. Jeanne was accustomed to fast. Had she abstained from food that morning and if so when had she last partaken of it? We cannot say.

On another day the voice spoke again and repeated, 'Jeannette, be good.'

The child did not know whence the voice came. But the third time, as she listened, she knew it was an angel's voice and she even recognized the angel to be St. Michael.

One day he said to her: 'Saint Catherine and Saint Margaret will come to thee. Act according to their advice; for they are appointed to guide thee and counsel thee in all thou hast to do, and thou mayest believe what they shall say unto thee.' And these things came to pass as the Lord had ordained.

This promise filled her with great joy, for she loved them both. Sainte Marguerite was highly honoured in the kingdom of France, where she was a great benefactress. She helped women in labour, and protected the peasant at work in the fields.

Sainte Catherine, whose coming the angel had announced to Jeanne at the same time as that of Sainte Marguerite, was the protectress of young girls and especially of servants and spinsters.

My Lord Saint Michael, the Archangel, did not forget his promise. The ladies Saint Catherine and Saint Margaret came as he had said. On their very first visit the young peasant maid vowed to them to preserve her virginity as long as it should please God.

The saints soon entered into familiar relations with her. They came to the village every day, and often several times a day. When she saw them appear in a ray of light coming down from heaven, shining and clad like queens, with golden crowns on their heads, wearing rich and precious jewels, the village maiden crossed herself devoutly and curtsied low. They addressed her courteously, as it seemed to Jeanne. They called the lowly damsel daughter of God. They taught her to live well and go to church. Without always having anything very new to say to her, since they came so constantly, they spoke to her of things which filled her with joy, and, after they had disappeared, Jeanne ardently pressed her lips to the ground their feet had trodden.

Since the two saints had been visiting Jeanne, my Lord Saint Michael had come less often; but he had not forsaken her. There came a time when he talked to her of love for the kingdom of France, of that love which she felt in her heart.

And the holy visitants, whose voices grew stronger and more ardent as the maiden's soul grew holier and more heroic, revealed to her her mission. 'Daughter of God,' they said, 'thou must leave thy village, and go to France.'

Jeanne at Domremy was acquainted with a prophecy foretelling that France would be ruined by a woman and saved by a maiden. It made an extraordinary impression upon her; and later she came to speak in a manner which proved that she not only believed it but was persuaded that she herself was the maiden designated by the prophecy.

Jeanne was in the habit of visiting her uncle, the priest of Sermaize, and of seeing in the Abbey of Cheminon, her cousin, a young ecclesiastic in minor orders, who was soon to follow her into France. She was in touch with a number of priests who would be very quick to recognize her exceptional piety, and her gift of beholding things invisible to the majority of Christians. They engaged her in conversations, which, had they been preserved, would doubtless present to us one of the sources whence she derived inspiration for her marvellous vocation.

Meanwhile Jeanne was living a life of illusion. Knowing nothing of the influences she was under, incapable of recognising in her Voices the echo of a human voice or the promptings of her own heart, she responded timidly to the saints when they bade her fare forth into France: 'I am a poor girl, and know not how to ride a horse or how to make war.'

As soon as she began to receive these revelations she gave up her games and her excursions. From early childhood she had shown signs of piety. Now she gave herself up to extreme devoutness; she confessed frequently, and communicated with ecstatic fervour; she heard mass in her parish church every day. At all hours she was to be found in church, sometimes prostrate on the ground, sometimes with her hands clasped, and her face turned towards the image of Our Lord or of Our Lady. The village priest, Messire Guillaume Frontey, could do nothing but praise the most guileless of his parishioners.

Everyone thought Jeanne odd and erratic. Among others, Isabellette, the young wife of Gérardin d'Epinal, roundly condemned a girl who cared so little for dancing. Colin, son of Jean Colin, and all the village lads made fun of her piety. Her fits of religious ecstasy raised a smile. She was regarded as a little mad. She suffered from this persistent raillery. But with her own eyes she beheld the dwellers in Paradise. And when they left her she would cry and wish that they had taken her with them.

'Daughter of God, thou must leave thy village and go forth into France.'

And the ladies Saint Catherine and Saint Margaret spoke again and said: 'Take the standard sent down to thee by the King of Heaven, take it boldly and God will help thee.' As she listened to these words of the ladies with the beautiful crowns, Jeanne was consumed with a desire for long expeditions on horseback, and for those battles in which angels hover over the heads of the warriors. But how was she to go to France? How was she to associate with men-at-arms? Ignorant and generously impulsive like herself, the Voices she heard merely revealed to her her own heart, and left her in sad agitation of mind.

And the Angel appeared unto her and said: 'Daughter of God, thou shalt lead the Dauphin to Reims that he may there receive worthily his anointing.'

The maid understood. The scales fell from her eyes; a bright light was shed abroad in her mind. Behold wherefore God had chosen her. Through her the Dauphin Charles was to be anointed at Reims. Henceforth Jeanne knew what great deeds she was to bring to pass. But as yet she discerned not the means by which she was to accomplish them.

'Thou must fare forth into France,' Saint Catherine and Saint Margaret said to her.

'Daughter of God, thou shalt lead the Dauphin to Reims that he may there receive worthily his anointing,' the Archangel Michael said to her.

She must obey them – but how? If at that time there were not just at hand some devout adviser to direct her, one incident quite personal and unimportant, which then occurred in her father's house, may have sufficed to point out the way to the young saint.

Tenant-in-chief of the Castle on the island in 1419, and in 1423 elder of the community, Jacques d'Arc was one of the notables of Domremy. The village folk held him in high esteem and readily entrusted him with difficult tasks. Towards the end of March, 1427, they sent him to Vaucouleurs as their authorised proxy in a lawsuit they were conducting before Robert de Baudricourt.

The result of the dispute is not known; but it is sufficient to note that Jeanne's father saw Sire Robert and had speech with him.

On his return home he must have more than once related these interviews, and told of the manners and words of so great a personage. And doubtless Jeanne heard many of these things. Assuredly she must have pricked up her ears at the name of Baudricourt. Then it was that her dazzling friend, the Archangel Knight, came once more to awaken the obscure thought slumbering within her: 'Daughter of God,' he said, 'go thou to the Captain Robert de Baudricourt, in the town of Vaucouleurs, that he may grant unto thee men who shall take thee to the gentle Dauphin.'

Resolved to obey faithfully the behest of the Archangel which accorded with her own desire, Jeanne foresaw that her mother, albeit pious, would grant her no aid in her design and that her father would strongly oppose it. Therefore she refrained from confiding it to them.

She thought that Durand Lassois would be the man to give her the succour of which she had need. In consideration of his age she called him uncle – he was her elder by 16 years.

Jeanne went to see him, told him of her design, and showed him that she must needs see Sire Robert de Baudricourt. That her kind kinsman might the more readily believe in her, she repeated to him the strange prophecy, of which we have already made mention: 'Was it not known of old,' she said, 'that a woman should ruin the kingdom of France and that a woman should re-establish it?'

During this visit to her cousin, Jeanne met with others besides her kinsfolk, the Vouthons and their children. She visited a young nobleman, by name Geoffroy de Foug, who dwelt in the parish of Maxey-sur-Vayse, of which the hamlet of Burey formed part. She confided to him that she wanted to go to France. My Lord Geoffroy did not know much of Jeanne's parents; he was ignorant even of their names. But the damsel seemed to him good, simple, pious, and he encouraged her in her marvellous undertaking. A week after her arrival at Burey she attained her object: Durand Lassois consented to take her to Vaucouleurs.

Chapter III
First Visit to Vaucouleurs – Flight to Neufchâteau –
Journey to Toul – Second Visit to Vaucouleurs

ROBERT DE BAUDRICOURT, who in those days commanded the town of Vaucouleurs for the Dauphin Charles, was the son of Liébault de Baudricourt deceased, once chamberlain of Robert, Duke of Bar,

governor of Pont-à-Mousson, and of Marguerite d'Aunoy, Lady of Blaise in Bassigny. Fourteen or 15 years earlier he had succeeded his two uncles, Guillaume, the Bastard of Poitiers, and Jean d'Aunoy as Bailie of Chaumont and Commander of Vaucouleurs. Sire Robert was like all the warriors of his time and country; he was greedy and cunning; he had many friends among his enemies and many enemies among his friends; he fought now for his own side, now against it, but always for his own advantage. For the rest he was no worse than his fellows, and one of the least stupid.

Without any difficulty Jeanne entered the castle, and she was led into the hall where was Sire Robert among his men-at-arms. She heard the Voice saying to her: 'That is he!' And immediately she went straight to him, and spoke to him fearlessly, beginning, doubtless, by saying what she deemed to be most urgent: 'I am come to you, sent by Messire,' she said, 'that you may send to the Dauphin and tell him to hold himself in readiness, but not to give battle to his enemies.'

Perfectly calm and self-possessed, Jeanne went on and uttered a prophecy concerning the Dauphin: 'Before mid-Lent my Lord will grant him aid.' Then straightway she added: 'But in very deed the realm belongs not to the Dauphin. Nathless it is Messire's will that the Dauphin should be king and receive the kingdom in trust – *en commande*. Notwithstanding his enemies, the Dauphin shall be king; and it is I who shall lead him to his anointing.'

Doubtless the title Messire, in the sense in which she employed it, sounded strange and obscure, since Sire Robert, failing to understand it, asked: 'Who is Messire?'

'The King of Heaven,' the damsel answered.

That word *commande* employed in matters connected with inheritance signified something given in trust. If the king received the kingdom *en commande* he would merely hold it in trust. Thus the maid's utterance agreed with the views of the most pious concerning Our Lord's government of kingdoms.

Touching things spiritual Jeanne held converse with several priests; among others with Messire Arnolin, of Gondrecourt-le-Château, and

Messire Dominique Jacob, priest of Moutier-sur-Saulx, who was her confessor. It is a pity we do not know what these ecclesiastics thought of the insatiable cruelty of the English, of the pride of my Lord Duke of Burgundy, of the misfortunes of the Dauphin, and whether they did not hope that one day Our Lord Jesus Christ at the prayer of the common folk would condescend to grant the kingdom *en commande* to Charles, son of Charles. It was possibly from one of these that Jeanne derived her theocratic ideas.

While she was speaking to Sire Robert there was present, and not by chance merely, a certain knight of Lorraine, Bertrand de Poulengy, who possessed lands near Gondrecourt and held an office in the provostship of Vaucouleurs. He was then about 36 years of age. He was a man who associated with churchmen; at least he was familiar with the manner of speech of devout persons. Perhaps he now saw Jeanne for the first time; but he must certainly have heard of her; and he knew her to be good and pious. Twelve years before he had frequently visited Domremy; he knew the country well and had been several times to the house of Jacques d'Arc and Romée, whom he held to be good honest farmer folk.

It may be that Bertrand de Poulengy was struck by the damsel's speech and bearing; it is more likely that the knight was in touch with certain ecclesiastics unknown to us, who were instructing the peasant seeress with an eye to rendering her better able to serve the realm of France and the Church. However that may be, in Bertrand she had a friend who was to be her strong support in the future.

For the [time being], however, if our information be correct, he did nothing and spoke not a word. Perhaps he judged it best to wait until the commander of the town should be ready to grant a more favourable hearing to the saint's request. Sire Robert understood nothing of all this; one point only appeared plain to him, that Jeanne would make a fine camp-follower and that she would be a great favourite with the men-at-arms.

In dismissing the villein who had brought her, he gave him a piece of advice quite in keeping with the wisdom of the time concerning the chastising of daughters: 'Take her back to her father and box her ears well.'

Sire Robert held such discipline to be excellent, for more than once he urged Uncle Lassois to take Jeanne home well whipped.

After a week's absence she returned to the village. Neither the Captain's contumely nor the garrison's insults had humiliated or discouraged her. Imagining that her Voices had foretold them, she held them to be proofs of the truth of her mission. Like those who walk in their sleep she was calm in the face of obstacles and yet quietly persistent. In the house, in the garden, in the meadow, she continued to sleep that marvellous slumber, in which she dreamed of the Dauphin, of his knights, and of battles with angels hovering above.

She found it impossible to be silent; on all occasions her secret escaped from her. She was always prophesying, but she was never believed. On St. John the Baptist's Eve, about a month after her return, she said sententiously to Michel Lebuin, a husbandman of Burey, who was quite a boy: 'Between Coussey and Vaucouleurs is a girl who in less than a year from now will cause the Dauphin to be anointed King of France.'

One day meeting Gérardin d'Epinal, the only man at Domremy not of the Dauphin's party, whose head according to her own confession she would willingly have cut off, although she was godmother to his son, she could not refrain from announcing even to him in veiled words her mystic dealing with God: 'Gossip, if you were not a Burgundian there is something I would tell you.'

The good man thought it must be a question of an approaching betrothal. Alas! how greatly would Jacques d'Arc have desired the secret to be of that nature. This upright man was very strict; he was careful concerning his children's conduct; and Jeanne's behaviour caused him anxiety. He knew not that she heard Voices. He had no idea that all day Paradise came down into his garden, that from Heaven to his house a ladder was let down, on which there came and went without ceasing more angels than had ever trodden the ladder of the Patriarch Jacob; neither did he imagine that for Jeannette alone, a mystery was being played, a thousand times richer and finer than those which on feast days were acted on platforms, in towns like Toul and Nancy. He was miles away from suspecting such incredible marvels. But what he did see was that his daughter was losing her senses, that her mind was wandering, and that she was giving utterance to wild words. He perceived that she could think of nothing but cavalcades and battles. He must have known something of the escapade at Vaucouleurs.

He was terribly afraid that one day the unhappy child would go off for good on her wanderings. This agonising anxiety haunted him even in his sleep. One night he dreamed that he saw her fleeing with men-at-arms; and this dream was so vivid that he remembered it when he awoke. For several days he said over and over again to his sons, Jean and Pierre: 'If I really believed that what I dreamed of my daughter would ever come true, I would rather see her drowned by you; and if you would not do it I would drown her myself.'

It is not uncommon for saints in their youth by the strangeness of their behaviour to give rise to such suspicions. And Jeanne displayed those signs of sainthood. She was the talk of the village. Folk pointed at her mockingly, saying: 'There goes she who is to restore France and the royal house.'

On the 22nd of June, from the Duke of Bedford, Regent of France for Henry VI, Antoine de Vergy, Governor of Champagne, received a commission to furnish forth 1,000 men-at-arms for the purpose of bringing the castellany of Vaucouleurs into subjection to the English.

On the march, as was his custom, Antoine de Vergy laid waste all the villages of the castellany with fire and sword. Threatened once again with a disaster with which they were only too well acquainted, the folk of Domremy and Greux already beheld their cattle captured, their barns set on fire, their wives and daughters ravished. Having experienced before that the Castle on the Island was not secure enough, they determined to flee and seek refuge in their market town of Neufchâteau, only eight kilometres (five miles) away from Domremy. Thus they set out towards the middle of July. Abandoning their houses and fields and driving their cattle before them, they followed the road, through the fields of wheat and rye and up the vine-clad hills to the town, wherein they lodged as best they could.

The d'Arc family was taken in by the wife of Jean Waldaires, who was called La Rousse. Handy and robust, Jeanne used also to help La Rousse in her household duties. This circumstance gave rise to the malicious report set on foot by the Burgundians that she had been serving maid in an inn frequented by drunkards and bad women. The truth is that Jeanne, when she was not tending the cattle, and helping her hostess, passed all her time in church.

During the fortnight Jeanne spent in the town of Neufchâteau, she frequented the church of the Grey Friars monastery, and two or three times confessed to brethren of the order. It has been stated that she belonged to the third order of St. Francis, and the inference has been drawn that her affiliation dated from her stay at Neufchâteau.

Such an inference is very doubtful; and in any case the affiliation cannot have been very ceremonious. It is difficult to see how in so short a time the friars could have instructed her in the practices of Franciscan piety. She was far too imbued with ecclesiastical notions concerning the spiritual and the temporal power, she was too full of mysteries and revelations to imbibe their spirit. Besides, her sojourn at Neufchâteau was troubled by anxiety and broken by absences.

In this town she received a summons to appear before the official of Toul, in whose jurisdiction she was, as a native of Domremy-de-Greux. A young bachelor of Domremy alleged that a promise of marriage had been given him by Jacques d'Arc's daughter. Jeanne denied it. He persisted in his statement, and summoned her to appear before the official.

The curious part of Jeanne's case is that her parents were against her, and on the side of the young man. It was in defiance of their wishes that she defended the suit and appeared before the official.

The journey from Neufchâteau to Toul and back involved travelling more than 20 leagues on foot, over roads infested with bands of armed men, through a country desolated by fire and sword, from which the peasants of Domremy had recently fled in a panic. To such a journey, however, she made up her mind against the will of her parents.

Possibly she may have appeared before the judge at Toul, not once but two or three times. And there was a great chance of her having to journey day and night with her so-called betrothed, for he was passing over the same road at the same time. Her Voices bade her fear nothing. Before the judge she swore to speak the truth, and denied having made any promise of marriage.

After a fortnight's sojourn at Neufchâteau, Jacques d'Arc and his family returned to Domremy. The orchard, the house, the monastery, the village, the fields – in what a state of desolation did they behold them! The soldiers had plundered, ravaged, burnt everything. Unable to exact ransom from the villeins who had taken flight, the men-at-arms had destroyed all their goods.

Meanwhile the English were laying siege to the town of Orléans, which belonged to their prisoner Duke Charles. By so doing they acted badly, for, having possession of his body, they ought to have respected his property. They built fortified towers round the city of Orléans, the very heart of France; and it was said that they had entrenched themselves there in great strength. Now Saint Catherine and Saint Margaret loved the Land of the Lilies; they were the sworn friends and gentle cousins of the Dauphin Charles. They talked to the shepherd maid of the misfortunes of the kingdom and continued to say: 'Leave thy village and go into France.'

Jeanne was all the more impatient to set forth because she had herself announced the time of her arrival in France, and that time was drawing near. She had told the Commander of Vaucouleurs that succour should come to the Dauphin before mid-Lent. She did not want to make her Voices lie.

Towards the middle of January occurred the opportunity she was looking for of returning to Burey. At this time Durand Lassois' wife was brought to bed. It was the custom in the country for the young kinswomen and friends of the mother to attend and wait upon her and her babe. Jeanne urged her uncle to ask her father that she might be sent to tend the sick woman, and Lassois consented: he was always ready to do what his niece asked him, and perhaps his complaisance was encouraged by pious persons of some importance. But how this father, who shortly before had said that he would throw his daughter into the Meuse rather than that she should go off with men-at-arms, should have allowed her to go to the gates of the town, protected by a kinsman of whose weakness he was well aware, is hard to understand.

Leaving the home of her childhood, which she was never to see again, Jeanne, in company with Durand Lassois, passed down her native valley in its winter bareness.

On her second arrival at Vaucouleurs, Jeanne imagined that she was setting foot in a town belonging to the Dauphin, and, in the language of the day, entering the royal antechamber. She was mistaken. Since the beginning of August 1428, the Commander of Vaucouleurs had yielded the fortress to Antoine de Vergy, but had not yet surrendered it to him.·

It was one of those promises to capitulate at the end of a given time. They were not uncommon in those days, and they ceased to be valid if the fortress were relieved before the day fixed for its surrender.

Jeanne went to Sire Robert in his castle just as she had done nine months before; and this was the revelation she made to him: 'My Lord Captain,' she said, 'know that God has again given me to wit, and commanded me many times to go to the gentle Dauphin, who must be and who is the true King of France, and that he shall grant me men-at-arms with whom I shall raise the siege of Orléans and take him to his anointing at Reims.'

This time she announces that it is her mission to deliver Orléans. And the anointing is not to come to pass until this the first part of her task shall have been accomplished. We cannot fail to recognize the readiness and the tact with which the Voices altered their commands previously given, according to the necessities of the moment. Robert's manner towards Jeanne had completely changed. He said nothing about boxing her ears and sending her back to her parents. He no longer treated her roughly; and if he did not believe her announcement at least he listened to it readily.

To judge from the few of her words handed down to us, in the early days of her mission the young prophetess spoke alternately two different languages. Her speech seemed to flow from two distinct sources. The one ingenuous, candid, naïve, concise, rustically simple, unconsciously arch, sometimes rough, alike chivalrous and holy, generally bearing on the inheritance and the anointing of the Dauphin and the confounding of the English. This was the language of her Voices, her own, her soul's language. The other, more subtle, flavoured with allegory and flowers of speech, critical with scholastic grace, bearing on the Church, suggesting the clerk and betraying some outside influence.

Jeanne lodged in the town with humble folk, Henri Leroyer and his wife Catherine, friends of her cousin Lassois. She used to occupy her time in spinning, being a good spinster; and the little she had she gave to the poor. She used to hear mass and remain long in prayer.

Under the chapel, in the crypt, there was an image of the Virgin, ancient and deeply venerated, called Notre-Dame-de-la-Voûte. It worked miracles, but especially on behalf of the poor and needy. Jeanne delighted to remain in this dark and lonely crypt, where the saints preferred to visit her.

In the garrison there was a man-at-arms of about 28 years of age, Jean de Novelompont or Nouillompont, who was commonly called Jean de Metz. By rank a freeman, albeit not of noble estate, he had acquired or inherited the lordship of Nouillompont and Hovecourt, situate in that part of Barrois which was outside the duke's domain; and he bore its name. Formerly in the pay of Jean de Wals, captain and provost of Stenay, he was now, in 1428, in the service of the commander of Vaucouleurs.

Of his morals and manner of life we know nothing, except that three years before he had sworn a vile oath and been condemned to pay a fine of two *sols*. Apparently when he took the oath he was in great wrath. He was more or less intimate with Bertrand de Poulengy, who had certainly spoken to him of Jeanne.

One day he met the damsel and said to her: 'Well, *ma mie*, what are you doing here? Must the king be driven from his kingdom and we all turn English?'

Such words from a young Lorraine warrior are worthy of notice. The Treaty of Troyes did not subject France to England; it united the two kingdoms. If war continued after as before, it was merely to decide between the two claimants, Charles de Valois and Henry of Lancaster. Whoever gained the victory, nothing would be changed in the laws and customs of France. Yet this poor freebooter of the German Marches imagined none the less that under an English king he would be an Englishman. Many French of all ranks believed the same and could not suffer the thought of being Anglicised; in their minds their own fates depended on the fate of the kingdom and of the Dauphin Charles.

Jeanne answered Jean de Metz: 'I came hither to the king's territory to speak with Sire Robert, that he may take me or command me to be taken to the Dauphin; but he heeds neither me nor my words.'

A report ran through the towns and villages. It was said that the son of the King of France, the Dauphin Louis, who had just entered his fifth year, had been recently betrothed to the daughter of the King of Scotland, the three-year-old Madame Margaret, and the common people celebrated this royal union with such rejoicings as were possible in a desolated country. Jeanne, when she heard these tidings, said to the man-at-arms: 'I must go to the Dauphin, for no one in the world, no king or duke or daughter of the King of Scotland, can restore the realm of France.'

Then straightway she added: 'In me alone is help, albeit for my part, I would far rather be spinning by my poor mother's side, for this life is not to my liking. But I must go; and so I will, for it is Messire's command that I should go.'

Jean de Metz asked, as Sire Robert had done: 'Who is Messire?'

'He is God,' she replied.

Then straightway, as if he believed in her, he said with a sudden impulse: 'I promise you, and I give you my word of honour, that God helping me I will take you to the king.'

He gave her his hand as a sign that he pledged his word and asked: 'When will you set forth?'

'This hour,' she answered, 'is better than tomorrow; tomorrow is better than after tomorrow.'

Jean de Metz himself, 27 years later, reported this conversation. If we are to believe him, he asked the damsel in conclusion whether she would travel in her woman's garb. It is easy to imagine what difficulties he would foresee in journeying with a peasant girl clad in a red frock over French roads infested with lecherous fellows, and that he would deem it wiser for her to disguise herself as a boy. She promptly divined his thought and replied: 'I will willingly dress as a man.'

There is no reason why these things should not have occurred. Only if they did, then a Lorraine freebooter suggested to the saint that idea concerning her dress which later she will think to have received from God.

Of his own accord, or rather, acting by the advice of some wise person, Sire Robert desired to know whether Jeanne was not being inspired by an evil spirit. For the devil is cunning and sometimes assumes the mark of innocence. And as Sire Robert was not learned in such matters, he determined to take counsel with his priest.

Now one day when Catherine and Jeanne were at home spinning, they beheld the Commander coming accompanied by the priest, Messire Jean Fournier. They asked the mistress of the house to withdraw; and when they were left alone with the damsel, Messire Jean Fournier put on his stole and pronounced some Latin words which amounted to saying: 'If thou be evil, away with thee; if thou be good, draw nigh.'

It was the ordinary formula of exorcism or, to be more exact, of conjuration. In the opinion of Messire Jean Fournier these words, accompanied by a few drops of holy water, would drive away devils, if there should unhappily be any in the body of this village maiden.

Having recited the formula and sprinkled the holy water, Messire Jean Fournier expected, if the damsel were possessed, to see her struggle, writhe and endeavour to take flight. In such a case he must needs have made use of more powerful formula, have sprinkled more holy water, and made more signs of the cross, and by such means have driven out the devils until they were seen to depart with a terrible noise and a noxious odour, in the shape of dragons, camels, or fish.

There was nothing suspicious in Jeanne's attitude. No wild agitation, no frenzy. Merely anxious and intreating, she dragged herself on her knees towards the priest. She did not flee before God's holy name. Messire Jean Fournier concluded that no devil was within her.

Left alone in the house with Catherine, Jeanne, who now understood the meaning of the ceremony, showed strong resentment towards Messire Jean Fournier. She reproached him with having suspected her: 'It was wrong of him,' she said to her hostess, 'for, having heard my confession, he ought to have known me.'

She would have thanked the priest of Vaucouleurs had she known how he was furthering the fulfilment of her mission by subjecting her to this ordeal. Convinced that this maiden was not inspired by the devil, Sire Robert must have been driven to conclude that she might be inspired by God; for apparently he was a man of simple reasoning. He wrote to the Dauphin Charles concerning the young saint; and doubtless he bore witness to the innocence and goodness he beheld in her.

Meanwhile Jeanne could not rest. She came and went from Vaucouleurs to Burey and from Burey to Vaucouleurs. She counted the days; time dragged for her as for a woman with child.

At the end of January, feeling she could wait no longer, she resolved to go to the Dauphin Charles alone. She clad herself in garments belonging to Durand Lassois, and with this kind cousin set forth on the road to France. A man of Vaucouleurs, one Jacques Alain, accompanied them. Probably these two men expected that the damsel would herself realise the impossibility of such a journey and that they would not go very far. That is what happened. The three travellers had barely journeyed a league from Vaucouleurs, when, near the Chapel of Saint Nicholas, which rises in the valley of Septfonds, in the middle of the great wood of Saulcy, Jeanne changed her mind and said to her comrades that it was not right of her to set out thus. Then they all three returned to the town.

At length a royal messenger brought King Charles's reply to the Commander of Vaucouleurs. The messenger was called Colet de Vienne. His name indicates that he came from the province which the Dauphin had governed before the death of the late king, and which had remained unswervingly faithful to the unfortunate prince. The reply was that Sire Robert should send the young saint to Chinon.

That which Jeanne had demanded and which it had seemed impossible to obtain was granted. She was to be taken to the king as she had desired and within the time fixed by herself. But this departure, for which she had so ardently longed, was delayed several days by a remarkable incident. The incident shows that the fame of the young prophetess had gone out through Lorraine; and it proves that in those days the great of the land had recourse to saints in their hour of need.

Jeanne was summoned to Nancy by my Lord the Duke of Lorraine. Furnished with a safe conduct that the duke had sent her, she set forth in rustic jerkin and hose on a nag given her by Durand Lassois and Jacques Alain. It had cost them 12 francs which Sire Robert repaid them later out of the royal revenue. From Vaucouleurs to Nancy is 24 leagues. Jean de Metz accompanied her as far as Toul; Durand Lassois went with her the whole way.

Chapter IV
The Journey to Nancy – The Itinerary of
Vaucouleur – To Sainte-Catherine-De-Fierbois

BY GIVING HIS ELDEST DAUGHTER, Isabelle, the heiress of Lorraine, in marriage to René, the second son of Madame Yolande, Queen of Sicily and of Jerusalem, and Duchess of Anjou, Duke Charles II of Lorraine, who was in alliance with the English, had recently done his

cousin and friend, the Duke of Burgundy, a bad turn. René of Anjou, now in his twentieth year, was a man of culture as much in love with sound learning as with chivalry, and withal kind, affable and gracious. When not engaged in some military expedition and in wielding the lance he delighted to illuminate manuscripts. He had a taste for flower-decked gardens and stories in tapestry; and like his fair cousin the Duke of Orléans he wrote poems in French. Invested with the duchy of Bar by the Cardinal Duke of Bar, his great-uncle, he would inherit the duchy of Lorraine after the death of Duke Charles which could not be far off.

This marriage was rightly regarded as a clever stroke on the part of Madame Yolande. But he who reigns must fight. The Duke of Burgundy, ill content to see a prince of the house of Anjou, the brother-in-law of Charles of Valois, established between Burgundy and Flanders, stirred up against René the Count of Vaudémont, who was a claimant of the inheritance of Lorraine. The Angevin policy rendered a reconciliation between the Duke of Burgundy and the King of France difficult. Thus was René of Anjou involved in the quarrels of his father-in-law of Lorraine. It befell that in this year, 1429, he was waging war against the citizens of Metz, the War of the Basketful of Apples. It was so called because the cause of war was a basketful of apples which had been brought into the town of Metz without paying duty to the officers of the Duke of Lorraine.

Meanwhile René's mother was sending convoys of victuals from Blois to the citizens of Orléans, besieged by the English. Although she was not then on good terms with the counsellors of her son-in-law, King Charles, she was vigilant in opposing the enemies of the kingdom when they threatened her own duchy of Anjou. René, Duke of Bar, had therefore ties of kindred, friendship and interest binding him at the same time to the English and Burgundian party as well as to the party of France. Such was the situation of most of the French nobles. René's communications with the Commander of Vaucouleurs were friendly and constant. It is possible that Sire Robert may have told him that he had a damsel at Vaucouleurs who was prophesying concerning the realm of France. It is possible that the Duke of Bar, curious to see her, may have had her sent to Nancy, where he was to be towards the 20th of February. In this month of February 1429, he was neither desirous nor able to concern himself greatly with the affairs of France; and although brother-in-law to King Charles, he was preparing not to succour the town of Orléans, but to besiege the town of Metz.

Old and ill, Duke Charles dwelt in his palace with his paramour Alison du Mai, a bastard and a priest's daughter, who had driven out the lawful wife, Dame Marguerite of Bavaria. Dame Marguerite was pious and high-born, but old and ugly, while Madame Alison was pretty. She had borne Duke Charles several children.

The following story appears the most authentic. There were certain worthy persons at Nancy who wanted Duke Charles to take back his good wife. To persuade him to do so they had recourse to the exhortations of a saint, who had revelations from Heaven, and who called herself the Daughter of God. By these persons the damsel of Domremy was represented to the enfeebled old Duke as being a saint who worked miracles of healing. By their advice he had her summoned in the hope that she possessed secrets which should alleviate his sufferings and keep him alive.

As soon as he saw her he asked whether she could not restore him to his former health and strength.

She replied that 'of such things' she knew nothing. But she warned him that his ways were evil, and that he would not be cured until he had amended them. She enjoined upon him to send away Alison, his concubine, and to take back his good wife.

Jeanne had come to the duke because it was his due, because a little saint must not refuse when a great lord wishes to consult her, and because in short she had been brought to Nancy. But her mind was elsewhere; of nought could she think but of saving the realm of France.

Reflecting that Madame Yolande's son with a goodly company of men-at-arms would be of great aid to the Dauphin, she asked the Duke of Lorraine, as she took her leave, to send this young knight with her into France.

'Give me your son,' she said, 'with men-at-arms as my escort. In return I will pray to God for your restoration to health.'

The duke did not give her men-at-arms; neither did he give her the Duke of Bar, the heir of Lorraine, the ally of the English, who was nevertheless to join her soon beneath the standard of King Charles. But he gave her four francs and a black horse.

Perhaps it was on her return from Nancy that she wrote to her parents asking their pardon for having left them. The fact that they received a letter and forgave is all that is known. One cannot forbear surprise that Jacques d'Arc, all through the month that his daughter was at Vaucouleurs, should have remained quietly at home, when previously, after having merely dreamed of her being with men-at-arms, he had threatened that if his sons did not drown her, he would with his own hands. For he must have been aware that at Vaucouleurs she was living with men-at-arms. Knowing her temperament, he had displayed great simplicity in letting her go.

Before or after her journey to Nancy (which is not known), certain of the townsfolk of Vaucouleurs who believed in the young prophetess either had made, or purchased for her ready-made, a suit of masculine clothing, a jerkin, cloth doublet, hose laced on to the coat, gaiters, spurs, a whole equipment of war. Sire Robert gave her a sword.

She had her hair cut round like a boy. Jean de Metz and Bertrand de Poulengy, with their servants Jean de Honecourt and Julien, were to accompany her as well as the king's messenger, Colet de Vienne, and the bowman Richard. There was still some delay and councils were held, for the soldiers of Antoine de Lorraine, Lord of Joinville, infested the country. Throughout the land there was nothing but pillage, robbery, murder, cruel tyranny, the ravishing of women, the burning of churches and abbeys, and the perpetration of horrible crimes. But the damsel was not afraid, and said: 'In God's name! take me to the gentle Dauphin, and fear not any trouble or hindrance we may meet.'

At length, on a day in February, so it is said, the little company issued forth from Vaucouleurs by La Porte de France.

Sire Robert was present at her departure. According to the customary formula he took an oath from each of the men-at-arms that they would surely and safely conduct her whom he confided to them. Then, being a man of little faith, he said to Jeanne in lieu of farewell: 'Go! and come what may.' And the little company went off into the mist, which at that season envelops the meadows of the Meuse.

They were obliged to avoid frequented roads and to beware especially of passing by Joinville, Montiers-en-Saulx and Sailly, where there were soldiers of the hostile party. Sire Bertrand and Jean de Metz were accustomed to such stealthy expeditions; they knew the byways and were acquainted with useful precautions, such as binding up the horses' feet in linen so as to deaden the sound of hoofs on the ground.

At nightfall, having escaped all danger, the company approached the right bank of the Marne and reached the Abbey of Saint-Urbain. From time immemorial it had been a place of refuge, and in those days its abbot was Arnoult of Aulnoy, a kinsman of Robert of Baudricourt. The gate of the plain edifice opened for the travellers who passed beneath the groined vaulting of its roof. The abbey included a building set apart for strangers. There they found the resting-place of the first stage of their journey.

They had still 125 leagues to cover and three rivers to cross, in a country infested with brigands. Through fear of the enemy, they journeyed by night. When they lay down on the straw the damsel, keeping her hose laced to her coat, slept in her clothes, under a covering, between Jean de Metz and Bertrand de Poulengy in whom she felt confidence. They said afterwards that they never desired the damsel because of the holiness they beheld in her; that may or may not be believed.

Jean de Metz was filled with no such ardent faith in the prophetess, since he inquired of her: 'Will you really do what you say?'

To which she replied: 'Have no fear. I do what I am commanded to do. My brethren in Paradise tell me what I have to do. It is now four or five years since my brethren in Paradise and Messire told me that I must go forth to war to deliver the realm of France.'

As they avoided high roads they were not often in the way of bridges; and they were frequently forced to ford rivers in flood. They crossed the Aube, near Bar-sur-Aube, the Seine near Bar-sur-Seine, the Yonne opposite Auxerre, where Jeanne heard mass in the church of Saint-Etienne; then they reached the town of Gien, on the right bank of the Loire.

At length these Lorrainers beheld a French town loyal to the King of France. They had travelled 75 leagues through the enemy's country without being attacked or molested. Afterwards this was considered miraculous.

From Gien, the little company followed the northern boundary of the duchy of Berry, crossed into Blésois, possibly passed through Selles-sur-Cher and Saint-Aignan, then, having entered Touraine, reached the green slopes of Fierbois. There one of the two heavenly ladies, who daily discoursed familiarly with the peasant girl, had her most famous sanctuary; there it was that Saint Catherine received multitudes of pilgrims and worked great miracles. According to popular belief the origin of her worship in this place was warlike and national and dated back to the beginning of French history. Prisoners who had become her votaries and whom she had delivered, hung the cords and chains with which they had been bound, their armour, and sometimes, in special cases, the armour of the enemy in the chapel at Fierbois.

Jeanne must have delighted to hear tell of such miracles, or others like them, and to see so many weapons hanging from the chapel walls. She must have been well pleased that the saint who visited her at all hours and gave her counsel should so manifestly appear the friend of poor soldiers and peasants cast into bonds, cages and pits, or hanged on trees by the *Godons*.

Chapter V
The Siege of Orléans from the 12th of October, 1428, till the 6th of March, 1429

SINCE THE VICTORY OF VERNEUIL and the conquest of Maine, the English had advanced but little in France and their actual possessions there were becoming less and less secure. If they spared the lands of the Duke of Orléans it was not on account of any scruple. Albeit on the banks of the Loire it was held dishonourable to seize the domains of a noble when he was a prisoner, everything is fair in war.

The regent had not scrupled to seize the duchy of Alençon when its duke was a prisoner. The truth is that by bribes and entreaties the good Duke Charles dissuaded the English from attacking his duchy. From 1424 until 1426 the citizens of Orléans purchased peace by money payments. The *Godons*, not being in a position to take the field, were all the more ready to enter into such agreements. During the minority of their half English and half French King, the Duke of Gloucester, the brother and deputy of the regent, and his uncle, the Bishop of Winchester, Chancellor of the Kingdom, were tearing out each other's hair, and their disputes were the occasion of bloodshed in the London streets. Towards the end of the year 1425 the regent returned to England, where he spent 17 months reconciling uncle and nephew and restoring public peace. By dint of craft and vigour he succeeded so far as to render his fellow countrymen desirous and hopeful of completing the conquest of France. With that object, in 1428, the English Parliament voted subsidies.

Now the most cunning, the most expert, the most fortunate in arms of all the English captains and princes was Thomas Montacute, Earl of Salisbury and of Perche. He had long waged war in Normandy, in Champagne and in Maine. At present he was gathering an army in England, intended for the banks of the Loire. He got as many bowmen as he wanted; but of horse and men-at-arms he was disappointed. Only those of low estate were willing to go and fight in a land ravaged by famine. At length the noble earl, the fair cousin of King Henry, crossed the sea with 449 men-at-arms and 2,250 archers. In France he found troops recruited by the regent, 400 horse of whom 200 were Norman, with three bowmen to each horseman, according to the English custom. He led his men to Paris where irrevocable resolutions were taken. Hitherto the plan had been to attack Angers; at the last moment it was decided to lay siege to Orléans.

Orléans sheltered 15,000 souls. Of Roman origin, the form of the town was still the same as in the days of the Emperor Aurelian. The southern side along the Loire and the northern side extended to some 914 metres (3,000 feet). The eastern and western boundaries were only 45 metres (150 feet) long. The city was surrounded by walls two metres (six feet) thick and from five to 10 metres (18 to 33 feet) high above the moat. These walls were flanked by 34 towers, pierced with five gates and two posterns. The stone bridge lined with houses which led from the town to the left bank of the Loire was famous all over the world. It had 19 arches of varying breadth. The first, on leaving the town by La Porte du Pont, was called l'Allouée or Pont Jacquemin-Rousselet; here was a drawbridge. The fifth arch abutted on an island which was long, narrow, and in the form of a boat, like all river islands. Above the bridge it was called Motte-Saint-Antoine, from a chapel built upon it dedicated to that saint; and below, Motte-des-Poissonniers, because in order to keep captured fish alive boats with holes in them were moored to it.

The suburbs of Orléans were the finest in the kingdom. On the south the fishermen's suburb of Le Portereau, with its Augustinian church and monastery, extended along the river at the foot of the vineyards of Saint-Jean-le-Blanc, which produced the best wine in the country. Above, on the gentle slopes ascending to the bleak plateau of Sologne, the Loiret, with its torrential springs, its limpid waters, its shady banks, the gardens and the brooks of Olivet, smiled beneath a mild and showery sky.

The *faubourg* of the Burgundian gate stretching eastwards was the best built and the most populous. Leaving this suburb and passing by the vineyards along the sandy branch of the Loire extending between the bank of the river and l'Île-aux-Bœufs about a quarter of a league further on, one comes to the steep slope of Saint-Loup; and, advancing still further towards the east, the belfries of Saint-Jean-de-Bray, Combleux and Chécy may be seen rising one beyond the other between the river and the Roman road from Autun to Paris. On the north of the city were fine monasteries and beautiful churches, the chapel of Saint-Ladre, in the cemetery; the Jacobins, the Cordeliers, the church of Saint-Pierre-Ensentelée. Directly north, the *faubourg* of La Porte Bernier lay along the Paris road, and close by there stretched the sombre city of the wolves, the deep forest of oaks, horn beams, beeches and willows, wherein were hidden, like woodcutters and charcoal-burners, the villages of Fleury and Samoy.

Towards the west the *faubourg* of La Porte Renard stretched out into the fields along the road to Châteaudun, and the hamlet of Saint-Laurent along the road to Blois.

These *faubourgs* were so populous and so extensive that when, on the approach of the English, the people from the suburbs took refuge within the city the number of its inhabitants was doubled.

The inhabitants of Orléans were resolved to fight, not for their honour indeed; in those days no honour redounded to a citizen from the defence of his own city; his only reward was the risk of terrible danger. When the town was captured the great and wealthy had but to pay ransom and the conqueror entertained them well; the lesser and poorer nobility ran greater risks. In this year, 1428, the knights, who defended Melun and surrendered after having eaten their horses and their dogs, were drowned in the Seine. 'Nobility was worth nothing,' ran a Burgundian song.

But generally being of noble birth saved one's life. As for those burghers brave enough to defend themselves, they were likely to perish. There were no fixed rules with regard to them; sometimes several were hanged; sometimes only one, sometimes all. It was also lawful to cut off their heads or to throw them into the water, sewn in a sack. In that same year, 1428, Captains La Hire and Poton had failed in their assault on Le Mans and decamped just in time. The citizens who had aided them were beheaded in the square du Cloître-Saint-Julien, on the Olet stone, by order of William Pole, Earl of Suffolk, who had already arrived at Olivet, and of John Talbot, the most courteous of English knights, who was shortly to come there too. Such an example was sufficient to warn the people of Orléans.

The people of Orléans were not taken by surprise. Their fathers had watched the English closely, and put their city in a state of defence. They themselves, in the year 1425, had so firmly expected a siege that they had collected arms in the Tower of Saint-Samson, while all, rich and poor alike, had been required to dig dykes and build ramparts. War has always been costly. They devoted three quarters of the yearly revenue of the town to keeping up the ramparts and other preparations for war. Hearing of the approach of the Earl of Salisbury, with marvellous energy they prepared to receive him.

The walls, except those along the river, were devoid of breastwork; but in the shops were stakes and crossbeams intended for the manufacture of balustrades. These were put up on the fortifications to form parapets, with barbicans of a pent-house shape so as to provide with cover the defenders firing from the walls. At the entrance to each suburb wooden barriers were erected, with a lodge for the porter whose duty it was to open and shut them. On the tops of the ramparts and in the towers were 71 pieces of artillery, including cannons and mortars, without counting culverins. The quarry of Montmaillard, three leagues from the town, produced stones which were made into cannon balls. At great expense there were brought into the city lead, powder and sulphur which the women prepared for use in the cannons and culverins. Every day there were manufactured in thousands, arrows, darts, stacks of bolts, armed with iron points and feathered with parchment, numbers of *pavas*, great shields made of pieces of wood mortised one into the other and covered with leather. Corn, wine and cattle were purchased in great quantities both for the inhabitants and the men-at-arms, the king's men and adventurers who were expected.

Adventurers from all parts responded to the magistrates' appeal. Thus the number of friends who entered the city was well-nigh as great as that of the expected foe. The defenders were paid; they were furnished with bread, meat, fish, forage in plenty and casks of wine were broached for them. In the beginning the inhabitants treated them like their own children. The citizens all contributed to the entertainment of the strangers, and gave them what they had. But this concord did not long endure. Whatever tradition alleges as to the friendly relations subsisting between the citizens and their military guests, affairs in Orléans were in truth not different from what they were in other besieged towns; before long the inhabitants began to complain of the garrison.

On the 5th of September the Earl of Salisbury reached Janville, having taken with ease towns, fortified churches or castles to the number of 40.

From Janville he sent two heralds to Orléans to summon the inhabitants to surrender. The magistrates lodged these heralds honourably in the faubourg Bannier, at the Hôtel de la Pomme and confided to them a present of wine for the Earl of Salisbury; they knew their duty to so great a prince. But they refused to open their gates to the English garrison, alleging, doubtless, as was the custom of citizens in those days, that they were not able to open them, having those within who were stronger than they.

On Tuesday, the 12th of this month, at the news that the enemy was coming through Sologne, the magistrates sent soldiers to pull down the houses of Le Portereau, the suburb on the left bank, also the Augustinian church and monastery of that suburb, as well as all other buildings in which the enemy might lodge or entrench himself.

When the army arrived it was greatly diminished by desertions, having shed runaways at each victory. Some returned to England, others roamed through the realm of France robbing and plundering. That very 12th of October orders had been despatched from Rouen to the Bailies and Governors of Normandy to arrest those English who had departed from the company of my Lord, the Earl of Salisbury.

The fort of Les Tourelles and its outworks barred the entrance to the bridge. The English established themselves in Le Portereau, placed their cannon and their mortars on the rising ground of Saint-Jean-le-Blanc, and, on the following Sunday, they hurled down upon the city a shower of stone cannonballs, which did great damage to the houses, but killed no one save a woman of Orléans, named Belles, who dwelt near the Chesneau postern on the river bank. Thus the siege, which was to be ended by a woman's victory, began with a woman's death.

That same week the English cannon destroyed 12 water mills near La Tour Neuve. Whereupon the people of Orléans constructed within the city 11 mills worked by horses, in order that there might be no lack of flour. There were a few skirmishes at the bridge. Then on Thursday, the 21st of October, the English attempted to storm the outworks of Les Tourelles. The little band of adventurers in the service of the town and the city troops made a gallant defence. The women helped; throughout the four hours that the assault lasted long lines of gossips might be seen hurrying to the bridge, bearing their pots and pans filled with burning coals and boiling oil and fat, frantic with joy at the idea of scalding the *Godons*. The attack was repulsed; but two days later the French perceived that the outworks were undermined; the English had dug subterranean passages, to the props of which they had afterwards set fire. The outworks having become untenable in the opinion of the soldiers, they were destroyed and abandoned. It was deemed impossible to defend Les Tourelles thus dismantled. Those towers which would once have arrested an army's progress for a whole month were now useless against cannon. In front of La Belle Croix the townsfolk erected a rampart of earth and wood. Beyond this outwork two arches of the bridge were cut and replaced by a movable platform. And when this was done, the fort of Les Tourelles was abandoned to the English with no great regret. The latter set up a rampart of earth and faggots on the bridge, breaking two of its arches, one in front, the other behind their earthwork.

On the Sunday, towards evening, a few hours after the flag of St. George had been planted on the fort, the Earl of Salisbury, with William Glasdale and several captains, went up one of the towers to observe the lie of the city. Looking from a window he beheld the walls armed with cannon; the towers vanishing into pinnacles or with terraces on their flat roofs; the battlements dry and grey; the suburbs adorned for a few days longer with the fine stonework of their churches and monasteries; the vineyards and the woods yellow with autumn tints; the Loire and its oval-shaped islands, all slumbering in the evening calm. He was looking for the weak point in the ramparts, the place where he might make a breach and put up his scaling ladders. For his plan was to take Orléans by assault. William Glasdale said to him, 'My Lord, look well at your city. You have a good bird's-eye view of it from here.'

At this moment a cannonball breaks off a corner of the window recess, a stone from the wall strikes Salisbury, carrying away one eye and one side of his face. The day after the taking of Les Tourelles and when its loss had been remedied as best might be, the king's lieutenant general entered the town. He was le Seigneur Jean, Count of Porcien and of Montaing, Grand Chamberlain of France, son of Duke Louis of Orléans, who had been assassinated in 1407 by order of Jean-Sans-Peur, and whose death had armed the Armagnacs against the Burgundians. Dame de Cany was his mother, but he ought to have been the son of the Duchess of Orléans since the Duke was his father. Not only was it no drawback to children to be born outside wedlock and of an adulterous union, but it was a great honour to be called the bastard of a prince. The Bastard of Orléans was then 26 at the most. The year before, with a small company, he had hastened to revictual the inhabitants of Montargis, who were besieged by the Earl of Warwick. He had not only revictualled the town; but with the help of Captain La Hire had driven away the besiegers.

After the death of its chief, Salisbury's army was paralysed by disunion and diminished by desertions. Winter was coming: the captains, seeing there was nothing to be done for the present, broke up their camp, and, with such men as remained to them, went off to shelter behind the walls of Meung and Jargeau. On the evening of the 8th of November all that remained before the city was the garrison of Les Tourelles, consisting of

500 Norman horse, commanded by William Molyns and William Glasdale. The French might besiege and take them: they would not budge. The Governor, the old Sire de Gaucourt, had just fallen on the pavement in La Rue des Hôtelleries and broken his arm; he couldn't move. But what about the rest of the defenders?

The truth is, no one knew what to do. These warriors were doubtless acquainted with many measures for the succour of a besieged town, but they were all measures of surprise. Their only devices were sallies, ambuscades, skirmishes and other such valiant feats of arms. Should they fail in raising a siege by surprise, then they remained inactive – at the end of their ideas and of their resources. Their most experienced captains were incapable of any common effort – of any concerted action, of any enterprise in short, requiring a continuous mental effort and the subordination of all to one. Each was for his own hand and thought of nothing but booty. The defence of Orléans was altogether beyond their intelligence.

For 21 days Captain Glasdale remained entrenched, with his 500 Norman horse, under the battered walls of Les Tourelles, between his earthworks on Le Portereau side, which couldn't have become very formidable as yet, and his barrier on the bridge, which being but wood, a spark could easily have set on fire.

Meanwhile the citizens were at work. After the departure of the English, they performed a huge and arduous task. Concluding, and rightly, that the enemy would return not through La Sologne this time, but through La Beauce, they destroyed all their suburbs on the west, north and east, as they had already destroyed or begun to destroy Le Portereau. They burned and pulled down 22 churches and monasteries, among others the church of Saint-Aignan and its monastery, so beautiful that it was a pity to see it spoiled, the church of Saint Euverte, the church of Saint-Laurent-des-Orgerils, not without promising the blessed patrons of the town that when they should have delivered the city from the English, the citizens would build them new and more beautiful churches.

On the 30th of November Captain Glasdale beheld Sir John Talbot approaching Les Tourelles. He brought 300 men furnished with cannon, mortars and other engines of war. Thenceforward the bombardment was resumed more violently than before: roofs were broken through, walls were battered, but there was more noise than work. The people of Orléans had wherewith to answer the besiegers. For the 70 cannon and mortars, of which the city artillery consisted, there were 12 professional gunners with servants to wait on them. A very clever founder named Guillaume Duisy had cast a mortar which from its position at the crook or spur by the Chesneau postern, hurled stone bullets of 120 livres on to Les Tourelles. Near this mortar were two cannon, one called Montargis because the town of Montargis had lent it, the other named *Rifflart* after a very popular demon. A culverin firer, a Lorrainer living at Angers, had been sent by the king to Orléans, where he was paid 12 livres a month. His name was Jean de Montesclère. He was held to be the best master of his trade. He had in his charge a huge culverin which inflicted great damage on the English.

On the 25th of December a truce was proclaimed for the celebration of the Nativity of Our Lord. Of one faith and one religion, on feast days the hostility of the combatants ceased, and courtesy reconciled the knights of the two camps whenever the calendar reminded them that they were Christians. Noël is a gay feast. Captain Glasdale wanted to celebrate it with carol singing according to the English custom. He asked my Lord Jean, the Bastard of Orléans, and Marshal de Boussac to send him a band of musicians, which they graciously did. The Orléans players went forth to Les Tourelles with their clarions and their trumpets; and they played the English such carols as rejoiced their hearts. To the folk of Orléans, who came on to the bridge to listen to the music, it sounded very melodious; but no sooner had the truce expired than every man looked to himself. For from one bank to the other the cannon burst from their slumber, hurling balls of stone and copper with renewed vigour.

That which the people of Orléans had foreseen happened on the 30th of December. On that day the English came in great force through La Beauce to Saint-Laurent-des-Orgerils. All the French knights went out to meet them and performed great feats of arms; but the English occupied Saint-Laurent, and then the siege really began. They erected a bastion on the left bank of the Loire, west of Le Portereau, in a place called the Field of Saint-Privé. Another they erected in the little island to the right of Saint-Laurent-des-Orgerils. On the right bank, at Saint-Laurent, they constructed an entrenched camp. At a bow-shot's distance on the road to Blois, in a place called la Croix-Boissée, they built another bastion. Two bowshots away, towards the north on the road to Mans, at a spot called Les Douze-Pierres, they raised a fort which they called London.

By these works half of Orléans was invested, which was as good as saying that it was not invested at all. People went in and out as they pleased. Small relieving companies despatched by the king arrived without let or hindrance.

It became evident to Lord Scales, William Pole and Sir John Talbot, who since Salisbury's death had been conducting the siege, that months and months must elapse ere the investment could be completed and the city surrounded by a ring of forts connected by a moat. Meanwhile the miserable *Godons*, up to the ears in mud and snow, were freezing in their wretched hovels. If things went on thus they were in danger of being worse off and more starved than the besieged. Therefore, following the example of the late Earl, from time to time they tried to bring matters to a crisis; without great hope of success they endeavoured to take the town by assault.

On the side of the Renard Gate the wall was lower than elsewhere; and, as their strongest force lay in this direction, they preferred to attack this part of the ramparts. They stormed the Renard Gate, rushing against the barriers with loud cries of Saint George; but the king's men and the city bands drove them back to their bastions. Each of these ill planned and useless assaults cost them many men. And they already lacked both soldiers and horses.

Meanwhile the French, English and Burgundian knights took delight in performing valiant deeds of prowess. Whenever the whim took them, and under the slightest protest, they sallied forth into the country, but always with the object of capturing some booty, for they thought of little else.

The king's council was making every effort to succour Orléans. The king summoned the nobles of Auvergne. They had been true to the Lilies ever since the day when the Dauphin, Canon of Notre-Dame-d'Ancis, and barely more than a child, had travelled over wild peaks to subdue two or three rebellious barons.

The next day, Saturday, the eve of the first Sunday in Lent, when the Count of Clermont's army was still some distance away, they reached Rouvray. There, early in the morning, the Gascons of Poton and La Hire perceived the head of the convoy advancing into the plain, along the Étampes road.

There they were, a line of 300 carts and wagons full of arms and victuals conducted by English soldiers and merchants and peasants from Normandy, Picardy and Paris, 1,500 men at the most, all tranquil and unsuspecting. There naturally occurred to the Gascons the idea of falling upon these people and making short work with them at the moment when they least expected it. In great haste they sent to the Count of Clermont for permission to attack. He foolishly sent word to the Gascons not to attack before his arrival. The Gascons obeyed greatly disappointed; they saw what was being lost by waiting. And at length, perceiving that they have walked into the lion's mouth, the English leaders, Sir John Fastolf, Sir Richard Gethyn, Bailie of Évreux, Sir Simon Morhier, Provost of Paris, place themselves in good battle array. With their wagons they make a long narrow enclosure in the plain. There they entrench their horsemen, posting the archers in front, behind stakes planted in the ground with their points inclined towards the enemy. Seeing these preparations, the Constable of Scotland loses patience and leads his 400 horsemen in a rush upon the stakes, where the horses' legs are broken. The English, discovering that it is only a small company they have to deal with, bring out their cavalry and charge with such force that they overthrow the French and slay 300. Meanwhile the men of Auvergne had reached Rouvray and were scouring the village, draining the cellars. The Bastard left them and came to the help of the Scots with 400 fighting men. But he was wounded in the foot, and in great danger of being taken.

There fell in this combat Lord William Stuart and his brother, the Lords of Verduzan, of Châteaubrun, of Rochechouart, Jean Chabot with many others of high nobility and great valour. The English, not yet satiated with slaughter, scattered in pursuit of the fugitives. La Hire and Poton, beholding the enemy's standards dispersed over the plain, gathered together as many men as they could, between 60 and 80, and threw themselves on a small part of the English force, which they overcame. If at this juncture the rest of the French had rallied they might have saved the honour and advantage of the day. But the Count of Clermont, who had not attempted to come to the aid of the Bastard and the Constable of Scotland, displayed his unfailing cowardice to the end. Having seen them all slain, he returned with his army to Orléans, where he arrived well on into the night of the 12th of February. There followed him with their troops in disorder, the Baron La Tour-d'Auvergne, the Viscount of Thouars, the Marshal de Boussac, the Lord of Gravelle and the Bastard, who with the greatest difficulty kept in the saddle. Jamet du Tillay, La Hire and Poton came last, watching to see that the English did not complete their discomfiture by falling upon them from the forts.

Albeit the Count of Clermont was the king's cousin, the people of Orléans received him but coldly. He was held to have acted shamefully and treacherously; and there were those who let him know what they thought. On the morrow he made off with his men of Auvergne and Bourbonnais amidst the rejoicings of the townsfolk who did not want to support those who would not fight. At the same time there left the city Sire Louis de Culant, High Admiral of France and Captain La Hire, with 2,000 men-at-arms. At their departure there arose from the citizens such howls of displeasure, that to appease them it was necessary to explain that the captains were going to fetch fresh supplies of men and victuals, which was the actual truth. Only the Lord Bastard and the Marshal de Boussac were left in the city. And even the Marshal was not to stay long. A month later he went, saying that the king had need of him and that he must go and take possession of broad lands fallen to him through his wife, by the death of his brother-in-law, the Lord of Châteaubrun, at the Battle of the Herrings. The townsfolk deemed the reason a good one. He promised to return before long, and they were content. Now the Marshal de Boussac was one of the barons who had the welfare of the kingdom most at heart. But he who has lands must needs do his duty by them.

Believing that they were betrayed and abandoned, the citizens bethought them of securing their own safety. Since the king was not able to protect them, they resolved that in order to escape from the English, they would give themselves to one more powerful than he. Therefore, to Lord Philip, Duke of Burgundy, they despatched Captain Poton of

Saintrailles, who was known to him because he had been his prisoner, and two magistrates of the city, Jean de Saint-Avy and Guion du Fossé. Their mission was to pray and entreat the Duke to look favourably on the town, and for the sake of his good kinsman, their Lord, Charles, Duke of Orléans, a prisoner in England, and thus prevented from defending his own domain, to induce the English to raise the siege until such time as the troubles of the realm should be set at rest. Thus they were offering to place their town as a pledge in the hands of the Duke of Burgundy. Such an offer was in accordance with the secret desire of the Duke, who, having sent a few hundred Burgundian horse to the walls of Orléans, was helping the English, and did not intend to do it for nothing.

Pending the uncertain and distant day when they might be thus protected, the people of Orléans continued to protect themselves as best they could. But they were anxious and not without reason. For although they might prevent the enemy from entering within the city, they could devise no means for speedily driving him away. In the early days of March they observed with concern that the English were digging a ditch to serve them as cover in passing from one bastion to another, from la Croix-Boissée to Saint-Ladre. This work they attempted to destroy. They vigorously attacked the *Godons* and took a few prisoners. With two shots from his culverin Maître Jean killed five persons, including Lord Gray, the nephew of the late Earl of Salisbury. But they could not hinder the English from completing their work. The siege continued with terrible vigour. Agitated by doubts and fears, consumed with anxiety, without sleep, without rest and succeeding in nothing, they began to despair. Suddenly a strange rumour arises, spreads and gains credence.

It is told that there had lately passed through the town of Gien a maid (*une pucelle*), who proclaimed that she was on her way to Chinon to the gentle Dauphin, and said that she had been sent by God to raise the siege of Orléans and take the king to his anointing at Reims.

The tidings that a little saint of lowly origin was bringing divine help to Orléans made a great impression on minds excited by the fevers of the siege and rendered religious through fear. The Maid inspired them with a burning curiosity, which the Lord Bastard, like a wise man, deemed it prudent to encourage. He despatched to Chinon two knights charged to inquire concerning the damsel. They set forth and the whole town anxiously awaited their return.

Chapter VI
The Maid at Chinon – Prophecies

FROM THE VILLAGE of Sainte-Catherine-de-Fierbois, Jeanne dictated a letter to the king, for she did not know how to write. In this letter she asked permission to come to him, and told him that to bring him aid she had travelled over 150 leagues, and that she knew of many things for his good.

Towards noon, when the letter had been sealed, Jeanne and her escort set out for Chinon. She went to the king, just as in those days there went to him the sons of poor widows of Azincourt and Verneuil riding lame horses found in some meadow – 15-year-old lads coming forth from their ruined towers to mend their own fortunes and those of France. Charles VII was France, the image and symbol of France. Yet he was but a poor creature withal, the eleventh of the miserable children born to the mad Charles VI and his prolific Bavarian queen. He had grown up among disasters, and had survived his four elder brethren. But he himself was badly bred, knock-kneed and bandy legged; a veritable king's son, if his looks only were considered, and yet it was impossible to swear to his descent. Through his presence on the bridge at Montereau on that day, when, according to a wise man, it were better to have died than to have been there, he had grown pale and trembling, looking dully at everything going to wrack and ruin around him. After their victory of Verneuil and their partial conquest of Maine, the English had left him four years' respite. But his friends, his defenders, his deliverers had alike been terrible. Pious and humble, well content with his plain wife, he led a sad, anxious life in his châteaux on the Loire. He was timid. And well might he be so, for no sooner did he show friendship towards or confidence in one of the nobility than that noble was killed.

King Charles, thin, dwarfed in mind and body, cowering, timorous, suspicious, cut a sorry figure. Yet he was as good as another; and perhaps at that time he was just the king that was needed. His great resource was to convoke the States General. The nobility gave nothing, alleging that it was beneath their dignity to pay money. When, notwithstanding their poverty, the clergy did contribute something, it was still, always the third estate that bore more than its share of the financial burden. That extraordinary tax, the *taille*, became annual. The king summoned the Estates every year, sometimes twice a year. They met not without difficulty. The roads were dangerous. At every corner, travellers might be robbed or murdered. The officers, who journeyed from town to town collecting the taxes, had an armed escort for fear of the Scots and other men-at-arms in the king's service.

By writs issued on the 8th of January, 1428, the king summoned the States General to meet six months hence, on the following 18th of July, at Tours. On the 18th of July no one attended. On the 22nd of July came a new summons from the king, commanding the Estates to meet at Tours on the 10th of September. But the meeting did not take place until October, at Chinon, just when the Earl of Salisbury was marching on the Loire. The States granted 500,000 livres.

But the time could not be far off when the good people would be unable to pay any longer. In those days of war and pillage many a field was lying fallow, many a shop was closed and few were the merchants ambling on their nags from town to town.

Regnault de Chartres will play an important part in this story; and his part would appear greater still if it were laid bare in its entirety. Son of Hector de Chartres, master of Woods and Waters in Normandy, he took orders, became archdeacon of Beauvais, then chamberlain of Pope John XXIII, and in 1414, at about 34, was raised to the archiepiscopal see of Reims. The following year three of his brothers fell on the gory field of Azincourt. In 1418 Hector de Chartres perished at Paris, assassinated by the Butchers. Regnault himself, cast into prison by the Cabochiens, expected to be put to death. He vowed that if he escaped he would fast every Wednesday, and drink water for breakfast every Friday and Saturday, for the rest of his life.

After 11 days' journey, Jeanne reached Chinon on the 6th of March. By the intercession of Saint Julien, and probably with the aid of Collet de Vienne, the king's messenger, Jeanne found a lodging in the town, near the castle, in an inn kept by a woman of good repute. With her soul comforted, Jeanne listened to the soft whisper of her Voices. The two days she spent in the inn were passed in retirement, on her knees. The banks of the Vienne and the broad meadows, still in their black wintry garb, the hillslopes over which light mists floated, did not tempt her. But when, on her way to church, climbing up a steep street, or merely grooming her horse in the inn yard, she raised her eyes to the north, there on a mountain close at hand, just about the distance that would be traversed by one of those stone cannon-balls which had been in use for the last 50 or 60 years, she saw the towers of the finest castle of the realm. Behind its proud walls there breathed that king to whom she had journeyed, impelled by a miraculous love.

Meanwhile the despatches brought from the Commander of Vaucouleurs by Colet de Vienne were presented to the king. These despatches instructed him concerning the deeds and sayings of the damsel. This was one of those countless matters to be examined by the council, one which, it appears, the king must himself investigate, as pertaining to his royal office and as interesting him especially, since it might be a question of a damsel of remarkable piety, and he was himself the highest ecclesiastical personage in France. His grandfather, wise prince that he was, would have been far from scorning the counsel of devout women in whom was the voice of God.

King Charles read the Commander of Vaucouleur's letters, and had the damsel's escort examined before him. Of her mission and her miracles, they could say nothing. But they spoke of the good they had seen in her during the journey, and affirmed that there was no evil in her.

Of a truth, God speaketh through the mouths of virgins. But in such matters it is necessary to act with extreme caution, to distinguish carefully between the true prophetesses and the false, not to take for messengers from heaven the heralds of the devil. The latter sometimes create illusions. Certain ecclesiastics briefly interrogated Jeanne and asked her wherefore she had come. At first she replied that she would say nothing save to the king. But when the clerks represented to her that they were questioning her in the king's name, she told them that the King of Heaven had bidden her do two things: one was to raise the siege of Orléans, the other to lead the king to Reims for his anointing and his coronation.

The ecclesiastics, who had examined Jeanne, held various opinions concerning her. Some declared that her mission was a hoax, and that the king ought to beware of her. Others on the contrary held that, since she said she was sent of God, and that she had something to tell the king, the king should at least hear her.

Two priests who were then with the king, Jean Girard, President of the Parlement of Grenoble, and Pierre l'Hermite, later subdean of Saint-Martin-de-Tours, judged the case difficult and interesting enough to be submitted to Messire Jacques Gélu, that Armagnac prelate who had long served the house of Orléans and the Dauphin of France both in council and in diplomacy.

Charles was pious, and on his knees devoutly heard three masses a day. Regularly at the canonical hours he repeated the customary prayers in addition to prayers for the dead and other orisons. Daily he confessed, and communicated on every feast day. But he believed in foretelling events by means of the stars, in which he did not differ from other princes of his time. Each one of them had an astrologer in his service.

At that very time the Dauphin Charles had with him at Chinon an old Norman astrologer, one Pierre, who may have been Pierre de Saint-Valerien, canon of Paris. The latter had recently returned from Scotland, whither, accompanied by certain nobles, he had gone to fetch the Lady Margaret, betrothed to the Dauphin Louis. Not long afterwards this Maître Pierre was, rightly or wrongly, believed to have read in the sky that the shepherdess from the Meuse valley was appointed to drive out the English.

Jeanne had not long to wait in her inn. Two days after her arrival, what she had so ardently desired came to pass: she was taken to the king. Many of his familiar advisers, and those not the least important, counselled him to beware of a strange woman whose designs might be evil. There were others who put it before him that this shepherdess was introduced by letters from Robert de Baudricourt carried through hostile provinces; that in journeying to the king she had forded many rivers in a manner almost miraculous. On these considerations the king consented to receive her.

The great hall was crowded. As at every audience given by the king the room was close with the breath of the assembled multitude. On hearing of Jeanne's approach, king Charles buried himself among his retainers, either because he was still mistrustful and hesitating, or because he had other persons to speak to, or for some other reason. Jeanne was presented by the Count of Vendôme. Robust, with a firm, short neck, her figure appeared full, although confined by her man's jerkin. She wore breeches like a man, but still more surprising than her hose was her headgear and the cut of her hair. Beneath a woollen hood, her dark hair hung cut round in soup-plate fashion like a page's. Women of all ranks and all ages were careful to hide their hair so that not one lock of it should escape from beneath the coif, the veil or the high headdress which was then the mode. Jeanne's flowing locks looked strange to the folk of those days. She went straight to the king, took off her cap, curtsied, and said: 'God send you long life, gentle Dauphin.'

Afterwards there were those who marvelled that she should have recognized him in the midst of nobles more magnificently dressed than he. It is possible that on that day he may have been poorly attired. We know that it was his custom to have new sleeves put to his old doublets. And in any case he did not show off his clothes. Very ugly, knock-kneed, with emaciated thighs, small, odd, blinking eyes and a large bulbous nose, on his bony, bandy legs tottered and trembled this prince of 26.

When she had made her rustic curtsey, the king asked her name and what she wanted. She replied: 'Fair Dauphin, my name is Jeanne the Maid; and the King of Heaven speaks unto you by me and says that you shall be anointed and crowned at Reims, and be lieutenant of the King of Heaven, who is King of France.' She asked to be set about her work, promising to raise the siege of Orléans.

The king took her apart and questioned her for some time. By nature he was gentle, kind to the poor and lowly, but not devoid of mistrust and suspicion.

It is said that during this private conversation, addressing him with the familiarity of an angel, she made him this strange announcement: 'My Lord bids me say unto thee that thou art indeed the heir of France and the son of a king; he has sent me to thee to lead thee to Reims to be crowned there and anointed if thou wilt.' Afterwards the Maid's chaplain reported these words, saying he had received them from the Maid herself. All that is certain is that the Armagnacs were not slow to turn them into a miracle in favour of the Line of the Lilies. It was asserted that these words spoken by God himself, by the mouth of an innocent girl, were a reply to the carking, secret anxiety of the king. Madame Ysabeau's son, it was said, distracted and saddened by the thought that perhaps the royal blood did not flow in his veins, was ready to renounce his kingdom and declare himself a usurper, unless by some heavenly light his doubts concerning his birth should be dispelled. Men told how his face shone with joy when it was revealed to him that he was the true heir of France.

Doubtless the Armagnac preachers were in the habit of speaking of Queen Ysabeau as *une grande gorre* and a Herodias of licentiousness; but one would like to know whence her son derived his curious misgiving. He had not manifested it on entering into his inheritance; and, had occasion required, the jurists of his party would have proved to him by reasons derived from laws and customs that he was by birth the true heir and the lawful successor of the late king; for filiation must be proved not by what is hidden, but by what is manifest, otherwise it would be impossible to assign the legal heir to a kingdom or to an acre of land. Nevertheless, it must be borne in mind that the king was very unfortunate at this time. Now misfortune agitates the conscience and raises scruples; and he might well doubt the justice of his cause since God was forsaking him. But if he were indeed assailed by painful doubts, how can he have been relieved from them by the words of a damsel who, as far as he then knew, might be mad or sent to him by his enemies? It is hard to reconcile such credulity with what we know of his suspicious nature. The first thought that occurred to him must have been that ecclesiastics had instructed the damsel.

A few moments after he had dismissed her, he assembled the Sire de Gaucourt and certain other members of his council and repeated to them what he had just heard: 'She told me that God had sent her to aid me to recover my kingdom.' He did not add that she had revealed to him a secret known to himself alone.

The king's Counsellors, knowing little of the damsel, decided that they must have her before them to examine her concerning her life and her belief. King Charles kept Jeanne in uncertainty as to what was believed of her. But he did not suspect her of craftiness and he received her willingly. She talked to him with the simplest familiarity. She called him gentle Dauphin, and by that term she implied nobility and royal magnificence. She also called him her *oriflamme*, because he was her *oriflamme*, or, as in modern language she would have expressed it, her standard. The *oriflamme* was the royal banner. No one at Chinon had seen it, but marvellous things were told of it. The *oriflamme* was in the form of a gonfanon with two wings, made of a costly silk, fine and light, called *sandal*, and it was edged with tassels of green silk. It had come down from heaven; it was the banner of Clovis and of Saint Charlemagne. When the king went to war it was carried before him. So great was its virtue that the enemy at its approach became powerless and fled in terror. It was remembered how, when in 1304 Philippe le Bel defeated the Flemings, the knight who bore it was slain. The next day he was found dead, but still clasping the standard in his arms. It had floated in front of King Charles VI before his misfortunes, and since then it had never been unfurled.

One day when the Maid and the king were talking together, the Duke of Alençon entered the hall. When he was a child, the English had taken him prisoner at Verneuil and kept him five years in the Crotoy Tower. Only recently set at liberty, he had been shooting quails near Saint-Florent-lès-Saumur, when a messenger had brought the tidings that God had sent a damsel to the king to turn the English out of France. This news interested him as much as anyone because he had married the Duke of Orléans' daughter; and straightway he had come to Chinon to see for himself. In the days of his graceful youth the Duke of Alençon appeared to advantage, but he was never renowned for his wisdom. He was weak-minded, violent, vain, jealous and extremely credulous. He believed that ladies find favour by means of a certain herb, the mountain-heath; and later he thought himself bewitched. He had a disagreeable, harsh voice; he knew it, and the knowledge annoyed him. As soon as she saw him approaching, Jeanne asked who this noble was. When the king replied that it was his cousin Alençon, she curtsied to the duke and said: 'Be

welcome. The more representatives of the blood royal are here the better.'
In this she was completely mistaken. The Dauphin smiled bitterly at her
words. Not much of the royal blood of France ran in the duke's veins.

On the next day Jeanne went to the king's mass. When she approached
her Dauphin she bowed before him. The king took her into a room
and sent everyone away except the Sire de la Trémouille and the Duke
of Alençon.

Then Jeanne addressed to him several requests. More especially did
she ask him to give his kingdom to the King of Heaven. 'And afterwards,'
she added, 'the King of Heaven will do for you what he has done for your
predecessors and will restore you to the condition of your fathers.'

That same day she rode out with the king and threw a lance in the
meadow with so fine a grace that the Duke of Alençon, marvelling, made
her a present of a horse.

She called the Duke of Alençon her fair duke, and loved him for the
sake of the Duke of Orléans, whose daughter he had married. She loved
him also because he believed in her when all others doubted or denied,
and because the English had done him wrong. She loved him too because
she saw he had a good will to fight. It was told how when he was a captive
in the hands of the English at Verneuil, and they proposed to give him
back his liberty and his goods if he would join their party, he had rejected
their offer. He was young like her; she thought that he like her must be
sincere and noble. And perhaps in those days he was, for doubtless he
was not then seeking to discover powders with which to dry up the king.

It was decided that Jeanne should be taken to Poitiers to be examined
by the doctors there. In this town the Parliament met. Here also were
gathered together many famous clerks learned in theology, secular as
well as regular, and grave doctors and masters were summoned to join
them. Jeanne set out under escort. At first she thought she was being
taken to Orléans. Her faith was like that of the ignorant but believing folk,
who, having taken the cross, went forth and thought every town they
approached was Jerusalem. Halfway she inquired of her guides where
they were taking her. When she heard that it was to Poitiers: 'In God's
name!' she said, 'much ado will be there, I know. But my Lord will help
me. Now let us go on in God's strength!'

Chapter VII
The Maid at Poitiers

✝

FOR 14 YEARS THE TOWN of Poitiers had been the capital of that part of France which belonged to the French. The Dauphin Charles had transferred his Parliament there, or rather had assembled there those few members who had escaped from the Parliament of Paris.

Here was a large assembly of doctors for the cross examination of one shepherdess. But we must remember that in those days theology subtle and inflexible dominated all human knowledge and forced the secular arm to give effect to its judgment. Therefore, as soon as an ignorant girl caused it to be believed that she had seen God, the Virgin, the saints and the angels, she must either pass from miracle to miracle, through an edifying death to beatification, or from heresy to heresy through an ecclesiastical prison, to be burnt as a witch. And, as the holy Inquisitors were fully persuaded that the Devil easily entered into a woman, the unhappy creature was more likely to be burnt alive than to die in an odour of sanctity. But Jeanne before the doctors at Poitiers was an exception; she ran no risk of being suspected in matters of faith. In her presence the illustrious masters drew in their theological claws. They were churchmen, but they were Armagnacs, for the most part businessmen, diplomatists, old councillors of the Dauphin. As priests, doubtless they were possessed of a certain body of dogma and morality, and of a code of rules for judging matters of faith. But now it was a question not of curing the disease of heresy, but of driving out the English. Jeanne was in favour with my Lord the Duke of Alençon and with my Lord the Bastard; the inhabitants of Orléans were looking to her for their deliverance. She promised to take the king to Reims; and it happened that the cleverest and the most powerful man in France, the Chancellor of the kingdom, my Lord Regnault de Chartres, was Archbishop and Count of Reims; and that had great weight.

In this Church holy and indivisible, there were the doctors of Poitiers who deliberately pronounced God to be on the side of the Dauphin, while the University of Paris as deliberately pronounced God to be on the side of the Burgundians and the English.

Jeanne was taken to the mansion where dwelt Maître Jean Rabateau, not far from the law-courts, in the heart of the town. Maître Jean Rabateau was lay attorney general; all criminal cases went to him, while civil cases went to the ecclesiastical attorney general, Jean Jouvenel.

Jean Rabateau's wife, in common with the wives of all lawyers, was a woman of good reputation While she was at La Rose, Jeanne would stay long on her knees every day after dinner. At night she would rise from her bed to pray, and pass long hours in the little oratory of the mansion. It was in this house that the doctors conducted her examination. When their coming was announced she was seized with cruel anxiety. The Blessed Saint Catherine was careful to reassure her.

The grave doctors and masters and the principal clerks of the Parliament of Poitiers, in companies of two and three, repaired to the house of Jean Rabateau, and each one of them in turn questioned Jeanne. The first to come were Jean Lombard, Guillaume le Maire, Guillaume Aimery, Pierre Turelure and Jacques Meledon. Brother Jean Lombard asked: 'Wherefore have you come? The king desires to know what led you to come to him.' Jeanne's reply greatly impressed these clerks.

Then the word fell to Brother Guillaume Aimery: 'According to what you have said, the Voice told you that God will deliver the people of France from their distress; but if God will deliver them he has no need of men-at-arms.'

'In God's name,' replied the Maid, 'the men-at-arms will fight, and God will give the victory.'

Maître Guillaume declared himself satisfied.

On the 22nd of March, Maître Pierre de Versailles and Maître Jean Érault went together to Jean Rabateau's lodging. The squire, Gobert Thibault, whom Jeanne had already seen at Chinon, came with them. He was a young man and very simple, one who believed without asking for a sign. As they came in Jeanne went to meet them, and, striking the squire on the shoulder, in a friendly manner, she said: 'I wish I had many men as willing as you.'

With men-at-arms she felt at her ease. But the doctors she could not tolerate, and she suffered torture when they came to argue with her. Although these theologians showed her great consideration, their eternal questions wearied her. She bore them a grudge for not believing in her straightway, without proof, and for asking her for a sign, which she could not give them, since neither Saint Michael nor Saint Catherine nor Saint Margaret appeared during the examination. She felt awkward in their presence, and their manners were the occasion of that irritation which is discernible in more than one of her replies. Sometimes when they questioned her she retreated to the end of her bench and sulked.

'We come to you from the king,' said Maître Pierre de Versailles.

She replied with a bad grace: 'I am quite aware that you are come to question me again. I don't know A from B.' But to the question: 'Wherefore do you come?' she made answer eagerly: 'I come from the King of Heaven to raise the siege of Orléans, and take the king to be crowned and anointed at Reims. Maître Jean Érault, have you ink and paper? Write what I shall tell you.' And she dictated a brief manifesto to the English captains: 'You, Suffort, Clasdas and La Poule, in the name of the King of Heaven I call upon you to return to England.' Maître Jean Érault, who wrote at her dictation, was, like most of the clerks, favourably disposed towards her.

The damsel was interrogated concerning her Voices, which she called her council, and her saints, whom she imagined in the semblance of those sculptured or painted figures peopling the churches. The doctors objected to her having cast off woman's clothing and had her hair cut round in the manner of a page. Now it is written: 'The woman shall not wear that which pertaineth unto a man, neither shall a man put on a woman's garment: for all that do so are abomination unto the Lord thy God' (Deuteronomy xxii, 5). The Council of Gangres, held in the reign of the Emperor Valens, had anathematised women who dressed as men and cut short their hair.

Certain of her questioners inquired why she called Charles Dauphin instead of giving him his title of king. This title had been his by right since the 30th of October, 1422; for on that day, the ninth since the death of the king his father, at Mehun-sur-Yèvre, in the chapel royal, he had put off his black gown and assumed the purple robe, while the heralds, raising aloft the banner of France, cried: 'Long live the king!'

She answered: 'I will not call him king until he shall have been anointed and crowned at Reims. To that city I intend to take him.'

Without this anointing there was no king of France for her. Of the miracles which had followed that anointing she had heard every year from the mouth of her priest as he recited the glorious deeds of the Blessed Saint Remi, the patron saint of her parish. This reply was such as to satisfy the interrogators because, both for things spiritual and temporal, it was important that the king should be anointed at Reims. And Messire Regnault de Chartres must have ardently desired it.

Brother Seguin of Seguin in his turn questioned the damsel. He was from Limousin, and his speech betrayed his origin. He spoke with a drawl and used expressions unknown in Lorraine and Champagne. Perhaps he had that dull, heavy air, which rendered the folk of his province somewhat ridiculous in the eyes of dwellers on the Loire, the Seine and the Meuse. To the question: 'What language do your Voices speak?' Jeanne replied: 'A better one than yours.'

Even saints may lose patience. If Brother Seguin did not know it before, he learnt it that day. And what business had he to doubt that Saint Catherine and Saint Margaret, who were on the side of the French, spoke French? Such a doubt Jeanne could not bear, and she gave her questioner to understand that when one comes from Limousin one does not inquire concerning the speech of heavenly ladies. Notwithstanding he pursued his interrogation: 'Do you believe in God?' 'Yes, more than you do,' said the Maid, who, knowing nothing of the good Brother, was somewhat hasty in esteeming herself better grounded in the faith than he.

But she was vexed that there should be any question of her belief in God, who had sent her. Her reply, if favourably interpreted, would testify to the ardour of her faith. Did Brother Seguin so understand it? His contemporaries represented him as being of a somewhat bitter disposition. On the contrary, there is reason to believe that he was good-natured.

'But after all,' he said, 'it cannot be God's will that you should be believed unless some sign appear to make us believe in you. On your word alone we cannot counsel the king to run the risk of granting you men-at-arms.'

'In God's name,' she answered, 'it was not to give a sign that I came to Poitiers. But take me to Orléans and I will show you the signs wherefore I am sent. Let me be given men, it matters not how many, and I will go to Orléans.'

And she repeated what she was continually saying: 'The English shall all be driven out and destroyed. The siege of Orléans shall be raised and the city delivered from its enemies, after I shall have summoned it to surrender in the name of the King of Heaven. The Dauphin shall be anointed at Reims, the town of Paris shall return to its allegiance to the king, and the Duke of Orléans shall come back from England.'

She said without ceasing: 'The sign that I will show you shall be Orléans relieved and the siege raised.'

Such persistency made an impression on most of her interrogators. They determined to make of it not a stone of stumbling, but rather an example of zeal and a subject of edification. Since she promised them a sign it behoved them in all humility to ask God to send it, and, filled with a like hope, joining with the king and all the people, to pray to the God, who delivered Israel, to grant them the banner of victory. Thus were overcome the arguments of Brother Seguin and of those who, led away by the precepts of human wisdom, desired a sign before they believed.

After an examination which had lasted six weeks, the doctors declared themselves satisfied.

There was one point it was necessary to ascertain; they must know whether Jeanne was, as she said, a virgin. Matrons had indeed already examined her on her arrival at Chinon. Then there was a doubt as to whether she were man or maid; and it was even feared that she might be an illusion in woman's semblance, produced by the art of demons, which scholars considered by no means impossible.

Chapter VIII
The Maid at Poitiers (*continued*)

✦

A BELIEF, COMMON TO LEARNED and ignorant alike, ascribed special virtues to the state of virginity.

The very economy of the Christian religion – the ordering of its mysteries, wherein humanity is represented as ruined by a woman and saved by a virgin, and all flesh is involved in Eve's curse – led to the triumph of virginity and the exaltation of a condition which, in the words of a Father of the Church, is in the flesh, yet not of the flesh.

'It is because of virginity,' says Saint Gregory of Nyssa, 'that God vouchsafes to dwell with men. It is virginity which gives men wings to soar towards heaven.'

While mystics and visionaries were glorifying virginity, the Church, bent on governing the body as well as the soul, condemned opinions denying the lawfulness of marriage, which she had constituted a sacrament. Those who would anathematise all works of the flesh she held to be abominable and impious. A maid deserved praise for preserving her virginity, provided always that her motives were praiseworthy.

It was then commonly believed that such maidens as gave themselves to the devil were straightway stripped of their virginity; and that thus he obtained power over these unhappy creatures. Such ways accorded with what was known of his libidinous disposition. These pleasures were tempered to his woeful state. And thereby he gained a further advantage – that of unarming his victim – for virginity is as a coat of mail against which the darts of hell are but blades of straw. Hence it was all but certain that a soul vowed to the devil could not reside within a maid. Wherefore, there was one infallible way of proving that the peasant girl from Vaucouleurs was not given up to magic or to sorcery, and had made no pact with the Evil One. Recourse was had to it.

Jeanne was seen, visited, privately inspected and thoroughly examined by wise women, *mulieres doctas*; by knowing virgins, *peritas virgines*; by widows and wives, *viduas et conjugates*. First among these matrons were: the Queen of Sicily and of Jerusalem, Duchess of Anjou; Dame Jeanne de Preuilly, wife of the Sire de Gaucourt, Governor of Orléans, who was about 57 years of age; and Dame Jeanne de Mortemer, wife of Messire Robert le Maçon, Lord of Trèves, a man full of years. The last was only 18, and one would have expected her to be better acquainted with the *Calendrier des Vieillards* than with the formulary of matrons. It is strange with what assurance the good wives of those days undertook the solution of a problem which had appeared difficult to King Solomon in all his wisdom.

Jeanne of Domremy was found to be a maid pure and intact.

While she herself was being subjected to the interrogatories of doctors and the examination of matrons, certain clerics who had been despatched to her native province were there prosecuting an inquiry concerning her birth, her life and her morals. The ecclesiastics had been chosen from those mendicant Friars who could pass freely along the highways and byways of the enemy's country without exciting the suspicion of English and Burgundians. And, indeed, they were in no way molested. From Domremy and from Vaucouleurs they brought back sure testimony to the humility, the devotion, the honesty and the simplicity of Jeanne. But, most important, they had found no difficulty in gleaning certain pious tales, such as commonly adorned the childhood of saints. To these monks we must attribute an important share in the development of those legends of Jeanne's early years, which were so soon to become popular. From this time, apparently, dates the story that when Jeanne was in her seventh year, wolves spared her sheep, and birds of the woods came at her call and ate crumbs from her lap. Such saintly flowers suggest a Franciscan origin; among them are the wolf of Gubbio and the birds preached to by Saint Francis. These mendicants may also have furnished examples of the Maid's prophetic gift. They may have spread abroad the story that, when she was at Vaucouleurs, on the day of the Battle of the Herrings, she knew of the great hurt inflicted on the French at Rouvray. The success of such little stories was immediate and complete.

After this examination and inquiry, the doctors came to the following conclusions: 'The king, beholding his own need and that of his realm, and considering the constant prayers to God of his poor subjects and all others who love peace and justice, ought not to repulse or reject the Maid.

'The king asked her for a sign, to which she replied that before Orléans she would give it, but neither earlier nor elsewhere, for thus it is ordained of God.

'Now, seeing that the king hath made trial of the aforesaid Maid as far as it was in his power to do, that he findeth no evil in her, and that her reply is that she will give a divine sign before Orléans; seeing her persistency, and the consistency of her words, and her urgent request that she be sent to Orléans to show there that the aid she brings is divine, the king should not hinder her from going to Orléans with men-at-arms, but should send her there in due state trusting in God. For to fear her or reject her when there is no appearance of evil in her would be to rebel against the Holy Ghost, and to render oneself unworthy of divine succour, as Gamaliel said of the Apostles in the Council of the Jews.'

In short, the doctors' conclusion was that as yet nothing divine appeared in the Maid's promises, but that she had been examined and been found humble, a virgin, devout, honest, simple and wholly good; and that, since she had promised to give a sign from God before Orléans, she must be taken there, for fear that in her the gift of the Holy Ghost should be rejected.

Of these conclusions a great number of copies were made and sent to the towns of the realm as well as to the princes of Christendom. The Emperor Sigismond, for example, received a copy.

If the doctors of Poitiers had intended this six weeks' inquiry, culminating in a favourable and solemn conclusion, to bring about the glorification of the Maid and the heartening of the French people by the preparation and announcement of the marvel they had before them, then they succeeded perfectly.

At the termination of the inquiries, a favourable opportunity for introducing the Maid into Orléans arrived in the beginning of April. For her arming and her accoutring, she was sent first to Tours.

Chapter IX
The Maid at Tours

✚

A T TOURS THE MAID LODGED in the house of a dame commonly called Lapau. She was Eléonore de Paul, a woman of Anjou, who had been lady-in-waiting to Queen Marie of Anjou. Married to Jean du Puy, Lord of La Roche-Saint-Quentin, councillor of the Queen of Sicily, she had remained in the service of the Queen of France.

The town of Tours belonged to the Queen of Sicily, who grew richer and richer as her son-in-law grew poorer and poorer. She aided him with money and with lands. In 1424, the duchy of Touraine with all its dependencies, except the castellany of Chinon, had come into her possession. The burgesses and commonalty of Tours earnestly desired peace. Meanwhile they made every effort to escape from pillage at the hands of men-at-arms. Neither King Charles nor Queen Yolande was able to defend them, so they must needs defend themselves. When the town watchmen announced the approach of one of those marauding chiefs who were ravaging Touraine and Anjou, the citizens shut their gates and saw to it that the culverins were in their places. Then there was a parley: the captain from the brink of the moat maintained that he was in the king's service and on his way to fight the English; he asked for a night's rest in the town for himself and his men. From the heights of the ramparts he was politely requested to pass on; and, in case he should be tempted to force an entry, a sum of money was offered him. Thus the citizens fleeced themselves for fear of being robbed.

In like manner, only a few days before Jeanne's coming, they had given the Scot, Kennedy, who was ravaging the district, 200 livres to go on. When they had got rid of their defenders, their next care was to fortify themselves against the English. On the 29th of February of this same year, 1429, these citizens lent 100 crowns to Captain La Hire, who was then doing his best for Orléans. And even on the approach of the English they consented to receive 40 archers belonging to the company of the Sire de Bueil, only on condition that Bueil should lodge in the castle with 20 men, and that the others should be quartered in the inns, where they were to have nothing without paying for it. Thus it was or was not; and the Sire de Bueil went off to defend Orléans.

In Jean du Puy's house, Jeanne was visited by an Augustinian monk, one Jean Pasquerel. He was returning from the town of Puy-en-Velay where he had met Isabelle Romée and certain of those who had conducted Jeanne to the king.

Jeanne's comrades, having made friends with Pasquerel, said to him: 'You must go with us to Jeanne. We will not leave you until you have taken us to her.' They travelled together. Brother Pasquerel went with them to Chinon, which Jeanne had left; then he went on to Tours, where his convent was.

Jeanne's comrades said to her: 'Jeanne, we have brought you this good father. You will like him well when you know him.'

She replied: 'The good father pleases me. I have already heard tell of him, and even tomorrow will I confess to him.' The next day the good father heard her in confession, and chanted mass before her. He became her chaplain, and never left her.

In the fifteenth century Tours was one of the chief manufacturing towns of the kingdom. Here it was that, by the king's command, the master armourer made Jeanne a suit of mail. The suit he furnished was of wrought iron; and, according to the custom of that time, consisted of a helmet, a cuirass in four parts, with epaulets, armlets, elbow pieces, fore armlets, gauntlets, cuisses, knee pieces, greaves and shoes. Possibly one of the skilful and renowned drapers of Tours took the Maid's measure for a *houppelande* or loose coat in silk or cloth of gold or silver, such as captains wore over the cuirass. To look well, the coat, which was open in front, must be cut in scallops that would float round the horseman as he rode. Jeanne loved fine clothes but still more fine horses.

The king invited her to choose a horse from his stables. A shield was out of the question. Since chain-armour, which was not proof against blows, had been succeeded by that plate-armour, on which nothing could make an impression, they had ceased to be used save in pageants. As for the sword – the noblest part of her accoutrement and the bright symbol of strength joined to loyalty – Jeanne refused to take that from the royal armourer; she was resolved to receive it from the hand of Saint Catherine herself.

We know that on her coming into France she had stopped at Fierbois and heard three masses in Saint Catherine's chapel. Therein the Virgin of Alexandria had many swords, without counting the one Charles Martel was said to have given her. The walls bristled with swords; and, as gifts had been flowing in for half a century, ever since the days of King Charles V, the sacristans were probably in the habit of taking down the old weapons to make room for the new, hoarding the old steel in some storehouse until an opportunity arrived for selling it. The Voices indicated one sword among the multitude of those in the Chapel at Fierbois. Messire Richard Kyrthrizian and Brother Gille Lecourt, both of them priests, were then custodians of the chapel. Jeanne in a letter caused them to be asked for the sword, which had been revealed to her. In the letter she said that it would be found underground, not very deep down, and behind the altar. At least these were all the directions she was able to give afterwards, and then she could not quite remember whether it was behind the altar or in front. Was she able to give the custodians of the chapel any signs by which to recognize the sword? She never explained this point, and her letter is lost.

It is certain, however, that she believed the sword had been shown to her in a vision and in no other manner. The priests were careful to offer it to the Maid with great ceremony before giving it to the armourer who had come for it. They enclosed it in a sheath of red velvet, embroidered with the royal flowers de luce. When Jeanne received it she recognized it to be the one revealed to her in a celestial vision and promised her by her Voices, and she failed not to let the little company of monks and soldiers who surrounded her know that it was so. This they took to be a good omen and a sign of victory. To protect Saint Catherine's sword the priests of the town gave her a second sheath; this one was of black cloth. Jeanne had a third made of very tough leather.

The king had given her no command. Acting according to the counsel of the doctors, he did not hinder her from going to Orléans with men-at-arms. He even had her taken there in state in order that she might give the promised sign. He granted her men to conduct her, not for her to conduct. How could she have conducted them since she did not know the way? Meanwhile she had a standard made according to the command of Saint Catherine and Saint Margaret, who had said: 'Take the standard in the name of the King of Heaven!' It was of a coarse white cloth, or buckram, edged with silk fringe. At the bidding of her Voices, Jeanne caused a painter of the town to represent on it what she called 'the World,' that is, Our Lord seated upon his throne, blessing with his right hand, and in his left holding the globe of the world. On his right and on his left were angels, both painted as they were in churches, and presenting Our Lord with flowers de luce. Above or on one side were the names Jhesus – Maria, and the background was strewn with the royal lilies in gold. She also had a coat-of-arms painted: on an azure shield a silver dove, holding in its beak a scroll on which was written: 'De par le Roi du Ciel.' This coat-of-arms she had painted on the reverse of the standard bearing on the front the picture of Our Lord.

The standard was the signal for rallying. For long only kings, emperors and leaders in war had had the right of raising it. The feudal suzerain had it carried before him; vassals ranged themselves beneath their lord's banners. But in 1429 banners had ceased to be used save in corporations, guilds, and parishes, borne only before the armies of peace. In war they were no longer needed. The meanest captain, the poorest knight had his own standard. When 50 French men-at-arms went forth from Orléans against a handful of English marauders, a crowd of banners like a swarm of butterflies waved over the fields.

Chapter X
The Siege of Orléans from the 7th of March to the 28th of April, 1429

SINCE THE TERRIBLE AND RIDICULOUS **discomfiture of the king's men in the Battle of the Herrings, the citizens of Orléans had lost all faith in their defenders. Their minds agitated, suspicious and credulous were possessed by phantoms of fear and wrath. Suddenly and without reason they believe themselves betrayed.**

One day it is announced that a hole big enough for a man to pass through has been made in the town wall just where it skirts the outbuildings of the Aumône. A crowd of people hasten to the spot; they see the hole and a piece of the wall which had been restored, with two loopholes; they fail to understand, and think themselves sold and betrayed into the enemy's hands; they rave and break forth into howls, and seek the priest in charge of the hospital to tear him to pieces. A few days after, on Holy Thursday, a similar rumour is spread abroad: traitors are about to deliver up the town into the hands of the English. The folk seize their weapons; soldiers, burgesses, villeins mount guard on the outworks, on the walls and in the streets. On the morrow, the day after that on which the panic had originated, fear still possesses them.

In the beginning of March the besiegers saw approaching the Norman vassals, summoned by the regent. But they were only 629 lances all told, and they were only bound to serve for 26 days. Under the leadership of

Scales, Pole and Talbot, the English continued the investment works as best they could. On the 10th of March, four kilometres (two and a half miles) east of the city, they occupied without opposition the steep slope of Saint-Loup and began to erect a bastion there, which should command the upper river and the two roads from Gien and Pithiviers, at the point where they meet near the Burgundian gate. On the 20th of March they completed the bastion named London, on the road to Mans. Between the 9th and 15th of April two new bastions were erected towards the west, Rouen 274 metres (900 feet) east of London, Paris 274 metres (900 feet) from Rouen. About the 20th they fortified Saint-Jean-le-Blanc across the Loire and established a watch to guard the crossing of the river. This was but little in comparison with what remained to be done, and they were short of men; for they had less than 3,000 round the town. Wherefore they fell upon the peasants. Now that the season for tending the vines was drawing near, the country folk went forth into the fields thinking only of the land; but the English lay in wait for them, and when they had taken them prisoners, set them to work.

In the opinion of those most skilled in the arts of war, these bastions were worthless. They were furnished with no stabling for horses. They could not be built near enough to render assistance to each other; the besieger was in danger of being himself besieged in them. In short, from these vexatious methods of warfare the English reaped nothing but disappointment and disgrace. In fact it was so easy to pass through the enemy's lines that merchants were willing to run the risk of taking cattle to the besieged. And more than once the besieged had carried off, in the very faces of the English, victuals and ammunition destined for the besiegers and including casks of wine, game, horses, bows, forage and even 26 head of large cattle.

The siege was costing the English dear – 40,000 *livres tournois* a month. They were short of money; they were obliged to resort to the most irritating expedients. By a decree of the 3rd of March, King Henry had recently ordered all his officers in Normandy to lend him one quarter of their pay. In their huts of wood and earth, the men-at-arms, who had endured much from the cold, now began to suffer hunger.

The wasted fields of La Beauce, of l'Île-de-France and of Normandy could furnish them with no great store of sheep or oxen. Their food was bad, their drink worse. The vintage of 1427 had been bad, that of the following year was poor and weak – more like sour grapes than wine. A sudden humiliation still further weakened the English. Captain Poton de Saintrailles and the two magistrates, Guyon du Fossé and Jean de Saint-Avy, who had gone on an embassy to the Duke of Burgundy, returned to Orléans on the 17th of April. The duke had granted their request and consented to take the town under his protection. But the regent, to whom the offer had been made, would not have it thus.

The ambassadors returned accompanied by a Burgundian herald who blew his trumpet in the English camp, and, in the name of his master, commanded all combatants who owed allegiance to the duke to raise the siege. Some hundreds of archers and men-at-arms, Burgundians, men of Picardy and of Champagne, departed forthwith.

On the next day, at four o'clock in the morning, the citizens emboldened and deeming the opportunity a good one, attacked the camp of Saint-Laurent-des-Orgerils. They slew the watch and entered the camp, where they found piles of money, robes of martin and a goodly store of weapons. Absorbed in pillage, they paid no heed to defending themselves and were surprised by the enemy, who in great force had hastened to the place. They fled pursued by the English who slew many.

Within those walls, in a space where there was room for not more than 15,000 inhabitants, 40,000 were huddled together, one vast multitude agonised by all manner of suffering; depressed by domestic sorrow; racked with anxiety; maddened by constant danger and perpetual panic. Although the wars of those days were not so sanguinary as they became later, the sallies of the inhabitants of Orléans were the occasion of constant and considerable loss of life. Since the middle of March the English bullets had fallen more into the centre of the town; and they were not always harmless.

The people of Orléans firmly believed that this war was sent to them of God to punish sinners, who had worn out his patience. They were aware both of the cause of their sorrows and of the means of remedying them. The remedy was to live well, to amend one's life, to have masses said and sung for the souls of those who had suffered death in the service of the realm, to renounce the sinful life, and to ask forgiveness of Our Lady and the saints. This remedy had been adopted by the people of Orléans. They had offered candles to Our Lady and to the patron saints of the town, and had carried the shrine of Saint-Aignan round the walls.

Every time they felt themselves in great danger, they brought it forth from the Church of Sainte-Croix, carried it in grand procession round the town and over the ramparts, then, having brought it back to the cathedral, they listened to a sermon preached in the porch by a good monk chosen by the magistrates. They said prayers in public and resolved to amend their lives.

The Lord of Villars and Messire Jamet du Tillay, having returned from Chinon, reported that they had with their own eyes seen the Maid; and they told of the marvels of her coming. They extolled her piety, her candour, that simplicity which testified that God dwelt with her, and that skill in managing a horse and wielding weapons which caused all men to marvel.

Certain of the captains, and certain even of the people, treated them with derision. But by so doing they ran the risk of ill-usage. The inhabitants of the city believed in the Maid as firmly as in Our Lord. From her they expected help and deliverance. They summoned her in a kind of mystic ecstasy and religious frenzy. The fever of the siege had become the fever of the Maid.

What was to become of Orléans? The siege, badly conducted, was causing the English the most grievous disappointments. Further, their captains perceived they would never succeed in taking the town by means of those bastions, between which anything, either men, victuals or ammunition, could pass, and with an army miserably quartered in mud hovels, ravaged by disease and reduced by desertions to 3,000, or at the most to 3,200 men. They had lost nearly all their horses. Far from being able to continue the attack it was hard for them to maintain the defensive and to hold out in those miserable wooden towers, which, as Le Jouvencel said, were more profitable to the besieged than to the besiegers.

Their only hope, and that an uncertain and distant one, lay in the reinforcements, which the regent was gathering with great difficulty. Meanwhile, time seemed to drag in the besieged town. The warriors who defended it were brave, but they had come to the end of their resources and knew not what more to do. The citizens were good at keeping guard, but they would not face fire. They did not suspect the miserable condition to which the besiegers had been reduced. Hardship, anxiety and an infected atmosphere depressed their spirits. At every moment they believed themselves betrayed. They were not calm and self-possessed enough to recognize the enormous advantages of their situation. The town's means of communication, whereby it could be indefinitely reinforced and revictualled, were still open. Besides, a relieving army, well in advance of that of the English, was on the point of arriving. It was bringing a goodly drove of cattle, as well as men and ammunition enough to capture the English fortresses in a few days.

With this army the king was sending the Maid who had been promised.

Chapter XI
The Maid at Blois – The Letter to the English – The Departure for Orléans

✣

WITH AN ESCORT OF SOLDIERS of fortune the Maid reached Blois at the same time as my Lord Regnault de Chartres, Chancellor of France, and the Sire de Gaucourt, Governor of Orléans. The Marshal de Boussac, the Captains La Hire and Poton came from Orléans. An army of 7,000 men assembled beneath the walls of the town. All that was now waited for was the money necessary to pay the cost of the victuals and the hire of the soldiers. Captains and men-at-arms did not give their services on credit. As for the merchants, if they risked the loss of their victuals and their life, it was only for ready money. No cash, no cattle – and the wagons stayed where they were.

In the month of March, Jeanne had dictated to one of the doctors at Poitiers a brief manifesto intended for the English. She expanded it into a letter, which she showed to certain of her companions and afterwards sent by a Herald from Blois to the camp of Saint-Laurent-des-Orgerils. This letter was addressed to King Henry, to the regent and to the three chiefs, who, since Salisbury's death, had been conducting the siege, Scales, Suffolk and Talbot. The following is the text of it:

† Jhesus Maria †

King of England, and you, Duke of Bedford, who call yourself Regent of the realm of France – you, Guillaume de la Poule, Earl of Sulford; Jehan, Sire de Talebot and you Thomas, Sire d'Escales, who call yourselves Lieutenants of the said Duke of Bedfort, do right in the sight of the King of Heaven. Surrender to the Maid sent hither by God, the King of Heaven, the keys of all the good towns in France that you have taken and ravaged. She is come here in God's name to claim the Blood Royal. She is ready to make peace if so be you will do her satisfaction by giving and paying back to France what you have taken from her. And you, archers, comrades-in-arms, gentle and otherwise, who are before the town of Orléans, go ye hence into your own land, in God's name. And if you will not, then hear the wondrous works of the Maid who will shortly come upon you to your very great hurt. And you, King of England, if you do not thus, I am a Chieftain of war – and in whatsoever place in France I meet with your men, I will force them to depart willy nilly; and if they will not, then I will have them all slain. I am sent hither by God, the King of Heaven, body for body, to drive them all out of the whole of France. And if they obey, then will I show them mercy. And think not in your heart that you will hold the kingdom of France [from] God the King of Heaven, Son of the Blessed Mary, for it is King Charles, the true heir, who shall so hold it. God, the King of Heaven, so wills it, and he hath revealed it unto King Charles by the Maid. With a goodly company the King shall enter Paris. If ye will not believe these wondrous works wrought by God and the Maid, then, in whatsoever place ye shall be, there shall we fight. And if ye do me not right, there shall be so great a noise as hath not been in France for a thousand years. And know ye that the King of Heaven will send such great power to the Maid, to her and to her good soldiers, that ye will not be able to overcome her in any battle; and in the end the God of Heaven will reveal who has the better right. You, Duke of Bedfort, the Maid prays and beseeches you that you bring not destruction upon yourself. If you do her right, you may come in her company where the French will do the fairest deed ever done for Christendom. And if ye will have peace in the city of Orléans, then make ye answer; and, if not, then remember it will be to your great hurt and that shortly. Written this Tuesday of Holy Week.

Such is the letter. It was written in a new spirit; for it proclaimed the kingship of Jesus Christ and declared a holy war. It is hard to tell whether it proceeded from Jeanne's own inspiration or was dictated to her by the council of ecclesiastics.

But at least it is certain that on this occasion the Maid is expressing her own sentiments. Afterwards we shall find her saying: 'I asked for peace, and when I was refused I was ready to fight.' But, as she dictated the letter and was unable to read it, we may ask whether the clerks who held the pen did not add to it.

Two or three passages suggest the ecclesiastical touch. Doubtless they desired the good of the kingdom of France; but certainly they desired much more the good of Christendom; and we shall see that, if those mendicant monks, Brother Pasquerel and later Friar Richard, follow the Maid, it will be in the hope of employing her to the Church's advantage. Thus it would be but natural that they should declare her at the outset commander in war, and even invest her with a spiritual power superior to the temporal power of the king, and implied in the phrase: 'Surrender to the Maid ... the keys of the good towns.'

The learned did not greatly appreciate the style of this letter. The Bastard of Orléans thought the words very simple; and a few years later a good French jurist pronounced it coarse, heavy and badly arranged. Nevertheless, we wonder whether it were not that her manner of expression seemed bad to them, merely because it differed from the style of legal documents. True it is that the letter from Blois indicates the poverty of the French prose of that time when not enriched by an Alain Chartier; but it contains neither term nor expression which is not to be met with in the good authors of the day. The words may not be correctly ordered, but the style is none the less vivacious. There is nothing to suggest that the writer came from the banks of the Meuse; no trace is there of the speech of Lorraine or Champagne. It is clerkly French.

In the army she was regarded as a holy maiden. Her company consisted of a chaplain, Brother Jean Pasquerel; two pages, Louis de Coutes and Raymond; her two brethren, Pierre and Jean; two heralds, Ambleville and Guyenne; two squires, Jean de Metz and Bertrand de Poulengy.

Jean de Metz kept the purse which was filled by the crown. She had also certain valets in her service. A squire, one Jean d'Aulon, whom the king gave her for a steward, joined her at Blois. He was the poorest squire of the realm. He was entirely dependent on the Sire de La Trémouille, who lent him money; but he was well known for his honour and his wisdom. Jeanne attributed the defeats of the French to their riding forth accompanied by bad women and to their taking God's holy name in vain. And this opinion, far from being held by her alone, prevailed among persons of learning and religion; according to whom the disaster of Nicopolis was occasioned by the presence of prostitutes in the army, and by the cruelty and dissoluteness of the knights.

The Maid had a banner made for the monks to assemble beneath and summon the men-at-arms to prayer. This banner was white, and on it were represented Jesus on the Cross between Our Lady and Saint John. The Duke of Alençon went back to the king to make known to him the needs of the company at Blois. The king sent the necessary funds; and at length they were ready to set out. At the start there were two roads open, one leading to Orléans along the right bank of the Loire, the other along the left bank. At the end of about 20–22 kilometres (12 or 14 miles) the road along the right bank came out on the edge of the Plain of La Beauce, occupied by the English who had garrisons at Marchenoir, Beaugency, Meung, Montpipeau, Saint-Sigismond and Janville. In that direction lay the risk of meeting the army, which was coming to the aid of the English round Orléans. After the experience of the Battle of the Herrings such a meeting was to be feared. If the road along the left bank were taken, the march would lie through the district of La Sologne, which still belonged to King Charles; and if the river were left well on one side, the army would be out of sight of the English garrisons of Beaugency and of Meung. True, it would involve crossing the Loire, but by going up the river eight kilometres (five miles) east of the besieged city a crossing could conveniently be affected between Orléans and Jargeau. On due deliberation it was decided that they should go by the left bank through La Sologne. It was decided to take in the victuals in two separate lots for fear the unloading near the enemy's bastions should take too long. On Wednesday, the 27th of April, they started. The priests in procession, with a banner at their head, led the march, singing the

Veni creator Spiritus. The Maid rode with them in white armour, bearing her standard. The men-at-arms and the archers followed, escorting 600 wagons of victuals and ammunition and 400 head of cattle. The long line of lances, wagons and herds defiled over the Blois bridge into the vast plain beyond. The first day the army covered 32 kilometres (20 miles) of rutty road. Then at curfew, when the setting sun, reflected in the Loire, made the river look like a sheet of copper between lines of dark reeds, it halted, and the priests sang *Gabriel angelus.*

That night they encamped in the fields. Jeanne, who had not been willing to take off her armour, awoke aching in every limb. She heard mass and received communion from her chaplain, and exhorted the men-at-arms always to confess their sins. Then the army resumed its march towards Orléans.

Chapter XII
The Maid at Orléans

✞

ON THE EVENING OF THURSDAY, the 28th of April, Jeanne was able to discern from the heights of Olivet the belfries of the town, the towers of Saint-Paul and Saint-Pierre-Empont, whence the watchmen announced her approach. The army descended the slopes towards the Loire and stopped at the Bouchet wharf, while the carts and the cattle continued their way along the bank as far as l'Île-aux-Bourdons, opposite Chécy, four kilometres (two and a half miles) further up the river. At a signal from the watchmen my Lord the Bastard, accompanied by Thibaut de Termes and certain other captains, left the town by the Burgundian Gate, took a boat at Saint-Jean-de-Braye, and came down to hold counsel with the Lords de Rais and de Loré, who commanded the convoy.

Meanwhile, the Maid had only just perceived that she was on the Sologne bank, and that she had been deceived concerning the line of march. Sorrow and wrath possessed her. She had been misled, that was certain. But had it been done on purpose? Had they really intended to deceive her? It is said that she had expressed a wish to go through La Beauce and not through La Sologne, and that she had received the answer: 'Jeanne, be reassured; we will take you through La Beauce.' Is it possible? Why should the barons have thus trifled with the holy damsel, whom the king had confided to their care, and who already inspired most of them with respect? Certain of them, it is true, believing her not to be in earnest, would willingly have turned her to ridicule; but if one of them had played her the trick of representing La Beauce as La Sologne, how was it there was no one to undeceive her? How could Brother Pasquerel, her chaplain, her steward and the honest squire d'Aulon, have become the accomplices of so clumsy a jest?

Jeanne knew no more of Orléans than she did of Babylon. We may therefore conjecture that there was a misunderstanding. She had spoken neither of Sologne nor of Beauce. Doubtless Jeanne had said to the captains and priests what she was soon to repeat to the Bastard: 'I must go to Talbot and the English.' For now she was angry and sad at finding herself separated from the town by the sands and waters of the river. What was there to vex her in this? Those who were with her then did not discover; and perhaps her reasons were misunderstood because they were spiritual and mystic. She certainly could not have judged that a military mistake had been made by the bringing of troops and victuals through La Sologne. As she did not know the roads, it was impossible for her to tell which was the best.

One may conclude that what really vexed her was that she had not been taken straight to Talbot and the English. She had just heard that Talbot with his camp was on the right bank. And when she spoke of Talbot and the English she meant only those English who were with Talbot. But still, it is not clear why she should have desired to appear first before Talbot and his English, and why she was now so annoyed at being separated from him by the Loire. Did she think that the entrenched camp, Saint-Laurent-des-Orgerils, commanded by Scales, Suffolk and Talbot would be attacked immediately? Such an idea would never of itself have occurred to her, since she did not know the place, and no soldier would ever have put such madness into her head. Neither, as has so often been asserted, can she have thought of forcing a passage between the bastion Saint-Pouair and the outskirts of the wood, since of the bastions and of the forest she knew as little as of the rest. If such had been her intention she would have announced it plainly to the Bastard. She came to require them to make peace, and if they would not make peace she was ready to fight. Perhaps even she may have hoped that by appearing to the English captains, her standard in hand, accompanied by Saint Catherine and Saint Margaret and Saint Michael the Archangel, she would persuade them to leave France. She may have believed that Talbot, falling on his knees, would obey not her, but Him who sent her; that thus she would accomplish that for which she came, without shedding one drop of that French blood which was so dear to her; neither would the English whom she pitied lose their bodies or their souls.

Even after the discomfiture of her arrival, in order that she might please God, she did not consider herself freed from the obligation of offering peace to her enemies. And since she could not go straight to Talbot's camp she wanted to appear before the fort of Saint-Jean-le-Blanc.

There was no one left behind the palisades. But if she had gone and found any of the enemy there she would first have offered them peace.

My Lord the Bastard who regarded Jeanne's mission as purely religious, and who would have been greatly astonished had anyone told him that he ought to consult this peasant on military matters, appeared as if he did not understand the reproaches she addressed to him.

Jeanne said confidently to those who were growing anxious: 'Wait a little, for in God's name everything shall enter the town.'

She was right. The wind changed: the sails were unfurled, and the barges were borne up the river by a favourable wind, so strong that one boat was able to tow two or three others. Without hindrance they passed the Saint-Loup bastion.

The lords who had brought the convoy decided that they would set out immediately after the unloading. Having accomplished the first part of its task, the army would return to Blois to fetch the remaining victuals and ammunition, for everything had not been brought at once. Hearing that the soldiers, with whom she had come, were going away, Jeanne wished to go with them; and, after having so urgently asked to be taken to Orléans, now that she was before the gates of the city, her one idea was to go back.

'As for entering the town,' she said, 'it would hurt me to leave my men, and I ought not to do it. They have all confessed, and in their company I should not fear the uttermost power of the English.'

She was confirmed in her resolution to return to Blois by the captains who had brought her and who wanted to take her back, alleging the king's command. They wished to keep her because she brought good luck. My Lord the Bastard, however, saw serious obstacles and even dangers in the way of her return. In the state in which he had left the people of Orléans, if their Maid were not straightway brought before them they would rise in fury and despair, with cries, threats, rioting and violence; everything was to be feared, even massacres. He entreated the captains, in the king's interest, to agree to Jeanne's entering Orléans; and without great difficulty, he induced them to return to Blois without her. But Jeanne did not give in so quickly. He besought her to decide to cross the Loire. She refused and with such insistence that he must have realised how difficult it is to influence a saint.

On the morning of the 29th the barges, which had been anchored at Chécy, crossed the Loire, and those who were with the convoy loaded them with victuals, ammunition and cattle. The river was high. The barges were able to drift down the navigable channel near the left bank. The birches and osiers of l'Île-aux-Bœufs hid them from the English in the Saint-Loup bastion. Besides, at that moment, the enemy was occupied elsewhere. The town garrison was skirmishing with them in order to distract their attention.

It was six o'clock in the evening before she left Chécy. The captains wanted her to enter the town at nightfall for fear of disorders and lest the crush around her should be too great. Doubtless they passed along the broad valleys leading from Semoy towards the south, on the borders of the parishes of Saint-Marc and Saint-Jean-de-Braye. On the way she said to those who rode with her: 'Fear nothing. No harm shall happen to you.' And indeed the only danger was for pedestrians. Horsemen ran little risk of being pursued by the English, who were short of horses in their bastions.

On that Friday, the 29th of April, in the darkness, she entered Orléans, by the Burgundian Gate. Bearing torches and rejoicing as heartily as if they had seen God himself descending among them, the townsfolk of

Orléans pressed around her. They had suffered great privations, they had feared that help would never come; but now they were heartened and felt as if the siege had been raised already by the divine virtue, which they had been told resided in this Maid. They looked at her with love and veneration; elbowing and pushing each other, men, women and children rushed forward to touch her and her white horse, as folk touch the relics of saints. Men-at-arms and citizens, enraptured, accompanied her in crowds to the Church of Sainte-Croix, whither she went first to give thanks, then to the house of Jacques Boucher, where she was to lodge. Into this house the Maid was received with her two brothers, the two comrades who had brought her to the king, and their valets.

As for the D'Arc brothers, they did not stay with their sister, but lodged in the house of Thévenin Villedart. The town paid all their expenses; for example, it furnished them with the shoes and gaiters they needed and gave them a few gold crowns. Three of the Maid's comrades, who were very destitute and came to see her at Orléans, received food.

On the next day, the 30th of April, the town bands of Orléans were early afoot. From morn till eve everything in the town was topsy-turvy; the rebellion, which had been repressed so long, now broke forth. As early as February the citizens had begun to mistrust and hate the knights; now at last they shook off their yoke and broke it. Henceforth they would recognize no king's lieutenant, no governor, no lords, no generals; there was but one power and one defence: the Maid. The town bands were waiting for the Maid to put herself at their head, and with her to march immediately against the *Godons*. The captains endeavoured to make them understand that they must wait for the army from Blois and the company of Marshal de Boussac, who that night had set out to meet the army. The citizens in arms would listen to nothing, and with loud cries clamoured for the Maid.

In the evening of the 30th she sent her herald Ambleville, to the camp of Saint-Laurent-des-Orgerils to ask for Guyenne, who had borne the letter from Blois and had not returned. Ambleville was also instructed to tell Sir John Talbot, the Earl of Suffolk, and the Lord Scales that in God's name the Maid required them to depart from France and go to England; otherwise they would suffer hurt. The English sent back Ambleville with an evil message.

'The English,' he said to the Maid, 'are keeping my comrade to burn him.' She made answer: 'In God's name they will do him no harm.' And she commanded Ambleville to return.

On Sunday, the 1st of May, my Lord the Bastard went to meet the army from Blois. He knew the country; and, being both energetic and cautious, he was desirous to superintend the entrance of this convoy as he had done that of the other. He set out with a small escort. He did not dare to take with him the Saint herself; but, in order, so to speak, to put himself under her protection and tactfully to flatter the piety and affections of the folk of Orléans, he took a member of her suite, her steward, Sire Jean d'Aulon. Thus he grasped the first opportunity of showing his good will to the Maid, feeling that henceforth nothing could be done except with her or under her patronage.

The fervour of the citizens was not abated. That very day, in their passionate desire to see the Saint, they crowded round Jacques Boucher's house as turbulently as the pilgrims from Puy pressed into the sanctuary of La Vierge Noire. There was a danger of the doors being broken in. The cries of the townsfolk reached her. Then she appeared: good, wise, equal to her mission, one born for the salvation of the people. In the absence of captains and men-at-arms, this wild multitude only awaited a sign from her to throw itself in tumult on the bastions and perish there. Notwithstanding the visions of war that haunted her, that sign she did not give. Child as she was, and as ignorant of war as of life, there was that within her which turned away disaster. She led this crowd of men, not to the English bastions, but to the holy places of the city. Down the streets she rode, accompanied by many knights and squires; men and women pressed to see her and could not gaze upon her enough. They marvelled at the manner of her riding and of her behaviour, in every point like a man-at-arms; and they would have hailed her as a veritable Saint George had they not suspected Saint George of turning Englishman.

That Sunday, for the second time, she went forth to offer peace to the enemies of the kingdom. She passed out by the Renard Gate and went along the Blois Road, through the suburbs that had been burnt down, towards the English bastion. Surrounded by a double moat, it was planted on a slope at the crossroads called La Croix Boissée or Buissée, because the townsfolk of Orléans had erected a cross there, which every Palm Sunday they dressed with a branch of box blessed by the priest. Doubtless she intended to reach this bastion, and perhaps to go on to the camp of Saint-Laurent-des-Orgerils situated between La Croix Boissée and the Loire, where, as she had said, were Talbot and the English. For she had not yet given up hope of gaining a hearing from the leaders of the siege. But at the foot of the hill, at a place called La Croix-Morin, she met some *Godons* who were keeping watch. And there, in tones grave, pious and noble, she summoned them to retreat before the hosts of the Lord. 'Surrender, and your lives shall be spared. In God's name go back to England. If ye will not I will make you suffer for it.'

These men-at-arms answered her with insults as those of Les Tourelles had done. One of them, the Bastard of Granville, cried out to her: 'Would you have us surrender to a woman?'

The French, who were with her, they dubbed pimps and infidels, to shame them for being in the company of a bad woman and a witch. But whether because they thought her magic rendered her invulnerable, or because they held it dishonourable to strike a messenger, now, as on other occasions, they forbore to fire on her.

Throughout this time of waiting the Maid never rested for a moment. On Monday, May 2nd, she mounted her horse and rode out into the country to view the English bastions. The people followed her in crowds; they had no fear and were glad to be near her. And when she had seen all that she wanted, she returned to the city, to the cathedral church, where she heard vespers.

On the morrow, the 3rd of May, the day of the Invention of the Holy Cross, which was the Cathedral Festival, she followed in the procession, with the magistrates and the townsfolk. It was then that Maître Jean de Mâcon, the precentor of the cathedral, greeted her with these words: 'My daughter, are you come to raise the siege?'

She replied: 'Yea, in God's name.'

'My daughter,' he said to the Maid, 'their force is great and they are strongly intrenched. It will be a difficult matter to turn them out.'

If notary Guillaume Girault, if draper Jean Luillier, if Messire Jean de Mâcon, instead of fostering these gloomy ideas, had counted the numbers of the besieged and the besieging, they would have found that the former were more numerous than the latter; and that the army of Scales, of Suffolk, of Talbot appeared mean and feeble when compared with the great besieging armies of the reign of King Henry V. Had they looked a little more closely they would have perceived that the bastions, with the formidable names of London and of Paris, were powerless to prevent either corn, cattle, pigs, or men-at-arms being brought into the city; and that these gigantic dolls were being mocked at by the dealers, who, with their beasts, passed by them daily. In short, they would have realised that the people of Orléans were for the moment better off than the English. But they had examined nothing for themselves. They were content to abide by public opinion which is seldom either just or correct.

What aggravated the trouble, the danger, and the panic of the situation, was that the citizens believed they were betrayed. They suspected the king's men of deserting them once again. After having done so much and spent so much they saw themselves given up to the English. This idea made them mad. It was said that the Chancellor of France wanted to disband the army. It was absurd. On the contrary, great efforts for the deliverance of the city were being made by the king's council and that of the Queen of Sicily. But the people's brains had been turned by their long suffering and their terrible danger. A more reasonable fear was lest any mishap should occur on the road from Blois like that which had overtaken the force at Rouvray. The Maid's comrades were infected with the anxieties of the townsfolk; one of them betrayed his fears to her, but she was not affected by them. With the radiant tranquillity of the illuminated, she said: 'The Marshal will come. I am confident that no harm will happen to him.'

On that day there entered into the city the little garrisons of Gien, of Château-Regnard and of Montargis. But the Blois army did not come. On the morrow, at daybreak, it was descried in the plain of La Beauce. And, indeed, the Sire de Rais and his company, escorted by the Marshal de Boussac and my Lord the Bastard, were skirting the Forest of Orléans. At these tidings the citizens must needs exclaim that the Maid had been right in wishing to march straight against Talbot since the captains now followed the very road she had indicated. But in reality it was not just as they thought. Only one part of the Blois army had risked forcing its way between the western bastions; the convoy, with its escort, like the first convoy, was coming through La Sologne and was to enter the town by water.

Jeanne dined at Jacques Boucher's house with her steward, Jean d'Aulon. When the table was cleared, the Bastard, who had come to the treasurer's house, talked with her for a moment. He was gracious and polite, but spoke with restraint.

'I have heard on good authority,' he remarked, 'that Fastolf is soon to join the English who are conducting the siege. He brings them supplies and reinforcements and is already at Janville.'

At these tidings Jeanne appeared very glad and said, laughing: 'Bastard, Bastard, in God's name, I command thee to let me know as soon as thou shalt hear of Fastolf's arrival. For should he come without my knowledge, I warn thee thou shalt lose thy head.'

Far from betraying any annoyance at so rude a jest, he replied that she need have no fear, he would let her know.

The approach of Sir John Fastolf had already been announced on the 26th of April. It was expressly in order to avoid him that the army had come through La Sologne. It is possible that on the 4th of May the tidings of his coming had no surer foundation. But the Bastard knew something else. The corn of the second convoy, like that of the first, was coming down the river. It had been resolved, in a council of war, that in the afternoon the captains should attack the Saint-Loup bastion, and divert the English as had been done on the 29th of April. The attack had already begun. But of this the Bastard breathed not a word to the Maid. He held her to be the one source of strength in the town. But he believed that in war her part was purely spiritual.

After he had withdrawn, Jeanne, worn out by her morning's expedition, lay down on her bed with her hostess for a short sleep. Sire Jean d'Aulon, who was very weary, stretched himself on a couch in the same room, thinking to take the rest he so greatly needed. But scarce had he fallen asleep when the Maid leapt from her bed and roused him with a great noise. He asked her what she wanted.

'In God's name,' she answered in great agitation, 'my council have told me to go against the English; but I know not whether I am to go against their bastions or against Fastolf, who is bringing them supplies.'

In her dreams she had been present at her council, that is to say, she had beheld her saints. She had seen Saint Catherine and Saint Margaret. There had happened to her what always happens. The saints had told her no more than she herself knew. They had revealed to her nothing of what she needed to know. They had not informed her how, at that very moment, the French were attacking the Saint-Loup bastion and suffering great hurt. The good Sire d'Aulon was not the one to relieve her from her embarrassment. He, too, was excluded from the councils of war.

In the street she found Brother Pasquerel, her chaplain, with other priests, and Mugot, her page, to whom she cried: 'Ha! cruel boy, you did not tell me that the blood of France was being shed!... In God's name, our people are hard put to it.'

She bade him bring her horse and leave the wife and daughter of her host to finish arming her. On his return the page found her fully accoutred. She sent him to fetch her standard from her room. He gave it her through the window. She took it and spurred on her horse into the high street, towards the Burgundian Gate, at such a pace that sparks flashed from the pavement.

Sire d'Aulon had not seen her start. He imagined, why, it is impossible to say, that she had gone out on foot, and, having met a page on horseback in the street, had made him dismount and give her his horse.

The Maid and Sire d'Aulon, with a few fighting men of their company, pressed on through the fields to Saint-Loup. On the way they saw certain of their party. The good squire, unaccustomed to great battles, never remembered having seen so many fighting men at once.

For an hour the Sire de Rais' Bretons and the men from Le Mans had been skirmishing before the bastion. As the custom was those who had arrived last were keeping watch. But if these combatants, who had reached the town only that very morning, had attacked without taking time to breathe, they must have been hard pressed. On the top of their high hill, in their strong fortress, the English had easily held out albeit they were but few; and the French king's men can hardly have been able to make head against them, since the Maid and Sire d'Aulon found them scattered through the fields. She gathered them together and led them back to the attack. They were her friends: they had journeyed together: they had sung psalms and hymns together: together they had heard mass in the fields. They knew that she brought good luck: they followed her. As she marched at their head her first idea was a religious one. The bastion was built upon the church and convent of the Ladies of Saint-Loup. With the sound of a trumpet, she had it proclaimed that nothing should be taken from the church. This was the first time she had seen fighting; and no sooner had she entered into the battle than she became the leader because she was the best. She did better than others, not because she knew more; she knew less. But her heart was nobler. When every man thought of himself, she alone thought of others: when every man took heed to defend himself, she defended herself not at all, having previously offered up her life. And thus this child – who feared suffering and death like every human being, who knew by her Voices and her presentiments that she would be wounded – went straight on and stood beneath showers of arrows and cannon-balls on the edge of the moat, her standard in hand, rallying her men. Through her what had been merely a diversion became a serious attack. The bastion was stormed.

The attack had lasted three hours. After the burning of the bastion the English climbed into the church belfry. The French had difficulty in dislodging them; but they ran no danger thereby. Of prisoners, they took two score, and the rest they slew. The Maid was very sorrowful when she saw so many of the enemy dead. She pitied these poor folk who had died unconfessed.

Before leaving the fort she confessed to Brother Pasquerel, her chaplain. And she charged him to make the following announcement to all the men-at-arms: 'Confess your sins and thank God for the victory. If you do not, the Maid will never help you more and will not remain in your company.'

The Saint-Loup bastion, attacked by 1,500 French, had been defended by only 300 English. That they made no vigorous defence is indicated by the fact that only two or three Frenchmen were slain. It was not by any severe mental effort or profound calculation that the French king's men had gained this advantage. It had cost them little, and yet it was immense. It meant the cutting off of the besiegers' communications with Jargeau: it meant the opening of the upper Loire: it was the first step towards the raising of the siege. Better still, it afforded positive proof that these devils who had inspired such fear were miserable creatures, who might be entrapped like mice and smoked out like wasps in their nest. Such unhoped-for good fortune was due to the Maid. She had done everything, for without her nothing would have been done. She it was, who, in ignorance wiser than the knowledge of captains and free-lances, had converted an idle skirmish into a serious attack and had won the victory by inspiring confidence.

When at night she returned to her lodging, Jeanne told her chaplain that on the morrow, which was the day of the Ascension of Our Lord, she would keep the festival by not wearing armour and by abstaining from fighting. She commanded that no one should think of quitting the town, of attacking or making an assault, until he had first confessed.

On the morrow, the captains held a council of war in the house of Chancellor Cousinot in the Rue de la Rose. There were present, as well as the Chancellor, my Lord the Bastard, the Sire de Gaucourt, the Sire de Rais, the Sire de Graville, Captain La Hire, my Lord Ambroise de Loré and several others. It was decided that Les Tourelles, the chief stronghold of the besiegers, should be attacked on the morrow. Meanwhile, it would be necessary to hold in check the English of the camp of Saint-Laurent-des-Orgerils. On the previous day, when Talbot set out from Saint-Laurent, he had not been able to reach Saint-Loup in time because he had been obliged to make a long circuit, going round the town from west to east. But, although, on that previous day, the enemy had lost command of the Loire above the town, they still held the lower river. They could cross it between Saint-Laurent and Saint-Privé as rapidly as the French could cross it by the Île-aux-Toiles; and thus the English might gather in force at Le Portereau. This, the French must prevent and, if possible, draw off the garrisons from Les Augustins and Les Tourelles to Saint-Laurent-des-Orgerils. With this object it was decided that the people of Orléans with the folk from the communes, that is, from the villages, should make a feigned attack on the Saint-Laurent camp, with mantelets, faggots and ladders. Meanwhile, the nobles would cross the Loire by l'Île-aux-Toiles, would land at Le Portereau under the watch of Saint-Jean-le-Blanc which had been abandoned by the English, and attack the bastion of Les Augustins; and when that was taken, the fort of Les Tourelles. Thus there would be one assault made by the citizens, another by the nobles; one real, the other feigned; both useful, but only one glorious and worthy of knights. When the plan was thus drawn up, certain captains were of opinion that it would be well to send for the Maid and tell her what had been decided. And, indeed, on the previous day, she had done so well that there was no longer need to hold her aloof. Others deemed that it would be imprudent to tell her what was contemplated concerning Les Tourelles. For it was important that the undertaking should be kept secret, and it was feared that the holy damsel might speak of it to her friends among the common people. Finally, it was agreed that she should know those decisions which affected the train-bands of Orléans, since, indeed, she was their captain, but that such matters as could not be safely communicated to the citizens should be concealed from her.

Jeanne was in another room of the house with the Chancellor's wife. Messire Ambroise de Loré went to fetch her; and, when she had come, the Chancellor told her that the camp of Saint-Laurent-des-Orgerils was to be attacked on the morrow. She divined that something was being kept back; for she possessed a certain acuteness. Besides, since they had hitherto concealed everything, it was natural she should suspect that something was still being kept from her. This mistrust annoyed her. Did they think her incapable of keeping a secret?

My Lord the Bastard deemed it well to avoid exasperating her by telling her the truth. He pacified her without incriminating anybody: 'Jeanne, do not rage. It is impossible to tell you everything at once. What the Chancellor has said has been concluded and ordained. But if those on the other side [of the water, the English of La Sologne] should depart to come and succour the great bastion of Saint-Laurent and the English who are encamped near this part of the city, we have determined that some of us shall cross the river to do what we can against those on the other side [those of Les Augustins and Les Tourelles]. And it seems to us that such a decision is good and profitable.'

The Maid replied that she was content, that such a decision seemed to her good, and that it should be carried out in the manner determined.

It will be seen that by this proceeding the secrecy of the deliberations had been violated, and that the nobles had not been able to do what they had determined or at least not in the way they had determined. On that Ascension Day the Maid for the last time sent a message of peace to the

English, which she dictated to Brother Pasquerel in the following terms: *Ye men of England, who have no right in the realm of France, the King of Heaven enjoins and commands you by me, Jeanne the Maid, to leave your forts and return to your country. If ye will not I will make so great a noise as shall remain for ever in the memory of man: This I write to you for the third and last time, and I will write to you no more.*

Signed thus: *Jhesus – Maria. Jeanne the Maid.*

And below: *I should have sent to you with more ceremony. But you keep my heralds. You kept my herald Guyenne. If you will send him back to me, I will send you some of your men taken at the bastion Saint-Loup; they are not all dead.*

Jeanne went to La Belle Croix, took an arrow, and tied her letter to it with a string, then told an archer to shoot it to the English, crying: 'Read! This is the message.'

The English received the arrow, untied the letter and having read it they cried: 'This a message from the Armagnac strumpet.'

When she heard them, tears came into Jeanne's eyes and she wept. But soon she beheld her saints, who spoke to her of Our Lord, and she was comforted. 'I have had a message from my Lord,' she said joyfully.

My Lord the Bastard himself demanded the Maid's herald, threatening that if he were not sent back he would keep the heralds whom the English had sent to treat for the exchange of prisoners. It is asserted that he even threatened to put those prisoners to death. But Ambleville did not return.

Chapter XIII
The Taking of Les Tourelles and the Deliverance of Orléans

O N THE MORROW, Friday the 6th of May, the Maid rose at daybreak. She confessed to her chaplain and heard mass sung before the priests and fighting men of her company. The zealous townsfolk were already up and armed. Whether or no she had told them, the

citizens, who were strongly determined to cross the Loire and attack Les Tourelles themselves, were pressing in crowds to the Burgundian Gate. They found it shut. The Sire de Gaucourt was guarding it with men-at-arms. The nobles had taken this precaution in case the citizens should discover their enterprise and wish to take part in it. The gate was closed and well defended. Bent on fighting and themselves recovering their precious jewel, Les Tourelles, the citizens had recourse to her before whom gates opened and walls fell; they sent for the Saint. She came, frank and terrible. She went straight to the old Sire de Gaucourt, and, refusing to listen to him, said: 'You are a wicked man to try to prevent these people from going out. But whether you will or no, they will go and will do as well as they did the other day.'

Excited by Jeanne's voice and encouraged by her presence, the citizens, crying slaughter, threw themselves on Gaucourt and his men-at-arms. When the old baron perceived that he could do nothing with them, and that it was impossible to bring them to his way of thinking, he himself joined them. He had the gates opened wide and cried out to the townsfolk: 'Come, I will be your captain.'

And with the Lord of Villars and Sire d'Aulon he went out at the head of the soldiers, who had been keeping the gate, and all the train-bands of the town. At the foot of La Tour-Neuve, at the eastern corner of the ramparts, there were boats at anchor. In them l'Île-aux-Toiles was reached, and thence on a bridge formed by two boats they crossed over the narrow arm of the river which separates l'Île-aux-Toiles from the Sologne bank. Those who arrived first entered the abandoned fort of Saint-Jean-le-Blanc, and, while waiting for the others, amused themselves by demolishing it. Then, when all had passed over, the townsfolk gayly marched against Les Augustins. But the enemy came out of their entrenchments and advanced within two bow-shots of the French, upon whom from their bows and cross-bows they let fly so thick a shower of arrows that the men of Orléans could not stand against them. They gave way and fled to the bridge of boats: then, afraid of being cast into the river, they crossed over to l'Île-aux-Toiles. The fighting men of the Sire de Gaucourt were more accustomed to war. With the Lord of Villars, Sire d'Aulon, and a valiant Spaniard, Don

Alonzo de Partada, they took their stand on the slope of Saint-Jean-le-Blanc and resisted the enemy. Although very few in number, they were still holding out when, about three o'clock in the afternoon, Captain La Hire and the Maid crossed the river with the free-lances. The townsfolk, taking heart, followed them and drove back the English. But at the foot of the bastion they were again repulsed. In great agitation the Maid galloped from the bastion to the bank, and from the bank to the bastion, calling for the knights; but the knights did not come. Their plans had been upset, their order of battle reversed, and they needed time to collect themselves. The artillery came too, and Master Jean de Montesclère with his culverin and his gunners, bringing all the engines needed for the assault. Four thousand men assembled round Les Augustins.

The Sire de Gaucourt's men were ranged behind, to cover the besiegers in case the English from the bridge end should come to the aid of their countrymen in Les Augustins. But a quarrel arose in de Gaucourt's company. Some, like Sire d'Aulon and Don Alonzo, judged it well to stay at their post. Others were ashamed to stand idle. Finally Don Alonzo and a man-at-arms, having challenged each other to see who would do the best, ran towards the bastion hand in hand. At one single volley Maître Jean's culverin overthrew the palisade. Straightway the two champions forced their way in.

'Enter boldly!' cried the Maid. And she planted her standard on the rampart. The Sire de Rais followed her closely.

The numbers of the French were increasing. They made a strong attack on the bastion and soon took it by storm. In the end all the English were slain or taken, except a few, who took refuge in Les Tourelles. In the huts the French found many of their own men imprisoned. After bringing them out, they set fire to the fort, and thus made known to the English their new disaster. It is said to have been the Maid who ordered the fire in order to put a stop to the pillage in which her men were mercilessly engaging.

The lords, captains and men-at-arms went back to the town to pass a quiet night. The archers and most of the townsfolk stayed at Le Portereau. The Maid would have liked to stay too, so as to be sure of beginning again on the morrow. Wounded in the foot by a caltrop, overcome with fatigue, she felt weak, and contrary to her custom she broke her fast, although the day was Friday. According to Brother Pasquerel, who in this matter is not very trustworthy, while she was finishing her supper in her lodging, there came to her a noble whose name is not mentioned and who addressed her thus: 'The captains have met in council. They recognize how few we were in comparison with the English, and that it was by God's great favour that we won the victory. Now that the town is plentifully supplied we may well wait for help from the king. Wherefore, the council deems it inexpedient for the men-at-arms to make a sally tomorrow.'

Jeanne replied: 'You have been at your council; I have been at mine. Now believe me the counsel of Messire shall be followed and shall hold good, whereas your counsel shall come to nought.' And turning to Brother Pasquerel who was with her, she said: 'Tomorrow rise even earlier than today, and do the best you can. Stay always at my side, for tomorrow I shall have much ado – more than I have ever had, and tomorrow blood shall flow from my body.'

It was not true that the English outnumbered the French. On the contrary they were far less numerous. There were scarce more than 3,000 men round Orléans.

On the morrow, Saturday the 7th of May, Jeanne heard Brother Pasquerel say mass and piously received the holy sacrament. Jacques Boucher's house was beset with magistrates and notable citizens. After a night of fatigue and anxiety, they had just heard tidings which exasperated them. They had heard tell that the captains wanted to defer the storming of Les Tourelles. The truth was that my Lord the Bastard and the captains, having observed during the night a great movement among the English on the upper Loire, were confirmed in their fears that Talbot would attack the walls near the Renard Gate while the French were occupied on the left bank.. The magistrates besought the Maid to complete without delay the deliverance she had already begun. They said to her: 'We have taken counsel and we entreat you to accomplish the mission you have received from God and likewise from the king.'

'In God's name, I will,' she said. And straightway she mounted her horse, and uttering a very ancient phrase, she cried: 'Let who loves me follow me!'

The townsfolk had been too quick to take alarm. Notwithstanding their fear of Talbot and the English of the Saint-Laurent camp, the nobles crossed the Loire in the early morning, and at Le Portereau rejoined their horses and pages who had passed the night there with the archers and trainbands. They were all there, the Bastard, the Sire de Gaucourt and the lords of Rais, Graville, Guitry, Coarraze, Villars, Illiers, Chailly, the Admiral de Culant, the captains La Hire and Poton. The Maid was with them. The magistrates sent them great store of engines of war: hurdles, all kinds of arrows, hammers, axes, lead, powder, culverins, cannon and ladders. The attack began early. What rendered it difficult was not the number of English entrenched in the bulwark and lodged in the towers: there were barely more than 500 of them. The assailants, citizens, men-at-arms and archers were 10 times more numerous. That so many combatants had been assembled was greatly to the credit of the French nation; but so great an army of men could not be employed at once. Knights were not much use against earthworks; and the townsfolk although very zealous, were not very tenacious. Finally, the Bastard, who was prudent and thoughtful, was afraid of Talbot.

At noon everyone went away to dinner. Then about one o'clock they set to work again. The Maid carried the first ladder. As she was putting it up against the rampart, she was struck on the shoulder over the right breast, by an arrow shot so straight that half a foot of the shaft pierced her flesh. She knew that she was to be wounded; she had foretold it to her king, adding that he must employ her all the same. She had announced it to the people of Orléans and spoken of it to her chaplain on the previous day; and certainly for the last five days she had been doing her best to make the prophecy come true. When the English saw that the arrow had pierced her flesh they were greatly encouraged: they believed that if blood were drawn from a witch all her power would vanish. It made the French very sad. As was usual when combatants were wounded in battle, a group of soldiers surrounded her; some wanted to charm her. It was a custom with men-at-arms to attempt to close wounds by muttering paternosters over them. Spells were cast by means of incantations and conjurations. Certain paternosters had the power of stopping hemorrhage. Papers covered with magic characters were also used. But it meant having recourse to the power of devils and committing mortal sin. Jeanne did not wish to be charmed.

'I would rather die,' she said, 'than do anything I knew to be sin or contrary to God's will.'

Her armour was taken off. The wound was anointed with olive oil and fat, and, when it was dressed, she confessed to Brother Pasquerel, weeping and groaning. Soon she beheld coming to her her heavenly counsellors, Saint Catherine and Saint Margaret. They wore crowns and emitted a sweet fragrance. She was comforted. She resumed her armour and returned to the attack.

The sun was going down; and since morning the French had been wearing themselves out in a vain attack upon the palisades of the bulwark. My Lord the Bastard, seeing his men tired and night coming on, and afraid doubtless of the English of the Saint-Laurent-des-Orgerils Camp, resolved to lead the army back to Orléans. He had the retreat sounded. The trumpet was already summoning the combatants to Le Portereau. The Maid came to him and asked him to wait a little.

Then, leaving her standard with a man of her company, she went alone up the hill into the vineyards, which it had been impossible to till this April, but where the tiny spring leaves were beginning to open. There, in the calm of evening, among the vine props tied together in sheaves and the lines of low vines drinking in the early warmth of the earth, she began to pray and listened for her heavenly voices. Too often tumult and noise prevented her from hearing what her angel and her saints had to say to her. She could only understand them well in solitude or when the bells were tinkling in the distance, and evening sounds soft and rhythmic were ascending from field and meadow.

During her absence Sire d'Aulon, who could not give up the idea of winning the day, devised one last expedient. He was the least of the nobles in the army; but in the battles of those days every man was a law unto himself. The Maid's standard was still waving in front of the bulwark. The man who bore it was dropping with fatigue and had passed it on to a soldier, surnamed the Basque, of the company of my Lord of Villars. It occurred to Sire d'Aulon, as he looked upon this standard blessed by priests and held to bring good luck, that if it were borne in front, the fighting men, who loved it dearly, would follow it and in order not to lose it would scale the bulwark. With this idea he went to the Basque and said: 'If I were to enter there and go on foot up to the bulwark would you follow me?'

The Basque promised that he would. Straightway Sire d'Aulon went down into the ditch and protecting himself with his shield, which sheltered him from the stones fired from the cannon, advanced towards the rampart.

After a quarter of an hour, the Maid, having offered a short prayer, returned to the men-at-arms and said to them: 'The English are exhausted. Bring up the ladders.'

She went towards the fort. But when she reached the ditch she suddenly beheld the standard so dear to her, a thousand times dearer than her sword, in the hands of a stranger. Thinking it was in danger, she hastened to rescue it and came up with the Basque just as he was going down into the ditch. There she seized her standard by the part known as its tail, that is the end of the flag, and pulled at it with all her might, crying:

'Ha! my standard, my standard!'

The Basque stood firm, not knowing who was pulling thus from above. And the Maid would not let it go. The nobles and captains saw the standard shake, took it for a sign and rallied. Meanwhile Sire d'Aulon had reached the rampart. He imagined that the Basque was following close behind. But, when he turned round he perceived that he had stopped on the other side of the ditch, and he cried out to him: 'Eh! Basque, what did you promise me?'

At this cry the Basque pulled so hard that the Maid let go, and he bore the standard to the rampart.

Jeanne understood and was satisfied. To those near her she said: 'Look and see when the flag of my standard touches the bulwark.'

A knight replied: 'Jeanne, the flag touches.'

Then she cried: 'All is yours. Enter.'

Straightway nobles and citizens, men-at-arms, archers, townsfolk threw themselves wildly into the ditch and climbed up the palisades so quickly and in such numbers that they looked like a flock of birds descending on a hedge. And the French, who had now entered within the fortifications, saw retreating before them, but with their faces turned proudly towards the enemy, the Lords Moleyns and Poynings, Sir Thomas Giffart, Baillie of Mantes and Captain Glasdale, who were covering the flight of their men to Les Tourelles. For the Maid was there, standing upon the rampart. And the English, panic-stricken, wondered what kind of a witch this could be whose powers did not depart with the flowing of her blood, and who with charms healed her deep wounds. Meanwhile she was looking at them kindly and sadly and crying out, her voice broken with sobs.

'Glassidas! Glassidas! surrender, surrender to the King of Heaven. Thou hast called me strumpet; but I have great pity on thy soul and on the souls of thy men.'

Having escaped from the French on the bulwark, across the burning planks the 600 were set upon by the French on the bridge. Four hundred were slain, the others taken. The day had cost the people of Orléans 100 men.

When in the black darkness, along the fire-reddened banks of the Loire, the last cries of the vanquished had died away, the French captains, amazed at their victory, looked anxiously towards Saint-Laurent-des Orgerils, for they were still afraid lest Sir John Talbot should sally forth from his camp to avenge those whom he had failed to succour. Throughout that long attack, which had lasted from sunrise to sunset, Talbot, the Earl of Suffolk and the English of Saint-Laurent had not left their entrenchments. Even when Les Tourelles were taken the conquerors remained on the watch, still expecting Talbot. But this Talbot, with whose name French mothers frightened their children, did not budge. He had been greatly feared that day, and he himself had feared lest, if he withdrew any of his troops to succour Les Tourelles, the French would capture his camp and his forts on the west.

The army prepared to return to the town. In three hours, the bridge, three arches of which had been broken, was rendered passable. Some hours after darkness, the Maid entered the city by the bridge as she had foretold. In like manner all her prophecies were fulfilled when their fulfilment depended on her own courage and determination. The bells of the city were ringing; the clergy and people sang the Te Deum. After God and his Blessed Mother, they gave thanks in all humility to Saint Aignan and Saint Euverte, who had been bishops in their mortal lives and were now the heavenly patrons of the city.

Jeanne was brought back to Jacques Boucher's house, where a surgeon again dressed the wound she had received above the breast. She took four or five slices of bread soaked in wine and water, but neither ate nor drank anything else.

On the morrow, Sunday, the 8th of May, being the Feast of the Appearance of St. Michael, it was announced in Orléans, in the morning, that the English issuing forth from those western bastions which were all that remained to them, were ranging themselves before the town moat in battle array and with standards flying.

The Maid went out into the country with the priests. Being unable to put on her cuirass because of the wound on her shoulder, she merely wore one of those light coats-of-mail called *jaserans*.

The men-at-arms inquired of her: 'Today being the Sabbath, is it wrong to fight?'

She replied: 'You must hear mass.'

She did not think the enemy should be attacked.

'For the sake of the holy Sabbath do not give battle. Do not attack the English, but if the English attack you, defend yourselves stoutly and bravely, and be not afraid, for you will overcome them.'

In the country, at the foot of a cross, where four roads met, one of those consecrated stones, square and flat, which priests carried with them on their journeys, was placed upon a table. Very solemnly did the officiating ecclesiastics sing hymns, responses and prayers; and at this altar the Maid with all the priests and all the men-at-arms heard mass.

After the *Deo gratias* she recommended them to observe the movements of the English. 'Now look whether their faces or their backs be towards you.'

She was told that they had turned their backs and were going away.

Three times she had told them: 'Depart from Orléans and your lives shall be saved.' Now she asked that they should be allowed to go without more being required of them.

'It is not well pleasing to my Lord that they should be engaged today,' she said. 'You will have them another time. Come, let us give thanks to God.'

The *Godons* were going. During the night they had held a council of war and resolved to depart. In order to put a bold front on their retreat and to prevent its being cut off, they had faced the folk of Orléans for an hour, now they marched off in good order. Captain La Hire and Sire de Loré, curious as to which way they would take and desiring to see whether they would leave anything behind them, rode five or six kilometres (three or four miles) in pursuit with 100 or 120 horse. The English were retreating towards Meung.

Thus, on the 8th of May, in the morning, was the town of Orléans delivered, 209 days after the siege had been laid and nine days after the coming of the Maid.

Chapter XIV
The Maid at Tours and at Selles-En-Berry – The Treatises of Jacques Gélu and of Jean Gerson

✙

O N THE MORNING of Sunday the 8th of May, the English departed, retreating towards Meung and Beaugency.

On the ninth of the same month, the combatants brought by the Sire de Rais, receiving neither pay nor entertainment, went off each man on his own account; and the Maid did not stay longer. After having taken part in the procession by which the townsfolk rendered thanks to God, she took her leave of those to whom she had come in the hour of distress and affliction and whom she now quitted in the hour of deliverance and rejoicing. They wept with joy and with gratitude and offered themselves to her for her to do with them and their goods whatever she would.

From Chinon the king caused to be sent to the inhabitants of the towns in his dominion and notably to those of La Rochelle and Narbonne, a letter written at three sittings, between the evening of the 9th of May and the morning of the 10th, as the tidings from Orléans were coming in. In this letter he announced the capture of the forts of Saint-Loup, Les Augustins and Les Tourelles and called upon the townsfolk to praise God and do honour to the great feats accomplished there, especially by the Maid, who 'had always been present when these deeds were done.' Thus did the royal power describe Jeanne's share in the victory. It was in no wise a captain's share; she held no command of any kind. But, sent by God, at least so it might be believed, her presence was a help and a consolation.

When, on the Friday before Whitsunday, she entered Tours, Charles, who had set out from Chinon, had not yet arrived. Banner in hand, she rode out to meet him and when she came to him, she took off her cap and bowed her head as far as she could over her horse. The king lifted his hood, bade her look up and kissed her. It is said that he felt glad to see her, but in reality we know not what he felt.

In this month of May, 1429, he received from Messire Jacques Gélu a treatise concerning the Maid, which he probably did not read, but which his confessor read for him. Messire Jacques Gélu, sometime Councillor to the Dauphin and now my Lord Archbishop of Embrun, had at first been afraid that the king's enemies had sent him this shepherdess to poison him, or that she was a witch possessed by demons. In the beginning he had advised her being carefully interrogated, not hastily repulsed, for appearances are deceptive and divine grace moves in a mysterious manner. Now, after having read the conclusions of the doctors of Poitiers, learnt the deliverance of Orléans, and heard the cry of the common folk, Messire Jacques Gélu no longer doubted the damsel's innocence and goodness. Seeing that the doctors were divided in their opinion of her, he drew up a brief treatise, which he sent to the king, with a very ample, a very humble and a very worthy dedicatory epistle.

The great doctor Gerson, former chancellor of the university, was then ending his days at Lyon in the monastery of Les Célestins, of which his brother was prior.

The deliverance of the city of Orléans must have gladdened the heart of the old Orleanist partisan. The Dauphin's councillors, eager to set the Maid to work, had told him of the deliberations at Poitiers, and asked him, as a good servant of the house of France, for his opinion concerning them. In reply he wrote a compendious treatise on the Maid.

In this work he is careful from the first to distinguish between matters of faith and matters of devotion. In questions of faith doubt is forbidden. With regard to questions of devotion the unbeliever, to use a colloquial expression, is not necessarily damned. Three conditions are necessary if a question is to be considered as one of devotion: first, it must be edifying; second, it must be probable and attested by popular report or the testimony of the faithful; third, it must touch on nothing contrary to faith. When these conditions are fulfilled, it is fitting neither persistently to condemn nor to approve, but rather to appeal to the church.

At the conclusion of his treatise, Gerson briefly examines one point of canon law which had been neglected by the doctors of Poitiers. He establishes that the Maid is not forbidden to dress as a man.

Firstly. The ancient law forbade a woman to dress as a man, and a man as a woman. This restriction, as far as strict legality is concerned, ceases to be enforced by the new law.

Secondly. In its moral bearing this law remains binding. But in such a case it is merely a matter of decency.

Thirdly. From a legal and moral standpoint this law does not refuse masculine and military attire to the Maid, whom the King of Heaven appoints His standard-bearer, in order that she may trample underfoot the enemies of justice. In the operations of divine power the end justifies the means.

Fourthly. Examples may be quoted from history alike sacred and profane, notably Camilla and the Amazons.

Jean Gerson completed this treatise on Whit-Sunday, a week after the deliverance of Orléans. It was his last work. He died in the July of that year, 1429, in the 65th year of his age.

During the 10 days he spent at Tours the king kept Jeanne with him. Meanwhile the council were deliberating as to their line of action. The royal treasury was empty. Charles could raise enough money to make gifts to the gentlemen of his household, but he had great difficulty in defraying the expenses of war. Pay was owing to the people of Orléans. They had received little and spent much. Their resources were exhausted and they demanded payment. In May and in June the king distributed among the captains, who had defended the town, sums amounting to 41,631 livres. He had gained his victory cheaply. The total cost of the defence of Orléans was 110,000 livres. The townsfolk did the rest; they gave even their little silver spoons.

It would doubtless have been expedient to attempt to destroy that formidable army of Sir John Fastolf which had lately terrified the good folk of Orléans. But no one knew where to find it. It had disappeared somewhere between Orléans and Paris. It would have been necessary to go forth to seek it; that was impossible, and no one thought of doing such a thing. An expedition to Normandy was suggested; and the idea was so natural that the king was already imagined to be at Rouen. Finally it was decided to attempt the capture of the châteaux the English held on the Loire, both below and above Orléans, Jargeau, Meung, Beaugency. A useful undertaking and one which presented no very great difficulties, unless it involved an encounter with Sir John Fastolf's army, and whether it would or no it was impossible to tell.

Without further delay my Lord the Bastard marched on Jargeau with a few knights and some of Poton's soldiers of fortune; but the Loire was high and its waters filled the trenches.

By the reasons of the captains the Maid set little store. She listened to her Voices alone, and they spoke to her words which were infinitely simple. Her one idea was to accomplish her mission. Saint Catherine, Saint Margaret and Saint Michael the Archangel, had sent her into France not to calculate the resources of the royal treasury, not to decree aids and taxes, not to treat with men-at-arms, with merchants and the conductors of convoys, not to draw up plans of campaign and negotiate truces, but to lead the Dauphin to his anointing. Wherefore it was to Reims that she wished to take him, not that she knew how to go there, but she believed that God would guide her. Delay, tardiness, deliberation saddened and irritated her. When with the king she urged him gently.

Many times she said to him: 'I shall live a year, barely longer. During that year let as much as possible be done.'

One day she grew impatient and went to the king when he was in one of those closets of carved wainscot constructed in the great castle halls for intimate or family gatherings. She knocked at the door and entered almost immediately. There she found the king conversing with Maître Gérard Machet, his confessor, my Lord the Bastard, the Sire de Trèves and a favourite noble of his household, by name Messire Christophe d'Harcourt. She knelt embracing the king's knees (for she was conversant with the rules of courtesy), and said to him: 'Fair Dauphin, do not so long and so frequently deliberate in council, but come straightway to Reims, there to receive your rightful anointing.'

The king looked graciously upon her but answered nothing. The Lord d'Harcourt, having heard that the Maid held converse with angels and saints, was curious to know whether the idea of taking the king to Reims had really been suggested to her by her heavenly visitants. Describing them by the word she herself used, he asked: 'Is it your council who speak to you of such things?'

She replied: 'Yes, in this matter I am urged forward.' Straightway my Lord d'Harcourt responded: 'Will you not here in the king's presence tell us the manner of your council when they speak to you?'

At this request Jeanne blushed.

Willing to spare her constraint and embarrassment, the king said kindly: 'Jeanne, does it please you to answer this question before these persons here present?'

But Jeanne addressing my Lord d'Harcourt said: 'I understand what you desire to know and I will tell you willingly.'

And straightway she gave the king to understand what agony she endured at not being understood and she told of her inward consolation: 'Whenever I am sad because what I say by command of Messire is not readily believed, I go apart and to Messire I make known my complaint, saying that those to whom I speak are not willing to believe me. And when I have finished my prayer, straightway I hear a voice saying unto me: "Daughter of God, go, I will be thy help." And this voice fills me with so great a joy, that in this condition I would forever stay.'

While she was repeating the words spoken by the Voice, Jeanne raised her eyes to heaven. The nobles present were struck by the divine expression on the maiden's face. But those eyes bathed in tears, that air of rapture, which filled my Lord the Bastard with amazement, was not an ecstasy, it was the imitation of an ecstasy. The scene was at once simple and artificial. It reveals the kindness of the king, who was incapable of wounding the child in any way, and the light-heartedness with which the nobles of the court believed or pretended to believe in the most wonderful marvels. It proves likewise that henceforth the little Saint's dignifying the project of the coronation with the authority of a divine revelation was favourably regarded by the royal council.

The Maid accompanied the king to Loches and stayed with him until after the 23rd of May.

The people believed in her. As she passed through the streets of Loches they threw themselves before her horse; they kissed the Saint's hands and feet. Maître Pierre de Versailles, a monk of Saint-Denys in France, one of her interrogators at Poitiers, seeing her receive these marks of veneration, rebuked her on theological grounds: 'You do wrong,' he said, 'to suffer such things to which you are not entitled. Take heed: you are leading men into idolatry.'

Then Jeanne, reflecting on the pride which might creep into her heart, said: 'In truth I could not keep from it, were not Messire watching over me.'

She was displeased to see certain old wives coming to salute her; that was a kind of adoration which alarmed her. But poor folk who came to her she never repulsed. She would not hurt them, but aided them as far as she could.

With marvellous rapidity the fame of her holiness had been spread abroad throughout the whole of France. Many pious persons were wearing medals of lead or some other metal, stamped with her portrait, according to the customary mode of honouring the memory of saints. Paintings or sculptured figures of her were placed in chapels. At mass the priest recited as a collect 'the Maid's prayer for the realm of France:'

From Loches the Maid went to Selles-en-Berry, a considerable town on the Cher. Here, shortly before had met the three estates of the kingdom; and here the troops were now gathering.

On Saturday, the 4th of June, she received a herald sent by the people of Orléans to bring her tidings of the English. As commander in war, they recognized none but her.

Meanwhile, surrounded by monks, and side by side with men-at-arms, like a nun she lived apart, a saintly life. She ate and drank little. She communicated once a week and confessed frequently. During mass at the moment of elevation, at confession and when she received the body of Our Lord she used to weep many tears. Every evening, at the hour of vespers, she would retire into a church and have the bells rung for about half an hour to summon the mendicant friars who followed the army. Then she would begin to pray while the brethren sang an anthem in honour of the Virgin Mary.

While practising as far as she was able the austerities required by extreme piety, she appeared magnificently attired, like a lord, for indeed she held her lordship from God. She wore the dress of a knight, a small hat, doublet and hose to match, a fine cloak of silk and cloth of gold well lined and shoes laced on the outer side of the foot. Such attire in no wise scandalised even the most austere members of the Dauphin's party. The English and Burgundian clerks on the other hand converted into scandal what was a subject of edification, and maintained that she was a woman dissolute in dress and in manners.

On the reverse of her standard, sprinkled by mendicants with holy water, she had had a dove painted, holding in its beak a scroll, whereon were written the words 'in the name of the King of Heaven.' These were the armorial bearings she had received from her council. The emblem and the device seemed appropriate to her, since she proclaimed that God had sent her, and since at Orléans she had given the sign promised at Poitiers. The king, notwithstanding, changed this shield for arms representing a crown supported upon a sword between two flowers-de-luce and indicating clearly what was the aid that the Maid of God was bringing to the realm of France. It is said that she regretted having to abandon the arms communicated to her by divine revelation.

She prophesied, and, as happens to all prophets, she did not always foretell what was to come to pass. It was the fate of the prophet Jonah himself. And doctors explain how the prophecies of true prophets cannot be all fulfilled.

She had said: 'Before Saint John the Baptist's Day, in 1429, there shall not be one Englishman, howsoever strong and valiant, to be seen throughout France, either in battle or in the open field.'

Chapter XV
The Taking of Jargeau – The Bridge of Meung – Beaugency

ON MONDAY, THE 6TH OF JUNE, the king lodged at Saint-Aignan near Selles-en-Berry. Among the gentlemen of his company were two sons of that Dame de Laval who, in her widowhood, had made the mistake of loving a landless cadet. André, the younger, at the age of 20, had just passed under the cloud of a disgrace common to nearly all

nobles in those days; his grandmother's second husband, Sire Bertrand Du Guesclin, had experienced it several times. Taken prisoner in the château of Laval by Sir John Talbot, he had incurred a heavy debt in order to furnish the 16,000 golden crowns of his ransom.

Being in great need of money, the two young nobles offered their services to the king, who received them very well, gave them not a crown, but said he would show them the Maid. And as he was going with them from Saint-Aignan to Selles, he summoned the Saint, who straightway, armed at all points save her head, and lance in hand, rode out to meet the king. She greeted the two young nobles heartily and returned with them to Selles. The eldest, Lord Guy, she received in the house where she was lodging, opposite the church, and called for wine. Such was the custom among princes. Cups of wine were brought, into which the guests dipped slices of bread called sops. When offering him the wine cup, the Maid said to Lord Guy: 'I will shortly give you to drink at Paris.'

That same day, at the hour of vespers, she set out from Selles for Romorantin with a numerous company of men-at-arms and train-bands, commanded by Marshal de Boussac. She was surrounded by mendicant friars and one of her brothers went with her. She wore white armour and a hood. Her horse was brought to her at the door of her house. It was a great black charger which resolutely refused to let her mount him. She had him led to the Cross by the roadside, opposite the church, and there she leapt into the saddle. Whereupon Lord Guy marvelled; for he saw that the charger was as still as if he had been bound. She turned her horse's head towards the church porch, and in her clear woman's voice cried: 'Ye priests and churchmen, walk in processions and pray to God.

Then, gaining the highroad: 'Go forward, go forward,' she said.

In her hand she carried a little axe. Her page bore her standard furled.

The meeting-place was Orléans. On Thursday, the 9th of June, in the evening, Jeanne passed over the bridge she had crossed on the 8th of May. Saturday, the 11th, the army set out for Jargeau. The young Duke of Alençon was placed in command. He was not remarkable for his intelligence. But he knew how to ride, and in those days that was the only knowledge indispensable to a general. Again the people of Orléans defrayed the cost of the expedition. For the payment of the fighting men they contributed 3,000 livres, for their feeding, seven hogsheads of corn. At their own request, the king imposed on them a new *taille* of 3,000 livres. At their own expense they despatched workmen of all trades – masons, carpenters, smiths. They lent their artillery. They sent culverins, cannons, La Bergère and the large mortar to which four horses were harnessed, with the gunners Megret and Jean Boillève. They furnished ammunition, engines, arrows, ladders, pickaxes, spades, mattocks; and all were marked, for they were a methodical folk. Everything for the siege was sent to the Maid. For in this undertaking she was the one commander they recognized, not the Duke of Alençon, not even the Bastard their own lord's noble brother. For the inhabitants of Orléans, Jeanne was the leader of the siege; and to Jeanne, before the besieged town, they despatched two of their citizens – Jean Leclerc and François Joachim. After the citizens of Orléans, the Sire de Rais contributed most to the expenses of the siege of Jargeau. This unfortunate noble spent thoughtlessly right and left, while rich burgesses made great profits by lending to him at a high rate of interest. The sorry state of his affairs was shortly to bring him to attempt their readjustment by vowing his soul to the devil.

The town of Jargeau, which was shortly to be taken after a severe siege, had surrendered to the English without resistance on the 5th of October in the previous year. The Duke of Alençon with 600 horse was at the head of the force, and with him, the Maid. The first night they slept in the woods. On the morrow, at daybreak, my Lord the Bastard, my Lord Florent d'Illiers and several other captains joined them. They were in a great hurry to reach Jargeau. Suddenly they hear that Sir John Fastolf is at hand, coming from Paris with 2,000 combatants, bringing supplies and artillery to Jargeau.

This was the army which had been the cause of Jeanne's anxiety on the 4th of May, because her saints had not told her where Fastolf was. The captains held a council of war. Many thought the siege ought to be abandoned and that the army should go to meet Fastolf. Some actually went off at once. Jeanne exhorted the men-at-arms to continue their march on Jargeau. Where Sir John Fastolf's army was, she knew no more than the others; her reasons were not of this world.

'Be not afraid of any armed host whatsoever,' she said, 'and make no difficulty of attacking the English, for Messire leads you.'

And again she said: 'Were I not assured that Messire leads, I would rather be keeping sheep than running so great a danger.'

She gained a better hearing from the Duke of Alençon than from any of the Orléans leaders. Those who had gone were recalled and the march on Jargeau was continued.

The suburbs of the town appeared undefended; but, when the French king's men approached, they found the English posted in front of the outbuildings, wherefore they were compelled to retreat. When the Maid beheld this, she seized her standard and threw herself upon the enemy, calling on the fighting men to take courage. That night, the French king's men were able to encamp in the suburbs. They kept no watch, and yet from the Duke of Alençon's own avowal they would have been in great danger if the English had made a sally.

The very next day, in the morning the besiegers brought their siege train and their mortars up to the walls. The Orléans cannon fired upon the town and did great damage. Three of La Bergère's volleys wrecked the greatest tower on the fortifications.

The trainbands reached Jargeau on Saturday, the 11th. Straightway, without staying to take counsel, they hastened to the trenches and began the assault. They were too zealous; consequently, they went badly to work, received no aid from the men-at-arms and were driven back in disorder.

On Saturday night, the Maid, who was accustomed to summon the enemy before fighting, approached the entrenchments, and cried out to the English: 'Surrender the town to the King of Heaven and to King Charles, and depart, or it will be the worse for you.'

To this summons the English paid no heed, albeit they had a great desire to come to some understanding. The Earl of Suffolk came to my Lord the Bastard, and told him that if he would refrain from the attack, the town should be surrendered to him. The English asked for a fortnight's respite, after which time, they would undertake to withdraw immediately, they and their horses, provided, doubtless, that by that time they had not been relieved. On both sides such conditional surrenders were common. The Sire de Baudricourt had signed one at Vaucouleurs just before Jeanne's arrival there. In this case it was mere trickery to ask the French to enter into such an agreement just when Sir John Fastolf was coming with artillery and supplies. It has been asserted that the Bastard was taken in this snare; but such a thing is incredible; he was far too wily for that. Nevertheless, on the morrow, which was Sunday and the 12th of the month, the Duke of Alençon and the nobles, who were holding a council concerning the measures for the capture of the town, were told that Captain La Hire was conferring with the Earl of Suffolk. They were highly displeased. Captain La Hire, who was not a general, could not treat in his own name, and had doubtless received powers from my Lord the Bastard. The latter commanded for the duke, a prisoner in the hands of the English, while the Duke of Alençon commanded for the king; and hence the disagreement.

The Maid, who was always ready to show mercy to prisoners when they surrendered and at the same time always ready to fight, said: 'If they will, let them in their jackets of mail depart from Jargeau with their lives! If they will not, the town shall be stormed.'

The Duke of Alençon, without even inquiring the terms of the capitulation, had Captain La Hire recalled.

He came, and straightway the ladders were brought. The heralds sounded the trumpets and cried: 'To the assault.'

The Maid unfurled her standard, and fully armed, wearing on her head one of those light helmets known as *chapelines*, she went down into the trenches with the king's men and the trainbands, well within reach of arrows and cannonballs. She kept by the Duke of Alençon's side, saying: 'Forward! fair duke, to the assault.'

The duke, who was not so courageous as she, thought that she went rather hastily to work; and this he gave her to understand.

Then she encouraged him: 'Fear not. God's time is the right time. When He wills it you must open the attack. Go forward, He will prepare the way.'

In the thick of the attack, she noticed on the wall one of those long thin mortars, which, from the manner of its charging, was called a breechloader. Seeing it hurl stones on the very spot where the king's fair cousin was standing, she realised the danger, but not for herself. 'Move away,' she said quickly. 'That cannon will kill you.'

The duke had not moved more than a few yards, when a nobleman of Anjou, the Sire Du Lude, having taken the place he had quitted, was killed by a ball from that same cannon.

The attack had lasted four hours, when Jeanne, standard in hand, climbed up a ladder leaning against the rampart. A stone fired from a cannon struck her helmet and knocked it with its escutcheon, bearing her arms, off her head. They thought she was crushed, but she rose quickly and cried to the fighting men: 'Up, friends, up! Messire has doomed the English. They are ours at this moment. Be of good cheer.'

The wall was scaled and the French king's men penetrated into the town. The English fled into La Beauce and the French rushed in pursuit of them. Guillaume Regnault, a squire of Auvergne, came up with the Earl of Suffolk on the bridge and took him prisoner.

'Are you a gentleman?' asked Suffolk.

'Yes.'

'Are you a knight?'

'No.'

The Earl of Suffolk dubbed him a knight and surrendered to him.

Very soon the rumour ran that the Earl of Suffolk had surrendered on his knees to the Maid. It was even stated that he had asked to surrender to her as to the bravest lady in the world. But it is more likely that he would have surrendered to the lowest menial of the army rather than to a woman whom he held to be a witch possessed of the devil.

The garrison surrendered at discretion. Now, as always, no great harm was done during the battle, but afterwards the conquerors made up for it. Five hundred English were massacred; the nobles alone were held to ransom. And over them, the French fell to quarrelling. The French nobles kept them all for themselves; the trainbands claimed their share, and, not getting it, began to destroy everything. What the nobles could save was carried off during the night, by water, to Orléans. The town was completely sacked; the old church, which had served the *Godons* as a magazine, was pillaged.

Including killed and wounded, the French had not lost 20 men.

Without disarming, the Maid and the knights returned to Orléans. To celebrate the taking of Jargeau, the magistrates organised a public procession.

As an acknowledgment of the good and acceptable services rendered by the holy maiden, the councillors of the captive Duke Charles of Orléans, gave her a green cloak and a robe of crimson Flemish cloth or fine Brussels purple. Jean Luillier, who furnished the stuff, asked eight crowns for two ells [roughly equivalent to 137.2 cm (54 in)] of fine Brussels at four crowns the ell; two crowns for the lining of the robe; two crowns for an ell of yellowish green cloth, making in all 12 golden crowns.

Jean Bourgeois, tailor, asked one golden crown for the making of the robe and the cloak, as well as for furnishing white satin, taffeta and other stuffs.

The town had previously given the Maid half an ell of cloth of two shades of green worth 35 *sous* of Paris to make 'nettles' for her gown. Nettles were the Duke of Orléans' device, green or purple or crimson his colours. This green was no longer the bright colour of earlier days, it had gradually been growing darker as the fortunes of the house declined. It had first been a vivid green, then a brownish shade, and, finally, the tint of the faded leaf with a suggestion of black in it which signified sorrow and mourning. The Maid's colour was *feuillemort*. She, like the officers of the duchy and the men of the trainbands wore the Orléans livery; and thus they made of her a kind of herald-at-arms or heraldic angel.

The cloak of yellowish green and the robe embroidered with nettles, she must have been glad to wear for love of Duke Charles, whom the English had treated with such sore despite. Having come to defend the heritage of the captive prince, she said that in Jesus' name, the good Duke of Orléans was on her mind and she was confident that she would deliver him.

Then, speaking of the captive duke she would say: 'My Voices have revealed much to me concerning him. Duke Charles hath oftener been the subject of my revelations than any man living except my king.'

In reality, all that Saint Catherine and Saint Margaret had done was to tell her of the well-known misfortunes of the Prince. Valentine of Milan's son and Isabelle Romée's daughter were separated by a gulf broader and deeper than the ocean which stretched between them. They dwelt at the antipodes of the world of souls, and all the saints of Paradise would have been unable to explain one to the other.

All the same Duke Charles was a good prince and a debonair; he was kind and he was pitiful. More than any other he possessed the gift of pleasing. He charmed by his grace, albeit but ill-looking and of weak constitution. His temperament was so out of harmony with his position that he may be said to have endured his life rather than to have lived it. His father assassinated by night in the Rue Barbette in Paris by order of Duke John; his mother a perennial fount of tears, dying of anger and of grief in a Franciscan nunnery; the two S's, standing for *Soupirs* (sighs) and *Souci* (care), the emblems and devices of her mourning, revealing her ingenious mind fancifully elegant even in despair; the Armagnacs, the Burgundians, the Cabochiens, cutting each other's throats around him; these were the sights he had witnessed when little more than a child. Then he had been wounded and taken prisoner at the Battle of Azincourt.

Now, for 14 years, dragged from castle to castle, from one end to the other of the island of fogs; imprisoned within thick walls, closely guarded, receiving two or three of his countrymen at long intervals, but never permitted to converse with one except before witnesses, he felt old before his time, blighted by misfortune. 'Fruit fallen in its greenness, I was put to ripen on prison straw. I am winter fruit,' he said of himself. In his captivity, he suffered without hope, knowing that on his death-bed Henry V had recommended his brother not to give him up at any price.

He was left in ignorance of the affairs of his duchy; and, if he ever concerned himself about it, it was when he collected the books of King Charles V which had been bought by the Duke of Bedford and resold to London merchants; or when he commanded that on the approach of the English to Blois, its fine tapestries and his father's library should be carried off to La Rochelle. After Beauty, rich hangings and delicate miniatures were what he loved most in the world. The bright sunshine of France, the lovely month of May, dancing and ladies were what he longed for most.

Some have wished to believe that from his duchy news reached him of the Maid's coming. They have gone so far as to imagine that a faithful servant kept him informed of the happy incidents of May and June 1429; but nothing is less certain. On the contrary, the probability is that the English refused to let him receive any message, and that he was totally ignorant of all that was going on in the two kingdoms.

Possibly he did not care for news of the war as much as one might expect. No, despite her revelations, the picture Jeanne imagined of her fair duke was not the true one. They were never to meet; but if they had met there would have been serious misunderstandings between them, and they would have remained incomprehensible one to the other. Jeanne's elemental, straightforward way of thinking could never have accorded with the ideas of so great a noble and so courteous a poet. They could never have understood each other because she was simple, he subtle; because she was a prophetess while he was filled with courtly knowledge and lettered grace; because she believed, and he was as one not believing; because she was a daughter of the common folk and a saint ascribing all sovereignty to God, while for him law consisted in feudal uses and customs, alliances and treaties; because, in short, they held conflicting ideas concerning life and the world. The Maid's mission, her being sent by Messire to recover his duchy for him, would never have appealed to the good duke; and Jeanne would never have understood his behaviour towards his English and Burgundian cousins. It was better they should never meet.

The capture of Jargeau had given the French control of the upper Loire. In order to free the city of Orléans from all danger, it was necessary to make sure of the banks of the lower river. There the English still held Meung and Beaugency. On Tuesday, the 14th of June, at the hour of vespers, the army took the field.

They passed through La Sologne, and that same evening gained the Bridge of Meung, situated above the town and separated from its walls by a broad meadow. Like most bridges, it was defended by a castlet at each end; and the English had provided it with an earthen outwork, as they had done for Les Tourelles at Orléans. They defended it badly, however, and the French king's men forced their way in before nightfall. They left a garrison there, and went out to encamp in Beauce, almost under the walls. The young Duke of Alençon lodged in a church with a few men-at-arms; and, as was his wont, did not keep watch. He was surprised and ran great danger.

The town garrison, which was a small one, was commanded by Lord Scales, and 'the Child of Warwick'. The next day, early in the morning, the king's men, passing within a cannon shot of the town of Meung, marched straight on Beaugency, which they reached in the morning.

The Duke of Alençon stationed sentinels in front of the castle to watch the English. Just then, he saw coming towards him, two nobles of Brittany, the Lords of Rostrenen and of Kermoisan, who said to him: 'The constable asks the besiegers for entertainment.'

Arthur of Brittany, Sire de Richemont, Constable of France, had spent the winter in Poitou waging war against the troops of the Sire de La Trémouille. Now in defiance of the king's prohibition the constable came to join the king's men. He had crossed the Loire at Amboise and arrived before Beaugency with 600 men-at-arms and 400 archers. His coming caused the captains great embarrassment. Some esteemed him a man of strong will and great courage. But many were dependent upon the Sire de La Trémouille, as for example the poor squire, Jean d'Aulon. The Duke of Alençon wanted to retreat, alleging that the king had commanded him not to receive the constable.

'If the constable comes, I shall retire,' he said to Jeanne.

To the Breton nobles he replied, that if the constable came into the camp, the Maid, and the besiegers would fight against him.

So decided was he that he mounted his horse to ride straight up to the Bretons. The Maid, out of respect for him and for the king, was preparing to follow him. But many of the captains restrained the Duke of Alençon deeming that now was not the time to break a lance with the Constable of France.

On the morrow a loud alarm was sounded in the camp. The heralds were crying: 'To arms!' The English were said to be approaching in great numbers. The young duke still wanted to retreat in order to avoid receiving the constable. This time Jeanne dissuaded him: 'We must stand together,' she said.

He listened to this counsel and went forth to meet the constable, followed by the Maid, my Lord the Bastard and the Lords of Laval. Near the leper's hospital at Beaugency they encountered a fine company. As they approached, a thick-lipped little man, dark and frowning, alighted from his horse. It was Arthur of Brittany. The Maid embraced his knees as she was accustomed to do when holding converse with the great ones of heaven and earth. Thus did every baron when he met one nobler than himself.

The constable spoke to her as a good Catholic, a devout servant of God and the Church, saying: 'Jeanne, I have heard that you wanted to fight against me. Whether you are sent by God I know not. If you are I do not fear you. For God knows that my heart is right. If you are sent by the devil, I fear you still less.'

He was entitled to speak thus, for he made a point of never acknowledging the devil's power over him. His love of God he showed by seeking out wizards and witches with a greater zeal than was displayed by bishops and Inquisitors. In France, in Poitou and in Brittany he had sent more to the stake than any other man living.

The Duke of Alençon dared not either dismiss him or grant him a lodging for the night. It was the custom for newcomers to keep the watch. The constable with his company kept watch that night in front of the castle.

Without more ado the young Duke of Alençon proceeded to the attack. Here, again, those who bore the brunt of the attack and provided for the siege were the citizens of Orléans. The magistrates of the town had sent by water from Meung to Beaugency the necessary siege train, ladders, pickaxes, mattocks and those great penthouses beneath which the besiegers protected themselves like tortoises under their shells. They had sent also cannons and mortars. On the 17th of June, at midnight, Sir Richard Gethyn, Bailie of Évreux, who commanded the garrison, offered to capitulate. It was agreed that the English should surrender the castle and bridge, and depart on the morrow, taking with them horses and harness with each man his property to the value of not more than one silver mark. Further, they were required to swear that they would not take up arms again before the expiration of 10 days. On these terms, the next day, at sunrise, to the number of 500, they crossed the drawbridge and retreated on Meung, where the castle, but not the bridge, remained in the hands of the English. The constable wisely sent a few men to reinforce the garrison on the Meung Bridge.

The Beaugency garrison had been in too great haste to surrender. Scarce had it gone when a man-at-arms of Captain La Hire's company came to the Duke of Alençon saying: 'The English are marching upon us. We shall have them in front of us directly. They are over there, full one thousand fighting men.'

Jeanne heard him speak but did not seize his meaning.

'What is that man-at-arms saying?' she asked.

And when she knew, turning to Arthur of Brittany, who was close by, she said: 'Ah! Fair constable, it was not my will that you should come, but since you are here, I bid you welcome.'

The force the French had to face was Sir John Talbot and Sir John Fastolf with the whole English army.

Chapter XVI
The Battle of Patay – Opinions of Italian and German Ecclesiastics – The Gien Army

HAVING LEFT PARIS on the 9th of June, Sir John Fastolf was coming through La Beauce with 5,000 fighting men. To the English at Jargeau he was bringing victuals and arrows in abundance. Learning by the way that the town had surrendered, he left his stores at Étampes and marched on to Janville, where Sir John Talbot joined him with 40 lances and 200 bowmen.

There they heard that the French had taken the Meung bridge and laid siege to Beaugency. Sir John Talbot wished to march to the relief of the inhabitants of Beaugency and deliver them with the aid of God and Saint George. Sir John Fastolf counselled abandoning Sir Richard Gethyn and his garrison to their fate; for the moment he deemed it wiser not to fight.

'In comparison with the French we are but a handful,' he said. 'If luck should turn against us, then we should be in a fair way to lose all those conquests won by our late King Henry after strenuous effort and long delay.'

His advice was disregarded and the army marched on Beaugency. The force was not far from the town on Friday, the 17th of June, just when the garrison was issuing forth with horses, armour and baggage to the amount of one silver mark's worth for each man.

Informed of the army's approach the French king's men went forth to meet it. Captain La Hire and the young Sire de Termes said to the Maid: 'The English are coming. They are in battle array and ready to fight.'

As was her wont, she made answer: 'Strike boldly and they will flee.'

And she added that the battle would not be long.

Believing that the French were offering them battle, the English took up their position. The archers planted their stakes in the ground, their points inclined towards the enemy.

The Duke of Alençon had by no means decided to descend into the plain. In presence of the constable, my Lord the Bastard and the captains, he consulted the holy Maid, who gave him an enigmatical answer: 'See to it that you have good spurs.'

Taking her to mean the Count of Clermont's spurs, the spurs of Rouvray, the Duke of Alençon exclaimed: 'What do you say? Shall we turn our backs on them?'

'Nay,' she replied.

According to the opinions of doctors and masters it was well to listen to the Maid, but at the same time to follow the course marked out by human wisdom.

The commanders of the army, either because they judged the occasion unfavourable or because, after so many defeats, they feared a pitched battle, did not come down from their hill. The two heralds sent by two English knights to offer single combat received the answer: 'For today you may go to bed, because it grows late. But tomorrow, if it be God's will, we will come to closer quarters.'

The English, assured that they would not be attacked, marched off to pass the night at Meung.

On the morrow, Saturday, the 18th, Saint Hubert's day, the French went forth against them. They were not there. The *Godons* had decamped early in the morning and gone off, with cannon, ammunition and victuals, towards Janville, where they intended to entrench themselves.

Straightway King Charles's army of 12,000 men set out in pursuit of them. Along the Paris road they went, over the plain of Beauce.

Now, as on the previous evening, she prophesied: 'Today our fair king shall win a victory greater than has been his for a long time. My council has told me that they are all ours.'

Captain Poton and Sire Arnault de Gugem went forth to reconnoitre. The most skilled men-of-war, and among them my Lord the Bastard and the Marshal de Boussac, mounted on the finest of war-steeds, formed the vanguard. Then under the leadership of Captain La Hire, who knew the country, came the horse of the Duke of Alençon, the Count of Vendôme, the Constable of France, with archers and crossbowmen. Last of all came the rear guard, commanded by the lords of Graville, Laval, Rais and Saint-Gilles.

The Maid, ever zealous, desired to be in the vanguard; but she was kept back. She did not lead the men-at-arms, rather the men-at-arms led her. They regarded her, not as captain of war but as a bringer of good luck.

After they had ridden 19 or 20 kilometres (12 or 13 miles) in overpowering heat and passed Saint-Sigismond on the left and got beyond Saint-Péravy, Captain Poton's 60 to 80 scouts reached a spot where the ground, which had been level hitherto, descends, and where the road leads down into a hollow called La Retrève. A league straight in front of them was the little town of Patay.

It is two o'clock in the afternoon. Poton's and Gugem's horse chance to raise a stag, which darts out of a thicket and plunges down into the hollow of La Retrève. Suddenly a clamour of voices ascends from the hollow. It proceeds from the English soldiers loudly disputing over the game which has fallen into their hands. Thus informed of the enemy's presence, the French scouts halt and straightway despatch certain of their company to go and tell the army that they have surprised the *Godons* and that it is time to set to work.

Now this is what had been happening among the English. They were retreating in good order on Janville, their vanguard commanded by a knight bearing a white standard. Then came the artillery and the victuals in waggons driven by merchants; then the main body of the army, commanded by Sir John Talbot and Sir John Fastolf. The rear-guard, which was likely to bear the brunt of the attack, consisted only of Englishmen from England. It followed at some distance from the rest. Its scouts, having seen the French without being seen by them, informed Sir John Talbot, who was then between the hamlet of Saint-Péravy and the town of Patay. On this information he called a halt and commanded the vanguard with waggons and cannon to take up its position on the edge of the Lignerolles wood. The position was excellent: backed by the forest, the combatants were secure against being attacked in the rear, while in front they were able to entrench themselves behind their waggons. The main body did not advance so far. It halted some little distance from Lignerolles, in the hollow of La Retrève. On this spot the road was lined with quickset hedges. Sir John Talbot with 500 picked bowmen stationed himself there to await the French who must perforce pass that way. His design was to defend the road until the rear-guard had had time to join the main body, and then, keeping close to the hedges, he would fall back upon the army.

The archers, as was their wont, were making ready to plant in the ground those pointed stakes, the spikes of which they turned against the chests of the enemy's horses, when the French, led by Poton's scouts, came down upon them like a whirlwind, overthrew them and cut them to pieces.

At this moment, Sir John Fastolf, at the head of the main body, was preparing to join the vanguard. Feeling the French cavalry at his heels, he gave spur and at full gallop led his men on to Lignerolles. When those of the white standard saw him arriving thus in rout, they thought he had been defeated. They took fright, abandoned the edge of the wood, rushed into the thickets of Climat-du-Camp and in great disorder came out on the Paris road. With the main body of the army, Sir John Fastolf pushed on in the same direction. There was no battle. Marching over the bodies of Talbot's archers, the French threw themselves on the English, who were as dazed as a flock of sheep and fell before the foe without resistance. When the main body of the French, commanded by La Hire, reached Lignerolles, they found only 800 foot whom they soon overthrew. Of the 12,000 to 13,000 French on the march, scarce 1,500 took part in the battle or rather in the massacre. Sir John Talbot, who had leapt on to his horse without staying to put on his spurs, was taken prisoner by the Captains La Hire and Poton. In all, there were between 1,200 and 1,500 prisoners.

Not more than 200 men-at-arms pursued the fugitives to the gates of Janville. Except for the vanguard, which had been the first to take flight, the English army was entirely destroyed. On the French side, the Sire de Termes, who was present, states that there was only one killed: a man of his own company.

The Maid arrived before the slaughter was ended. She saw a Frenchman, who was leading some prisoners, strike one of them such a blow on the head that he fell down as if dead. She dismounted and procured the

Englishman a confessor. She held his head and comforted him as far as she could. Such was the part she played in the Battle of Patay.

A few breathless *Godons* succeeded in reaching Janville. But the townsfolk, with whom on their departure they had deposited their money and their goods, shut the gates in their faces and swore loyalty to King Charles.

From Patay the victorious army marched to Orléans. The inhabitants were expecting the king. But the king and his chamberlain, fearing and not without reason, some aggressive movement on the part of the constable, held themselves secure in the Château of Sully. Thence they started for Châteauneuf on the 22nd of June. That same day the Maid joined the king at Saint-Benoit-sur-Loire. He received her with his usual kindness and said: 'I pity you because of the suffering you endure.' And he urged her to rest.

At these words she wept. It has been said that her tears flowed because of the indifference and incredulity towards her that the king's urbanity implied. But we must beware of attributing to the tears of the enraptured and the illuminated a cause intelligible to human reason. To her Charles appeared clothed in an ineffable splendour like that of the holiest of kings. How, since she had shown him her angels, invisible to ordinary folk, could she for one moment have thought that he lacked faith in her?

'Have no doubt,' she said to him, confidently, 'you shall receive the whole of your kingdom and shortly shall be crowned.'

True, Charles seemed in no great haste to employ his knights in the recovery of his kingdom. But his council just then had no idea of getting rid of the Maid. On the contrary, they were determined to use her cleverly, so as to put heart into the French, to terrify the English, and to convince the world that God, Saint Michael and Saint Catherine, were on the side of the Armagnacs. In announcing the victory of Patay to the good towns, the royal councillors said not one word of the constable, neither did they mention my Lord the Bastard. They described as leaders of the army, the Maid, with the two Princes of the Blood Royal, the Duke of Alençon and the Duke of Vendôme. In such wise did they exalt her. And, indeed, she must have been worth as much and more than a great captain, since the constable attempted to seize her.

Probably she herself knew nothing of this plot. She besought the king to pardon the constable – a request which proves how great was her naïveté.

By royal command Richemont received back his lordship of Parthenay.

Duke John of Brittany, who had married a sister of Charles of Valois, was not always pleased with his brother-in-law's counsellors. In 1420, considering him too Burgundian, they had devised for him a Bridge of Montereau. In reality, he was neither Armagnac nor Burgundian nor French nor English, but Breton. In 1423 he recognized the Treaty of Troyes; but two years later, when his brother, the Duke of Richemont, had gone over to the French king and received the constable's sword from him, Duke John went to Charles of Valois, at Saumur, and did homage for his duchy. In short, he extricated himself cleverly from the most embarrassing situations and succeeded in remaining outside the quarrel of the two kings who were both eager to involve him in it. While France and England were cutting each other's throats, he was raising Brittany from its ruins.

The Maid filled him with curiosity and admiration. Shortly after the Battle of Patay, he sent to her, Hermine, his herald-at-arms, and Brother Yves Milbeau, his confessor, to congratulate her on her victory. The good Brother was told to question Jeanne.

He asked her whether it was God who had sent her to succour the king. Jeanne replied that it was.

'If it be so,' replied Brother Yves Milbeau, 'my Lord the Duke of Brittany, our liege lord, is disposed to proffer his service to the king. He cannot come in person for he is sorely infirm. But he is to send his son with a large army.'

On hearing these words, the little Saint made a curious mistake. She thought that Brother Yves had meant that the Duke of Brittany was her liege lord as well as his, which would have been altogether senseless. Her loyalty revolted: 'The Duke of Brittany is not my liege lord,' she replied sharply. 'The king is my liege lord.'

A few days later, the Sire de Rostrenen, who had accompanied the constable to Beaugency and to Patay, came from Duke John to treat of the prospective marriage between his eldest son, François, and Bonne de Savoie, daughter of Duke Amédée. With him was Comment-Qu'il-Soit, herald of Richard of Brittany, Count of Étampes. The herald was commissioned to present the Maid with a dagger and horses.

Jeanne maintained her resolution to go to Reims and take the king to his anointing. She did not stay to consider whether it would be better to wage war in Champagne than in Normandy. She did not know enough of the configuration of the country to decide such a question, and it is not likely that her saints and angels knew more of geography than she did. She was in haste to take the king to Reims for his anointing, because she believed it impossible for him to be king until he had been anointed. The idea of leading him to be anointed with the holy oil had come to her in her native village, long before the siege of Orléans. This inspiration was wholly of the spirit, and had nothing to do with the state of affairs created by the deliverance of Orléans and the victory of Patay.

The best course would have been to march straight on Paris after the 18th of June. The French were then only 145 kilometres (90 miles) from the great city, which at that juncture would not have thought of defending itself. Considering it as good as lost, the regent shut himself up in the Fort of Vincennes. They had missed their opportunity. The French king's councillors, Princes of the Blood, were deliberating, surprised by victory, not knowing what to do with it. Certain it is that not one of them thought of conquering, and that speedily, the whole inheritance of King Charles. The forces at their disposal, and the very conditions of the society in which they lived, rendered it impossible for them to conceive of such an undertaking. The king's councillors were no dreamers; they did not believe in the end of the war, neither did they desire it. But they intended to conduct it with the least possible risk and expenditure. Such were the opinions of the good servants of King Charles.

Certain among them wished the war to be carried on in Normandy. The idea had occurred to them as early as the month of May, before the Loire campaign, and indeed there was much to be said for it. In Normandy they would cut the English tree at its root. It was quite possible that they might immediately recover a part of that province where the English had but few fighting men. In 1424 the Norman garrisons consisted of not more than 400 lances and 1,200 bowmen. Since then they had received but few reinforcements. The regent was recruiting men everywhere and displaying marvellous activity, but he lacked money, and his soldiers were always deserting. In the conquered province, as soon as the *Coués* came out of their strongholds they found themselves in the enemy's territory. From the borders of Brittany, Maine, Perche as far as Ponthieu and Picardy, on the banks of the Mayenne, Orne, the Dive, the Touque, the Eure, the Seine, the partisans of the various factions held the country, watching the roads, robbing, ravaging and murdering. Everywhere the French would have found these brave fellows ready to espouse their cause; the peasants and the village priests would likewise have wished them well. But the campaign would involve long sieges of towns, strongly defended, albeit held by but small garrisons. Now the men-at-arms dreaded the delays of sieges, and the royal treasury was not sufficient for such costly undertakings. Normandy was ruined, stripped of its crops, and robbed of its cattle. Were the captains and their men to go into this famine-stricken land? And why should the king reconquer so poor a province?

Other nobles clamoured for an expedition into Champagne. And in spite of all that has been said to the contrary, the Maid's visions had no influence whatever on this determination. The king's councillors led Jeanne and were far from being led by her. Once before they had diverted her from the road to Reims by providing her with work on the Loire. Once again they might divert her into Normandy, without her even perceiving it, so ignorant was she of the roads and of the lie of the land. If there were certain who recommended a campaign in Champagne, it was not on the faith of saints and angels, but for purely human reasons. Is it possible to discover these reasons? There were doubtless certain lords and captains who considered the interest of the King and the kingdom, but everyone found it so difficult not to confound it with his own interest, that the best way to discover who was responsible for the march on Reims is to find out who was to profit by it. It was certainly not the Duke of Alençon, who would have greatly preferred to take advantage of the Maid's help for the conquest of his own duchy. Neither was it my Lord the Bastard, nor the Sire de Gaucourt, nor the king himself, for they must have desired the securing of Berry and the Orléanais by the capture of La Charité held by the terrible Perrinet Gressart. On the other hand, we may conclude that the Queen of Sicily would not be unfavourable to the march of the king, her son-in-law, in a north easterly direction. This Spanish lady was possessed by the Angevin mania. Reassured for the moment concerning the fate of her duchy of Anjou, she was pursuing eagerly, and to the great hurt of the realm of France, the establishment of her son René in the duchy of Bar and in the inheritance of Lorraine. She cannot have been displeased, therefore, when she saw the king keeping her an open road between Gien and Troyes and Châlons. But since the constable's exile she had lost all influence over her son-in-law, and it is difficult to discover who could have watched her interests in the council of May, 1429. Besides, without seeking further, it is obvious that there was one person, who above all others must have desired the anointing of the king, and who more than any was in a position to make his opinion prevail. That person was the man on whom devolved the duty of holding in his consecrated hands the Sacred Ampulla, my Lord Regnault de Chartres, Archbishop Duke of Reims, Chancellor of the Kingdom.

He was a man of rare intelligence, skilled in business, a very clever diplomatist, greedy of wealth, caring less for empty honours than for solid advantage, avaricious, unscrupulous, one who at the age of about 50 had lost nothing of his consuming energy; he had recently displayed it by spending himself nobly in the defence of Orléans. Thus gifted, how could he fail to exercise a powerful control over the government?

While the coronation campaign was attended with grave drawbacks and met with serious obstacles, it nevertheless brought great gain and a certain subtle advantage to the royal cause. Unfortunately, it left free from attack the rest of France occupied by the English, and it gave the latter time to recover themselves and procure aid from over sea. As to the advantages of the expedition, they were many and various. First, Jeanne truly expressed the sentiments of the poor priests and the common folk when she said that the Dauphin would reap great profit from his anointing. From the oil of the holy Ampulla the king would derive a splendour, a majesty which would impress the whole of France, yea, even the whole of Christendom. In those days royalty was alike spiritual and temporal; and multitudes of men believed with Jeanne that kings only became kings by being anointed with the holy oil. Thus it would not be wrong to say that Charles of Valois would receive greater power from one drop of oil than from 10,000 lances. On a consideration like this, the king's councillors must needs set great store. They had also to take into account the time and the place. Might not the ceremony be performed in some other town than Reims?

Therefore, it was necessary to go to Reims. To attain the city of the Blessed Saint Remi 400 kilometres (250 miles) of hostile country must be traversed.

But for some time the army would be in no danger of meeting the enemy on the road. The English and Burgundians were engaged in using every means both fair and foul for the raising of troops. For the moment the French need fear no foe. The rich country of Champagne, sparsely wooded, well cultivated, teemed with corn and wine and abounded in fat cattle. Champagne had not been devastated like Normandy. There was a likelihood of obtaining food for the men-at-arms, especially if, as was hoped, the good towns supplied victuals. They were very wealthy; their barns overflowed with corn. While owing allegiance to King Henry, no bonds of affection united them to the English or to the Burgundians. They governed themselves. They were rich merchants, who only longed for peace and who did their best to bring it about. Just now they were beginning to suspect that the Armagnacs were growing the stronger party. These folk of Champagne had a clergy and a *bourgeoisie* who might be appealed to. It was not a question of storming their towns with artillery, mines and trenches, but of getting round them with amnesties, concessions to the merchants and elaborate engagements to respect the privileges of the clergy. The townsfolk were expected to throw open their gates and partly from love, partly from fear, to give money to their lord the king.

The campaign was already arranged, and that very skilfully. Communications had been opened with Troyes and Châlons. By letters and messages from a few notables of Reims it was made known to King Charles that if he came they would open to him the gates of their town. He even received three or four citizens, who said to him, 'Go forth in confidence to our city of Reims. It shall not be our fault if you do not enter therein.'

Such assurances emboldened the royal council; and the march into Champagne was resolved upon.

The army assembled at Gien; it increased daily. The nobles of Brittany and Poitou came in in great numbers, most of them mounted on sorry steeds and commanding but small companies of men. The poorest equipped themselves as archers, and in default of better service were ready to act as bowmen. Villeins and tradesmen came likewise. From the Loire to the Seine and from the Seine to the Somme the only cultivated land was round *châteaux* and fortresses. Most of the fields lay fallow. In many places fairs and markets had been suspended. The king went to Gien and summoned the queen who was at Bourges.

His idea was to take her to Reims and have her crowned with him, following the example of Queen Blanche of Castille, of Jeanne de Valois and of Queen Jeanne, wife of King John. But queens had not usually been crowned at Reims. The queen, who had come to Gien, was sent back to Bourges. The king set out without her.

On Friday, the 24th of June, the Maid set out from Orléans for Gien. On the morrow she dictated from Gien a letter to the inhabitants of Tournai, telling them how the English had been driven from all their strongholds on the Loire and discomfited in battle. In this letter she invited them to come to the anointing of King Charles at Reims and called upon them to continue loyal Frenchmen. Here is the letter:

† Jhesus † Maria

Fair Frenchmen and loyal, of the town of Tournay, from this place the Maid maketh known unto you these tidings: that in eight days, by assault or otherwise, she hath driven the English from all the strongholds they held on the River Loire. Know ye that the Earl of Suffort, Lapoulle his brother, the Sire of Tallebord, the Sire of Scallez and my lords Jean Falscof and many knights and captains have been taken, and the brother of the Earl of Suffort and Glasdas slain. I beseech you to remain good and loyal Frenchmen; and I beseech and entreat you that ye make yourselves ready to come to the anointing of the fair King Charles at Rains, where we shall shortly be, and come ye to meet us when ye know that we draw nigh. To God I commend you. God keep you and give you his grace that ye may worthily maintain the good cause of the realm of France. Written at Gien the xxvth day of June.

Addressed 'to the loyal Frenchmen of the town of Tournay.'

An epistle in the same tenor must have been sent by the Maid's monkish scribes to all the towns which had remained true to King Charles, and the priests themselves must have drawn up the list of them. The town of Tournai, ceded to Philip the Good by the English government, in 1423, had not recognized its new master. Jean de Thoisy, its bishop, resided at Duke Philip's court; but it remained the king's town, and the well-known attachment of its townsfolk to the Dauphin's fortunes was exemplary and famous. The Consuls of Albi, in a short note concerning the marvels of 1429, were careful to remark that this northern city, so remote that they did not exactly know where it was, still held out for France, though surrounded by France's enemies. 'The truth is that the English occupy the whole land of Normandy, and of Picardy, except Tournay', they wrote.

There is no doubt that the Maid herself dictated this letter. It will be noticed that therein she takes to herself the credit and the whole credit for the victory. Her candour obliged her to do so. In her opinion God had done everything, but he had done everything through her. 'The Maid hath driven the English out of all their strongholds.' She alone could reveal so naïve a faith in herself. Brother Pasquerel would not have written with such saintly simplicity.

On the 27th of June, or about then, the Maid caused letters to be despatched to the Duke of Burgundy, inviting him to come to the king's coronation. She received no reply. Duke Philip was the last man in the world to correspond with the Maid. And that she should have written to him courteously was a sign of her goodness of heart.

Chapter XVII
The Convention of Auxerre – Friar Richard – The Surrender of Troyes

AFTER HAVING SPENT THREE DAYS under the walls of Auxerre, the army being refreshed, crossed the Yonne and came to the town of Saint-Florentin, which straightway submitted to the king. On the 4th of July, they reached the village of Saint-Phal, four hours' journey from Troyes.

In this strong town there was a garrison of between 500 and 600 men at the most. A bailie, Messire Jean de Dinteville, two captains, the Sires de Rochefort and de Plancy, commanded in the town for King Henry and for the Duke of

Burgundy. Troyes was a manufacturing town; the source of its wealth was the cloth manufacture. True, this industry had long been declining through competition and the removal of markets; its ruin was being precipitated by the general poverty and the insecurity of the roads. Nevertheless, the cloth workers' guild maintained its importance and sent a number of magistrates to the council.

In 1420, these merchants had sworn to the treaty which promised the French crown to the House of Lancaster; they were then at the mercy of English and Burgundians. For the holding of those great fairs, to which they took their cloth, they must needs live at peace with their Burgundian neighbours, and if the *Godons* had closed the ports of the Seine against their bales, they would have died of hunger. Wherefore the notables of the town had turned English, which did not mean that they would always remain English.

The Bishop of Troyes was my lord Jean Laiguisé, one of the first to swear to the treaty of 1420. The Chapter had elected him without waiting for the permission of the regent, who declared against the election, not that he disliked the new pontiff; Messire Jean Laiguisé had sucked hatred of the Armagnacs and respect for the Rose of Lancaster from his *alma mater* of Paris. But my Lord of Bedford could not forgive any slighting of his sovereign rights.

Shortly afterwards he incurred the censure of the whole Church of France and was judged by the bishops worse than the cruellest tyrants of Scripture. More wicked than they and more sacrilegious, my Lord of Bedford threatened the privileges of the Gallican Church, when, on behalf of the Holy See, he robbed the bishops of their patronage, levied a double tithe on the French clergy, and commanded churchmen to surrender to him the contributions they had been receiving for 40 years. The episcopal lords resolved to appeal from a Pope ill-informed to one with wider knowledge; for they held the authority of the Bishop of Rome to be insignificant in comparison with the authority of the council. In order to pacify the Church of France thus roused against him, my lord of Bedford convoked at Paris the bishops of the ecclesiastical province of Sens, which included the dioceses of Paris, Troyes, Auxerre, Nevers, Meaux, Chartres and Orléans.

Messire Jean Laiguisé attended this Convocation. The Synod was held at Paris, in the Priory of Saint-Eloi, under the presidency of the Archbishop, from the 1st of March till the 23rd of April, 1429. The assembled bishops represented to my Lord the regent the sorry plight of the ecclesiastical lords: the peasants, pillaged by soldiers, no longer paid their dues; the lands of the Church were lying waste; divine service had ceased to be held because there was no money with which to support public worship. Unanimously they refused to pay the Pope and the regent the double tithe; and they threatened to appeal from the Pope to the council. As for despoiling the clergy of all the contributions they had received during the last 40 years, that, they declared, would be impious; and with great charity they reminded my Lord of Bedford of the fate reserved by God's judgment for the impious even in this world.

Jean Laiguisé's sentiments towards the English regent were those of the Synod. It would be wrong, however, to conclude that the Bishop of Troyes desired the death of the sinner, or even that he was hostile to the English.

King Charles had not ventured to enter Champagne without taking measures for his safety; he knew on what he could rely in the town of Troyes. He had received information and promises; he maintained secret relations with several burgesses of the city, and those none of the least. During the first fortnight of May, a royal notary, 10 clerks and leading merchants, on their way to the king, were arrested just outside the walls, on the Paris road, by the Sire de Chateauvillain, a captain in the English service. This mission was probably fulfilled by others more fortunate. It is easy to divine what questions were discussed at these audiences. The merchants would ask whether Charles, if he became their Lord, would guarantee absolute freedom to their trade; the clerks would ask his promise to respect the goods of the Church. And the king doubtless was not sparing of his pledges.

The Maid, with one division of the army, halted before the stronghold of Saint-Phal, belonging to Philibert de Vaudrey, commander of the town of Tonnerre, in the service of the Duke of Burgundy. In that place of Saint-Phal, Jeanne beheld approaching her a Franciscan friar, who was crossing himself and sprinkling holy water, for he feared lest she were the devil, and dared not draw near without having first exorcised the evil spirit. It was Friar Richard who was coming from Troyes.

The place of his birth is unknown. A disciple of Brother Vincent Ferrier and of Brother Bernardino of Sienna, like them, he taught the imminent coming of Antichrist and the salvation of the faithful by the adoration of the holy name of Jesus. After having been on a pilgrimage to Jerusalem, he returned to France, and preached at Troyes, during the Advent of 1428.

'Sow, sow your seed, my good folk,' he said. 'Sow beans ready for the harvest, for He who is to come will come quickly.' Friar Richard thundered most loudly against the draught boards of the men and the ornaments of the women. The good Brother likewise caused to be burnt the mandrake roots which many folk kept in their houses. Witches made much of them; and those who believed that the Maid was a witch accused her of carrying a mandrake on her person. Friar Richard hated these magic roots all the more strongly because he believed in their power of attracting wealth, the root of all evil.

On Sunday, the 1st of May, he was to preach to the devout Parisians. When the morning came no Friar Richard appeared, and in vain they waited for him. Disappointed and sad, at length they learnt that the Friar had been forbidden to preach. Friar Richard had gone off to Auxerre. Thence he went preaching through Burgundy and Champagne.

When Jeanne saw the good Brother crossing himself and sprinkling holy water she knew that he took her for something evil. However, she was by no means offended. Besides, she was growing accustomed to such treatment. It was without a trace of anger, although in a slightly ironical tone, that she said to the preacher: 'Approach boldly, I shall not fly away.'

Meanwhile Friar Richard, by the ordeal of holy water and by the sign of the cross, had proved that the damsel was not a devil and that there was no devil in her. And when she said she had come from God he believed her with all his heart and esteemed her an angel of the Lord.

He confided to her the reason for his coming. The inhabitants of Troyes doubted whether she were of God; to resolve their doubts he had come to Saint-Phal. Now he knew she was of God. From that moment he threw in his lot with the party of the Maid and the Dauphin.

To the burgesses and inhabitants of the town of Troyes Jeanne dictated a letter. Herein, calling herself the servant of the King of Heaven and speaking in the name of God Himself, in terms gentle yet urgent, she called upon them to render obedience to King Charles of France, and warned them that whether they would or no she with the king would enter into all the towns of the holy kingdom and bring them peace. Here is the letter:

Jhesus † Maria

Good friends and beloved, an it please you, ye lords, burgesses and inhabitants of the town of Troies, Jehanne the Maid doth call upon and make known unto you on behalf of the King of Heaven, her sovereign and liege Lord, in whose service royal she is every day, that ye render true obedience and fealty to the Fair King of France. Whosoever may come against him, he shall shortly be in Reins and in Paris, and in his good towns of his holy kingdom, with the aid of King Jhesus. Ye loyal Frenchmen, come forth to King Charles and fail him not. And if ye come have no fear for your bodies nor for your goods. An if ye come not, I promise you and on your lives I maintain it, that with God's help we shall enter into all the towns of the holy kingdom and shall there establish peace, whosoever may oppose us. To God I commend you. God keep you if it be his will. Answer speedily. Before the city of Troyes, written at Saint-Fale, Tuesday the fourth day of July.

The Maid gave this letter to Friar Richard, who undertook to carry it to the townsfolk.

From Saint-Phal the army advanced towards Troyes along the Roman road. When they heard of the army's approach, the council of the town assembled on Tuesday, the 5th, early in the morning, and sent the people of Reims a missive of which the following is the purport:

'This day do we expect the enemies of King Henry and the Duke of Burgundy who come to besiege us. In view of the design of these our foes and having considered the just cause we support and the aid of our princes promised unto us, we have resolved in council, no matter what may be the strength of our enemies, to continue in our obedience waxing ever greater to King Henry and to the Duke of Burgundy, even until death. And this have we sworn on the precious body of Our Lord Jesus Christ. Wherefore we pray the citizens of Reims to take thought for us as brethren and loyal friends, and to send to my Lord the regent and the Duke of Burgundy to beseech and entreat them to take pity on their poor subjects and come to their succour.'

On that same day, in the morning, from his lodging at Brinion-l'Archevêque, King Charles despatched his heralds bearing closed letters, signed by his hand, sealed with his seal, addressed to the members of the council of the town of Troyes. Therein he made known unto them that by the advice of his council, he had undertaken to go to Reims, there to receive his anointing, that his intention was to enter the city of Troyes on the morrow, wherefore he summoned and commanded them to render the obedience they owed him and prepare to receive him. He wisely made a point of reassuring them as to his intentions, which were not to avenge the past. Such was not his will, he said, but let them comport themselves towards their sovereign as they ought, and he would forget all and maintain them in his favour.

The council refused to admit King Charles' heralds within the town; but they received his letters, read them, deliberated over them and made known to the heralds the result of their deliberations which was the following:

'The lords, knights and squires who are in the town, on behalf of King Henry and the Duke of Burgundy, have sworn with us, inhabitants of the city, that we will not receive into the town any who are stronger than we, without the express command of the Duke of Burgundy. Having regard to their oath, those who are in the town would not dare to admit King Charles.'

The councillors had King Charles' letter posted up and below it their reply. In council they read the letter the Maid had dictated at Saint-Phal and entrusted to Friar Richard. The monk had not prepared them to give it a favourable reception, for they laughed at it heartily. 'There is no rhyme or reason in it,' they said. ''Tis but a jest.' They threw it in the fire without sending a reply. Jeanne was a braggart, they said. And they added: 'We certify her to be mad and possessed of the devil.'

That same day, at nine o'clock in the morning, the army began to march by the walls and take up its position round the town.

When the French arrived, most of the townsfolk were on the ramparts looking more curious than hostile and apparently fearing nothing. They desired above all things to see the king.

The town was strongly defended. The Duke of Burgundy had long been keeping up the fortifications. In 1417 and 1419 the people of Troyes, like those of Orléans in 1428, had pulled down their suburbs and destroyed all the houses outside the town for 200 or 300 paces from the ramparts. The arsenal was well furnished; the stores overflowed with victuals; but the Anglo-Burgundian garrison amounted only to between 500 and 600 men.

On that day also, at five o'clock in the afternoon, the councillors of the town of Troyes sent to inform the people of Reims of the arrival of the Armagnacs, and despatched to them copies of the letter from Charles of Valois, of their reply to it and of the Maid's letter, which they cannot therefore have burned immediately. They likewise communicated to them their resolution to resist to the death in case they should receive succour. In like manner they wrote to the people of Châlons to tell them of the Dauphin's coming; and to them they made known that the letter of Jeanne the Maid had been brought to Troyes by Friar Richard the preacher.

These writings amounted to saying: like all citizens in such circumstances, we are in danger of being hanged either by the Burgundians or by the Armagnacs, which would be very grievous. To avoid this calamity as far as in us lies, we give King Charles of Valois to understand that we do not open our gates to him because the garrison prevents us and that we are the weaker, which is true. And we make known to our Lords, the regent and the Duke of Burgundy, that the garrison being too weak to defend us, which is true, we ask for succour, which is loyal; and we trust that the succour will not be sent, for if it were we should have to endure a siege, and risk being taken by assault which for us merchants would be grievous. But, having asked for succour and not receiving it, we may then surrender without reproach. The important point is to cause the garrison, fortunately a small one, to make off. Five hundred men are too few for defence, but too many for surrender. Such were the crafty thoughts of those dwellers in Champagne.

Meanwhile King Charles' army was stricken with famine. There were between 6,000 and 7,000 men in camp who had not broken bread for a week. The men-at-arms were reduced to feeding on pounded ears of corn still green and on the new beans they found in abundance.

The king, who had been lodging at Brinion since the 4th of July, arrived before Troyes in the afternoon of Friday the 8th. That very day he held council of war with the commanders and princes of the blood to decide whether they should remain before the town until by dint of promises or threats they obtained its submission, or whether they should pass on, leaving it to itself, as they had done at Auxerre.

The discussion had lasted long when the Maid arrived and prophesied:

'Fair Dauphin,' said she, 'command your men to attack the town of Troyes and delay no further in councils too prolonged, for, in God's name, before three days, I will cause you to enter the town, which shall be yours by love or by force and courage. And false Burgundy shall look right foolish.'

The council over, she mounted her horse, and lance in hand hurried to the moat, followed by a crowd of knights, squires and craftsmen. The point of attack was to be the north-west wall, between the Madeleine and the Comporté Gates. Jeanne, who firmly believed that the town would be taken by her, spent the night inciting her people to bring faggots and put the artillery in position. 'To the assault,' she cried, and signed to them to throw hurdles into the trenches.

This threat had the desired effect. The lower orders, imagining the town already taken, and expecting the French to come to pillage, massacre and ravish, as was the custom, took refuge in the churches. As for the clerics and notables, this was just what they wanted.

Being assured by Charles of Valois that they might come to him in safety, the Lord Bishop Jean Laiguisé, my Lord Guillaume Andouillette, Master of the Hospital, the Dean of the Chapter, the clergy and the notables went to the king. Jean Laiguisé was the spokesman.

It is not their fault, he said, if the king enter not according to his good pleasure. The Bailie and those of the garrison, some 300 or 400, guard the gates, and forbid their being opened. Let it please the king to have patience until I have spoken to those of the town. I trust that as soon as I have spoken to them, they will open the gates and render the king such obedience as he shall be pleased withal.

In replying to the bishop, the king set forth the reasons for the expedition and the rights he held over the town of Troyes.

Without exception, he said, I will forgive all the deeds of past times, and, according to the example of Saint Louis, I will maintain the people of Troyes in peace and liberty.

Jean Laiguisé demanded that such revenues and patronage as had been bestowed on churchmen by the late king, Charles VI, should be retained by them, and that those who had received the same from King Henry of England should be given charters by King Charles authorizing them to keep their benefices, even in cases where the king had bestowed them on others.

The king consented. This conference he reported to the council of the Town. Whereupon the council sent letters to the citizens of Reims making known to them this resolution and exhorting them to take a similar one.

Friar Richard went to find the Maid. As soon as he saw her, and when he was still afar off, he knelt before her. When he returned to the town, the good Friar preached to the folks at length and exhorted them to obey King Charles.

The townsfolk had great faith and confidence in this good Brother who spoke so eloquently. What he said of the Maid appeared to them admirable, and won their obedience to a king so powerfully accompanied. With one voice they all cried aloud, 'Long live King Charles of France!'

The town opened its gates to Charles. On Sunday, the 10th of July, very early in the morning, the Maid entered first into Troyes and with her the common folk whom she so dearly loved. Friar Richard accompanied her. She posted archers along the streets which the procession was to follow, so that the King of France should pass through the town between a double row of those foot soldiers of his army who had so nobly aided him.

While Charles of Valois was entering by one gate, the Burgundian garrison was going out by the other. As had been agreed, the men of King Henry and Duke Philip bore away their arms and other possessions.

On that same Sunday, about nine o'clock in the morning, King Charles entered the city. He had put on his festive robes, gleaming with velvet, with gold and with precious stones. The Duke of Alençon and the Maid, holding her banner in her hand, rode at his side.

Chapter XVIII
The Surrender of Châlons and of Reims – The Coronation

⚜

EAVING TROYES, the royal army entered into the poorer part of Champagne, crossed the Aube near Arcis, and took up its quarters at Lettrée, 20 kilometres (12½ miles) from Châlons.

The towns of Champagne were as closely related as the fingers of one hand. When the Dauphin was at Brinion-l'Archevêque, the people of Châlons had heard of it from their friends of Troyes. The latter had even told them that Friar Richard, the preacher, had brought them a letter from Jeanne the Maid. Whereupon the folk of Châlons wrote to those of Reims:

'We are amazed at Friar Richard. We esteemed him a man right worthy. But he has turned sorcerer. We announce unto you that the citizens of Troyes are making war against the Dauphin's men. We are resolved to resist the enemy with all our strength.'

On the 14th of July the king and his army entered the town of Châlons. There the Maid found four or five peasants from her village come to see her. The people of Châlons, following the example of their friends of Troyes, wrote to the inhabitants of Reims that they had received the King of France and that they counselled them to do likewise. In this letter they said they had found King Charles kind, gracious, pitiful and merciful; and of a truth the king was dealing leniently with the towns of Champagne.

The citizens of Reims acted with extreme caution.

King Charles adopted towards the citizens of Reims that same wise benignity he had shown to the citizens of Troyes, promising them full pardon and oblivion.

'Be not deterred,' he said, 'by matters that are past and the fear that we may remember them. Be assured that if now ye act towards us as ye ought, ye shall be dealt with as becometh good and loyal subjects.' On the delivery of this letter the council was convoked, but it so befell that there were not enough aldermen to deliberate.

The Bailie declared that the citizens of Reims, desirous to communicate with their captains, were willing to receive him if he were accompanied by no more than 50 horse. Herein they displayed their goodwill, being entitled to refuse to receive a garrison within their walls; this privilege notwithstanding, they consented to admit 50 horse, which meant about 200 fighting men. The Sire de Chastillon demanded as the conditions of his coming that the town should be victualled and put in a state of defence, that he should enter it with 300 or 400 combatants, that the defence of the city as well as of the castle should be entrusted to him, and that there should be delivered up to him five or six notables as hostages. On these conditions he declared himself ready to live and die for them.

The English were indeed recruiting troops wherever they could and pressing all manner of folk into their service. They were said to be arming even priests; and the regent was certainly pressing into his service the crusaders disembarked in France, whom the Cardinal of Winchester was intending to lead against the Hussites. As we may imagine, King Henry's council did not fail to inform the inhabitants of Reims of the armaments which were being assembled. On the 3rd of July they were told that the troops were crossing the sea, and on the 10th Colard de Mailly, Bailie of Vermandois, announced that they had landed. But these tidings failed to inspire the folk of Champagne with any great confidence in the power of the English. While the Sire de Chastillon was promising that in 40 days they should have a fine large army from beyond the seas, King Charles with 30,000 combatants was but a few miles from their gates. Nothing remained for him but to turn round and join the English.

On the 12th of July, from my Lord Regnault de Chartres, Archbishop and Duke of Reims, the townsfolk received a letter requesting them to make ready for the king's coming.

The council of the city having assembled on that day, the clerk proceeded to draw up an official report of its deliberations:

'... After having represented to my Lord of Chastillon that he is the Commander and that the lords and the mass of the people who....'

He wrote no more. Finding it difficult to protest their loyalty to the English while making ready King Charles's coronation, and considering it imprudent to recognize a new prince without being forced to it, the citizens abruptly renounced the silver of speech and took refuge in the gold of silence.

On Saturday, the 16th, King Charles took up his quarters in the Castle of Sept-Saulx, 16 kilometres (10 miles) from the city where he was to be crowned. There the king received the citizens of Reims, who came in great numbers to do him homage. Then, with the Maid and his whole army, he resumed his march. Having traversed the last stage of the highroad which wound along the bank of the Vesle, he entered the great city of Champagne at nightfall.

According to tradition the coronation should take place on a Sunday. The citizens of Reims worked all night in order that everything might be ready on the morrow. They were urged on by their sudden affection for the King of France and likewise by their fear lest he and his army should spend many days in their city. Their horror of receiving and maintaining men-at-arms within their gates they shared with the citizens of all towns, who in their panic were incapable of distinguishing Armagnac soldiers from English and Burgundians.

The royal ornaments, which, after the coronation of the late king, had been deposited in the sacristy of Saint-Denys, were in the hands of the English. The crown of Charlemagne, brilliant with rubies, sapphires and emeralds, adorned with four flowers-de-luce, which the Kings of France received on their coronation, the English wished to place on the head of their King Henry. In English hands likewise were the sceptre surmounted by a golden Charlemagne in imperial robes, the rod of justice terminated by a hand in horn of unicorn, the golden clasp of Saint Louis' mantle and the golden spurs and the Pontifical, containing within its enamelled binding of silver-gilt the ceremonial of the coronation. The French must needs make shift with a crown kept in the sacristy of the cathedral.

Kings were anointed with oil, because oil signifies renown, glory and wisdom. In the morning the Sires de Rais, de Boussac, de Graville and de Culant were deputed by the king to go and fetch the Holy Ampulla.

It was a crystal flask which the Grand Prior of Saint-Remi kept in the tomb of the Apostle, behind the high altar of the Abbey Church. This flask contained the sacred chrism with which the Blessed Remi had anointed King Clovis. It was known that with use the oil became no less, that the flask remained always full, as a premonition and a pledge that the kingdom of France would endure for ever. According to the observation of witnesses, at the time of the coronation of the late King Charles, the oil had not diminished after the anointing.

At nine o'clock in the morning Charles of Valois entered the church with a numerous retinue. The king-at-arms of France called by name the 12 peers of the realm to come before the high altar. Of the six lay peers not one replied. In their places came the Duke of Alençon, the Counts of Clermont and of Vendôme, the Sires de Laval, de La Trémouille and de Maillé.

Of the six ecclesiastical peers, three replied to the summons of the king-at-arms – the Archbishop Duke of Reims, the Bishop Count of Châlons, the Bishop Duke of Laon. For the missing bishops of Langres and Noyon were substituted those of Seez and Orléans. In the absence of Arthur of Brittany, Constable of France, the sword was held by Charles, Sire d'Albret.

In front of the altar was Charles of Valois, wearing robes open on the chest and shoulders. He swore, first, to maintain the peace and privileges of the Church; second, to preserve his people from exactions and not to burden them too heavily; third, to govern with justice and mercy.

From his cousin d'Alençon he received the arms of a knight. Then the Archbishop anointed him with the holy oil, with which the Holy Ghost makes strong priests, kings, prophets and martyrs. This pouring out of the oil had rendered the kings of most Christian France burning and shining lights since the time of Charlemagne, yea, even since the days of Clovis. And Charles received the anointing, the sign of power and victory.

During the mystery, as it was called in the old parlance, the Maid stayed by the king's side. Her white banner, before which the ancient standard of Chandos had retreated, she held for a moment unfurled. Then others in their turn held her standard, her page Louis de Coutes, who never left her, and Friar Richard the preacher. In one of her dreams she had lately given a crown to the king; she was looking for this crown to be brought into the church by heavenly messengers. But the crown curiously rich and magnificent that Jeanne looked for came not.

From the altar the archbishop took the crown of no great value provided by the chapter, and with both hands raised it over the king's head. The 12 peers, in a circle round the prince, stretched forth their arms to hold it. The trumpets blew and the folk cried: 'Noël'.

Thus was anointed and crowned Charles of France.

Two hours after noon the mystery came to an end. We are told that then the Maid knelt low before the king, and, weeping said:

'Fair king, now is God's pleasure accomplished. It was His will that I should raise the siege of Orléans and bring you to this city of Reims to receive your holy anointing, making manifest that you are the true king and he to whom the realm of France should belong.'

The king made the customary gifts. To the Chapter he presented hangings of green satin as well as ornaments of red velvet and white damask. Moreover, he placed upon the altar a silver vase with 13 golden crowns. After the ceremony King Charles put the crown on his head and over his shoulders the royal mantle, blue as the sky, flowered with lilies of gold; and on his charger he passed down the streets of Reims city. The people in great joy cried, 'Noël'! as they had cried when my Lord the Duke of Burgundy entered. On that day the Sire de Rais was made marshal of France and the Sire de la Trémouille count. The eldest of Madame de Laval's two sons, he to whom the Maid had offered wine at Selles-en-Berry, was likewise made count. Captain La Hire received the county of Longueville with such parts of Normandy as he could conquer.

King Charles dined in the archiepiscopal palace in the ancient hall of Tau and as was customary, the royal table extended into the street, and there was feasting throughout the town. At every coronation the ancient stag, made of bronze and hollow, which stood in the courtyard of the archiepiscopal palace was carried into the Rue du Parvis; it was filled with wine and the people drank from it as from a fountain.

Jacques d'Arc had come to see the coronation for which his daughter had so zealously laboured. As well as his daughter, he saw once more his son Pierre.

Jacques d'Arc was one of the notables and perhaps the best businessman of his village. It was not merely to see his daughter riding through the streets in man's attire that he had come to Reims. He had come doubtless for himself and on behalf of his village to ask the king for an exemption from taxation. Out of the public funds the magistrates of the town paid Jacques d'Arc's expenses, and when he was about to depart, they gave him a horse to take him home.

From Gien, about June the 27th, the Maid had had a letter written to the Duke of Burgundy, calling upon him to come to the king's anointing.

Having received no reply, on the day of the coronation she dictated a second letter to the duke. Here it is:

† Jhesus Maria

'*High and greatly to be feared Prince, Duke of Burgundy, Jehanne the Maid, in the name of the King of Heaven, her rightful and liege lord, requires you and the King of France to make a good peace which shall long endure. Forgive one another heartily and entirely as becometh good Christians; an if it please you to make war, go ye against the Saracens. Prince of Burgundy, I pray you, I entreat you, I beseech you as humbly as lieth in my power, that ye make war no more against the holy realm of France, and that forthwith and speedily ye withdraw those your men who are in any strongholds and fortresses of the said holy kingdom; and in the name of the fair King of France, he is ready to make peace with you, saving his honour if that be necessary. And in the name of the King of Heaven, my Sovereign liege Lord, for your good, your honour and your life, I make known unto you, that ye will never win in battle against the loyal French and that all they who wage war against the holy realm of France, will be warring against King Jhesus, King of Heaven and of the world, my lawful liege lord. And with clasped hands I beseech and entreat you that ye make no battle nor wage war against us, neither you, nor your people, nor your subjects; and be assured that whatever number of folk ye bring against us, they will gain nothing, and it will be sore pity for the great battle and the blood that shall be shed of those that come against us. And three weeks past, I did write and send you letters by a herald, that ye should come to the anointing of the King, which today, Sunday, the 17th day of this present month, is made in the city of Reims: to which letter I have had no answer, neither news of the said herald. To God I commend you; may he keep you, if it be his will; and I pray God to establish good peace. Written from the said place of Reims, on the said seventeenth of July.*'

    Addressed: 'to the Duke of Burgundy.'

Esteeming King Charles, master of Champagne, to be a prince worthy of consideration, Duke Philip sent to Reims, David de Brimeu, Bailie of Artois, at the head of an embassy, to greet him and open negotiations for peace. The Burgundians received a hearty welcome from the chancellor and the council. It was hoped that peace would be concluded before their departure. The Angevin lords announced it to their queens, Yolande and Marie. By so doing they showed how little they knew the consummate old fox of Dijon. The French were not strong enough yet, neither were the English weak enough. It was agreed that in August an embassy should be sent to the Duke of Burgundy in the town of Arras. After four days negotiation, a truce for 15 days was signed and the embassy left Reims. At the same time, the duke at Paris solemnly renewed his complaint against Charles of Valois, his father's assassin, and undertook to bring an army to the help of the English.

Leaving Antoine de Hellande, nephew of the duke archbishop to command Reims, the King of France departed from the city on the 20th of July and went to Saint-Marcoul-de-Corbeny, where on the day after their coronation, the kings were accustomed to touch for the evil.

King Charles worshipped and presented offerings at the shrine of Saint Marcoul, and there touched for the evil. At Corbeny he received the submission of the town of Laon. Then, on the morrow, the 22nd, he went off to a little stronghold in the valley of the Aisne, called Vailly, which belonged to the Archbishop Duke of Reims. At Vailly he received the submission of the town of Soissons.

Chapter XIX
Rise of the Legend

⚜

IT IS ALWAYS DIFFICULT to ascertain what happens in war. Guillaume Girault, former magistrate of the town and notary at the Châtelet, wrote and signed, with his own hand, a brief account of the deliverance of Orléans. Herein he states that on Wednesday, Ascension

Eve, the bastion of Saint-Loup was stormed and taken as if by miracle, 'there being present, and aiding in the fight, Jeanne the Maid, sent of God'; and that, on the following Saturday, the siege laid by the English to Les Tourelles at the end of the bridge was raised by the most obvious miracle since the Passion. And Guillaume Girault testifies that the Maid led the enterprise. When eyewitnesses, participators in the deeds themselves, had no clear idea of events, what could those more remote from the scene of action think of them?

The tidings of the French victories flew with astonishing rapidity. The Loire campaign and the coronation expedition were scarcely known at first save by fabulous reports, and the people only thought of them as supernatural events.

In the letters sent by royal secretaries to the towns of the realm and the princes of Christendom, the name of Jeanne the Maid was associated with all the deeds of prowess.

It was believed that everything had been done through her, that the king had consulted her in all things, when in truth the king's counsellors and the captains rarely asked her advice, listened to it but seldom, and brought her forth only at convenient seasons. Everything was attributed to her alone. Her personality, associated with deeds attested and seemingly marvellous, became buried in a vast cycle of astonishing fables and disappeared in a forest of heroic stories.

They ascribed to her edifying words she had never uttered. 'When the Maid came to the king,' they said, 'she caused him to make three promises: the first was to resign his kingdom, to renounce it and give it back to God, from whom he held it; the second, to pardon all such as had turned against him and afflicted him; the third, to humiliate himself so far as to receive into favour all such as should come to him, poor and rich, friend and foe.'

It was believed that Jeanne had prophesied that on Saint John the Baptist's Day, 1429, not an Englishman should be left in France. These simple folk expected their saint's promises to be fulfilled on the day she had fixed. They maintained that on the 23rd of June she had entered the city of Rouen, and that on the morrow, Saint John the Baptist's day, the inhabitants of Paris had of their own accord, opened their gates to the King of France. In the month of July these stories were being told in

Avignon. Reformers, numerous it would seem in France and throughout Christendom, believed that the Maid would organise the English and French on monastic lines and make of them one nation of pious beggars, one brotherhood of penitents.

During the coronation campaign, nothing being known of the agreement between the king's men and the people of Auxerre, towards the end of July, it was related that the town having been taken by storm, 4,500 citizens had been killed and likewise 1,500 men-at-arms, knights as well as squires belonging to the parties of Burgundy and Savoy. Stories were told of treasons and massacres, horrible adventures in which the Maid was associated with that knave of hearts who was already famous. She was said to have had 12 traitors beheaded. Such tales were real romances of chivalry.

Three months after her coming to Chinon, Jeanne had her legend, which grew and increased and extended into Italy, Flanders and Germany. In the summer of 1429 this legend was already formed. All the scattered parts of what may be described as the gospel of her childhood existed.

At the age of seven Jeanne kept sheep; the wolves did not molest her flock; the birds of the field, when she called them, came and ate bread from her lap. The wicked had no power over her. No one beneath her roof need fear man's fraud or ill-will.

Moreover, an attempt was made to represent the wonders that had heralded the nativity of Jesus as having been repeated on the birth of Jeanne. It was imagined that she was born on the night of the Epiphany. The shepherds of her village, moved by an indescribable joy, the cause of which was unknown to them, hastened through the darkness towards the marvellous mystery. The cocks, heralds of this new joy, sing at an unusual season and, flapping their wings, seem to prophesy for two hours.

Of her coming into France there was much to tell. It was related that in the Château of Chinon she had recognized the king, whom she had never seen before, and had gone straight to him, although he was but poorly clad and surrounded by his baronage. It was said that she had given the king a sign, that she had revealed a secret to him; and that on the revelation of the secret, known to him alone, he had been illuminated with a heavenly joy. Concerning this interview at Chinon, while those present had little to say, the stories of many who were not there were interminable.

Seen through this chaos of stories more indistinct than the clouds in a stormy sky, Jeanne appeared a wondrous marvel. She prophesied and many of her prophecies had already been fulfilled. She had foretold the deliverance of Orléans and Orléans had been delivered. She had prophesied that she would be wounded, and an arrow had pierced her above the right breast. She had prophesied that she would take the king to Reims, and the king had been crowned in that city. Other prophecies had she uttered touching the realm of France, to wit, the deliverance of the Duke of Orléans, the entering into Paris, the driving of the English from the holy kingdom, and their fulfilment was expected.

Every day she prophesied and notably concerning various persons who had failed in respect towards her and had come to a bad end.

Maiden, at once a warrior and a lover of peace, *béguine*, prophetess, sorceress, angel of the Lord, ogress, every man beholds her according to his own fashion, creates her according to his own image. Pious souls clothe her with an invincible charm and the divine gift of charity; simple souls make her simple too; men gross and violent figure her a giantess, burlesque and terrible. Shall we ever discern the true features of her countenance?

The Life of Joan of Arc Volume II

Despite having lifted the siege of Orléans and gotten the Dauphin anointed, Joan still needed to fulfil her vow to rid France of the English. It was clear that Charles VII felt that she had exhausted her usefulness; he and his counsellors sidelined her almost completely so that she was neither consulted nor briefed on new situations. This was not apparent to the population, who continued to see her as a heroine.

When Joan was captured at Compiègne in May 1430 and sold to the English for 10,000 francs, the French king made no attempt to retrieve or assist her. The English believed she was a witch and brought her to trial at Rouen where she was found guilty and burned at the stake. Those in judgement were repeatedly astonished by the perspicacity of her answers, her confidence and her obstinacy in refusing to dress as a woman.

Years after her death, Charles VII wanted to clear her name, not for her but because he did not want it said that a witch had got him anointed. To save face all round, Joan's mother, Isabelle Romée, was sent to Paris to plead her daughter's cause. On 16 June 1455, the sentence of the 1431 trial was declared unjust, unfounded and iniquitous.

Chapter I
The Royal Army from Soissons to Compiègne –
Poem and Prophecy

ON THE 22ND OF JULY King Charles received the keys of the town of Soissons. Of its dukes, one was a prisoner in the hands of the English; the other was connected with the French party through his brother-in-law, King Charles, and with the Burgundian party through his father-in-law, the Duke of Lorraine. The Burgundians set fire to the houses, pillaged the churches, chastised the most notable burgesses; then came the Armagnacs, who sacked everything, made great slaughter of men, women and children ravished nuns, worthy wives and honest maids.

It would seem that at that time the leaders of the royal army had the intention of marching on Compiègne. Indeed it was important to capture this town from Duke Philip, for it was the key to l'Île-de-France and ought to be taken before the duke had time to bring up an army. But throughout this campaign the King of France was resolved to recapture his towns rather by diplomacy and persuasion than by force. Between the 22nd and the 25th of July he three times summoned the inhabitants of Compiègne to surrender. Being desirous to gain time and to have the air of being constrained, they entered into negotiations.

Having quitted Soissons, the royal army reached Château-Thierry on the 29th. On Monday, the 1st of August, the king crossed the Marne, over the Château-Thierry Bridge, and that same day took up his quarters at Montmirail. Meanwhile, the people of Reims received tidings that King Charles was leaving Château-Thierry and was about to cross the Seine. Believing that they had been abandoned, they were afraid lest the English and Burgundians should make them pay dearly for the coronation of the King of the Armagnacs; and in truth they stood in great danger. On the 3rd of August, they resolved to send a message to King Charles to entreat him not to forsake those cities which had submitted to him.

On the 5th of August, while the king is still at Provins or in the neighbourhood, Jeanne addresses to the townsfolk of Reims a letter dated from the camp, on the road to Paris and promises not to desert her friends faithful and beloved. She appears to have no suspicion of the projected retreat on the Loire.

Wherefore it is clear that the magistrates of Reims have not written to her and that she is not admitted to the royal counsels. She has been instructed, however, that the king has concluded a fifteen days' truce with the Duke of Burgundy, and thereof she informs the citizens of Reims. This truce that so highly displeased her we know not when it was concluded, whether at Soissons or Château-Thierry, on the 30th or 31st of July, or at Provins between the 2nd and 5th of August. It would appear that it was to last 15 days, at the end of which time the duke was to undertake to surrender Paris to the King of France. The Maid had good reason for her mistrust.

King Charles eagerly returned to his plan of retreating into Poitou. From La Motte-Nangis he sent his quartermasters to Bray-sur-Seine, which had just submitted. This town had a bridge over the river, across which the royal army was to pass on the 5th of August or in the morning of the 6th; but the English came by night and took possession of the bridge; with its retreat cut off, the royal army had to retrace its march.

Within this army, which had not fought and which was being devoured by hunger, there existed a party of zealots, led by those whom Jeanne fondly called the Royal Blood. They were the Duke of Alençon, the Duke of Bourbon, the Count of Vendôme and likewise the Duke of Bar, who had just come from the War of the Apple Baskets. Among the others were the two sons of the Lady of Laval, Gui, the eldest to whom she had offered wine at Selles-en-Berry, promising soon to give him to drink at Paris, and André, who afterwards became Marshal of Lohéac. This was the army of the Maid: a band of youths, scarcely more than children, who ranged their banners side by side with the banner of a girl younger than they.

On learning that the retreat had been cut off, it is said that these youthful princes were well content and glad. This was valour and zeal; but it was a curious position and a false when the knighthood wished for war while the royal council was desiring to treat.

Its retreat cut off, the royal army fell back on Brie.

Riding by the side of the Archbishop of Reims, the Maid looked with a friendly eye on the peasants crying 'Noël!' After saying that she had nowhere seen folk so joyful at the coming of the fair king, she sighed: 'Would to God I were so fortunate as, when I die, to find burial in this land.'

During the march on La Ferté and Crépy, King Charles received a challenge from the regent, then at Montereau, calling upon him to fix a meeting at whatsoever place he should appoint. 'We, who with all our hearts,' said the Duke of Bedford, 'desire the end of the war, summon and require you, if you have pity and compassion on the poor folk, who in your cause have so long time been cruelly treated, downtrodden and oppressed, to appoint a place suitable either in this land of Brie, where we both are, or in l'Île-de-France. There will we meet. And if you have any proposal of peace to make unto us, we will listen to it.'

This arrogant and insulting letter had not been penned by the regent in any desire or hope of peace, but rather to throw on King Charles's shoulders the responsibility for the miseries and suffering the war was causing the commonalty.

Writing to the king crowned in Reims Cathedral, from the beginning he addresses him in this disdainful manner: 'You who were accustomed to call yourself Dauphin of Viennois and who now without reason take unto yourself the title of king.' He declares that he wants peace and then adds forthwith: 'Not a peace hollow, corrupt, feigned, violated, perjured, like that of Montereau, on which, by your fault and your consent, there followed that terrible and detestable murder, committed contrary to all law and honour of knighthood, on the person of our late dear and greatly loved Father, Jean, Duke of Burgundy.'

For the moment the Duke of Bedford's most serious grievance against Charles was that he was accompanied by the Maid and Friar Richard. 'You cause the ignorant folk to be seduced and deceived, for you are supported by superstitious and reprobate persons, such as this woman of ill fame and disorderly life, wearing man's attire and dissolute in manners, and likewise by that apostate and seditious mendicant friar, they both alike being abominable in the sight of God.'

Thus wrote the Regent of England; albeit he had a mind, subtle, moderate and graceful, he was moreover a good Catholic and a believer in all manner of devilry and witchcraft.

His horror at the army of Charles of Valois being commanded by a witch and a heretic monk was certainly sincere, and he deemed it wise to publish the scandal. There were doubtless only too many, who, like him, were ready to believe that the Maid of the Armagnacs was a heretic, a worshipper of idols and given to the practice of magic.

This letter shows how the English had transformed an innocent child into a being unnatural, terrible, redoubtable, into a spectre of hell causing the bravest to grow pale.

Senlis was subject to the English. It was said that the regent was approaching with a great company of men-at-arms, commanded by the Earl of Suffolk, the Lord Talbot and the Bastard Saint Pol. With him were the crusaders of the Cardinal of Winchester, the late king's uncle, between 3,500 and 4,000, paid with the Pope's money to go and fight against the Hussites in Bohemia. The Cardinal judged it well to use them against the King of France, a very Christian king forsooth, but one whose hosts were commanded by a witch and an apostate.

According to the established rule, the army was in several divisions: the vanguard, the archers, the main body, the rear guard and the three wings. Further, and according to the same rule, there had been formed a skirmishing company, destined if need were to succour and reinforce the other divisions. With this company was the Maid. At the Battle of Patay, despite her entreaties, she had been forced to keep with the rear-guard; now she rode with the bravest and ablest, with those skirmishers or scouts, whose duty it was, says Jean de Bueil, to repulse the scouts of the opposite party and to observe the number and the ordering of the enemy. At length justice was done her; at length she was assigned the place which her skill in horsemanship and her courage in battle merited; and yet she hesitated to follow her comrades.

Her perplexity is easily comprehensible. The little Saint could not bring herself to decide whether to ride forth to battle on the day of our Lady's Feast or to fold her arms while fighting was going on around her. Her Voices intensified her indecision. In the end she went with the men-at-arms, not one of whom appears to have shared her scruples. On both sides there were wounded, and prisoners were taken. This hand-to-hand fighting continued the whole day; at sunset the most serious skirmish happened, and so much dust was raised that it was impossible to see anything.

At nightfall the skirmishing ceased, and the two armies slept at a crossbow-shot from each other. Then King Charles went off to Crépy, leaving the English free to go and relieve the town of Évreux, which had agreed to surrender on the 27th of August.

Their loss of the opportunity of conquering Normandy was the price the French had to pay for the royal coronation procession, for that march to Reims, which was at once military, civil and religious.

Chapter II
The Maid's First Visit to Compiègne – The Three Popes – Saint Denys – Truces

AFTER THE ENGLISH ARMY had departed for Normandy, King Charles sent from Crépy to Senlis the Count of Vendôme, the Maréchal de Rais and the Maréchal de Boussac with their men-at-arms. The inhabitants gave them to wit that they inclined to favour the Flowers de Luce. Henceforth the submission of Compiègne was sure. The king summoned the citizens to receive him; on Wednesday the 18th, the keys of the town were brought to him; on the next day he entered.

One by one, the king was recovering his good towns. He charged the folk of Beauvais to acknowledge him as their lord. When they saw the flowers-de-luce borne by the heralds, the citizens cried: 'Long live Charles of France!' The clergy chanted a *Te Deum* and there was great rejoicing. Those who refused fealty to King Charles were put out of the town with permission to take away their possessions.

Having entered Compiègne with the king, Jeanne lodged at the Hôtel du Boeuf, the house of the King's proctor. She longed to march on Paris, which she was sure of taking since her Voices had promised it to her. It is related that at the end of two or three days she grew impatient, and, calling the Duke of Alençon, said to him: 'My fair duke, command your men and likewise those of the other captains to equip themselves,' then she is said to have cried: 'By my staff! I must to Paris.' But this could not have happened: the Maid never gave orders to the men-at-arms. The truth of the matter is that the Duke of Alençon, with a goodly company of fighting men, took his leave of the king and that Jeanne was to accompany him. She was ready to mount her horse when on Monday the 22nd of August, a messenger from the Count of Armagnac brought her a letter in which he asked her which was the true Pope [the Papacy was disputed].

She had never seen this messenger, and doubtless she had never heard of him.

It is not easy to discover why he should have asked Jeanne to indicate the true pope. Doubtless it was customary in those days to consult on all manner of questions those holy maids to whom God vouchsafed illumination. Such a one the Maid appeared, and her fame as a prophetess had been spread abroad in a very short time.

The Count of Armagnac's letter, which she had read to her as she was mounting her horse, must have struck her as very obscure. The Saints, Catherine and Margaret, with whom she was constantly holding converse, revealed to her nothing concerning the Pope. They spoke to her of nought save of the realm of France; and Jeanne's prudence generally led her to confine her prophecies to the subject of the war. She told him that at that moment she was unable to instruct him concerning the true pope, but that later she would inform him in which of the three he must believe, according as God should reveal it unto her. In short, she in a measure followed the example of such soothsayers as postpone the announcement of the oracle to a future day.

On the morrow, Tuesday the 23rd of August, the Maid and the Duke of Alençon took leave of the king and set out from Compiègne with a goodly company of fighting men. Before marching on Saint-Denys in France, they went to Senlis to collect a company of men-at-arms whom the king had sent there.

The Lord Bishop of Senlis was Jean Fouquerel. Hitherto, he had been on the side of the English and entirely devoted to the Lord Bishop of Beauvais. On the approach of the royal army, Jean Fouquerel, who was a cautious person, had gone off to Paris to hide a large sum of money. He was careful of his possessions. Someone in the army took his nag and gave it to the Maid. Hearing of his displeasure, the Maid caused a letter to be written to him, saying that he might have back his nag if he liked; she did not want it for she found it not sufficiently hardy for men-at-arms.

To the north of Paris, about eight kilometres (five miles) distant from the great city, there rose the towers of Saint-Denys. On the 26th of August, the army of the Duke of Alençon arrived there, and entered without resistance, albeit the town was strongly fortified.

In this abbey everything proclaimed the dignity, the prerogatives and the high worship of the house of France. Jeanne must joyously have wondered at the insignia, the symbols and signs of the royalty of the Lilies gathered together in this spot, if indeed those eyes, occupied with celestial visions, had leisure to perceive the things of earth, and if her Voices, endlessly whispering in her ear, left her one moment's respite.

Here again, at Saint-Denys, she distributed banners to the men-at-arms. Churchmen on the English side strongly suspected her of charming those banners.

The Maid and the Duke of Alençon lost no time. Immediately after their arrival at Saint-Denys they went forth to skirmish before the gates of Paris. Two or three times a day they engaged in this desultory warfare, notably by the windmill at the Saint-Denys Gate and in the village of La Chapelle.

Out of respect for the seventh commandment, the Maid forbade the men of her company to commit any theft whatsoever. And she always refused victuals offered her when she knew they had been stolen. In reality she, like the others, lived on pillage, but she did not know it.

On the 28th of August a truce was concluded. It was to last till Christmas and was to extend over the whole country north of the Seine, from Nogent to Harfleur, with the exception of such towns as were situated where there was a passage over the river. Concerning the city of Paris it was expressly stated that 'Our Cousin of Burgundy, he and his men, may engage in the defence of the town and in resisting such as shall make war upon it or do it hurt.' The Chancellor Regnault de Chartres, the Sire de la Trémouille, Christophe d'Harcourt, the Bastard of Orléans, the Bishop of Séez and likewise certain young nobles very eager for war, such as the Counts of

Clermont and of Vendôme and the Duke of Bar, in short all the counsellors of the king and the Princes of the Blood who signed this article, were apparently giving the enemy a weapon against them and renouncing any attempt upon Paris. What did it profit King Charles to recognize his cousin's rights over Paris? We fail to see precisely; but after all this truce was no better and no worse than others. In sooth it did not give Paris to the king, but neither did it prevent the king from taking it. Did truces ever hinder Armagnacs and Burgundians from fighting when they had a mind to fight? Was one of those frequent truces ever kept? After having signed this one, the king advanced to Senlis.

Chapter III
The Attack on Paris

IN THE DAYS when King John was a prisoner in the hands of the English, the townsfolk of Paris, beholding the enemy in the heart of the land, feared lest their city should be besieged. In all haste therefore they proceeded to put it in a state of defence; they surrounded it with trenches and counter trenches.

The work was superintended by Hugues Aubriot, Provost of Paris, to whom was entrusted also the building of the Saint-Antoine bastion, completed under King Charles VI.

The Parisians did not like the English and were sorely grieved by their occupation of the city. The folk murmured when, after the funeral of the late king, Charles VI, the Duke of Bedford had the sword of the King of France borne before him. But what cannot be helped must be endured. The Parisians may have disliked the English; they admired Duke Philip, a prince of comely countenance and the richest potentate of Christendom. As for the little King of Bourges, mean-looking and sad-faced, strongly suspected of treason at Montereau, there was nothing pleasing in him; he was despised and his followers were regarded with fear and horror.

On the morrow of their victory at Patay, those terrible Armagnacs had only to march straight on the town to take it. In the mind of the regent, it was as if they had already taken it. He went off and shut himself in the Castle of Vincennes with the few men who remained to him.

Just in the nick of time the regent surrendered the town to Duke Philip, not, we may be sure, without many regrets for having recently refused him Orléans. He realised that thus, by returning to its French allegiance, the chief city of the realm would make a more energetic defence against the Dauphin's men. The Parisians' old liking for the magnificent duke would revive, and so would their old hatred of the disinherited son of Madame Ysabeau. In the Palais de Justice the duke read the story of his father's death, punctuated with complaints of Armagnac treason and violated treaties; those who were present swore to be right loyal to him and to the regent. On the following days the same oath was taken by the regular and secular clergy.

But the citizens were strengthened in their resistance more by their remembrance of Armagnac cruelty than by their affection for the fair duke. A rumour ran and was believed by them that Messire Charles of Valois had abandoned to his mercenaries the city and the citizens of all ranks, high and low, men and women, and that he intended to plough up the very ground on which Paris stood. Such a rumour represented him very falsely; on all occasions he was pitiful and debonair; his council had prudently converted the coronation campaign into an armed and peaceful procession. But the Parisians were incapable of judging sanely when the intentions of the King of France were concerned; and they knew only too well that once their town was taken there would be nothing to prevent the Armagnacs from laying it waste with fire and sword.

While the Dauphin had been away at his coronation an army had come from England into France. The regent intended it to overrun Normandy. In its march on Rouen he commanded it in person.

On the 10th of August, on Saint-Laurence's Eve, while the Armagnacs were encamped at La Ferté-Milon, the Saint-Martin Gate, flanked by four towers and a double drawbridge, was closed; and all men were forbidden to go to Saint-Laurent, either to the procession or to the fair, as in previous years.

On the 28th of the same month, the royal army occupied Saint-Denys. Henceforth no one dared leave the city, neither for the vintage nor for the gathering of anything in the kitchen gardens, which covered the plain north of the town. Prices immediately went up.

In the early days of September, the *quarteniers*, each one in his own district, had the trenches set in order and the cannons mounted on walls, gates and towers. At the command of the aldermen, the hewers of stone for the cannon made thousands of balls.

On Wednesday, the 7th of September, the Eve of the Virgin's Nativity, there was a procession to Sainte-Geneviève-du-Mont with the object of counteracting the evil of the times and allaying the animosity of the enemy. In it walked the canons of the Palace, bearing the True Cross.

That very day the army of the Duke of Alençon and of the Maid was skirmishing beneath the walls. It retreated in the evening; and on that night the townsfolk slept in peace, for on the morrow Christians celebrated the Nativity of the Blessed Virgin.

The people of Paris thought that even the Armagnacs would do no work on so high a festival and would keep the third commandment.

On this Thursday, the 8th of September, about eight o'clock in the morning, the Maid, the dukes of Alençon and of Bourbon, who with their men, to the number of 10,000 and more, had encamped in the village of La Chapelle, half-way along the road from Saint-Denys to Paris, set out on the march. At the hour of high mass, between 11 and 12 o'clock, they reached the height of Les Moulins, at the foot of which the Swine Market was held.

They came to attempt in broad daylight the escalading and the storming of the greatest, the most illustrious, and the most populous town of the realm; an undertaking of vast importance, proposed doubtless and decided in the royal council and with the knowledge of the king, who can have been neither indifferent nor hostile to it. Charles of Valois wanted to retake Paris. It remains to be seen whether for the accomplishment of his desire he depended merely on men-at-arms and ladders.

It would seem that the Maid had not been told of the resolutions taken. She was never consulted and was seldom informed of what had been decided. But she was as sure of entering the town that day as of going to

Paradise when she died. For more than three years her Voices had been drumming the attack on Paris in her ears. But the astonishing point is that, saint as she was, she should have consented to arm and fight on the day of the Nativity.

True it is that afterwards, at Montepilloy, she had engaged in a skirmish on the Day of the Assumption, and thus scandalized the masters of the university. She acted according to the counsel of her Voices and her decisions depended on the vaguest murmurings in her ear. Nothing is more inconstant and more contradictory than the inspirations of such visionaries, who are but the playthings of their dreams. What is certain at least is that Jeanne now as always was convinced that she was doing right and committing no sin.

When she reached the top of the mound, she cried out to the folk in Paris: 'Surrender the town to the King of France.'

On the mound she remained, sounding the great dyke with her lance and marvelling to find it so full and so deep. And yet for 11 days she and her men-at-arms had been reconnoitring round the walls and seeking the most favourable point of attack. That she should not have known how to plan an attack was quite natural. But what is to be thought of the men-at-arms, who were there on the mound, taken by surprise, as baffled as she, and all aghast at finding so much water close to the Seine when the river was in flood?

Certain among them idly threw fagots into the moat. Meanwhile the defenders assailed by flights of arrows, disappeared one after the other. But towards four o'clock in the afternoon, the citizens arrived in crowds. The cannon of the Saint-Denys Gate thundered. Arrows and abuse flew between those above and those below. The hours passed; the sun was sinking. The Maid never ceased sounding the moat with the staff of her lance and crying out to the Parisians to surrender.

'There, wanton! There, minx!' cried a Burgundian.

And planting his crossbow in the ground with his foot, he shot an arrow which split one of her greaves and wounded her in the thigh. Another Burgundian took aim at the Maid's standard-bearer and wounded him in the foot. The wounded man raised his visor to see whence the arrow came and straightway received another between the eyes.

After she had been wounded, Jeanne cried all the more loudly that the walls must be reached and the city taken. She was placed out of reach of the arrows in the shelter of a breastwork. There she urged the men-at-arms to throw fagots into the water and make a bridge. About 10 or 11 o'clock in the evening, the Sire de la Trémouille charged the combatants to retreat. The Maid would not leave the place. She was doubtless listening to her Saints and beholding celestial hosts around her.

The French returned to La Chapelle, whence they had set out in the morning. They carried their wounded on some of the carts which they had used for the transport of fagots and ladders. In the hands of the enemy they left 300 hand-carts, 660 ladders, 4,000 hurdles and large fagots, of which they had used but a small number. Their retreat must have been somewhat hurried, seeing that, when they came to the Barn of Les Mathurins, near The Swine Market, they forsook their baggage and set fire to it. With horror it was related that, like pagans of Rome, they had cast their dead into the flames. Nevertheless, the Parisians dared not pursue them. In those days men-at-arms who knew their trade never retreated without laying some snare for the enemy. Consequently, the king's men posted a considerable company in ambush by the roadside, to lie in wait for the light troops who should come in pursuit of the retreating army.

If we regard only the military tactics of the day, there is no doubt that the French had blundered and had lacked energy. But it was not on military tactics that the greatest reliance had been placed. Those who conducted the war, the king and his council, certainly expected to enter Paris that day. But how? As they had entered Châlons, as they had entered Reims, as they had entered all the king's good towns from Troyes to Compiègne. King Charles had shown himself determined to recover his towns by means of the townsfolk; towards Paris he acted as he had acted towards his other towns.

On the morrow, Friday the 9th, the Maid, rising with the dawn, despite her wound, asked the Duke of Alençon to have the call to arms sounded; for she was strongly determined to return to the walls of Paris, swearing not to leave them until the city should be taken. Meanwhile the French captains sent a herald to Paris, charged to ask for a safe conduct for the removing of the bodies of the dead left behind in great numbers.

Notwithstanding that they had suffered cruel hurt, after a retreat unmolested it is true, but none the less disastrous and involving the loss of all their siege train, several of the leaders were, like the Maid, inclined to attempt a new assault. Others would not hear of it. While they were disputing, they beheld a baron coming towards them and with him 50 nobles; it was the Sire de Montmorency, the first Christian peer of France, that is the first among the ancient vassals of the bishop of Paris. He was transferring his allegiance from the Cross of St. Andrew to the Flowers-de-luce. His coming filled the king's men with courage and a desire to return to the city.

Before his departure, the king appointed the Count of Clermont commander of the district with several lieutenants in the town of Senlis. Having thus disposed, the king quitted Saint-Denys on the 13th of September. The Maid followed him against her will notwithstanding that she had the permission of her Voices to do so.

Chapter IV
The Taking of Saint-Pierre-Le-Moustier – Friar Richard's Spiritual Daughters – The Siege of La Charité

⚜

THE KING SLEPT at Lagny-sur-Marne on the 14th of September, then crossed the Seine at Bray, forded the Yonne near Sens and went on through Courtenay, Châteaurenard and Montargis. On the 21st of September he reached Gien. There he disbanded the army he could no longer pay, and each man went to his own home. The Duke of Alençon withdrew into his viscounty of Beaumont-sur-Oise.

Learning that the queen was coming to meet the king, Jeanne went before her and greeted her at Selles-en-Berry. She was afterwards taken to Bourges, where my Lord d'Albret, half-brother of the Sire de la Trémouille, lodged her with Messire Régnier de Bouligny. Régnier was then receiver general. He had been one of those whose dismissal the university had requested in 1408, as being worse than useless, for they held him responsible for many of the disorders in the kingdom. He had entered the Dauphin's service, passed from the administration of the royal domain to that of taxes and attained the highest rank in the control of the finances. His wife, who had accompanied the queen to Selles, beheld the Maid and wondered. Jeanne seemed to her a creature sent by God for the relief of the king and those of France who were loyal to him. She remembered the days not so very long ago when she had seen the Dauphin and her husband not knowing where to turn for money. Her name was Marguerite La Touroulde; she was demoiselle, not dame; a comfortable *bourgeoise* and that was all.

Three weeks Jeanne sojourned in the receiver general's house. She slept there, drank there, ate there. Nearly every night, Demoiselle Marguerite La Touroulde slept with her; the etiquette of those days required it. No night-gowns were worn; folk slept naked in those vast beds. It would seem that Jeanne disliked sleeping with old women. Demoiselle La Touroulde, although not so very old, was of matronly age; she had moreover a matron's experience, and further she claimed, as we shall see directly, to know more than most matrons knew. Several times she took Jeanne to the bath and to the sweating room. That also was one of the rules of etiquette; a host was not considered to be making his guests good cheer unless he took them to the bath. In this point of courtesy princes set an example; when the king and queen supped in the house of one of their retainers or ministers, fine baths richly ornamented were prepared for them before they came to table. Mistress Marguerite doubtless did not possess what was necessary in her own house; wherefore she took Jeanne out to the bath and the sweating room. Such are her own expressions; and they probably indicate a vapour bath not a bath of hot water.

At Bourges the sweating-rooms were in the Auron quarter, in the lower town, near the river. Jeanne was strictly devout, but she did not observe conventual rule; she, like chaste Suzannah therefore, might permit herself to bathe and she must have had great need to do so after having slept on straw. What is more remarkable is that, after having seen Jeanne in the bath, Mistress Marguerite judged her a virgin according to all appearances.

In Messire Régnier de Bouligny's house and likewise wherever she lodged, she led the life of a *béguine* but did not practise excessive austerity. She confessed frequently. Many a time she asked her hostess to come with her to matins. In the cathedral and in collegiate churches there were matins every day, between four and six, at the hour of sunset. The two women often talked together; the receiver general's wife found Jeanne very simple and very ignorant. She was amazed to discover that the maiden knew absolutely nothing.

Among other matters, Jeanne told of her visit to the old Duke of Lorraine, and how she had rebuked him for his evil life; she spoke likewise of the interrogatory to which the doctors of Poitiers had subjected her. She was persuaded that these clerks had questioned her with extreme severity, and she firmly believed that she had triumphed over their ill will. Alas! she was soon to know clerks even less accommodating.

Mistress Marguerite said to her one day: 'If you are not afraid when you fight, it is because you know you will not be killed.' Whereupon Jeanne answered: 'I am no surer of that than are the other combatants.'

Oftentimes women came to the Bouligny house, bringing paternosters and other trifling objects of devotion for the Maid to touch.

Jeanne used to say laughingly to her hostess: 'Touch them yourself. Your touch will do them as much good as mine.'

This ready repartee must have shown Mistress Marguerite that Jeanne, ignorant as she may have been, was none the less capable of displaying a good grace and common sense in her conversation.

While in many matters this good woman found the Maid but a simple creature, in military affairs she deemed her an expert. Whether, when she judged the saintly damsel's skill in wielding arms, she was giving her own opinion or merely speaking from hearsay, as would seem probable, she at any rate declared later that Jeanne rode a horse and handled a lance as well as the best of knights and so well that the army marvelled. Indeed, most captains in those days could do no better.

Probably there were dice and dice boxes in the Bouligny house, otherwise Jeanne would have had no opportunity of displaying that horror of gaming which struck her hostess. On this matter Jeanne agreed with her comrade, Friar Richard, and indeed with everyone else of good life and good doctrine.

What money she had Jeanne distributed in alms. 'I am come to succour the poor and needy,' she used to say.

When the multitude heard such words they were led to believe that this Maid of God had been raised up for something more than the glorification of the Lilies, and that she was come to dispel such ills as murder, pillage and other sins grievous to God, from which the realm was suffering. Mystic souls looked to her for the reform of the Church and the reign of Jesus Christ on earth. She was invoked as a saint, and throughout the loyal provinces were to be seen carved and painted images of her which were worshipped by the faithful. Thus, even during her lifetime, she enjoyed certain of the privileges of beatification.

North of the Seine meanwhile, English and Burgundians were at their old work. The Duke of Vendôme and his company fell back on Senlis, the English descended on the town of Saint-Denys and sacked it once more. In the Abbey Church they found and carried off the Maid's armour, thus, according to the French clergy, committing undeniable sacrilege and for this reason: because they gave the monks of the Abbey nothing in exchange.

The king was then at Mehun-sur-Yèvre, quite close to Bourges, in one of the finest châteaux in the world, rising on a rock and overlooking the town. The late Duke Jean of Berry, a great builder, had erected this château with the care that he never failed to exercise in matters of art. Mehun was King Charles's favourite abode.

The Duke of Alençon, eager to reconquer his duchy, was waiting for troops to accompany him into Normandy, across the marches of Brittany and Maine. He sent to the king to know if it were his good pleasure to grant him the Maid. 'Many there be,' said the duke, 'who would willingly come with her, while without her they will not stir from their homes.' Her discomfiture before Paris had not therefore, entirely ruined her prestige. The Sire de la Trémouille opposed her being sent to the Duke of Alençon, whom he mistrusted, and not without cause. He gave her into the care of his half-brother, the Sire d'Albret, lieutenant of the king in his own country of Berry.

The Royal Council deemed it necessary to recover La Charité, left in the hands of Perrinet Gressart at the time of the coronation campaign; but it was decided first to attack Saint-Pierre-le-Moustier, which commanded the approaches to Bec-d'Allier. The garrison of this little town was composed of English and Burgundians, who were constantly plundering the villages and laying waste the fields of Berry and Bourbonnais. The army for this expedition assembled at Bourges. It was commanded by my Lord d'Albret, but popular report attributed the command to Jeanne. The common folk, the burgesses of the towns, especially the citizens of Orléans knew no other commander.

After two or three days' siege, the king's men stormed the town. But they were repulsed. Squire Jean d'Aulon, the Maid's steward, who some time before had been wounded in the heel and consequently walked on crutches, had retreated with the rest. He went back and found Jeanne who had stayed almost alone by the side of the moat. Fearing lest harm should come to her, he leapt on to his horse, spurred towards her and cried: 'What are you doing, all alone? Wherefore do you not retreat like the others?'

Jeanne doffed her sallet and replied: 'I am not alone. With me are fifty thousand of my folk. I will not quit this spot till I have taken the town.'

Casting his eyes around, Messire Jean d'Aulon saw the Maid surrounded by but four or five men.

More loudly he cried out to her: 'Depart hence and retreat like the others.'

Her only reply was a request for fagots and hurdles to fill up the moat. And straightway in a loud voice she called: 'To the fagots and the hurdles all of ye, and make a bridge!'

The men-at-arms rushed to the spot, the bridge was constructed forthwith and the town taken by storm with no great difficulty. At any rate that is how the good Squire, Jean d'Aulon, told the story. He was almost persuaded that the Maid's 50,000 shadows had taken Saint-Pierre-le-Moustier.

With the little army on the Loire at that time were certain holy women who like Jeanne led a singular life and held communion with the Church Triumphant. They constituted, so to speak, a kind of flying squadron of *béguines*, which followed the men-at-arms. One of these women was called Catherine de La Rochelle; two others came from Lower Brittany.

They all had miraculous visions; Jeanne saw my Lord Saint Michael in arms and Saint Catherine and Saint Margaret wearing crowns; Pierronne beheld God in a long white robe and a purple cloak. Catherine de La Rochelle saw a white lady, clothed in cloth of gold; and, at the moment of the consecration of the host all manner of marvels of the high mystery of Our Lord were revealed unto her.

Jean Pasquerel was still with Jeanne in the capacity of chaplain. He hoped to take his penitent to fight in the Crusade against the Hussites, for it was against these heretics that he felt most bitterly. But he had been entirely supplanted by the Franciscan, Friar Richard, who, after Troyes, had joined the mendicants of Jeanne's earlier days. Friar Richard dominated this little band of the illuminated. He was called their good Father. He it was who instructed them. His designs for these women did not greatly differ from those of Jean Pasquerel: he intended to conduct them to those wars of the Cross, which he thought were bound to precede the impending end of the world.

Meanwhile, it was his endeavour to foster a good understanding between them, which, eloquent preacher though he was, he found very difficult. Within the sisterhood there were constant suspicions and disputes. Jeanne had been on friendly terms with Catherine de la Rochelle at Montfaucon in Brie and at Jargeau; but now she began to suspect her of being a rival, and immediately she assumed an attitude of mistrust. Possibly she was right. At any moment either Catherine or the Breton women might be made use of as she had been. In those days a prophetess was useful in so many ways: in the edification of the people, the reformation of the Church, the leading of men-at-arms, the circulation of money, in war, in peace; no sooner did one appear than each party tried to get hold of her. It seems as if, after having employed the Maid Jeanne to deliver Orléans, the king's councillors were now thinking of employing Dame Catherine to make peace with the Duke of Burgundy. Such a task was deemed fitting for a saint less chivalrous than Jeanne. Catherine was married and the mother of a family. In this circumstance there need be no cause for astonishment; for if the gift of prophecy be more especially reserved for virgins, the example of Judith proves that the Lord may raise up strong matrons for the serving of his people.

If we believe that, as her surname indicates, she came from La Rochelle, her origin must have inspired the Armagnacs with confidence. The inhabitants of La Rochelle, all pirates more or less, were too profitably engaged in preying upon English vessels to forsake the Dauphin's party. Moreover, he rewarded their loyalty by granting them valuable commercial privileges. They had sent gifts of money to the people of Orléans; and when, in the month of May, they learned the deliverance of Duke Charles's city, they instituted a public festival to commemorate so happy an event.

The first duty of a saint in the army, it would appear, was to collect money. Jeanne was always sending letters asking the good towns for money or for munitions of war; the burgesses always promised to grant her request and sometimes they kept their promise. Catherine de la Rochelle appears to have had special revelations concerning the funds of the party; her mission, therefore, was financial, while Jeanne's was martial. She announced that she was going to the Duke of Burgundy to conclude peace. If one may judge from the little that is known of her, the inspirations of this holy dame were not very elevated, not very orderly, not very profound.

Meeting Jeanne at Montfaucon in Berry (or at Jargeau) she addressed her thus:

'There came unto me a white lady, attired in cloth of gold, who said to me: 'Go thou through the good towns and let the king give unto thee heralds and trumpets to cry: 'Whosoever has gold, silver or hidden treasure, let him bring it forth instantly.''

Dame Catherine added: 'Such as have hidden treasure and do not thus, I shall know their treasure, and I shall go and find it.'

She deemed it necessary to fight against the English and seemed to believe that Jeanne's mission was to drive them out of the land, since she obligingly offered her the whole of her miraculous takings.

'Wherewithal to pay your men-at-arms,' she said. But the Maid answered disdainfully:

'Go back to your husband, look after your household, and feed your children.'

Disputes between saints are usually bitter. In her rival's missions Jeanne refused to see anything but folly and futility. Nevertheless it was not for her to deny the possibility of the white lady's visitations; for to Jeanne herself did there not descend every day as many saints, angels and archangels as were ever painted on the pages of books or the walls of monasteries? In order to make up her mind on the subject, she adopted the most effectual measures. A learned doctor may reason concerning matter and substance, the origin and the form of ideas, the dawn of impressions in the intellect, but a shepherdess will resort to a surer method; she will appeal to her own eyesight.

Jeanne asked Catherine if the white lady came every night, and learning that she did: 'I will sleep with you,' she said.

When night came, she went to bed with Catherine, watched till midnight, saw nothing and fell asleep, for she was young, and she had great need of sleep. In the morning, when she awoke, she asked: 'Did she come?'

'She did,' replied Catherine; 'you were asleep, so I did not like to wake you.'

'Will she not come tomorrow?'

Catherine assured her that she would come without fail.

This time Jeanne slept in the day in order that she might keep awake at night; so she lay down at night in the bed with Catherine and kept her eyes open. Often she asked: 'Will she not come?'

And Catherine replied: 'Yes, directly.'

But Jeanne saw nothing. She held the test to be a good one. Nevertheless, she could not get the white lady attired in cloth of gold out of her head. When Saint Catherine and Saint Margaret came to her, as they delayed not to do, she spoke to them concerning this white lady and asked them what she was to think of her. The reply was such as Jeanne expected:

'This Catherine,' they said, 'is naught but futility and folly.'

Then was Jeanne constrained to cry: 'That is just what I thought.'

The strife between these two prophetesses was brief but bitter. Jeanne always maintained the opposite of what Catherine said. When the latter was going to make peace with the Duke of Burgundy, Jeanne said to her:

'Me seemeth that you will never find peace save at the lance's point.'

There was one matter at any rate wherein the White Lady proved a better prophetess than the Maid's council, to wit, the siege of La Charité. When Jeanne wished to go and deliver that town, Catherine tried to dissuade her.

'It is too cold,' she said; 'I would not go.'

Catherine's reason was not a high one; and yet it is true Jeanne would have done better not to go to the siege of La Charité.

Taken from the Duke of Burgundy by the Dauphin in 1422, La Charité had been retaken in 1424, by Perrinet Gressart, a successful captain, who had risen from the rank of mason's apprentice to that of pantler to the Duke of Burgundy and had been created Lord of Laigny by the King of England. On the 30th of December, 1425, Perrinet's men arrested the Sire de La Trémouille, when he was on his way to the Duke of Burgundy, having been appointed ambassador in one of those eternal negotiations, forever in process between the king and the duke. He was for several months kept a prisoner in the fortress which his captor commanded. He must needs pay a ransom of 14,000 golden crowns; and, albeit he took this sum from the royal treasury, he never ceased to bear Perrinet a grudge. Wherefore it may be concluded that when he sent men-at-arms to La Charité it was in good sooth to capture the town and not with any evil design against the Maid.

The army despatched against this Burgundian captain and this great plunder of pilgrims was composed of no mean folk. Its leaders were Louis of Bourbon, Count of Montpensier and Charles II, Sire d'Albret, La Trémouille's half-brother and Jeanne's companion in arms during the coronation campaign. The army was doubtless but scantily supplied with stores and with money. That was the normal condition of armies in those days. When the king wanted to attack a stronghold of the enemy, he must needs apply to his good towns for the necessary material. The Maid, at once saint and warrior, could beg for arms with a good grace; but possibly she overrated the resources of the towns which had already given so much.

On the 7th of November, she and my Lord d'Alençon signed a letter asking the folk of Clermont in Auvergne for powder, arrows and artillery. Churchmen, magistrates and townsfolk sent 90 kilograms (200 pounds) of saltpetre, 45 kilograms (100 pounds) of sulphur, two cases of arrows; to these they added a sword, two poniards and a battle-axe for the Maid; and they charged Messire Robert Andrieu to present this contribution to Jeanne and to my Lord d'Albret.

On the 9th of November, the Maid was at Moulins in Bourbonnais. What was she doing there? No one knows. There was at that time in the town an abbess very holy and very greatly venerated. Her name was Colette Boilet. She had won the highest praise and incurred the grossest insults by attempting to reform the order of Saint Clare. Colette lived in the convent of the Sisters of Saint Clare, which she had recently founded in this town. It has been thought that the Maid went to Moulins on purpose to meet her. But we ought first to ascertain whether these two saints had any liking for each other. They both worked miracles and miracles which were occasionally somewhat similar; but that was no reason why they should take the slightest pleasure in each other's society. One was called *La Pucelle*, the other *La Petite Ancelle*. But these names, both equally humble, described persons widely different in fashion of attire and in manner of life. *La Petite Ancelle* wended her way on foot, clothed in rags like a beggar-woman; *La Pucelle*, wrapped in cloth of gold, rode forth with lords on horseback. That Jeanne, surrounded by Franciscans who observed no rule, felt any veneration for the reformer of the Sisters of Saint Clare, there is no reason to believe; neither is there anything to indicate that the pacific Colette, strongly attached to the Burgundian house, had any desire to hold converse with one whom the English regarded as a destroying angel.

From this town of Moulins, Jeanne dictated a letter by which she informed the inhabitants of Riom that Saint-Pierre-le-Moustier was taken, and asked them for materials of war as she had asked the folk of Clermont.

Here is the letter:

> *Good friends and beloved, ye wit how that the town of Saint Père le Moustier hath been taken by storm; and with God's help it is our intention to cause to be evacuated the other places contrary to the King; but for this there hath been great expending of powder, arrows and other munition of war before the said town, and the lords who are in this town are but scantily provided for to go and lay siege to La Charité, whither we wend presently; I pray you as ye love the welfare and honour of the King and likewise of all others here, that ye will straightway help and send for the said siege powder, saltpetre, sulphur, arrows, strong cross-bows and other munition of war. And do this lest by failure of the said powder and other habiliments of war, the siege should be long and ye should be called in this matter negligent or unwilling. Good friends and beloved, may our Lord keep you. Written at Molins, the ninth day of November.*
>
> *Jehanne.*

Addressed to: My good friends and beloved, the churchmen, burgesses and townsfolk of the town of Rion.

The magistrates of Riom, in letters sealed with their own seal, undertook to give Jeanne the Maid and my Lord d'Albret the sum of 60 crowns; but when the masters of the siege-artillery came to demand this sum, the magistrates would not give a farthing.

The folk of Orléans, on the other hand, once more appeared both zealous and munificent; for they eagerly desired the reduction of a town commanding the Loire for 120 kilometres (75 miles) above their own city. They deserve to be considered the true deliverers of the kingdom; had it not been for them neither Jargeau nor Beaugency would have been taken in June. Quite in the beginning of July, when they thought the Loire campaign was to be continued, they had sent their great mortar, La Bougue, to Gien. With it they had despatched ammunition and victuals; and now, in the early days of December, at the request of the king addressed to the magistrates, they sent to La Charité all the artillery brought back from Gien; likewise 89 soldiers of the municipal troops, wearing the cloak with the Duke of Orléans' colours, the white cross on the breast; with their trumpeter at their head and commanded by Captain Boiau; craftsmen of all conditions, master-masons and journeymen, carpenters, smiths; the cannoneers Fauveau, Gervaise Lefèvre and Brother Jacques, monk of the Gray friars monastery, at Orléans. What became of all this artillery and of these brave folk?

On the 24th of November, the Sire d'Albret and the Maid, being hard put to it before the walls of La Charité, likewise solicited the town of Bourges. On receipt of their letter, the burgesses decided to contribute 1,300 golden crowns. To raise this sum they had recourse to a measure by no means unusual; it had been employed notably by the townsfolk of Orléans when, sometime previously, to furnish forth Jeanne with munition of war, they had bought from a certain citizen a quantity of salt which they had put up to auction in the city barn. The townsfolk of Bourges sold by auction the annual revenue of a 13th part of the wine sold retail in the town. But the money thus raised never reached its destination.

A right goodly knighthood was gathered beneath the walls of La Charité; besides Louis de Bourbon and the Sire d'Albret, there was the Maréchal de Broussac, Jean de Bouray, Seneschal of Toulouse and Raymon de Montremur, a Baron of Dauphiné, who was slain there. It was bitterly cold and the besiegers succeeded in nothing. At the end of a month Perrinet Gressart, who was full of craft, caused them to fall into an ambush. They raised the siege, abandoning the artillery furnished by the good towns, those fine cannon bought with the savings of thrifty citizens. Their action was the less excusable because the town which had not been relieved and could not well expect to be, must have surrendered sooner or later. They pleaded that the king had sent them no victuals and no money; but that was not considered an excuse and their action was deemed dishonourable. According to a knight well acquainted with points of honour in war: 'One ought never to besiege a place without being sure of victuals and of pay beforehand. For to besiege a stronghold and then to withdraw is great disgrace for an army, especially when there is present with it a king or a king's lieutenant.'

On the 13th of December there preached to the people of Périgueux a Dominican friar, Brother Hélie Boudant, Pope Martin's Penitentiary in that town. He took as his text the great miracles worked in France by the intervention of a Maid, whom God had sent to the king. On this occasion the Mayor and the magistrates heard mass sung and presented two candles. Now for two months Brother Hélie had been under order to appear before the Parlement of Poitiers. On what charge we do not know. Mendicant monks of those days were for the most part irregular in faith and in morals. The doctrine of Friar Richard himself was not altogether beyond suspicion.

At Christmas, in the year 1429, the flying squadron of *béguines* being assembled at Jargeau, this good Brother said mass and administered the communion thrice to Jeanne the Maid and twice to that Pierronne of Lower Brittany, with whom our Lord conversed as friend with friend. Such an action might well be regarded, if not as a formal violation of the Church's laws, at any rate as an unjustifiable abuse of the sacrament. A menacing theological tempest was then gathering and was about to break over the heads of Friar Richard's daughters in the spirit. A few days after the attack on Paris, the venerable university had had composed or rather transcribed a treatise, *De bono et maligno spiritu*, with a view probably to finding therein arguments against Friar Richard and his prophetess Jeanne, who had both appeared before the city with the Armagnacs.

About the same time, a clerk of the faculty of law had published a summary reply to Chancellor Gerson's memorial concerning the Maid. 'It sufficeth not,' he wrote, 'that one simply affirm that he is sent of God; every heretic maketh such a claim; but he must prove the truth of that mysterious mission by some miraculous work or by some special testimony in the Bible.' This Paris clerk denies that the Maid has presented any such proof, and to judge her by her acts, he believes her rather to have been sent by the Devil than by God. He reproaches her with wearing a dress forbidden to women under penalty of anathema, and he refutes the excuses for her conduct in this matter urged by Gerson. He accuses her of having excited between princes and Christian people a greater war than there had ever been before. He holds her to be an idolatress using enchantments and making false prophecies. He charges her with having induced men to slay their fellows on the two high festivals of the Holy Virgin, the Assumption and the Nativity. 'Sins committed by the Enemy of Mankind, through this woman, against the Creator and his most glorious Mother. And albeit there ensued certain murders, thanks be to God they were not so many as the Enemy had intended.'

'All these things do manifestly prove error and heresy,' adds this devout son of the university. Whence he concludes that the Maid should be taken before the bishop and the Inquisitor; and he ends by quoting this text from Saint Jérôme: 'The unhealthy flesh must be cut off; the diseased sheep must be driven from the fold.'

Such was the unanimous opinion of the University of Paris concerning her in whom the French clerks beheld an Angel of the Lord. At Bruges, in November, a rumour ran and was eagerly welcomed by ecclesiastics that the University of Paris had sent an embassy to the Pope at Rome to denounce the Maid as a false prophetess and a deceiver, and likewise those who believed in her. We do not know the veritable object of this mission. But there is no doubt whatever that the doctors and masters of Paris were henceforward firmly resolved that if ever they obtained possession of the damsel they would not let her go out of their hands, and certainly would not send her to be tried at Rome, where she might escape with a mere penance, and even be enlisted as one of the Pope's mercenaries.

In English and Burgundian lands, not only by clerks but by folk of all conditions, she was regarded as a heretic; in those countries the few who thought well of her had to conceal their opinions carefully. After the retreat from Saint-Denys, there may have remained some in Picardy, and notably at Abbeville, who were favourable to the prophetess of the French; but such persons must not be spoken of in public.

Colin Gouye, surnamed Le Sourd, and Jehannin Daix, surnamed Le Petit, a man of Abbeville, learned this to their cost. In this town about the middle of September, Le Sourd and Le Petit were near the blacksmith's forge with divers of the burgesses and other townsfolk, among whom was a herald. They fell to talking of the Maid who was making so great a stir throughout Christendom. To certain words the herald uttered concerning her, Le Petit replied eagerly:

'Well! well! Everything that woman does and says is nought but deception.'

Le Sourd spoke likewise: 'That woman,' he said, 'is not to be trusted. Those who believe in her are mad, and there is a smell of burning about them.'

By that he meant that their destiny was obvious, and that they were sure to be burned at the stake as heretics.

Then he had the misfortune to add: 'In this town there be many with a smell of burning about them.'

Such words were for the dwellers in Abbeville a slander and a cause of suspicion. When the mayor and the aldermen heard of this speech, they ordered Le Sourd to be thrown into prison. Le Petit must have said something similar, for he too was imprisoned.

By saying that divers of his fellow-citizens were suspect of heresy, Le Sourd put them in danger of being sought out by the bishop and the Inquisitor as heretics and sorcerers of notoriously evil repute. As for the Maid, she must have been suspect indeed, for a smell of burning to be caused by the mere fact of being her partisan.

While Friar Richard and his spiritual daughters were thus threatened with a bad end should they fall into the hands of the English or Burgundians, serious troubles were agitating the sisterhood. On the subject of Catherine, Jeanne entered into an open dispute with her spiritual father. Friar Richard wanted the holy dame of La Rochelle to be set to work. Fearing lest his advice should be adopted, Jeanne wrote to her king to tell him what to do with the woman, to wit that he should send her home to her husband and children.

When she came to the king the first thing she had to say to him was: 'Catherine's doings are nought but folly and futility.'

Friar Richard made no attempt to hide from the Maid his profound displeasure. He was thought much of at court, and it was doubtless with the consent of the Royal Council that he was endeavouring to compass the employment of Dame Catherine. The Maid had succeeded. Why should not another of the illuminated succeed?

Meanwhile the council had by no means renounced the services Jeanne was rendering to the French cause. Even after the misfortunes of Paris and of La Charité, there were many who now as before held her power to be supernatural; and there is reason to believe that there was a party at Court intending still to employ her. And even if they had wished to discard her she was now too intimately associated with the royal lilies for her rejection not to involve them too in dishonour. On the 29th of December, 1429, at Mehun-sur-Yèvre, the king gave her a charter of nobility sealed with the great seal in green wax, with a double pendant, on a strip of red and green silk.

The grant of nobility was to Jeanne, her father, mother, brothers even if they were not free, and to all their posterity, male and female. It was a singular grant corresponding to the singular services rendered by a woman.

In the title she is described as Johanna d'Ay, doubtless because her father's name was given to the king's scribes by Lorrainers who would speak with a soft drawl; but whether her name were Ay or Arc, she was seldom called by it, and was commonly spoken of as Jeanne the Maid.

Chapter V
Letter to the Citizens of Reims – Letter to the Hussites – Departure from Sully

THE FOLK OF ORLÉANS were grateful to the Maid for what she had done for them. Far from reproaching her with the unfortunate conclusion of the siege of La Charité, they welcomed her into

their city with the same rejoicing and with as good cheer as before. On the 19th of January, 1430, they honoured her and likewise Maître Jean de Velly and Maître Jean Rabateau with a banquet, at which there was abundance of capons, partridges, hares and even a pheasant. The burgesses loved and honoured Jeanne, but they cannot have observed her very closely during the repast or they would not eight years later, when an adventuress gave herself out to be the Maid, have mistaken her for Jeanne, and offered her wine in the same manner and at the hands of the same city servant, Jacques Leprestre, as now presented it.

At a time which it is impossible to fix exactly the Maid bought a house at Orléans. To be more precise she took it on lease. The house that Jeanne acquired in this manner belonged to the Chapter of the Cathedral. It was in the centre of the town, in the parish of Saint-Malo, close to the Saint-Maclou Chapel. What price did the Maid give for this house? Apparently six crowns of fine gold (at 60 crowns to the mark), due half-yearly at Midsummer and Christmas, for 59 years. In addition, she must according to custom have undertaken to keep the house in good condition and to pay out of her own purse the ecclesiastical dues as well as rates for wells and paving and all other taxes.

There is no reason to believe that the Maid did not herself negotiate this agreement. Saint as she was, she knew well what it was to possess property. She counted up her possessions in arms and horses, valued them at 12,000 crowns, and, apparently made a pretty accurate reckoning.

On the third of March she followed King Charles to Sully.

During the first fortnight of March, from the townsfolk of Reims she received a message in which they confided to her fears only too well grounded. On the 8th of March the regent had granted to the Duke of Burgundy the counties of Champagne and of Brie on condition of his reconquering them. Armagnacs and English vied with each other in offering the biggest and most tempting morsels to this Gargantuan Duke. Not being able to keep their promise and deliver to him Compiègne which refused to be delivered, the French offered him in its place Pont-Sainte-Maxence. But it was Compiègne that he wanted.

In a manner concise and vivacious the Maid replied to the townsfolk of Reims:

> '*Dear friends and beloved and mightily desired. Jehenne the Maid hath received your letters making mention that ye fear a siege. Know ye that it shall not so betide, and I may but encounter them shortly. And if I do not encounter them and they do not come to you, if you shut your gates firmly, I shall shortly be with you: and if they be there, I shall make them put on their spurs so hastily that they will not know where to take them and so quickly that it shall be very soon. Other things I will not write unto you now, save that ye be always good and loyal. I pray God to have you in his keeping. Written at Sully, the 16th day of March.*
>
> *I would announce unto you other tidings at which ye would mightily rejoice; but I fear lest the letters be taken on the road, and the said tidings be seen.*
>
> *Signed. Jehanne.*
>
> *Addressed to my dear friends and beloved, churchmen, burgesses and other citizens of the town of Rains.*'

There can be no doubt that the scribe wrote this letter faithfully as it was dictated by the Maid, and that he wrote her words as they fell from her lips. In her haste she now and again forgot words and sometimes whole phrases; but the sense is clear all the same. And what confidence! 'You will have no siege if I encounter the enemy.' How completely is this the language of chivalry! On the eve of Patay she had asked: 'Have you good spurs?' Here she cries: 'I will make them put on their spurs.' She says that soon she will be in Champagne, that she is about to start. Surely we can no longer think of her shut up in the Castle of La Trémouille as in a kind of gilded cage. In conclusion, she tells her friends at Reims that she does not write unto them all that she would like for fear lest her letter should be captured on the road. She knew what it was to be cautious. Sometimes she affixed a cross to her letters to warn her followers to pay no heed to what she wrote, in the hope that the missive would be intercepted and the enemy deceived.

The partisans of Duke Philip were at that time hatching plots in the towns of Champagne, notably at Troyes and at Reims. On the 22nd of February, 1430, a canon and a chaplain were arrested and brought before the chapter for having conspired to deliver the city to the English.

It was well for them that they belonged to the Church, for having been condemned to perpetual imprisonment, they obtained from the king a mitigation of their sentence, and the canon a complete remittance. The aldermen and ecclesiastics of the city, fearing they would be thought badly of on the other side of the Loire, wrote to the Maid entreating her to speak well of them to the king. The following is her reply to their request:

'Very good friends and beloved, may it please you to wit that I have received your letters, the which make mention how it hath been reported to the King that within the city of Reims there be many wicked persons. Therefore I give you to wit that it is indeed true that even such things have been reported to him and that he grieves much that there be folk in alliance with the Burgundians; that they would betray the town and bring the Burgundians into it. But since then the King has known the contrary by means of the assurance ye have sent him, and he is well pleased with you. And ye may believe that ye stand well in his favour; and if ye have need, he would help you with regard to the siege; and he knows well that ye have much to suffer from the hardness of those treacherous Burgundians, your adversaries: thus may God in his pleasure deliver you shortly, that is as soon as may be. So I pray and entreat you my friends dearly beloved that ye hold well the said city for the King and that ye keep good watch. Ye will soon have good tidings of me at greater length. Other things for the present I write not unto you save that the whole of Brittany is French and that the Duke is to send to the King three thousand combatants paid for two months. To God I commend you, may he keep you.

Written at Sully, the 28th of March.

Jehanne.

Addressed to: My good friends and dearly beloved, the churchmen, aldermen, burgesses and inhabitants and masters of the good town of Reyms.'

Touching the succour to be expected from the Duke of Brittany, the Maid was labouring under a delusion. Like all other prophetesses she was ignorant of what was passing around her. Despite her failures, she believed in her good fortune; she doubted herself no more than she doubted God; and she was eager to pursue the fulfilment of her mission. 'Ye shall soon have tidings of me,' she said to the townsfolk of Reims. A few days after, and she left Sully to go into France and fight, on the expiration of the truces.

Chapter VI
The Maid in the Trenches of Melun – Le Seigneur de L'Ours – The Child of Lagny

IN EASTER WEEK, Jeanne, at the head of a band of mercenaries, is before the walls of Melun. She arrives just in time to fight. The truces have expired. Is it possible that the town which was subject to King Charles can have refused to admit the Maid with her company when she came to it so generously? Apparently, it was so. Was Jeanne able to communicate with the Carmelites of Melun? Probably. What misfortune befell her at the gates of the town? Did she suffer ill treatment at the hands of a Burgundian band? We know not. But when she was in the trenches, she heard Saint Catherine and Saint Margaret saying unto her: 'Thou wilt be taken before Saint John's Day.'

And she entreated them: 'When I am taken, let me die immediately without suffering long.' And the Voices repeated that she would be taken and thus it must be.

And they added gently: 'Be not troubled, be resigned. God will help thee.'

Saint John's Day was the 24th of June, in less than 10 weeks. Many a time after that, Jeanne asked her saints at what hour she would be taken; but they did not tell her; and thus doubting she ceased to follow her own ideas and consulted the captains.

On her way from Melun to Lagny-sur-Marne, in the month of May, she had to pass Corbeil. It was probably then, and in her company, that the two devout women from Lower Brittany, Pierronne and her younger sister in the spirit, were taken at Corbeil by the English.

For eight months the town of Lagny had been subject to King Charles and governed by Messire Ambroise de Loré, who was energetically waging war against the English of Paris and elsewhere. For the [time being] Messire Ambroise de Loré was absent; but his lieutenant, Messire Jean Foucault, commanded the garrison. Shortly after Jeanne's coming to this town, tidings were brought that a company of between 300 and 400 men of Picardy and of Champagne, fighting for the Duke of Burgundy, after having ranged through l'Île de France, were now on their way back to Picardy with much booty. Their captain was a valiant man-at-arms, one Franquet d'Arras. The French determined to cut off their retreat. Under the command of Messire Jean Foucault, Messire Geoffroy de Saint-Bellin, Lord Hugh Kennedy, a Scotchman and Captain Baretta, they sallied forth from the town.

The Maid went with them. They encountered the Burgundians near Lagny, but failed to surprise them. Messire Franquet's archers had had time to take up their position with their backs to a hedge, in the English manner. King Charles's men barely outnumbered the enemy. A certain clerk of that time, a Frenchman, writes of the engagement. His innate ingeniousness was invincible. With candid common sense he states that this very slight numerical superiority rendered the enterprise very arduous and difficult for his party. And the battle was strong indeed. The Burgundians were mightily afraid of the Maid because they believed her to be a witch and in command of armies of devils; notwithstanding, they fought right valiantly. Twice the French were repulsed; but they returned to the attack, and finally the Burgundians were all slain or taken.

The conquerors returned to Lagny, loaded with booty and taking with them their prisoners, among whom was Messire Franquet d'Arras. Of noble birth and the lord of a manor, he was entitled to expect that he would be held to ransom, according to custom. Both Jean de Troissy, Bailie of Senlis and the Maid demanded him from the soldier who was his captor. It was to the Maid that he was finally delivered. Did she obtain him in return for money? Probably, for soldiers were not accustomed to give up noble and profitable prisoners for nothing. Nevertheless, the Maid, when questioned on this subject, replied, that being neither mistress nor steward of France, it was not for her to give out money. We must suppose, therefore, that some one paid for her. However that may be, Captain Franquet d'Arras was given up to her, and she endeavoured to exchange him for a prisoner in the hands of the English. The man whom she thus desired to deliver was a Parisian who was called Le Seigneur de l'Ours.

He was not of gentle birth and his arms were the sign of his hostelry. It was the custom in those days to give the title of Seigneur to the masters of the great Paris inns. Thus Colin, who kept the inn at the Temple Gate, was known as Seigneur du Boisseau. The hôtel de l'Ours stood in the Rue Saint-Antoine, near the Gate properly called La Porte Baudoyer, but commonly known as Porte Baudet, Baudet possessing the double advantage over Baudoyer of being shorter and more comprehensible. It was an ancient and famous inn, equal in renown to the most famous, to the inn of L'Arbre Sec, in the street of that name, to the Fleur de Lis near the Pont Neuf, to the Epée in the Rue Saint-Denis, and to the Chapeau Fétu of the Rue Croix-du-Tirouer. As early as King Charles V's reign the inn was much frequented. Before huge fires the spits were turning all day long, and there were hot bread, fresh herrings and wine of Auxerre in plenty. But since then the plunderings of men-at-arms had laid waste the countryside, and travellers no longer ventured forth for fear of being robbed and slain. Knights and pilgrims had ceased coming into the town. Only wolves came by night and devoured little children in the streets. There were no fagots in the grate, no dough in the kneading-trough. Armagnacs and Burgundians had drunk all the wine, laid waste all the vineyards, and nought was left in the cellar save a poor piquette of apples and of plums.

The Seigneur de l'Ours, whom the Maid demanded, was called Jaquet Guillaume. Although Jeanne, like other folk, called him Seigneur, it is not certain that he personally directed his inn, nor even that the inn was open through these years of disaster and desolation. The only ascertainable fact is that he was the proprietor of the house with the sign of the Bear (*l'Ours*). He held it by right of his wife Jeannette, and had come into possession of it in the following manner.

Fourteen years before, when King Henry with his knighthood had not yet landed in France, the host of the Bear Inn had been the king's sergeant-at-arms, one Jean Roche, a man of wealth and fair fame. He was a devoted follower of the Duke of Burgundy, and that was what ruined him. Paris was then occupied by the Armagnacs. In the year 1416, in order to turn them out of the city, Jean Roche concerted with various burgesses. The plot was to be carried out on Easter Day, which that year fell on the 29th of April. But the Armagnacs discovered it. They threw the conspirators into prison and brought them to trial. On the first Saturday in May the Seigneur de l'Ours was carried to the marketplace in a tumbrel with Durand de Brie, a dyer, master of the 60 crossbowmen of Paris, and Jean Perquin, pin-maker and brasier. All three were beheaded, and the body of the Seigneur de l'Ours was hanged at Montfaucon where it remained until the entrance of the Burgundians. Six weeks after their coming, in July 1418, his body was taken down from the gibbet and buried in consecrated ground.

Now the widow of Jean Roche had a daughter by a first marriage. Her name was Jeannette; she took for her first husband a certain Bernard le Breton; for her second, Jaquet Guillaume, who was not rich. He owed money to Maître Jean Fleury, a clerk at law and the king's secretary. His wife's affairs were not more prosperous; her father's goods had been confiscated and she had been obliged to redeem a part of her maternal inheritance. In 1424, the couple were short of money, and they sold a house, concealing the fact that it was mortgaged. Being charged by the purchaser, they were thrown into prison, where they aggravated their offence by suborning two witnesses, one a priest, the other a chambermaid. Fortunately for them, they procured a pardon.

The Jaquet Guillaume couple, therefore, were in a sorry plight. There remained to them, however, the inheritance of Jean Roche, the inn near the Place Baudet, at the sign of the Bear, the title of which Jaquet Guillaume bore. This second Seigneur de l'Ours was to be as strongly Armagnac as the other had been Burgundian, and was to pay the same price for his opinions.

Six years had passed since his release from prison, when, in the March of 1430, there was plotted by the Carmelites of Melun and certain burgesses of Paris that conspiracy which we mentioned on the occasion of Jeanne's departure for l'Île de France. It was not the first plot into which the Carmelites had entered; they had plotted that rising which had been on the point of breaking out on the Day of the Nativity, when the Maid was leading the attack near La Porte Saint-Honoré; but never before had so many burgesses and so many notables entered into a conspiracy. A clerk of the Treasury, Maître Jean de la Chapelle, two magistrates of the Châtelet, Maître Renaud Savin and Maître Pierre Morant, a very wealthy man, named Jean de Calais, burgesses, merchants, artisans, more than 150 persons, held the threads of this vast web, and among them, Jaquet Guillaume, Seigneur de l'Ours.

The Carmelites of Melun directed the whole. Clad as artisans, they went from king to burgesses, from burgesses to king; they kept up the communications between those within and those without, and regulated all the details of the enterprise. One of them asked the conspirators for a written undertaking to bring the king's men into the city. Such a demand looks as if the majority of the conspirators were in the pay of the Royal Council.

In exchange for this undertaking these monks brought acts of oblivion signed by the king. For the people of Paris to be induced to receive the prince, whom they still called Dauphin, they must needs be assured of a full and complete amnesty. For more than 10 years, while the English and Burgundians had been holding the town, no one had felt altogether free from the reproach of their lawful sovereign and the men of his party. And all the more desirous were they for Charles of Valois to forget the past when they recalled the cruel vengeance taken by the Armagnacs after the suppression of the Butchers.

One of the conspirators, Jaquet Perdriel, advocated the sounding of a trumpet and the reading of the acts of oblivion on Sunday at the Porte Baudet.

'I have no doubt,' he said, 'but that we shall be joined by the craftsmen, who, in great numbers will flock to hear the reading.'

He intended leading them to the Saint Antoine Gate and opening it to the king's men who were lying in ambush close by.

Some 80 or 100 Scotchmen, dressed as Englishmen, wearing the Saint Andrew's cross, were then to enter the town, bringing in fish and cattle.

'They will enter boldly by the Saint-Denys Gate,' said Perdriel, 'and take possession of it. Whereupon the king's men will enter in force by the Porte Saint Antoine.'

The plan was deemed good, except that it was considered better for the king's men to come in by the Saint-Denys Gate.

On Sunday, the 12th of March, the second Sunday in Lent, Maître Jean de la Chapelle invited the magistrate Renaud Savin to come to the tavern of *La Pomme de Pin* and meet various other conspirators in order to arrive at an understanding touching what was best to be done. They decided that on a certain day, under pretext of going to see his vines at Chapelle-Saint-Denys, Jean de Calais should join the king's men outside the walls, make himself known to them by unfurling a white standard and bring them into the town. It was further determined that Maître Morant and a goodly company of citizens with him, should hold themselves in readiness in the taverns of the Rue Saint-Denys to support the French when they came in. In one of the taverns of this street must have been the Seigneur de l'Ours, who, dwelling nearby, had undertaken to bring together various folk of the neighbourhood.

The conspirators were acting in perfect agreement. All they now awaited was to be informed of the day chosen by the Royal Council; and they believed the attempt was to be made on the following Sunday. But on the 21st of March Brother Pierre d'Allée, Prior of the Carmelites of Melun, was taken by the English. Put to the torture, he confessed the plot and named his accomplices. On the information he gave, more than 150 persons were arrested and tried. On the 8th of April, the Eve of Palm Sunday, seven of the most important were taken to the marketplace on a tumbrel. They were: Jean de la Chapelle, clerk of the Treasury; Renaud Savin and Pierre Morant, magistrates at the Châtelet; Guillaume Perdriau; Jean le François, called Baudrin; Jean le Rigueur, baker, and Jaquet Guillaume, Seigneur de l'Ours. All seven were beheaded by the executioner, who afterwards quartered the bodies of Jean de la Chapelle and of Baudrin.

Jaquet Perdriel was merely deprived of his possessions. Jean de Calais soon procured a pardon Jeannette, the wife of Jaquet Guillaume, was banished from the kingdom and her goods confiscated.

How can the Maid have known the Seigneur de l'Ours? Possibly the Carmelites of Melun had recommended him to her, and perhaps it was on their advice that she demanded his surrender. She may have seen him in the September of 1429, at Saint-Denys or before the walls of Paris, and he may have then undertaken to work for the Dauphin and his party. Why were attempts made at Lagny to save this man alone of the 150 Parisians arrested on the information of Brother Pierre d'Allée? Rather than Renaud Savin and Pierre Morant, magistrates at the Châtelet, rather than Jean de la Chapelle, clerk of the Treasury, why choose the meanest of the band? And how could they look to exchange a man accused of treachery for a prisoner of war? All this seems to us mysterious and inexplicable.

In the early days of May, Jeanne did not know what had become of Jaquet Guillaume. When she heard that he had been tried and put to death she was sore grieved and vexed. None the less, she looked upon Franquet as a captive held to ransom. But the Bailie of Senlis, who for some unknown reason was determined on the captain's ruin, took advantage of the Maid's vexation at Jaquet Guillaume's execution, and persuaded her to give up her prisoner.

He represented to her that this man had committed many a murder, many a theft, that he was a traitor and that consequently he ought to be brought to trial.

'You will be neglecting to execute justice,' he said, 'if you set this Franquet free.'

These reasons decided her, or rather she yielded to the Bailie's entreaty.

'Since the man I wished to have is dead,' she said, 'do with Franquet as justice shall require you.'

Thus she surrendered her prisoner. Was she right or wrong? Before deciding we must ask whether it were possible for her to do otherwise than she did. She was the Maid of God, the angel of the Lord of Hosts, that is clear. But the leaders of war, the captains, paid no great heed to what she said. As for the Bailie, he was the king's man, of noble birth and passing powerful.

Assisted by the judges of Lagny, he himself conducted the trial. The accused confessed that he was a murderer, a thief and a traitor. We must believe him; and yet we cannot forbear a doubt as to whether he really was, any more than the majority of Armagnac or Burgundian men-at-arms, any more than a Damoiseau de Commercy or a Guillaume de Flavy, for example. He was condemned to death.

Jeanne consented that he should die, if he had deserved death, and seeing that he had confessed his crimes he was beheaded.

When they heard of the scandalous treatment of Messire Franquet, the Burgundians were loud in their sorrow and indignation. It would seem that in this matter the Bailie of Senlis and the judges of Lagny did not act according to custom. We, however, are not sufficiently acquainted with the circumstances to form an opinion. There may have been some reason, of which we are ignorant, why the King of France should have demanded this prisoner. He had a right to do so on condition that he paid the Maid the amount of the ransom. A soldier of those days, well informed in all things touching honour in war, was the author of *Le Jouvencel*. In his chivalrous romances he writes approvingly of the wise Amydas, King of Amydoine, who, learning that one of his enemies, the Sire de Morcellet, has been taken in battle and held to ransom, cries out that he is the vilest of traitors, ransoms him with good coins of the realm, and hands him over to the provost of the town and the officers of his council that they may execute justice upon him. Such was the royal prerogative.

Whether it was that camp life was hardening her, or whether, like all mystics, she was subject to violent changes of mood, Jeanne showed at Lagny none of that gentleness she had displayed on the evening of Patay. The virgin who once had no other arm in battle than her standard, now wielded a sword found there, at Lagny, a Burgundian sword and a trusty. Those who regarded her as an angel of the Lord, good Brother Pasquerel, for example, might justify her by saying that the Archangel Saint Michael, the standard-bearer of celestial hosts, bore a flaming sword. And indeed, Jeanne remained a saint.

While she was at Lagny, folk came and told her that a child had died at birth, unbaptized. Having entered into the mother at the time of her conception, the devil held the soul of this child, who, for lack of water, had died the enemy of its Creator. The greatest anxiety was felt concerning the fate of this soul. Some thought it was in limbo, banished forever from God's sight, but the more general and better-founded opinion was that it was seething in hell; for has not Saint Augustine demonstrated that souls, little as well as great, are damned because of original sin. And how could it be otherwise, seeing that Eve's fall had effaced the divine likeness in this child? He was destined to eternal death. And to think that with a few drops of water this death might have been avoided! So terrible a disaster afflicted not only the poor creature's kinsfolk, but likewise the neighbours and all good Christians in the town of Lagny. The body was carried to the Church of Saint-Pierre and placed before the image of Our Lady, which had been highly venerated ever since the plague of 1128. It was called Notre-Dame-des-Ardents because it cured burns, and when there were no burns to be cured it was called Notre-Dame-des-Aidants, or rather Des Aidances, that is, Our Lady the Helper, because she granted succour to those in dire necessity.

The maidens of the town knelt before her, the little body in their midst, beseeching her to intercede with her divine Son so that this little child might have his share in the Redemption brought by our Saviour. In such cases the Holy Virgin did not always deny her powerful intervention. Here it may not be inappropriate to relate a miracle she had worked 37 years before.

At Paris, in 1393, a sinful creature, finding herself with child, concealed her pregnancy, and, when her time was come, was without aid delivered. Then, having stuffed linen into the throat of the girl she had brought forth, she went and threw her on to the dust-heap outside La Porte Saint-Martin-des-Champs. But a dog scented the body, and scratching away the other refuse, discovered it. A devout woman, who happened to be passing by, took this poor little lifeless creature, and, followed by more than 400 people, bore it to the Church of Saint-Martin-des-Champs, there placed it on the altar of Our Lady, and kneeling down with the multitude of folk and the monks of the Abbey, with all her heart prayed the Holy Virgin not to suffer this innocent babe to be condemned eternally. The child stirred a little, opened her eyes, loosened the linen, which gagged her, and cried aloud. A priest baptized her on the altar of Our Lady, and gave her the name of Marie. A nurse was found, and she was fed from the breast. She lived three hours, then died and was carried to consecrated ground.

In those days resurrections of unbaptized children were frequent. That saintly Abbess, Colette of Corbie, who, when Jeanne was at Lagny, dwelt at Moulins with the reformed Sisters of Saint Clare, had brought back to life two of these poor creatures: a girl, who received the name of Colette at the font and afterwards became a nun, then abbess at Pont-à-Mousson; a boy, who was said to have been two days buried and whom the servant of the poor declared to be one of the elect. He died at six months, thus fulfilling the prophecy made by the saint.

With this kind of miracle Jeanne was doubtless acquainted. About 40 kilometres (25 miles) from Domremy, in the duchy of Lorraine, near Lunéville, was the sanctuary of Notre-Dame-des-Aviots, of which she had probably heard. Notre-Dame-des-Aviots, or Our Lady of those brought back to life, was famed for restoring life to unbaptized children. By means of her intervention they lived again long enough to be made Christians.

In the duchy of Luxembourg, near Montmédy, on the hill of Avioth, multitudes of pilgrims worshipped an image of Our Lady brought there by angels. On this hill a church had been built for her, with slim pillars and elaborate stonework in trefoils, roses and light foliage. This statue worked all manner of miracles. At its feet were placed children born dead; they were restored to life and straightway baptized.

The folk, gathered in the Church of Saint-Pierre de Lagny, around the statue of Notre-Dame-des-Aidances, hoped for a like grace. The damsels of the town prayed round the child's lifeless body. The Maid was asked to come and join them in praying to Our Lord and Our Lady. She went to the church, and knelt down with the maidens and prayed. The child was black, 'as black as my coat,' said Jeanne. When the Maid and the damsels had prayed, it yawned three times and its colour came back. It was baptized and straightway it died; it was buried in consecrated ground. Throughout the town this resurrection was said to be the work of the Maid. According to the tales in circulation, during the three days since its birth the child had given no sign of life; but the gossips of Lagny had doubtless extended the period of its comatose condition, like those good wives who of a single egg laid by the husband of one of them, made 100 before the day was out.

Chapter VII
Soissons and Compiègne – Capture of the Maid

LEAVING LAGNY, THE MAID presented herself before Senlis, with her own company and with the fighting men of the French nobles whom she had joined, in all some 1,000 horse. And for this force

she demanded entrance into the town. The folk of Senlis made answer to the Maid that, seeing the poverty of the town in forage, corn, oats, victuals and wine, they offered her an entrance with 30 or 40 of the most notable of her company and no more.

It is said that from Senlis Jeanne went to the Castle of Borenglise in the parish of Elincourt, between Compiègne and Ressons; and, in ignorance as to what can have taken her there, it is supposed that she made a pilgrimage to the Church of Elincourt, which was dedicated to Saint Margaret; and it is possible that she wished to worship Saint Margaret there as she had worshipped Saint Catherine at Fierbois, in order to do honour to one of those heavenly ladies who visited her every day and every hour.

The Council of King Charles had made over Pont-Sainte-Maxence to the Duke of Burgundy, in lieu of Compiègne, which they were unable to deliver to him since that town absolutely refused to be delivered, and remained the king's despite the king. The Duke of Burgundy kept Pont-Sainte-Maxence which had been granted him and resolved to take Compiègne.

On the 17th of April, when the truce had expired, he took the field with a goodly knighthood and a powerful army, four thousand Burgundians, Picards and Flemings, and 1,500 English, commanded by Jean de Luxembourg, Count of Ligny.

Compiègne, then one of the largest and strongest towns in France, was defended by a garrison of between 400 and 500 men, commanded by Guillaume de Flavy. Scion of a noble house of that province, forever in dispute with the nobles his neighbours, and perpetually picking quarrels with the poor folk, he was as wicked and cruel as any Armagnac baron. The citizens would have no other captain, and in that office they maintained him in defiance of King Charles and his chamberlains. They did wisely, for none was better able to defend the town than my Lord Guillaume, none was more set on doing his duty. When the King of France had commanded him to deliver the place he had refused point-blank; and when later the duke promised him a good round sum and a rich inheritance in exchange for Compiègne, he made answer that the town was not his, but the king's.

On the 13th of May, the Maid entered Compiègne, where she lodged in the Rue de l'Etoile. On the morrow, the Attorneys offered her four pots of wine. They thereby intended to do her great honour, for they did no more for the Lord Archbishop of Reims, Chancellor of the realm, who was then in the town with the Count of Vendôme, the king's lieutenant and various other leaders of war. These noble lords resolved to send artillery and other munitions to the Castle of Choisy, which could not hold out much longer and now, as before, the Maid was made use of.

The army marched towards Soissons in order to cross the Aisne. The captain of the town was a squire of Picardy, called by the French Guichard Bournel, by the Burgundians Guichard de Thiembronne; he had served on both sides. On the approach of King Charles's barons and men-at-arms, Captain Guichard made the folk of Soissons believe that the whole army was coming to encamp in their town. Wherefore they resolved not to receive them. Then happened what had already befallen at Senlis: Captain Bournel received the Lord Archbishop of Reims, the Count of Vendôme and the Maid, with a small company, and the rest of the army abode that night outside the walls. On the morrow, failing to obtain command of the bridge, they endeavoured to ford the river, but without success; for it was spring and the waters were high. The army had to turn back. When it was gone, Captain Bournel sold to the Duke of Burgundy the city he was charged to hold for the King of France; and he delivered it into the hand of Messire Jean de Luxembourg for 4,000 golden *saluts*.

At the tidings of this treacherous and dishonourable action on the part of the Captain of Soissons, Jeanne cried out that if she had him, she would cut his body into four pieces, which was no empty imagining of her wrath.

Before Soissons, Jeanne and the generals separated. The latter with their men-at-arms went to Senlis and the banks of the Marne. The country between the Aisne and the Oise was no longer capable of supporting so large a number of men or such important personages. Jeanne and her company wended their way back to Compiègne. Scarcely had she entered the town when she sallied forth to ravage the neighbourhood.

After returning to Compiègne, Jeanne, who never rested for a moment, hastened to Crépy-en-Valois, where were gathering the troops intended for the defence of Compiègne. Then, with these troops, she marched through the Forest of Guise, to the besieged town and entered it on the 23rd, at daybreak, without having encountered any Burgundians.

A little band of Burgundians commanded by a knight, Messire Baudot de Noyelles, occupied the high ground of the village of Margny. Most renowned among the men of war of the Burgundian party was Messire Jean de Luxembourg. He with his Picards was posted at Clairoix, on the banks of the Aronde, at the foot of Mount Ganelon. The 500 English of Lord Montgomery watched the Oise at Venette. Duke Philip occupied Coudun, a good four kilometres (two and a half miles) from the town, towards Picardy. Such dispositions were in accordance with the precepts of the most experienced captains. It was their rule that when besieging a fortified town a large number of men-at-arms should never be concentrated in one spot, in one camp, as they said. In case of a sudden attack, it was thought that a large company, if it has but one base, will be surprised and routed just as easily as a lesser number, and the disaster will be grievous. Wherefore it is better to divide the besiegers into small companies and to place them not far apart, in order that they may aid one another.

That same day, the 23rd of May, towards five o'clock in the evening riding a fine dapple-grey horse, Jeanne sallied forth, across the bridge, on to the causeway over the meadow. With her were her standard-bearer and her company of Lombards, Captain Baretta and his 300 or 400 men, both horse and foot, who had entered Compiègne by night. She was girt with the Burgundian sword, found at Lagny, and over her armour she wore a surcoat of cloth of gold. Such attire would have better beseemed a parade than a sortie; but in the simplicity of her rustic and religious soul she loved all the pompous show of chivalry.

The enterprise had been concerted between Captain Baretta, the other leaders of the party and Messire Guillaume de Flavy. The last named, in order to protect the line of retreat for the French, had posted archers, crossbowmen and cannoneers at the head of the bridge, while on the river he launched a number of small, covered boats, intended if need were to bring back as many men as possible. Jeanne was not consulted in the matter; her advice was never asked. Without being told anything she was taken with the army as a bringer of good luck; she was exhibited to the enemy as a powerful enchantress, and they, especially if they were in mortal sin, feared lest she should cast a spell over them.

This time she had not the remotest idea of what was to be done. With her head full of dreams, she imagined she was setting forth for some great and noble emprise.

It was five o'clock in the afternoon when the French set out on the march.

Having climbed up to Margny, the assailants found the Burgundians scattered and unarmed. They took them by surprise; and the French set to work to strike here and there haphazard. The Maid, for her part, overthrew everything before her.

Having stormed the camp and pillaged it, the assailants should in all haste have fallen back on the town with their booty; but they dallied at Margny, for what reason is not difficult to guess: that reason which so often transformed the robber into the robbed. The wearers of the white cross as well as those of the red, no matter what danger threatened them, never quitted a place as long as anything remained to be carried away.

If the mercenaries of Compiègne incurred peril by their greed, the Maid on her side by her valour and prowess ran much greater risk; never would she consent to leave a battle; she must be wounded, pierced with bolts and arrows, before she would give in.

The men of Clairoix appeared. Duke Philip himself came up with the band from Coudun. The French, outnumbered, abandoned Margny, and retreated slowly. It may be that their booty impeded their march. But suddenly espying the *Godons* from Venette advancing over the meadowland, they were seized with panic; they broke into one mad rush and in utter rout reached the bank of the Oise. The English followed so hard on the fugitives that the defenders on the ramparts dared not fire their cannon for fear of striking the French.

The latter having forced the barrier of the bulwark, the English were about to enter on their heels, cross the bridge and pass into the town. The captain of Compiègne saw the danger and gave the command to close the town gate. The bridge was raised and the portcullis lowered.

In the meadow, Jeanne still laboured under the heroic delusion of victory. Surrounded by a little band of kinsmen and personal retainers, she was withstanding the Burgundians, and imagining that she would overthrow everything before her.

Her comrades shouted to her: 'Strive to regain the town or we are lost.'

But her eyes were dazzled by the splendour of angels and archangels, and she made answer: 'Hold your peace; it will be your fault if we are discomfited. Think of nought but of attacking them.'

Her men took her horse by the bridle and forced her to turn towards the town. It was too late; the bulwarks commanding the bridge could not be entered: the English held the head of the causeway. The Maid with her little band was penned into the corner between the side of the bulwark and the embankment of the road. Her assailants were men of Picardy, who, striking hard and driving away her protectors, succeeded in reaching her. A bowman pulled her by her cloak of cloth of gold and threw her to the ground.

Urged to give her parole, she replied: 'I have plighted my word to another, and I shall keep my oath.'

She was disarmed and taken to Margny. At the tidings that the witch of the Armagnacs had been taken, cries and rejoicings resounded throughout the Burgundian camp. Duke Philip wished to see her. When he drew near to her, there were certain of his clergy and his knighthood who praised his piety, extolled his courage, and wondered that this mighty duke was not afraid of the spawn of Hell.

Jeanne remained in the custody of Messire Jean de Luxembourg, to whom she belonged henceforward. When he held the Maid to ransom, he was 39 years of age, covered with wounds and one-eyed.

That very evening from his quarters at Coudun the Duke of Burgundy caused letters to be written to the towns of his dominions telling of the capture of the Maid. 'Of this capture shall the fame spread far and wide,' is written in the letter to the people of Saint-Quentin; 'and there shall be bruited abroad the error and misbelief of all such as have approved and favoured the deeds of this woman.'

In like manner did the duke send the tidings to the Duke of Brittany by his herald Lorraine; to the Duke of Savoy and to his good town of Ghent.

The survivors of the company the Maid had taken to Compiègne abandoned the siege, and on the morrow returned to their garrisons.

Chapter VIII
The Maid at Beaulieu – The Shepherd of Gévaudan

✠

THE TIDINGS THAT JEANNE was in the hands of the Burgundians reached Paris on the morning of May the 25th. On the morrow, the 26th, the university sent a summons to Duke Philip requiring him to give up his prisoner to the vicar general of the Grand Inquisitor of France. At the same time, the vicar general himself by letter required the redoubtable duke to bring prisoner before him the young woman suspected of various crimes savouring of heresy.

At Beaulieu, Jeanne was treated courteously and ceremoniously. Her steward, Messire Jean d'Aulon, waited on her in her prison; one day he said to her pitifully:

'That poor town of Compiègne, which you so dearly loved, will now be delivered into the hands of the enemies of France, whom it must needs obey.'

She made answer: 'No, that shall not come to pass. For not one of those places, which the King of Heaven hath conquered through me and restored to their allegiance to the fair King Charles, shall be recaptured by the enemy, so diligently will he guard them.'

One day she tried to escape by slipping between two planks. She had intended to shut up her guards in the tower and take to the fields, but the porter saw and stopped her. She concluded that it was not God's will that she should escape this time.

Great was the mourning on the Loire when the inhabitants of the towns loyal to King Charles learnt the disaster which had befallen the Maid.

The councillors of the town of Tours ordered public prayers to be offered for the deliverance of the Maid. There was a public procession in which took part the canons of the cathedral church, the clergy of the town, secular and regular, all walking barefoot.

In the towns of Dauphiné prayers for the Maid were said at mass.

Learning that the Maid, whom he had once suspected of evil intentions and then recognized to be wholly good, had just fallen into the hands of the enemy of the realm, Messire Jacques Gélu, my Lord Archbishop of Embrun, despatched to King Charles a messenger bearing a letter touching the line of conduct to be adopted in such an unhappy conjuncture.

He beseeches him to examine his conscience and see whether he has in any wise sinned against the grace of God. For it may be that in wrath against the king the Lord hath permitted this virgin to be taken. For his own honour he urges him to strain every effort for her deliverance.

'I commend unto you,' he said, 'that for the recovery of this damsel and for her ransom, ye spare neither measures nor money, nor any cost, unless ye be ready to incur the ineffaceable disgrace of an ingratitude right unworthy.'

And why should the Lord Chamberlain and the Lord Archbishop have wanted to get rid of the Maid? She did not trouble them; on the contrary they found her useful and employed her. By her prophecy that she would cause the king to be anointed at Reims, she rendered an immense service to my Lord Regnault, who more than any other profited from the Champagne expedition, more even than the king, who, while he succeeded in being crowned, failed to recover Paris and Normandy. Notwithstanding this great advantage, the Lord Archbishop felt no gratitude towards the Maid; he was a hard man and an egoist. But did he wish her harm? Had he not need of her? At Senlis he was maintaining the king's cause; and he was maintaining it well, we may be sure, since, with the towns that had returned to their liege lord, he was defending his own episcopal and ducal city, his benefices and his canonries. Did he not intend to use her against the Burgundians?

Meanwhile Messire Regnault de Chartres believed himself possessed of a marvel far surpassing the marvel he had lost. He wrote a letter to the inhabitants of his town of Reims telling them that the Maid had been taken at Compiègne.

This misfortune had befallen her through her own fault, he added. 'She would not take advice, but would follow her own will.'

Chapter IX
The Maid at Beaurevoir – Catherine De La Rochelle at Paris – Execution of La Pierronne

✠

THE MAID HAD BEEN TAKEN CAPTIVE in the diocese of Beauvais. At that time the Bishop Count of Beauvais was Pierre Cauchon of Reims, a great and pompous clerk of the University of Paris, which had elected him rector in 1403. Standing equally high in the favour of the English, Messire Pierre was councillor of King Henry VI, Almoner of France and Chancellor to the Queen of England. Since 1423, his usual residence had been at Rouen. By their submission to King Charles the people of Beauvais had deprived him of his episcopal revenue. And, as the English said and believed that the army of the King of France was at that time commanded by Friar Richard and the Maid, Messire Pierre Cauchon, the impoverished Bishop of Beauvais, had a personal grievance against Jeanne.

It would have been better for his own reputation that he should have abstained from avenging the Church's honour on a damsel who was possibly an idolatress, a soothsayer and the invoker of devils, but who had certainly incurred his personal ill will. He was in the regent's pay; and the regent was filled with bitter hatred of the Maid. Again for his reputation's sake, my Lord Bishop of Beauvais should have reflected that in prosecuting Jeanne for a matter of faith he was serving his master's wrath and furthering the temporal interests of the great of this world. On these things he did not reflect; on the contrary, this case at once temporal and spiritual, as ambiguous as his own position, excited his worst passions. He flung himself into it with all the thoughtlessness of the violent. A maiden to be denounced, a heretic and an Armagnac to boot, what a feast for the prelate, the councillor of King Henry! After having concerted with the doctors and masters of the University of Paris, on the 14th of July, he presented himself before the camp of Compiègne and demanded the Maid as subject to his jurisdiction.

At the same time the Bishop of Beauvais was charged to offer money. To us it seems strange indeed that just at the very time when, by the mouth of the university, he was representing to the Lord of Luxembourg that he could not sell his prisoner without committing a crime, the bishop should himself offer to purchase her. According to these ecclesiastics, Jean would incur terrible penalties in this world and in the next, if in conformity with the laws and customs of war he surrendered a prisoner held to ransom in return for money, and he would win praise and blessing if he treacherously sold his captive to those who wished to put her to death. But at least we might expect that this Lord Bishop who had come to buy this woman for the Church, would purchase her with the Church's money. Not at all! The purchase money is furnished by the English. In the end therefore she is delivered not to the Church but to the English. And it is a priest, acting in the interests of God and of his Church, by virtue of his episcopal jurisdiction, who concludes the bargain. He offers 10,000 golden francs, a sum in return for which, he says, according to the custom prevailing in France, the king has the right to claim any prisoner even were he of the blood royal.

There can be no doubt whatever that the high and solemn ecclesiastic, Pierre Cauchon, suspected Jeanne of witchcraft. Wishing to bring her to trial, he exercised his ecclesiastical functions. This was not a question of faith. In the provinces ruled over by King Charles the Holy Inquisition prosecuted heresy in a curious manner and the secular arm saw to it that the sentences pronounced by the Church did not remain a dead letter. The Armagnacs burned witches just as much as the French and the Burgundians. For the present doubtless they did not believe the Maid to be possessed by devils; most of them on the contrary were inclined to regard her as a saint. But might they not be undeceived? Would it not be good Christian charity to present them with fine canonical arguments? If the Maid's case were really a case for the ecclesiastical court why not join with Churchmen of both parties and take her before the Pope and the council? And just at that time a council for the reformation of the Church and the establishment of peace in the kingdom was sitting in the town of Bâle; the university was sending its delegates, who would there meet the ecclesiastics of King Charles, also Gallicans and firmly attached to the privileges of the Church of France. Why not have this Armagnac prophetess tried by the assembled Fathers? The regent's councillors were already accusing Jeanne of witchcraft when she summoned them in the name of the King of Heaven to depart out of France. During the siege of Orléans, they wanted to burn her heralds and said that if they had her they would burn her also at the stake. Such in good sooth was their firm intent and their unvarying intimation. This does not look as if they would be likely to hand her over to the Church as soon as she was taken. In their own kingdom they burned as many witches and wizards as possible; but they had never suffered the Holy Inquisition to be established in their land, and they were ill acquainted with that form of justice. Informed that Jeanne was in the hands of the Sire de Luxembourg, the Great Council of England were unanimously in favour of her being purchased at any price. Various lords recommended that as soon as they obtained possession of the Maid she should be sewn in a sack and cast into the river. But one of them (it is said to have been the Earl of Warwick) represented to them that she ought first to be tried, convicted of heresy and witchcraft by an ecclesiastical tribunal, and then solemnly degraded in order that her king might be degraded with her. What a disgrace for Charles of Valois, calling himself King of France, if the University of Paris, if the French ecclesiastical dignitaries, bishops, abbots, canons, if in short the Church Universal were to declare that a witch had sat in his council and that a witch led his host, that one possessed had conducted him to his impious, sacrilegious and void anointing! Thus would the trial of the Maid be the trial of Charles VII, the condemnation of the Maid the condemnation of Charles VII. The idea seemed good to them and was adopted.

Early in August, the Sire de Luxembourg had the Maid taken from Beaulieu, which was not safe enough, to Beaurevoir, near Cambrai. There dwelt Dame Jeanne de Luxembourg and Dame Jeanne de Béthune.

These two ladies treated Jeanne kindly. They offered her woman's clothes or cloth with which to make them; and they urged her to abandon a dress which appeared to them unseemly. Jeanne refused, alleging that she had not received permission from Our Lord and that it was not yet time; later she admitted that had she been able to quit man's attire, she would have done so at the request of these two dames rather than for any other dame of France, the queen excepted.

Confined in the castle keep, Jeanne's mind was for ever running on her return to her friends at Compiègne; her one idea was to escape. Somehow there reached her evil tidings from France. She got the idea that all the inhabitants of Compiègne over seven years of age were to be massacred, 'to perish by fire and sword,' she said; and indeed such a fate was bound to overtake them if the town were taken.

What she had heard of their fate caused her infinite distress; she herself would rather die than continue to live after such a destruction of worthy people. For this reason she was strongly tempted to leap from the top of the keep. And because she knew all that could be said against it, she heard her Voices putting her in mind of those arguments.

Nearly every day, Saint Catherine said to her: 'Do not leap, God will help both you and those of Compiègne.'

And Jeanne replied to her: 'Since God will help those of Compiègne, I want to be there.'

One day she heard a rumour that the English had come to fetch her. Straightway Jeanne became frantic and beside herself. She ceased to listen to her Voices, who forbade her the fatal leap. The keep was at least 21 metres (70 feet) high; she commended her soul to God and leapt.

Having fallen to the ground, she heard cries: 'She is dead.'

The guards hurried to the spot. Finding her still alive, in their amazement they could only ask: 'Did you leap?'

She felt sorely shaken; but Saint Catherine spoke to her and said: 'Be of good courage. You will recover.'

Henceforth Jeanne believed that it was her saints who had helped her and guarded her from death. She knew well that she had been wrong in attempting such a leap, despite her Voices.

Saint Catherine said to her: 'You must confess and ask God to forgive you for having leapt.'

Jeanne did confess and ask pardon of Our Lord. And after her confession Saint Catherine made known unto her that God had forgiven her. For three or four days she remained without eating or drinking; then she took some food and was whole.

Whether Jeanne was or was not aided by the devil was a matter to be decided between herself and the doctors of the church. But it is certain that her one thought was to burst her bonds, and that she was ceaselessly imagining means of escape.

Chapter X
Beaurevoir – Arras – Rouen – The Trial for Lapse

✚

A T THAT TIME IT WAS rare for prisoners to be kept in isolation. At Arras, Jeanne received visitors; and among others, a Scotsman, who showed her her portrait, in which she was represented kneeling on one knee and presenting a letter to her king. This letter might be supposed to have been from the Sire de Baudricourt, or from any other clerk or captain by whom the painter may have thought Jeanne to have been sent to the Dauphin; it might have been a letter announcing to the king the deliverance of Orléans or the victory of Patay.

This was the only portrait of herself Jeanne ever saw and, for her own part, she never had any painted; but during the brief duration of her power, the inhabitants of the French towns placed images of her, carved and painted, in the chapels of the saints, and wore leaden medals on which she was represented; thus in her case following a custom established in honour of the saints canonised by the Church.

Many Burgundian lords, and among them a knight, one Jean de Pressy, Controller of the Finances of Burgundy, offered her woman's dress, as the Luxembourg dame had done, for her own good and in order to avoid scandal; but for nothing in the world would Jeanne have cast off the garb which she had assumed according to divine command.

Neither the capture of the Maid nor the retreat of the men-at-arms she had brought, put an end to the siege of Compiègne.

At length, about the middle of November Jeanne was delivered up to the English. It was decided to take her to Rouen, through Ponthieu, along the seashore, through the north of Normandy, where there would be less risk of falling in with the scouts of the various parties.

From Arras she was taken to the Château of Drugy, where the monks of Saint-Riquier were said to have visited her in prison. She was afterwards taken to Crotoy, where the castle walls were washed by the ocean waves. The Duke of Alençon, whom she called her fair duke, had been imprisoned there after the Battle of Verneuil. At the time of her arrival, Maître Nicolas Gueuville, Chancellor of the Cathedral church of Notre Dame d'Amiens, was a prisoner in that castle in the hands of the English. He heard her confess and administered the Communion to her. It was said that the damsels and burgesses of Abbeville went to see her in the castle where she was imprisoned.

The doctors and masters of the university pursued her with a bitterness hardly credible. Filled with faith and zeal for the avenging of God's honour, these clerks were, as they said, always ready to burn witches. They feared the devil; but, perchance, though they may not have admitted it even to themselves, they feared him 20 times more when he was Armagnac.

Jeanne was taken out of Crotoy at high tide and conveyed by boat to Saint-Valery, then to Dieppe, as is supposed, and certainly in the end to Rouen.

She was conducted to the old castle, built in the time of Philippe-Auguste on the slope of the Bouvreuil hill. Jeanne was placed in a tower looking on to the open country. Her room was on the middle storey, between the dungeon and the state apartment. It extended over the whole of that floor, which was 13 metres (43 feet) across, including the walls. A stone staircase approached it at an angle. There was but a dim light, for some of the window slits had been filled in. On her feet they put shackles and round her waist a chain padlocked to a beam nearly two metres (five or six feet) long. At night this chain was carried over the foot of her bed and attached to the principal beam.

Five English men-at-arms guarded the prisoner. They mocked her and she rebuked them, a circumstance they must have found consolatory. At night two of them stayed behind the door; three remained with her, and constantly troubled her by saying first that she would die, then that she would be delivered. No one could speak to her without their consent.

Nevertheless, folk entered the prison as if it were a fair; people of all ranks came to see Jeanne as they pleased.

Maître Pierre Manuel felt called upon to tell her that for certain she would never have come there if she had not been brought. Sensible persons were always surprised when they saw witches and soothsayers falling into a trap like any ordinary Christian. The king's advocate must have been a sensible person, since his surprise appeared in the questions he put to Jeanne.

'Did you know you were to be taken?' he asked her.

'I thought it likely,' she replied.

'Then why,' asked Maître Pierre again, 'if you thought it likely, did you not take better care on the day you were captured?'

'I knew neither the day nor the hour when I should be taken, nor when it should happen.'

The Sire Jean de Luxembourg came to Rouen.

'Jeanne,' said the Sire de Luxembourg, 'I have come to ransom you if you will promise never again to bear arms against us.'

These words do not accord with our knowledge of the negotiation for the purchase of the Maid. They seem to indicate that even then the contract was not complete, or at any rate that the vendor thought he could break it if he chose. But the most remarkable point about the Sire de Luxembourg's speech is the condition on which he says he will ransom the Maid. He asks her to promise never again to fight against England and Burgundy. From these words it would seem to have been his intention to sell her to the King of France or to his representative.

There is no evidence, however, of this speech having made any impression on the English. Jeanne set no store by it.

'In God's name, you do but jest,' she replied 'for I know well that it lieth neither within your will nor within your power.'

It is related that when he persisted in his statement, she replied:

'I know that these English will put me to death, believing that afterwards they will conquer France.'

Since she certainly did not believe it, it seems highly improbable that she should have said that the English would have put her to death. Throughout the trial she was expecting, on the faith of her Voices, to be delivered. She knew not how or when that deliverance would come to pass, but she was as certain of it as of the presence of Our Lord in the Holy Sacrament. She may have said to the Sire de Luxembourg: 'I know that the English want to put me to death.' Then she repeated courageously what she had already said a thousand times:

'But were there one hundred thousand *Godons* more than at present, they would not conquer the kingdom.'

On hearing these words, the Earl of Stafford unsheathed his sword and the Earl of Warwick had to restrain his hand. That the English Constable of France should have raised his sword against a woman in chains would be incredible.

On the 3rd of January, 1431, by royal decree, King Henry ordered the Maid to be given up to the Bishop and Count of Beauvais, reserving to himself the right to bring her before him, if she should be acquitted by the ecclesiastical tribunal.

'You must do the king good service. It is our intention to institute an elaborate prosecution against this Jeanne.'

As to the king's service, the Lord Bishop did not mean that it should be rendered at the expense of justice; he was a man of some priestly pride and was not likely to reveal his own evil designs. If he spoke thus, it was because in France, for a century at least, the jurisdiction of the Inquisition had been regarded as the jurisdiction of the king

Charged by the bishop to choose another registrar to assist him, Guillaume Manchon selected as his colleague Guillaume Colles, surnamed Boisguillaume, who like him was a notary of the Church.

Jean Massieu, priest, ecclesiastical dean of Rouen, was appointed usher of the court.

In that kind of trial, which was very common in those days, there were strictly only two judges, the Ordinary and the Inquisitor. But it was the custom for the bishop to summon as councillors and assessors persons learned in both canon and civil law. The number and the rank of those councillors varied according to the case.

On Tuesday, the 9th of January, my Lord of Beauvais summoned eight councillors to his house: the abbots of Fécamp and of Jumièges, the prior of Longueville, the canons Roussel, Venderès, Barbier, Coppequesne and Loiseleur.

'Before entering upon the prosecution of this woman,' he said to them, 'we have judged it good, maturely and fully to confer with men learned and skilled in law, human and divine, of whom, thank God, there be great number in this city of Rouen.'

The opinion of the doctors and masters was that information should be collected concerning the deeds and sayings publicly imputed to this woman.

The Lord Bishop informed them that already certain information had been obtained by his command, and that he had decided to order more to be collected, which would be ultimately presented to the council.

It is certain that a scribe of Andelot in Champagne, Nicolas Bailly, requisitioned by Messire Jean de Torcenay, Bailie of Chaumont for King Henry, went to Domremy, and with Gérard Petit, provost of Andelot, and divers mendicant monks, made inquiry touching Jeanne's life and reputation.

Abundant information was forthcoming, not only from Lorraine and from Paris, but from the districts loyal to King Charles, from Lagny, Beauvais, Reims and even from so far as Touraine and Berry; which was information enough to burn 10 heretics and 20 witches. Devilries were discovered which filled the priests with horror: the finding of a lost cup and gloves, the exposure of an immoral priest, the sword of Saint Catherine, the restoration of a child to life. There was also a report of a rash letter concerning the Pope and there were many other indications of witchcraft, heresy and religious error. Such information was not to be included among the documents of the trial. It was the custom of the Holy Inquisition to keep secret the evidence and even the names of the witnesses. In this case the Bishop of Beauvais might have pleaded as an excuse for so doing the safety of the deponents, who might have suffered had he published information gathered in provinces subject to the Dauphin Charles. Even if their names were concealed, they would be identified by their evidence. For the purposes of the trial, Jeanne's own conversation in prison was the best source of information: she spoke much and without any of the reserve which prudence might have dictated.

A painter, whose name is unknown, came to see her in her tower. He asked her aloud and before her guards what arms she bore, as if he wished to represent her with her escutcheon. In those days portraits were very seldom painted from life, except of persons of very high rank, and they were generally represented kneeling and with clasped hands in an attitude of prayer. Though in Flanders and in Burgundy there may have been a few portraits bearing no signs of devotion, they were very rare. A portrait naturally suggested a person praying to God, to the Holy Virgin, or to some saint. Wherefore the idea of painting the Maid's picture doubtless must have met with the stern disapproval of her ecclesiastical judges. All the more so because they must have feared that the painter would represent this excommunicated woman in the guise of a saint, canonised by the Church, as the Armagnacs were wont to do.

A careful consideration of this incident inclines us to think that this man was no painter but a spy. Jeanne told him of the arms which the king had granted to her brothers: an azure shield bearing a sword between two golden *fleurs de lis*. And our suspicion is confirmed when at the trial she is reproached with pomp and vanity for having caused her arms to be painted.

One visitor, a Maître Nicolas Loiseleur, confided to her that he, like herself, was a native of the Lorraine Marches, a shoemaker by trade, one who held to the French party and had been taken prisoner by the English. From King Charles he brought her tidings which were the fruit of his own imagination. Thus having won her confidence, the pseudo-shoemaker asked her sundry questions concerning the angels and saints who visited her. She answered him confidingly, speaking as friend to friend, as countryman to countryman. He gave her counsel, advising her not to believe all these churchmen and not to do all that they asked her; 'For,' he said, 'if thou believest in them thou shalt be destroyed.'

Many a time did Nicolas Loiseleur act the part of the Lorraine shoemaker. Afterwards he dictated to the registrars all that Jeanne had said, providing thus a valuable source of information of which a memorandum was made to be used during the examination. It would even appear that during certain of these visits the registrars were stationed at a peep-hole in an adjoining room.

He may not have been proud of such deceptions, but at any rate he made no secret of them. Afterwards the registrars pretended that it had been extremely repugnant to them thus to overhear in hiding a conversation so craftily contrived.

The duty of registrars was laid down in the following manner:

'Matters shall be ordained thus, that certain persons shall be stationed in a suitable place so as to surprise the confidences of heretics and to overhear their words.'

Maître Nicolas Loiseleur also often came to her in monkish dress. In this guise he inspired her with great confidence; she confessed to him devoutly and had no other confessor. She saw him sometimes as a shoemaker and sometimes as a canon and never perceived that he was the same person. Wherefore we must indeed believe her to have been incredibly simple in certain respects; and these great theologians must have realised that it was not difficult to deceive her.

Then they resolved that the Bishop of Beauvais should order a preliminary inquiry as to the deeds and sayings of Jeanne.

On Tuesday, the 13th of February, Jean d'Estivet, called Bénédicité, promoter, Jean de la Fontaine, Commissioner, Boisguillaume and Manchon, Registrars and Jean Massieu, Usher, took the oath faithfully to discharge their various offices. Then straightway Maître Jean de la Fontaine, assisted by two registrars, proceeded to the preliminary inquiry.

On Monday, the 19th of February, at eight o'clock in the morning, the doctors and masters assembled, to the number of 11, in the house of the Bishop of Beauvais; there they heard the reading of the articles and the preliminary information. Whereupon they gave it as their opinion, and, in conformity with this opinion, the bishop decided that there was matter sufficient to justify the woman called the Maid being cited and charged touching a question of faith.

But now a fresh difficulty arose. In such a trial it was necessary for the accused to appear at once before the Ordinary and before the Inquisitor. The two judges were equally necessary for the validity of the trial. Now the Grand Inquisitor for the realm of France, Brother Jean Graverent, was then at Saint-Lô, prosecuting on a religious charge a citizen of the town, one Jean Le Couvreur. In the absence of Brother Jean Graverent, the Bishop of Beauvais had invited the Vice Inquisitor for the diocese of Rouen to proceed against Jeanne conjointly with himself. Meanwhile the Vice Inquisitor seemed not to understand; he made no response; and the bishop was left in embarrassment with his lawsuit on his hands.

This Vice Inquisitor was Brother Jean Lemaistre, Prior of the Dominicans of Rouen, bachelor of theology, a monk right prudent and scrupulous. At length in answer to a summons from the Usher, at four o'clock on the 19th of February, he appeared in the house of the Bishop of Beauvais. He declared himself ready to intervene provided that he had the right to do so, which he doubted. As the reason for his uncertainty he alleged that he was the Inquisitor of Rouen. He declared that he would ask the Grand Inquisitor of France for an authorisation which should hold good for the diocese of Beauvais. Meanwhile he consented to act in order to satisfy his own conscience and to prevent the proceedings from lapsing, which, in the opinion of all, must have ensued had the trial been instituted without the concurrence of the Holy Inquisition. All preliminary difficulties were now removed. The Maid was cited to appear on Wednesday, the 21st of February, 1431.

On that day, at eight o'clock in the morning, the Bishop of Beauvais, the Vicar of the Inquisitor, and 41 councillors and assessors assembled in the castle chapel. Fifteen of them were doctors in theology, five doctors in civil and canon law, six bachelors in theology, 11 bachelors in canon law, four licentiates in civil law. The bishop sat as judge. At his side were the councillors and assessors, clothed either in the fine camlet of canons or in the coarse cloth of mendicants, expressive, the one of sacerdotal solemnity, the other of evangelical meekness. Some glared fiercely, others cast down their eyes. Brother Jean Lemaistre, Vice Inquisitor of the Faith, was among them, silent, in the black and white livery of poverty and obedience.

Before bringing in the accused, the usher informed the bishop that Jeanne, to whom the citation had been delivered, had replied that she would be willing to appear, but she demanded that an equal number of ecclesiastics of the French party should be added to those of the English party. She requested also the permission to hear mass. The bishop refused both demands; and Jeanne was brought in, dressed as a man, with her feet in shackles. She was made to sit down at the table of the registrars.

And now from the very outset these theologians and this damsel regarded each other with mutual horror and hatred. Contrary to the custom of her sex, a custom which even loose women did not dare to infringe, she displayed her hair, which was brown and cut short over the ears. It was possibly the first time that some of those young monks seated behind their elders had ever seen a woman's hair. She wore hose like a youth. To them her dress appeared immodest and abominable. She exasperated and irritated them. This man's attire brought before their minds the works performed by the Maid in the camp of the Dauphin Charles, calling himself king. By the stroke of a magic wand she had deprived the English men-at-arms of all their strength, and thereby she had inflicted sore hurt on the majority of the churchmen who were to judge her. Some among them were thinking of the benefices of which she had despoiled them; others, doctors and masters of the university, recalled how she had been about to lay Paris waste with fire and sword; others again, canons and abbots, could not forgive her perchance for having struck fear into their hearts even in remote Normandy. Was it possible for them to pardon the havoc she had thus wrought in a great part of the Church of France, when they knew she had done it by sorcery, by divination and by invoking devils? As they were very learned, they saw magicians and wizards where others would never have suspected them; they held that to doubt the power of demons over men and things was not only heretical and impious, but tending to subvert the whole natural and social order. These doctors, seated in the castle chapel, had burned each one of them 10, 20, 50 witches, all of whom had confessed their crimes. Would it not have been madness after that to doubt the existence of witches?

To us it seems curious that beings capable of causing hailstorms and casting spells over men and animals should allow themselves to be taken, judged, tortured, and burned without making any defence; but it was constantly occurring; every ecclesiastical judge must have observed it. Very learned men were able to account for it: they explained that wizards and witches lost their power as soon as they fell into the hands of churchmen. The hapless Maid had lost her power like the others; they feared her no longer.

At least Jeanne hated them as bitterly as they hated her. It was natural for unlettered saints, for the fair inspired, frank of mind, capricious and enthusiastic to feel an antipathy towards doctors all inflated with knowledge and stiffened with scholasticism. Such an antipathy Jeanne had recently felt towards clerks, even when as at Poitiers they had been on the French side, and had not wished her evil and had not greatly troubled her. Wherefore we may easily imagine how intense was the repulsion with which the clerks of Rouen now inspired her. She knew that they sought to compass her death. But she feared them not; confidently she awaited from her saints and angels the fulfilment of their promise, their coming for her deliverance. She knew not when nor how her deliverance should come; but that come it would she never once doubted.

The bishop required her to swear, according to the prescribed form with both hands on the holy Gospels, that she would reply truly to all that should be asked her.

She could not. Her Voices forbade her telling any one of the revelations they had so abundantly vouchsafed to her.

She answered: 'I do not know on what you wish to question me. You might ask me things that I would not tell you.'

And when the bishop insisted on her swearing to tell the whole truth:

'Touching my father and mother and what I did after my coming into France I will willingly swear,' she said; 'but touching God's revelations to me, those I have neither told nor communicated to any man, save to Charles my king. And nought of them will I reveal, were I to lose my head for it.'

Then, either because she wished to gain time or because she counted on receiving some new directions from her *council*, she added that in a week she would know whether she might so reveal those things.

At length she took the oath, according to the prescribed form, on her knees, with both hands on the missal. Then she answered concerning her name, her country, her parents, her baptism, her godfathers and godmothers. She said that to the best of her knowledge she was about nineteen years of age.

Questioned concerning her education, she replied: 'From my mother I learnt my Paternoster, my Ave Maria and my Credo.'

But, asked to repeat her Paternoster, she refused, for, she said, she would only say it in confession. This was because she wanted the bishop to hear her confess.

The assembly was profoundly agitated; all spoke at once. Jeanne with her soft voice had scandalised the doctors.

The bishop forbade her to leave her prison, under pain of being convicted of the crime of heresy.

She refused to submit to this prohibition. 'If I did escape,' she said, 'none could reproach me with having broken faith, for I never gave my word to anyone.'

Afterwards she complained of her chains.

The bishop told her they were on account of her attempt to escape.

She agreed: 'It is true that I wanted to escape, and I still want to, just like every other prisoner.'

Such a confession was very bold, if she had rightly understood the judge when he said that by flight from prison she would incur the punishment of a heretic. To escape from an ecclesiastical prison was to commit a crime against the Church, but it was folly as well as crime; for the prisons of the Church are penitentiaries, and the prisoner who refuses salutary penance is as foolish as he is guilty; for he is like a sick man who refuses to be cured. But Jeanne was not, strictly speaking, in an ecclesiastical prison; she was in the castle of Rouen, a prisoner of war in the hands of the English. Could it be said that if she escaped she would incur excommunication and the spiritual and temporal penalties inflicted on the enemies of religion? There lay the difficulty. The Lord Bishop removed it forthwith by an elaborate legal fiction. Three English men-at-arms, John Grey, John Berwoist and William Talbot, were appointed by the king to be Jeanne's custodians. The bishop, acting as an ecclesiastical judge, himself delivered to them their charge, and made them swear on the holy Gospels to bind the damsel and confine her. In this wise the Maid became the prisoner of our holy Mother, the Church; and she could not burst her bonds without falling into heresy. The second sitting was appointed for the next day, the 22nd of February.

Chapter XI
The Trial for Lapse (*continued*)

WHEN A RECORD OF THE PROCEEDINGS came to be written down after the first sitting, a dispute arose between the ecclesiastical notaries and the two or three royal registrars who had likewise

taken down the replies of the accused. As might be expected, the two records differed in several places. It was decided that on the contested points Jeanne should be further examined. The notaries of the Church complained also that they experienced great difficulty in seizing Jeanne's words on account of the constant interruptions of the bystanders.

Jeanne was brought in by the Usher, Messire Jean Massieu. Again she endeavoured to avoid taking the oath to tell everything; but she had to swear on the Gospel.

She was examined by Maître Jean Beaupère, doctor in theology. In his University of Paris he was regarded as a scholar of light and leading.

Interrogated as to the occupations of her childhood, she replied that she was busy with household duties and seldom went into the fields with the cattle.

'For spinning and sewing,' she said, 'I am as good as any woman in Rouen.'

In order to take her unawares, Maître Jean Beaupère proceeded without method, passing abruptly from one subject to another. Suddenly he spoke of her Voices. She gave him the following reply:

'Being thirteen years of age, I heard the Voice of God, bidding me lead a good life. And the first time I was sore afeard. And the Voice came almost at the hour of noon, in summer, in my father's garden....'

She heard the Voice on the right towards the church. Rarely did she hear it without seeing a light. This light was in the direction whence the Voice came.

Thinking to embarrass Jeanne, he asked how she came to see the light if it appeared at her side. Jeanne made no reply, and as if distraught, she said:

'If I were in a wood I should easily hear the Voices coming towards me.... It seems to me to be a Voice right worthy. I believe that this Voice was sent to me by God. After having heard it three times I knew it to be the voice of an angel.'

'What instruction did this Voice give you for the salvation of your soul?'

'It taught me to live well, to go to church, and it told me to fare forth into France.'

In the beginning of her career, she believed that Our Lord, the true King of France, had ordained her to deliver the government of the realm to Charles of Valois, as His deputy. Interrogated concerning her coming to Chinon, she replied:

'Without let or hindrance I went to my king. When I reached the town of Sainte-Catherine de Fierbois, I sent first to the town of Château-Chinon, where my king was. I arrived there about the hour of noon and lodged in an inn, and, after dinner, I went to my king who was in his castle.'

With regard to this audience in the castle of Chinon, she told her judges she had recognized the king as she had recognized the Sire de Baudricourt, by revelation.

The interrogator asked her: 'When the Voice revealed your king to you, was there any light?'

'Saw you any angel above the king?'

She refused to reply.

She never spoke of her Voices without describing them as her refuge and relief, her consolation and her joy.

And the Maid added: 'Never have I required of them any other final reward than the salvation of my soul.'

The examination ended with a capital charge: the attack on Paris on a feast day. It was in this connection possibly that Brother Jacques of Touraine, a friar of the Franciscan order, who from time to time put a question, asked Jeanne whether she had ever been in a place where Englishmen were being slain.

'In God's name, was I ever in such a place?' Jeanne responded vehemently. 'How glibly you speak. Why did they not depart from France and go into their own country?'

A nobleman of England, who was in the chamber, on hearing these words, said to his neighbours: 'By my troth she is a good woman. Why is she not English?'

At the third sitting, held in the Robing Chamber, there were present 62 assessors, of whom 20 were new.

Jeanne showed a greater repugnance than before to swearing on the holy Gospels to reply to all that should be asked her. In charity the bishop warned her that this obstinate refusal caused her to be suspected, and he required her to swear, under pain of being convicted upon all the charges.

Still the bishop failed to force an unconditional oath from the Maid; she swore to tell the truth on all she knew concerning the trial, reserving to herself the right to be silent on everything which in her opinion did not concern it.

Maître Jean Beaupère asked her whether she saw anything when she heard her Voices.

She replied: 'I cannot tell you everything. I am not permitted. The Voice is good and worthy.... To this question I am not bound to reply.'

And she asked them to give her in writing the points concerning which she had not given an immediate reply.

What use did she intend to make of this writing? She did not know how to read; she had no counsel.

Maître Beaupère asked: 'Do you know whether you stand in God's grace?'

This was an extremely insidious question; it placed Jeanne in the dilemma of having to avow herself sinful or of appearing unpardonably bold. One of the assessors, Maître Jean Lefèvre of the Order of the Hermit Friars, observed that she was not bound to reply. There was murmuring throughout the chamber.

But Jeanne said: 'If I be not, then may God bring me into it; if I be, then may God keep me in it.'

The assessors were astonished at so ready an answer. And yet no improvement ensued in their disposition towards her. They admitted that touching her king she spoke well, but for the rest she was too subtle, and with a subtlety peculiar to women.

Maître Jean Beaupère asked: 'Jeanne, will you have a woman's dress?'

She answered: 'Give me one; and I will accept it and depart. Otherwise I will not have it. I will be content with this one, since God is pleased for me to wear it.'

On this reply, which contained two errors tending to heresy, the Lord Bishop adjourned the court.

Maître Jean Beaupère, as on the previous Saturday, was curious to know whether Jeanne had heard her Voices. She heard them every day.

He asked her: 'Is it an angel's voice that speaketh unto you, or the voice of a woman saint or of a man saint? Or is it God speaking without an interpreter?'

Said Jeanne: 'This voice is the voice of Saint Catherine and of Saint Margaret; and on their heads are beautiful crowns, right rich and right precious. I am permitted to tell you so by Messire. If you doubt it send to Poitiers, where I was examined.'

She was right in appealing to the clerks of France. The Armagnac doctors had no less authority in matters of faith than the English and Burgundian doctors. Were they not all to meet at the council?

When she was asked whether her saints were both clothed alike, whether they were of the same age, whether they spoke at once, whether one of them appeared before the other, she refused to reply, saying she had not permission to do so.

She was asked whether she had received permission from God to go into France and whether God had commanded her to put on man's dress.

By keeping silence on this point she became liable to be suspected of heresy, and however she replied she laid herself open to serious charges – she either took upon herself homicide and abomination, or she attributed it to God, which manifestly was to blaspheme.

Then they passed on to the sword she had captured from a Burgundian.

'I wore it at Compiègne,' she said, 'because it was good for dealing sound clouts and good buffets.' The buffet was a flat blow, the clout was a side stroke. Some moments later, on the subject of her banner, she said that, in order to avoid killing anyone, she bore it herself when they charged the enemy. And she added: 'I have never slain anyone.'

The examinations were long; they lasted between three and four hours. Before closing this one, Maître Jean Beaupère wished to know whether Jeanne had been wounded at Orléans. This was an interesting point. It was generally admitted that witches lost their power when they shed blood.

A famous Norman clerk, Maître Jean Lohier, having come to Rouen, the Count Bishop of Beauvais commanded that he should be informed concerning the trial.

'Have you seen anything of the records of the trial?'

'I have,' replied Maître Jean. 'This trial is void. It is impossible to support it on many grounds: firstly, it is not in regular form.'

'Secondly,' continued Maître Jean Lohier, 'the judges and assessors when they are trying this case are shut up in the castle, where they are not free to utter their opinions frankly. Thirdly, the trial involves divers persons who are not called, notably it touches the reputation of the King of France, to whose party Jeanne belonged, yet neither he nor his representative is cited. Fourthly, neither documents nor definite written charges have been produced, wherefore this woman, this simple girl, is left to reply without guidance to so many masters, to such great doctors and on such grave matters, especially those concerning her revelations. For all these reasons the trial appears to me to be invalid.' Then he added: 'You see how they proceed. They will catch her if they can in her words. They take advantage of the statements in which she says, "I know for certain," concerning her apparitions. But if she were to say, "It seems to me," instead of "I know for certain," it is my opinion that no man could convict her. I perceive that the dominant sentiment which actuates them is one of hatred. Their intention is to bring her to her death. Wherefore I shall stay here no longer. I cannot witness it.'

The fifth session of the court took place in the usual chamber on the 1st of March, in the presence of 58 assessors, of whom nine had not sat previously.

In her prison the Maid prophesied before her guard, John Grey. Informed of these prophecies, the judges wished to hear them from Jeanne's own mouth.

'Before seven years have passed,' she said to them, 'the English shall lose a greater wager than any they lost at Orléans. They shall lose everything in France. They shall suffer greater loss than ever they have suffered in France, and that shall come to pass because God shall vouchsafe unto the French great victory.'

'How do you know this?'

'I know it by revelation made unto me and that this shall befall within seven years. And greatly should I sorrow were it further delayed. I know it by revelation as surely as I know that you are before my eyes at this moment.'

'When shall this come to pass?'

'I know neither the day nor the hour.'

'But the year?'

'That ye shall not know for the present. But I should wish it to be before Saint John's Day.'

They also wanted to make her admit that she had caused herself to be honoured as a saint. She disconcerted them by the following reply: 'The poor folk came to me readily, because I did them no hurt, but aided them to the best of my power.'

Then the examination ranged over many and various subjects: Friar Richard; the children Jeanne had held over the baptismal fonts; the good wives of the town of Reims who touched rings with her; the butterflies caught in a standard at Château Thierry.

In this town, certain of the Maid's followers were said to have caught butterflies in her standard. Now doctors in theology knew for a certainty that necromancers sacrificed butterflies to the devil.

Then the Lord Bishop declared the examination concluded. He added, however, that should it appear expedient to interrogate Jeanne more fully, certain doctors and masters would be appointed for that purpose.

Accordingly, on Saturday, March the 10th, Maître Jean de la Fontaine, the bishop's commissioner, went to the prison. He was accompanied by Nicolas Midi, Gérard Feuillet, Jean Fécard and Jean Massieu. She was examined concerning the paintings on her standard, and she replied:

'Saint Catherine and Saint Margaret bade me take the standard and bear it boldly, and have painted upon it the King of Heaven. And this, much against my will, I told to my king. Touching its meaning I know nought else.'

They tried to make her out avaricious, proud and ostentatious because she possessed a shield and arms, a stable, chargers, demi-chargers and hackneys, and because she had money with which to pay her household, some 10,000 or 12,000 livres. But the point on which they questioned her most closely was the sign which had already been twice discussed in the public examinations. On this subject the doctors displayed an insatiable curiosity. For the sign was the exact reverse of the coronation at Reims; it was an anointing, not with divine unction but with magic charm, the crowning of the King of France by a witch.

Chapter XII
The Trial for Lapse (*continued*)

✠

ON MONDAY, THE 12TH OF MARCH, Brother Jean Lemaistre received from Brother Jean Graverent, Inquisitor of France, an order to proceed against and to pronounce the final sentence on a certain woman, named Jeanne, commonly called the Maid. On that same day,

in the morning, Maître Jean de la Fontaine, in presence of the bishop, for the second time examined Jeanne in her prison. [He asked her many of the same questions from the previous interview.]

Then they reverted to the question of her wearing man's dress.

'Which would you prefer, to wear a woman's dress and hear mass, or to continue in man's dress and not to hear mass?'

'Promise me that I shall hear mass if I am in woman's dress, and then I will answer you.'

'I promise you that you shall hear mass when you are in woman's dress.'

'And what do you say if I have promised and sworn to our king not to put off these clothes? Nevertheless, I say unto you: "Have me a robe made, long enough to touch the ground, but without a train. I will go to mass in it; then, when I come back, I will return to my present clothes."'

'You must wear woman's dress altogether and without conditions.'

'Send me a dress like that worn by your burgess's daughters, to wit, a long *houppelande*; and I will take it and even a woman's hood to go and hear mass. But with all my heart I entreat you to leave me these clothes I am now wearing, and let me hear mass without changing anything.'

Her aversion to putting off man's dress is not to be explained solely by the fact that this dress preserved her best against the violence of the men-at-arms; it is possible that no such objection existed. She was averse to wearing woman's dress because she had not received permission from her Voices; and we may easily divine why not. Was she not a chieftain of war? How humiliating for such an one to wear petticoats like a townsman's wife!

Then they came to the question which they held to be the most difficult of all:

'If the devil were to take upon himself the form of an angel, how would you know whether he were a good angel or a bad?'

She replied with a simplicity which appeared presumptuous: 'I should easily discern whether it were Saint Michael or an imitation of him.'

Once again, the examiner put to Jeanne that question on which her life or death depended:

'Will you submit all your deeds and sayings, good or bad, to the judgment of our mother, Holy Church?'

'As for the Church, I love her and would maintain her with all my power, for religion's sake,' the Maid replied; 'and I am not one to be kept from church and from hearing mass. But as for the good works which I have wrought, and touching my coming, for them I must give an account to the King of Heaven, who has sent me to Charles, son of Charles, King of France.'

'Will you submit to the judgment of the Church?'

'I appeal to Our Lord, who hath sent me, to Our Lady and to all the blessed saints in Paradise. To my mind Our Lord and his Church are one, and no distinction should be made. Wherefore do you essay to make out that they are not one?'

In justice to Maître Jean de la Fontaine we are bound to admit the lucidity of his reply. 'There is the Church Triumphant, in which are God, his saints, the angels and the souls that are saved,' he said. 'There is also the Church Militant, which is our Holy Father, the Pope, the Vicar of God on earth; the cardinals, the prelates of the Church and the clergy, with all good Christians and Catholics; and this Church in its assembly cannot err, for it is moved by the Holy Ghost. Will you appeal to the Church Militant?'

'I am come to the King of France from God, from the Virgin Mary and all the blessed saints in Paradise and from the Church Victorious above and by their command. To this Church I submit all the good deeds I have done and shall do. As to replying whether I will submit to the Church Militant, for the present, I will make no further answer.'

Again she was offered a woman's dress in which to hear mass; she refused it.

At this point the examination was adjourned. The last interrogation in the prison took place after dinner. She had now endured 15 in 25 days, but her courage never flagged.

Now that the inquiries and examinations were concluded, it was announced that the preliminary trial was at an end. The so-called trial in ordinary opened on the Tuesday after Palm Sunday, the 27th of March, in a room near the great hall of the castle.

Before ordering the deed of accusation to be read, my Lord of Beauvais offered Jeanne the aid of an advocate. If this offer had been postponed till then, it was doubtless because in his opinion Jeanne had not previously needed such aid. It is well known that a heretic's advocate, if he would himself escape falling into heresy, must strictly limit his methods of defence.

We may notice that my Lord of Beauvais offered the accused an advocate on the ground of her ignorance of things divine and human, but without taking her youthfulness into account. In other courts of law proceedings against a minor – that is, a person under 25 – who was not assisted by an advocate, were legally void.

Jeanne did not accept the judge's offer: 'First,' she said, 'touching what you admonish me for my good and in matters of religion, I thank you and the company here assembled. As for the advocate you offer me, I also thank you, but it is not my intent to depart from the counsel of Our Lord. As for the oath you wish me to take, I am ready to swear to speak the truth in all that concerns your suit.'

Thereupon Maître Thomas de Courcelles began to read in French the indictment drawn up in 70 articles. This text set forth in order the deeds with which Jeanne had already been reproached and which were groundlessly held to have been confessed by her and duly proved. There were no less than 70 distinct charges of horrible crimes committed against religion and Holy Mother Church. Questioned on each article, Jeanne with heroic candour repeated her previous replies.

On Wednesday, the 9th of May, Jeanne was taken to the great tower of the castle, into the torture-chamber. There my Lord of Beauvais, in the presence of the Vice Inquisitor and nine doctors and masters, read her the articles, to which she had hitherto refused to reply; and he threatened her that if she did not confess the whole truth she would be put to the torture.

The instruments were prepared; the two executioners, Mauger Leparmentier, a married clerk, and his companion, were in readiness close by her, awaiting the bishop's orders.

Six days before Jeanne had received great comfort from her Voices. Now she replied resolutely: 'Verily, if you were to tear my limbs asunder and drive my soul out of my body, naught else would I tell you, and if I did say anything unto you, I would always maintain afterwards that you had dragged it from me by force.'

My Lord of Beauvais decided to defer the torture, fearing that it would do no good to so hardened a subject. On the following Saturday, he deliberated in his house, with the Vice Inquisitor and 13 doctors and masters; opinion was divided. Maître Raoul Roussel advised that Jeanne should not be tortured lest ground for complaint should be given against a trial so carefully conducted. It would seem that he anticipated the Devil's granting Jeanne the gift of taciturnity, whereby in diabolical silence she would be able to brave the tortures of the Holy Inquisition.

On the 28th of April, the university, meeting in its general assembly at Saint-Bernard, charged the Holy Faculty of Theology and the Venerable Faculty of Decrees with the examination of the 12 articles.

According to the Sacred Faculty of Theology, Jeanne's apparitions were fictitious, lying, deceptive, inspired by devils. The sign given to the king was a presumptuous and pernicious lie, derogatory to the dignity of angels. Jeanne's belief in the visitations of Saint Michael, Saint Catherine and Saint Margaret was an error rash and injurious because Jeanne placed it on the same plane as the truths of religion. Jeanne's predictions were but superstitions, idle divinations and vain boasting. Her statement that she wore man's dress by the command of God was blasphemy, a violation of divine law and ecclesiastical sanction, a contemning of the sacraments and tainted with idolatry. In the letters she had dictated, Jeanne appeared treacherous, perfidious, cruel, sanguinary, seditious, blasphemous and in favour of tyranny. In setting out for France she had broken the commandment to honour father and mother, she had given an occasion for scandal, she had committed blasphemy and had fallen from the faith. In the leap from Beaurevoir, she had displayed a pusillanimity bordering on despair and homicide; and, moreover, it had caused her to utter rash statements touching the remission of her sin and erroneous pronouncements concerning free will. By proclaiming her confidence in her salvation, she uttered presumptuous and pernicious lies; by saying that Saint Catherine and Saint Margaret did not speak English, she blasphemed these saints and violated the precept: 'Thou shalt love thy neighbour.' The honours she rendered these saints were nought but idolatry and the worship of devils. Her refusal to submit her doings to the Church tended to schism, to the denial of the unity and authority of the Church and to apostasy.

Meanwhile, where were the clerks of France? Had they nothing to say in this matter? Had they no decision to submit to the Pope and to the council? Why did they not urge their opinions in opposition to those of the Faculties of Paris? Why did they keep silence? Jeanne demanded the record of the Poitiers trial. Wherefore did those Poitiers doctors, who had recommended the king to employ the Maid lest, by rejecting her, he should refuse the gift of the Holy Spirit, fail to send the record to Rouen? Where were Brother Pasquerel, Friar Richard and all those churchmen who but lately surrounded her in France and who looked to go with her to the Crusade against the Bohemians and the Turks? Why did they not demand a safe-conduct and come and give evidence at the trial? Or at least why did they not send their evidence? Why did not the Archbishop of Embrun, who but recently gave such noble counsels to the king, send some written statement in favour of the Maid to the judges at Rouen? My Lord of Reims, Chancellor of the Kingdom, had said that she was proud but not heretical. Wherefore now, acting contrary to his own interests and honour, did he refrain from testifying in favour of her through whom he had recovered his episcopal city? Wherefore did he not assert his right and do his duty as metropolitan and censure and suspend his suffragan, the Bishop of Beauvais, who was guilty of prevarication in the administration of justice? Why did not the illustrious clerics, whom King Charles had appointed deputies at the Council of Bâle, undertake to bring the cause of the Maid before the council? And finally, why did not the priests, the ecclesiastics of the realm, with one voice demand an appeal to the Holy Father?

Chapter XIII
The Abjuration – The First Sentence

✠

ON SATURDAY, THE 19TH OF MAY, the doctors and masters, to the number of 50, assembled in the archiepiscopal chapel of Rouen. There they unanimously declared their agreement with the decision of the University of Paris; and my Lord of Beauvais ordained that a new charitable admonition be addressed to Jeanne. Accordingly, on Wednesday the 23rd, the bishop, the Vice Inquisitor and the Promoter

went to a room in the castle, near Jeanne's cell. They were accompanied by seven doctors and masters, by the Lord Bishop of Noyon and by the Lord Bishop of Thérouanne.

The accused was brought in, and Maître Pierre Maurice, doctor in theology, read to her the 12 articles as they had been abridged and commented upon, in conformity with the deliberations of the university; the whole was drawn up as a discourse addressed to Jeanne directly:

Article I

First, Jeanne, thou saidst that at about the age of thirteen, thou didst receive revelations and behold apparitions of angels and of the Saints, Catherine and Margaret, that thou didst behold them frequently with thy bodily eyes, that they spoke unto thee and do still oftentimes speak unto thee, and that they have said unto thee many things that thou hast fully declared in thy trial.

The clerks of the University of Paris and others have considered the manner of these revelations and apparitions, their object, the substance of the things revealed, the person to whom they were revealed; all points touching them have they considered. And now they pronounce these revelations and apparitions to be either lying fictions, deceptive and dangerous, or superstitions, proceeding from spirits evil and devilish.

Article II

Item, thou hast said that thy King received a sign, by which he knew that thou wast sent of God: to wit that Saint Michael, accompanied by a multitude of angels, certain of whom had wings, others crowns, and with whom were Saint Catherine and Saint Margaret, came to thee in the town of Château-Chinon; and that they all entered with thee and went up the staircase of the castle, into the chamber of thy King, before whom the angel who wore the crown made obeisance. And once didst thou say that this crown which thou callest a sign, was delivered to the Archbishop of Reims who gave it to thy King, in the presence of a multitude of princes and lords whom thou didst call by name.

Now concerning this sign, the aforesaid clerks declare it to lack verisimilitude, to be a presumptuous lie, deceptive, pernicious, a thing counterfeited and attacking the dignity of angels.

Article III

Item, thou hast said that thou knewest the angels and the saints by the good counsel, the comfort and the instruction they gave thee, because they told thee their names and because the saints saluted thee. Thou didst believe also that it was Saint Michael who appeared unto thee; and that the deeds and sayings of this angel and these saints are good thou didst believe as firmly as thou believest in Christ.

Now the clerks declare such signs to be insufficient for the recognition of the said saints and angels.

Article IV

Item, thou hast said thou art assured of certain things which are to come, that thou hast known hidden things, that thou hast also recognized men whom thou hadst never seen before, and this by the Voices of Saint Catherine and Saint Margaret.

Thereupon the clerks declare that in these sayings are superstition, divination, presumptuous assertion and vain boasting.

Article V

Item, thou hast said that by God's command and according to his will, thou hast worn and dost still wear man's apparel. Because thou hast God's commandment to wear this dress thou hast donned a short tunic, jerkin, and hose with many points. Thou dost even wear thy hair cut short above the ears, without keeping about thee anything to denote the feminine sex, save what nature hath given thee. And oftentimes hast thou in this garb received the Sacrament of the Eucharist. And albeit thou hast been many times admonished to leave it, thou wouldest not, saying that thou wouldst liefer [gladly] die than quit this apparel, unless it were by God's command; and that if thou wert still in this dress and with those of thine own party it would be for the great weal of France. Thou sayest also that for nothing wouldst thou take an oath not to wear this dress and bear these arms; and for all this that thou doest thou dost plead divine command.

In such matters the clerks declare that thou blasphemest against God, despising him and his Sacraments, that thou dost transgress divine law, Holy Scripture and the canons of the Church, that thou thinkest evil and dost err from the faith, that thou art full of vain boasting, that thou art addicted to idolatry and worship of thyself and thy clothes, according to the customs of the heathen.

Article VI

Item, thou hast often said, that in thy letters thou hast put these names, Jhesus Maria, and the sign of the cross, to warn those to whom thou didst write not to do what was indicated in the letter. In other letters thou hast boasted that thou wouldst slay all those who did not obey thee, and that by thy blows thou wouldst prove who had God on his side. Also hast thou oftentimes said that all thy deeds were by revelation and according to divine command.

Touching such affirmations the clerks declare thee to be a traitor, perfidious, cruel, desiring human bloodshed, seditious, an instigator of tyranny, a blasphemer of God's commandments and revelations.

Article VII

Item, thou sayest that according to revelations vouchsafed unto thee at the age of seventeen, thou didst leave thy parents' house against their will, driving them almost mad. Thou didst go to Robert de Baudricourt, who, at thy request, gave thee man's apparel and a sword, also men-at-arms to take thee to thy King. And being come to the King, thou didst say unto him that his enemies should be driven away, thou didst promise to bring him into a great kingdom, to make him victorious over his foes, and that for this God had sent thee. These things thou sayest thou didst accomplish in obedience to God and according to revelation.

In such things the clerks declare thee to have been irreverent to thy father and mother, thus disobeying God's command; to have given occasion for scandal, to have blasphemed, to have erred from the faith and to have made a rash and presumptuous promise.

Article VIII

Item, thou hast said, that voluntarily thou didst leap from the Tower of Beaurevoir, preferring rather to die than to be delivered into the hands of the English and to live after the destruction of Compiègne. And albeit Saint Catherine and Saint Margaret forbade thee to leap, thou couldst not restrain thyself. And despite the great sin thou hast committed in offending these saints, thou didst know by thy Voices, that after thy confession, thy sin was forgiven thee.

This deed the clerks declare thee to have committed through cowardice turning to despair and probably to suicide. In this matter likewise thou didst utter a rash and presumptuous statement in asserting that thy sin is forgiven, and thou dost err from the faith touching the doctrine of free will.

Article IX

Item, thou hast said that Saint Catherine and Saint Margaret promised to lead thee to Paradise provided thou didst remain a virgin; and that thou hadst vowed and promised them to cherish thy virginity, and of that thou art as well assured as if already thou hadst entered into the glory of the Blessed. Thou believest that thou hast not committed mortal sin. And it seemeth to thee that if thou wert in mortal sin the saints would not visit thee daily as they do.

Such an assertion the clerks pronounce to be a pernicious lie, presumptuous and rash, that therein lieth a contradiction of what thou hadst previously said, and that finally thy beliefs do err from the true Christian faith.

Article X

Item, thou hast declared it to be within thy knowledge that God loveth certain living persons better than thee, and that this thou hast learnt by revelation from Saint Catherine and Saint Margaret: also that those saints speak French, not English, since they are not on the side of the English. And when thou knewest that thy Voices were for thy King, you didst fall to disliking the Burgundians.

Such matters the clerks pronounce to be a rash and presumptuous assertion, a superstitious divination, a blasphemy uttered against Saint Catherine and Saint Margaret, and a transgression of the commandment to love our neighbours.

Article XI

Item, thou hast said that to those whom thou callest Saint Michael, Saint Catherine and Saint Margaret, thou didst do reverence, bending the knee, taking off thy cap, kissing the ground on which they trod, vowing to them thy virginity: that in the instruction of these saints, whom thou didst invoke and kiss and embrace, thou didst believe as soon as they appeared unto thee, and without seeking counsel from thy priest or from any other ecclesiastic. And, notwithstanding, thou believest that these Voices came from God as firmly as thou believest in the Christian religion and the Passion of Our Lord Jesus Christ. Moreover thou hast said that did any evil spirit appear to thee in the form of Saint Michael thou wouldest know such a spirit and distinguish him from the saint. And again hast thou said, that of thine own accord, thou hast sworn not to reveal the sign thou gavest to thy King. And finally thou didst add: 'Save at God's command.'

Now touching these matters, the clerks affirm that supposing thou hast had the revelations and beheld the apparitions of which thou boastest and in such a manner as thou dost say, then art thou an idolatress, an invoker of demons, an apostate from the faith, a maker of rash statements, a swearer of an unlawful oath.

Article XII

Item, thou hast said that if the Church wished thee to disobey the orders thou sayest God gave thee, nothing would induce thee to do it; that thou knowest that all the deeds of which thou hast been accused in thy trial were wrought according to the command of God and that it was impossible for thee to do otherwise. Touching these deeds, thou dost refuse to submit to the judgment of the Church on earth or of any living man, and will submit therein to God alone. And moreover thou didst declare this reply itself not to be made of thine own accord but by God's command; despite the article of faith: Unam sanctam Ecclesiam catholicam, *having been many times declared unto thee, and notwithstanding that it behoveth all Christians to submit their deeds and sayings to the Church militant especially concerning revelations and such like matters.*

Wherefore the clerks declare thee to be schismatic, disbelieving in the unity and authority of the Church, apostate and obstinately erring from the faith.

Having completed the reading of the articles, Maître Pierre Maurice, on the invitation of the bishop, proceeded to exhort Jeanne. He had been rector of the University of Paris in 1428. He was esteemed an orator.

In terms of calculated simplicity did this illustrious doctor call upon Jeanne to reflect on the effects of her words and sayings, and tenderly did he exhort her to submit to the Church. After the wormwood he offered her the honey; he spoke to her in words kind and familiar. With remarkable adroitness he entered into the feelings and inclinations of the maiden's heart. Seeing her filled with knightly enthusiasm and loyalty to King Charles, whose coronation was her doing, he drew his comparisons from chivalry, thereby essaying to prove to her that she ought rather to believe in the Church Militant than in her Voices and apparitions.

Thus did Maître Pierre Maurice endeavour to make Jeanne understand him. He did not succeed. Against the courage of this child all the reasons and all the eloquence of the world would have availed nothing. When Maître Pierre had finished speaking, Jeanne, being asked whether she did not hold herself bound to submit her deeds and sayings to the Church, replied:

'What I have always held and said in the trial that will I maintain.... If I were condemned and saw the fagots lighted, and the executioner ready to stir the fire, and I in the fire, I would say and maintain till I died nought other than what I said during the trial.'

At these words the bishop declared the discussion at an end, and deferred the pronouncing of the sentence till the morning.

The next day, the Thursday after Whitsuntide and the 24th day of May, early in the morning, Maître Jean Beaupère visited Jeanne in her prison and warned her that she would be shortly taken to the scaffold to hear a sermon.

'If you are a good Christian,' he said, 'you will agree to submit all your deeds and sayings to Holy Mother Church, and especially to the ecclesiastical judges.'

Maître Jean Beaupère thought he heard her reply, 'So I will.'

If such were her answer, then it must have been because, worn out by a flight of agony, her physical courage quailed at the thought of death by burning.

She was taken in a cart and with an armed guard to that part of the town called Bourg-l'Abbé, lying beneath the castle walls. And but a short distance away the cart was stopped, in the cemetery of Saint-Ouen, also called *les aitres Saint-Ouen*. Here it was that Jeanne was to hear the sermon, as so many other unhappy creatures had done before her.

On the great scaffold the two judges, the Lord Bishop and the Vice Inquisitor, took their places. The other scaffold was a kind of pulpit. To it ascended the doctor who, according to the use and custom of the Holy Inquisition was to preach the sermon against Jeanne. He was Maître Guillaume Erard, doctor in theology, canon of the churches of Langres and of Beauvais. At this time, he was very eager to go to Flanders, where he was urgently needed; and he confided to his young servitor, Brother Jean de Lenisoles, that the preaching of this sermon caused him great inconvenience. 'I want to be in Flanders,' he said. 'This affair is very annoying for me.'

From one point of view, however, he must have been pleased to perform this duty, since it afforded him the opportunity of attacking the King of France, Charles VII, and of thereby showing his devotion to the English cause, to which he was strongly attached.

Jeanne, dressed as a man, was brought up and placed at his side, before all the people.

Maître Guillaume Erard began his sermon in the following manner:

'I take as my text the words of God in the Gospel of Saint John, chapter xv: 'The branch cannot bear fruit of itself, except it abide in the vine.' Thus it behoveth all Catholics to remain abiding in Holy Mother Church, the true vine, which the hand of Our Lord Jesus Christ hath planted. Now this

Jeanne, whom you see before you, falling from error into error, and from crime into crime, hath become separate from the unity of Holy Mother Church and in a thousand manners hath scandalised Christian people.'

Then he reproached her with having failed, with having sinned against royal Majesty and against God and the Catholic Faith; and all these things must she henceforth eschew under pain of death by burning.

He declaimed vehemently against the pride of this woman. He said that never had there appeared in France a monster so great as that which was manifest in Jeanne; that she was a witch, a heretic, a schismatic, and that the king, who protected her, risked the same reproach from the moment that he became willing to recover his throne with the help of such a heretic.

Towards the middle of his sermon, he cried out with a loud voice:

'Ah! right terribly hast thou been deceived, noble house of France, once the most Christian of houses! Charles, who calls himself thy head and assumes the title of king hath, like a heretic and schismatic, received the words of an infamous woman, abounding in evil works and in all dishonour. And not he alone, but all the clergy in his lordship and dominion, by whom this woman, so she sayeth, hath been examined and not rejected. Full sore is the pity of it.'

Two or three times did Maître Guillaume repeat these words concerning King Charles. Then pointing at Jeanne with his finger he said:

'It is to you, Jeanne, that I speak; and I say unto you that your king is a heretic and a schismatic.'

At these words Jeanne was deeply wounded in her love for the Lilies of France and for King Charles. She was moved with great feeling, and she heard her Voices saying unto her:

'Reply boldly to the preacher who is preaching to you.'

Then obeying them heartily, she interrupted Maître Jean:

'By my troth, Messire,' she said to him, 'saving your reverence, I dare say unto you and swear at the risk of my life, that he is the noblest Christian of all Christians, that none loveth better religion and the Church, and that he is not at all what you say.'

Maître Guillaume ordered the Usher, Jean Massieu, to silence her. Then he went on with his sermon, and concluded with these words: 'Jeanne, behold my Lords the Judges, who oftentimes have summoned you and required you to submit all your acts and sayings to Mother Church. In these acts and sayings were many things which, so it seemed to these clerics, were good neither to say nor to maintain.'

'I will answer you,' said Jeanne. Touching the article of submission to the Church, she recalled how she had asked for all the deeds she had wrought and the words she had uttered to be reported to Rome, to Our Holy Father the Pope, to whom, after God, she appealed. Then she added: 'And as for the sayings I have uttered and the deeds I have done, they have all been by God's command.'

She declared that she had not understood that the record of her trial was being sent to Rome to be judged by the Pope.

'I will not have it thus,' she said. 'I know not what you will insert in the record of these proceedings. I demand to be taken to the Pope and questioned by him.'

They urged her to incriminate her king. But they wasted their breath.

'For my deeds and sayings I hold no man responsible, neither my king nor another.'

'Will you abjure all your deeds and sayings? Will you abjure such of your deeds and sayings as have been condemned by the clerks?'

'I appeal to God and to Our Holy Father, the Pope.'

Admonished with yet a third admonition, Jeanne refused to recant. With confidence she awaited the deliverance promised by her Voices, certain that of a sudden there would come men-at-arms from France and that in one great tumult of fighting-men and angels she would be liberated. That was why she had insisted on retaining man's attire.

Two sentences had been prepared: one for the case in which the accused should abjure her error, the other for the case in which she should persevere. By the first there was removed from Jeanne the ban of excommunication. By the second, the tribunal, declaring that it could do nothing more for her, abandoned her to the secular arm. The Lord Bishop had them both with him.

He took the second and began to read …

Meanwhile, as he read, the clerks who were round Jeanne urged her to recant, while there was yet time Maître Nicolas Loiseleur exhorted her to do as he had recommended, and to put on woman's dress.

Maître Guillaume Erard was saying: 'Do as you are advised and you will be delivered from prison.'

Then straightway came the Voices unto her and said: 'Jeanne, passing sore is our pity for you! You must recant what you have said, or we abandon you to secular justice.... Jeanne, do as you are advised. Jeanne, will you bring death upon yourself!'

The sentence was long and the Lord Bishop read slowly:

'We judges, having Christ before our eyes and also the honour of the true faith, in order that our judgment may proceed from the Lord himself, do say and decree that thou hast been a liar, an inventor of revelations and apparitions said to be divine; a deceiver, pernicious, presumptuous, light of faith, rash, superstitious, a soothsayer, a blasphemer against God and his saints. We declare thee to be a contemner of God even in his sacraments, a prevaricator of divine law, of sacred doctrine and of ecclesiastical sanction, seditious, cruel, apostate, schismatic, having committed a thousand errors against religion, and by all these tokens rashly guilty towards God and Holy Church.'

Time was passing. Already the Lord Bishop had uttered the greater part of the sentence. The executioner was there, ready to take off the condemned in his cart.

Then suddenly, with hands clasped, Jeanne cried that she was willing to obey the Church.

The judge paused in the reading of the sentence.

An uproar arose in the crowd, consisting largely of English men-at-arms and officers of King Henry. Ignorant of the customs of the Inquisition, which had not been introduced into their country, these *Godons* could not understand what was going on; all they knew was that the witch was saved. Now they held Jeanne's death to be necessary for the welfare of England; wherefore the unaccountable actions of these doctors and the Lord Bishop threw them into a fury. In their Island witches were not treated thus; no mercy was shown them, and they were burned speedily. Angry murmurs arose; stones were thrown at the registrars of the trial. Maître Pierre Maurice, who was doing his best to strengthen Jeanne in the resolution she had taken, was threatened and the *coués* very nearly made short work with him.

He threatened to suspend the trial.

'I have been insulted,' he said. 'I will proceed no further until honourable amends have been done me.'

In the tumult, Maître Guillaume Erard unfolded a double sheet of paper, and read Jeanne the form of abjuration, written down according to the opinion of the masters. It was no longer than the Lord's Prayer and consisted of six or seven lines of writing. It was in French and began with these words: 'I, Jeanne....' The Maid submitted therein to the sentence, the judgment and the commandment of the Church; she acknowledged having committed the crime of high treason and having deceived the people. She undertook never again to bear arms or to wear man's dress or her hair cut round her ears.

When Maître Guillaume had read the document, Jeanne declared she did not understand it, and wished to be advised thereupon. She was heard to ask counsel of Saint Michael. She still believed firmly in her Voices, albeit they had not aided her in her dire necessity, neither had spared her the shame of denying them. For, simple as she was, at the bottom of her heart she knew well what the clerks were asking of her; she realised that they would not let her go until she had pronounced a great recantation. All that she said was merely in order to gain time and because she was afraid of death; yet she could not bring herself to lie.

Without losing a moment Maître Guillaume said to Messire Jean Massieu, the Usher: 'Advise her touching this abjuration.'

And he passed him the document.

Messire Jean Massieu at first made excuse, but afterwards he complied and warned Jeanne of the danger she was running by her refusal to recant.

'You must know,' he said, 'that if you oppose any of these articles you will be burned. I counsel you to appeal to the Church Universal as to whether you should abjure these articles or not.'

Maître Guillaume Erard asked Jean Massieu: 'Well, what are you saying to her?'

Jean Massieu replied: 'I make known unto Jeanne the text of the deed of abjuration and I urge her to sign it. But she declares that she knoweth not whether she will.'

At this juncture, Jeanne, who was still being pressed to sign, said aloud: 'I wish the Church to deliberate on the articles. I appeal to the Church Universal as to whether I should abjure them. Let the document be read by the Church and the clerks into whose hands I am to be delivered. If it be their counsel that I ought to sign it and do what I am told, then willingly will I do it.'

Maître Guillaume Erard replied: 'Do it now, or you will be burned this very day.'

And he forbade Jean Massieu to confer with her any longer.

Whereupon Jeanne said that she would liefer sign than be burned.

Then straightway Messire Jean Massieu gave her a second reading of the deed of abjuration. And she repeated the words after the Usher. As she spoke her countenance seemed to express a kind of sneer. It may have been that her features were contracted by the violent emotions which swayed her and that the horrors and tortures of an ecclesiastical trial may have overclouded her reason, subject at all times to strange vagaries, and that after such bitter suffering there may have come upon her the actual paroxysm of madness. On the other hand, it may have been that with sound sense and calm mind she was mocking at the clerks of Rouen; she was quite capable of it, for she had mocked at the clerks of Poitiers. At any rate she had a jesting air, and the bystanders noticed that she pronounced the words of her abjuration with a smile. And her gaiety, whether real or apparent, roused the wrath of those burgesses, priests, artisans and men-at-arms who desired her death.

''Tis all a mockery. Jeanne doth but jest,' they cried.

On the platform a chaplain of the Cardinal violently accused the Lord Bishop. 'You do wrong to accept such an abjuration. 'Tis a mere mockery,' he said.

'You lie,' retorted my Lord Pierre. 'I, the judge of a religious suit, ought to seek the salvation of this woman rather than her death.'

The Cardinal silenced his chaplain.

It is said that the Earl of Warwick came up to the judges and complained of what they had done, adding: 'The king is not well served, since Jeanne escapes.'

And it is stated that one of them replied: 'Have no fear, my Lord. She will not escape us long.'

With a pen that Massieu gave her Jeanne made a cross at the bottom of the deed.

In the midst of howls and oaths from the English my Lord of Beauvais read the more merciful of the sentences. It relieved Jeanne from excommunication and reconciled her to Holy Mother Church. Further the sentence ran:

'... Because thou hast rashly sinned against God and Holy Church, we, thy judges, that thou mayest do salutary penance, out of our Grace and moderation, do condemn thee finally and definitely to perpetual prison, with the bread of sorrow and the water of affliction, so that there thou mayest weep over thy offences and commit no other that may be an occasion of weeping.'

This penalty, like all other penalties, save death and mutilation, lay within the power of ecclesiastical judges.

Jeanne, turning towards them, said: 'Now, you Churchmen, take me to your prison. Let me be no longer in the hands of the English.'

The Lord Bishop gave the order: 'Take her back to the place whence you brought her.'

Thereafter, the Vice Inquisitor and with him divers doctors and masters, went to her prison and charitably exhorted her. She promised to wear woman's apparel, and to let her head be shaved.

The Duchess of Bedford, knowing that she was a virgin, saw to it that she was treated with respect. As the ladies of Luxembourg had done formerly, she essayed to persuade her to wear the clothing of her sex. By a certain tailor, one Jeannotin Simon, she had had made for Jeanne a gown which she had hitherto refused to wear. Jeannotin brought the garment to the prisoner, who this time did not refuse it.

Chapter XIV
The Trial for Relapse – Second Sentence – Death of the Maid

ON THE FOLLOWING SUNDAY, which was Trinity Sunday, there arose a rumour that Jeanne had resumed man's apparel. The report spread rapidly from the castle down the narrow streets where lived

the clerks in the shadow of the cathedral. Straightway notaries and assessors hastened to the tower which looked on the fields.

In the outer court of the castle they found some 100 men-at-arms, who welcomed them with threats and curses. These fellows did not yet understand that the judges had conducted the trial so as to bring honour to old England and dishonour to the French. They did not see how great was the advantage to their country when it was published abroad throughout the world that Charles of Valois had been conducted to his coronation by a heretic. But no, the only idea these brutes were capable of grasping was the burning of the girl prisoner who had struck terror into their hearts.

The next day, Monday the 25th, there came to the castle the Vice Inquisitor, accompanied by various doctors and masters. The Registrar, Messire Guillaume Manchon, was summoned. They found Jeanne wearing man's apparel, jerkin and short tunic, with a hood covering her shaved head. Her face was in tears and disfigured by terrible suffering.

She was asked when and why she had assumed this attire.

'I put it on of my own will and without constraint. I had liefer wear man's dress than woman's.'

'Wherefore did you return to it?'

'Because it is more seemly to take it and wear man's dress, being amongst men, than to wear woman's dress.... I returned to it because the promise made me was not kept, to wit, that I should go to mass and should receive my Saviour and be loosed from my bonds.'

'Did you not abjure, and promise not to return to this dress?'

'I had liefer die than be in bonds. But if I be allowed to go to mass and taken out of my bonds and put in a prison of grace, and given a woman to be with me, I will be good and do as the Church shall command.'

Thus spake Jeanne in sore sorrow.

Still the English were seriously to blame for having left her man's clothes. It would have been more humane to have taken them from her, since if she wore them she must needs die. They had taken away all her few possessions, even her poor brass ring, everything save that suit which meant death to her.

On the morrow, Tuesday the 29th, my Lord of Beauvais assembled the tribunal in the chapel of the archbishop's house.

Maître Nicholas de Venderès, canon, archdeacon, was the first to state his opinion.

'Jeanne is and must be held a heretic. She must be delivered to the secular authority.'

The Lord Bishop, having listened to opinions, concluded that Jeanne must be proceeded against as one having relapsed. Accordingly, he summoned her to appear on the morrow, the 30th of May, in the old Market Square.

On the morning of that Wednesday, the 30th of May, by the command of my Lord of Beauvais, the two young friars preachers, bachelors in theology, Brother Martin Ladvenu and Brother Isambart de la Pierre, went to Jeanne in her prison. Brother Martin told her that she was to die that day.

At the approach of this cruel death, amidst the silence of her Voices, she understood at length that she would not be delivered. Cruelly awakened from her dream, she felt heaven and earth failing her, and fell into a deep despair.

While she was lamenting, the doctors and masters entered the prison; they came by order of my Lord of Beauvais. On the previous day 39 counsellors out of 42, declaring that Jeanne had relapsed, had added that they deemed it well she should be reminded of the terms of her abjuration. Wherefore, according to the counsel of these clerics, the Lord Bishop had sent certain learned doctors to the relapsed heretic and had resolved to come to her himself.

She must needs submit to one last examination.

Brother Martin Ladvenu heard Jeanne's confession. Then he sent Messire Massieu, the Usher, to my Lord of Beauvais, to inform him that she asked to be given the body of Jesus Christ.

The bishop assembled certain doctors to confer on this subject; and after they had deliberated, he replied to the Usher: 'Tell Brother Martin to give her the communion and all that she shall ask.'

Contrite and sorrowful she said to Maître Pierre Maurice: 'Maître Pierre, where shall I be this evening?'

'Do you not trust in the Lord?' asked the canon.

'Yea, God helping me, I shall be in Paradise.'

Maître Nicolas Loiseleur exhorted her to correct the error she had caused to grow up among the people.

'To this end you must openly declare that you have been deceived and have deceived the folk and that you humbly ask pardon.'

Then, fearing lest she might forget when the time came for her to be publicly judged, she asked Brother Martin to put her in mind of this matter and of others touching her salvation.

It was about nine o'clock in the morning when Brother Martin and Messire Massieu took Jeanne out of the prison, wherein she had been in bonds 178 days. She was placed in a cart, and, escorted by 80 men-at-arms, was driven along the narrow streets to the Old Market Square, close to the river. On the scaffold Jeanne was to be stationed, there to listen to the sermon. Another and a larger scaffold had been erected adjoining the cemetery. There the judges and the prelates were to sit. The third scaffold, opposite the second, was of plaster, and stood in the middle of the square, on the spot whereon executions usually took place. On it was piled the wood for the burning. On the stake which surmounted it was a scroll bearing the words:

'Jehanne, who hath caused herself to be called the Maid, a liar, pernicious, deceiver of the people, soothsayer, superstitious, a blasphemer against God, presumptuous, miscreant, boaster, idolatress, cruel, dissolute, an invoker of devils, apostate, schismatic and heretic.'

The square was guarded by 160 men-at-arms. A crowd of curious folk pressed behind the guards, the windows were filled and the roofs covered with onlookers. Jeanne was brought on to the scaffold which had its back to the market-house gable. She wore a long gown and hood.

Then my Lord of Beauvais, in his own name and that of the Vice Inquisitor, pronounced the sentence.

He declared Jeanne to be a relapsed heretic.

'We declare that thou, Jeanne, art a corrupt member, and in order that thou mayest not infect the other members, we are resolved to sever thee from the unity of the Church, to tear thee from its body, and to deliver thee to the secular power. And we reject thee, we tear thee out, we abandon thee, beseeching this same secular power, that touching death and the mutilation of the limbs, it may be pleased to moderate its sentence....'

Things had now come to such a pass that had the city of Rouen belonged to King Charles, he himself could not have saved the Maid from the stake.

When the sentence was announced Jeanne breathed heart-rending sighs. Weeping bitterly, she fell on her knees, commended her soul to God, to Our Lady, to the blessed saints of Paradise, many of whom she mentioned by name. Very humbly did she ask for mercy from all manner of folk, of whatsoever rank or condition, of her own party and of the enemy's, entreating them to forgive the wrong she had done them and to pray for her. She asked pardon of her judges, of the English, of King Henry, of the English princes of the realm. Addressing all the priests there present she besought each one to say a mass for the salvation of her soul.

The Bailie, Messire le Bouteiller, who was present, waved his hand and said: 'Take her, take her.' Straightway, two of the king's sergeants dragged her to the base of the scaffold and placed her in a cart which was waiting. On her head was set a great fool's cap made of paper, on which were written the words: *'Hérétique, relapse, apostate, idolâtre'*; and she was handed over to the executioner.

The two young friars preachers and the Usher Massieu accompanied Jeanne to the stake.

She asked for a cross. An Englishman made a tiny one out of two pieces of wood, and gave it to her. She took it devoutly and put it in her bosom, on her breast. Then she besought Brother Isambart to go to the neighbouring church to fetch a cross, to bring it to her and hold it before her, so that as long as she lived, the cross on which God was crucified should be ever in her sight.

Massieu asked a priest of Saint-Sauveur for one, and it was brought. Jeanne weeping kissed it long and tenderly, and her hands held it while they were free.

When she saw a light put to the stake, she cried loudly, 'Jesus!' This name she repeated six times. She was also heard asking for holy water.

It was usual for the executioner, in order to cut short the sufferings of the victim, to stifle him in dense smoke before the flames had had time to ascend; but the Rouen executioner was too terrified of the prodigies worked by the Maid to do thus; and besides he would have found it difficult to reach her, because the Bailie had had the plaster scaffold made unusually high. Wherefore the executioner himself, hardened man that he was, judged her death to have been a terribly cruel one.

Once again Jeanne uttered the name of Jesus; then she bowed her head and gave up her spirit.

As soon as she was dead the Bailie commanded the executioner to scatter the flames in order to see that the prophetess of the Armagnacs had not escaped with the aid of the devil or in some other manner. Then, after the poor blackened body had been shown to the people, the executioner, in order to reduce it to ashes, threw on to the fire coal, oil and sulphur.

In such an execution the combustion of the corpse was rarely complete. Among the ashes, when the fire was extinguished, the heart and entrails were found intact. For fear lest Jeanne's remains should be taken and used for witchcraft or other evil practices, the Bailie had them thrown into the Seine.

Chapter XV
After the Death of the Maid – The End of the Shepherd – La Dame Des Armoises

✣

THE WAR CONTINUED. Twenty days after Jeanne's death the English in great force marched to recapture the town of Louviers. They had delayed till then, not, as some have stated, because they despaired of succeeding in anything as long as the Maid lived, but because they needed time to collect money and engines for the siege. In the July and August of this same year, at Senlis and at Beauvais, my Lord of Reims, Chancellor of France and the Maréchal de Boussac, were upholding the French cause. And we may be sure that my Lord of Reims was upholding it with no little vigour since at the same time he was defending the benefices which were so dear to him.

In 1433, the constable, with the assistance of the Queen of Sicily, caused the capture and planned the assassination of La Trémouille. It was the custom of the nobles of that day to appoint counsellors for King Charles and afterwards to kill them. However, the sword which was to have caused the death of La Trémouille, owing to his corpulence, failed to inflict a mortal wound. His life was saved, but his influence was dead. King Charles tolerated the constable as he had tolerated the Sire de la Trémouille.

The latter left behind him the reputation of having been grasping and indifferent to the welfare of the kingdom. Perhaps his greatest fault was that he governed in a time of war and pillage, when friends and foes alike were devouring the realm. He was charged with the destruction of the Maid, of whom he was said to have been jealous. This accusation proceeds from the House of Alençon, with whom the Lord Chamberlain was not popular. On the contrary, it must be admitted, that after the Lord Chancellor, La Trémouille was the boldest in employing the Maid, and if later she did thwart his plans there is nothing to prove that it was his intention to have her destroyed by the English. She destroyed herself and was consumed by her own zeal.

Now, one month after Paris had returned to her allegiance to King Charles, there appeared in Lorraine a certain damsel. She was about 25 years old. Hitherto she had been called Claude; but she now made herself known to various lords of the town of Metz as being Jeanne the Maid.

At this time, Jeanne's father and eldest brother were dead. Isabelle Romée was alive. Her two youngest sons were in the service of the King of France, who had raised them to the rank of nobility and given them the name of Du Lys. Jean, the eldest, called Petit-Jean, had been appointed Bailie of Vermandois, then Captain of Chartres. About this year, 1436, he was provost and captain of Vaucouleurs.

The youngest, Pierre, or Pierrelot, who had fallen into the hands of the Burgundians before Compiègne at the same time as Jeanne, had just been liberated from the prison of the Bastard of Vergy.

Both brothers believed that their sister had been burned at Rouen. But when they were told that she was living and wished to see them, they appointed a meeting at La-Grange-aux-Ormes, a village in the meadows of the Sablon, between the Seille and the Moselle, about four kilometres (two and a half miles) south of Metz. They reached this place on the 20th of May. There they saw her and recognized her immediately to be their sister; and she recognized them to be her brothers.

She was accompanied by certain lords of Metz, among whom was a man right noble, Messire Nicole Lowe, who was chamberlain to Charles VII. By divers tokens these nobles recognized her to be the Maid Jeanne who had taken King Charles to be crowned at Reims. These tokens were certain signs on the skin. Now there was a prophecy concerning Jeanne which stated her to have a little red mark beneath the ear. But this prophecy was invented after the events to which it referred. Consequently, we may believe the Maid to have been thus marked. Was this the token by which the nobles of Metz recognized her?

We do not know by what means she claimed to have escaped death; but there is reason to think that she attributed her deliverance to her holiness. Did she say that an angel had saved her from the fire? It might be read in books how, in the ancient amphitheatres, lions licked the bare feet of virgins, how boiling oil was as soothing as balm to the bodies of holy martyrs; and how according to many of the old stories nothing short of the sword could take the life of God's maidens. These ancient histories rested on a sure foundation. But if such tales had been related of the fifteenth century, they might have appeared less credible. And this damsel does not seem to have employed them to adorn her adventure. She was probably content to say that another woman had been burned in her place.

According to a confession she made afterwards, she came from Rome, where, accoutred in harness of war, she had fought valiantly in the service of Pope Eugenius. She may even have told the Lorrainers of the feats of prowess she had there accomplished.

Messire Nicole Lowe gave her a charger and a pair of hose. The charger was worth 30 francs – a sum wellnigh royal – for of the two horses which at Soissons and at Senlis the king gave the Maid Jeanne, one was worth 38 livres 10 sous, and the other 37 livres 10 sous. Not more than 16 francs had been paid for the horse with which she had been provided at Vaucouleurs.

She rode her horse with the same skill which seven years earlier, if we may believe some rather mythical stories, had filled with wonder the old Duke of Lorraine. And she spoke certain words to Messire Nicole Lowe which confirmed him in his belief that she was indeed that same Maid Jeanne who had fared forth into France. She had the ready tongue of a prophetess, and spoke in symbols and parables, revealing nought of her intent.

Her power would not come to her before Saint John the Baptist's Day, she said. Now this was the very time which the Maid, after the Battle of Patay, in 1429, had fixed for the extermination of the English in France.

This prophecy had not been fulfilled and consequently had not been mentioned again. Jeanne, if she ever uttered it, and it is quite possible that she did, must have been the first to forget it. Moreover, Saint John's Day was a term commonly cited in leases, fairs, contracts, hirings, etc., and it is quite conceivable that the calendar of a prophetess may have been the same as that of a labourer.

The day after their arrival at La Grange-aux-Ormes, Monday, the 21st of May, the Du Lys brothers took her, whom they held to be their sister, to that town of Vaucouleurs whither Isabelle Romée's daughter had gone to see Sire Robert de Baudricourt. In this town, in the year 1436, there were still living many persons of different conditions, such as the Leroyer couple and the Seigneur Aubert d'Ourches, who had seen Jeanne in February 1429.

After a week at Vaucouleurs she went to Marville, a small town between Corny and Pont-à-Mousson. There she spent Whitsuntide and abode for three weeks in the house of one Jean Quenat. On her departure she was visited by sundry inhabitants of Metz, who gave her jewels, recognising her to be the Maid of France. Jeanne, it will be remembered, had been seen by various knights of Metz at the time of King Charles's coronation at Reims. At Marville, Geoffroy Desch, following the example of Nicole Lowe, presented the so-called Jeanne with a horse. Geoffroy Desch belonged to one of the most influential families of the Republic of Metz.

From Marville, she went on a pilgrimage to Notre Dame de Liance. At Liance was worshipped a black image of the Virgin, which, according to tradition, had been brought by the crusaders from the Holy Land.

For the generality of men, Jeanne's life and death were surrounded by marvels and mysteries. Many had from the first doubted her having perished by the hand of the executioner. Certain were curiously reticent on this point; they said: 'the English had her publicly burnt at Rouen, or some other woman like her.' Others confessed that they did not know what had become of her.

Thus, when throughout Germany and France the rumour spread that the Maid was alive and had been seen near Metz, the tidings were variously received. Some believed them, others did not. An ardent dispute, which arose between two citizens of Arles, gives some idea of the emotion aroused by such tidings. One maintained that the Maid was still alive; the other asserted that she was dead; each one wagered that what he said was true. This was no light wager, for it was made and registered in the presence of a notary.

Meanwhile, in the beginning of August, the Maid's eldest brother, Jean du Lys, called Petit-Jean, had gone to Orléans to announce that his sister was alive. As a reward for these good tidings, he received for himself and his followers 10 pints of wine, 12 hens, two goslings and two leverets.

Messengers were passing to and fro between the town of Duke Charles and the town of the Duchess of Luxembourg. On the 9th of August a letter from Arlon reached Orléans. About the middle of the month a pursuivant arrived at Arlon. The magistrates of Orléans had sent him to Jeanne with a letter, the contents of which are unknown. Jeanne gave him a letter for the king, in which she probably requested an audience.

Jean du Lys proceeded just as if his miracle-working sister had in very deed been restored to him. He went to the king, to whom he announced the wonderful tidings. Charles cannot have entirely disbelieved them since he ordered Jean du Lys to be given a gratuity of 100 francs. Whereupon Jean promptly demanded 300 francs from the king's treasurer, who gave him 20.

Having returned to Orléans, Jean appeared before the town council. He gave the magistrates to wit that he had only eight francs, a sum by no means sufficient to enable him and four retainers to return to Lorraine. The magistrates gave him 12 francs.

While these things were occurring in France, Jeanne was still with the Duchess of Luxembourg. There she met the young Count Ulrich of Wurtemberg, who refused to leave her. He had a handsome cuirasse made for her and took her to Cologne. She still called herself the Maid of France sent by God.

Since the 24th of June, Saint John the Baptist's Day, her power had returned to her. Count Ulrich, recognising her supernatural gifts, entreated her to employ them on behalf of himself and his friends. Being very contentious, he had become seriously involved in the schism which was then rending asunder the diocese of Trèves.

Count Ulrich of Wurtemberg questioned the Maid of God concerning him. The second Jeanne replied with even more assurance; she declared that she knew who was the true archbishop and boasted that she would enthrone him.

Unfortunately, the Maid's intervention in this dispute attracted the attention of the Inquisitor General of the city of Cologne, Heinrich Kalt Eysen, an illustrious professor of theology. He inquired into the rumours which were being circulated in the city touching the young prince's protégée; and he learnt that she wore unseemly apparel, danced with men, ate and drank more than she ought, and practised magic. He was informed notably that in a certain assembly the Maid tore a tablecloth and straightway restored it to its original condition, and that having broken a glass against the wall she with marvellous skill put all its pieces together again. Such deeds caused Kalt Eysen to suspect her strongly of heresy and witchcraft. He summoned her before his tribunal; she refused to appear. This disobedience displeased the Inquisitor General, and he sent to fetch the defaulter. But the young Count of Wurtemberg hid his Maid in his house, and afterwards contrived to get her secretly out of the town. Thus she escaped the fate of her whom she was willing only partially to imitate. As he could do nothing else, the Inquisitor excommunicated her. She took refuge at Arlon with her protectress, the Duchess of Luxembourg. There she met Robert des Armoises, Lord of Tichemont. She may have seen him before, in the spring, at Marville, where he usually resided. Nothing is known of him, save that he surrendered this territory to the foreigner without the Duke of Bar's consent, and then beheld it confiscated and granted to the Lord of Apremont on condition that he should conquer it.

The so-called Maid married him apparently with the approval of the Duchess of Luxembourg. According to the opinion of the Holy Inquisitor of Cologne, this marriage was contracted merely to protect the woman against the interdict and to save her from the sword of the Church.

If the folk of Orléans did actually take her for the real Maid, Jeanne, then it must have been more on account of the evidence of the Du Lys brothers, than on that of their own eyes. For, when one comes to think of it, they had seen her but very seldom. During that week in May, she had only appeared before them armed and on horseback. Afterwards, in June

1429 and January 1430, she had merely passed through the town. True it was she had been offered wine and the magistrates had sat at table with her; but that was nine years ago. And the lapse of nine years works many a change in a woman's face. They had seen her last as a young girl, now they found her a woman and the mother of two children. Moreover, they were guided by the opinion of her kinsfolk. Their attitude provokes some astonishment, however, when one thinks of the conversation at the banquet, and of the awkward and inconsistent remarks the dame must have uttered. If they were not then undeceived, these burgesses must have been passing simple and strongly prejudiced in favour of their guest.

Later she was examined, tried and sentenced to be publicly exhibited. The usual sermon was preached at her and she was forced to confess publicly.

She declared that she was not the Maid, that she was married to a knight and had two sons.

The success of this fraud had endured four years. But folk would not have been imposed upon so long by this pseudo-Jeanne had it not been for the support given her by the Du Lys brothers. Were they her dupes or her accomplices? Dull-witted as they may have been, it seems hardly credible that the adventuress could have imposed upon them.

Chapter XVI
The Pragmatic Sanction – The Rehabilitation Trial – The Maid of Sarmaize – The Maid of Le Mans

KING CHARLES, BECOME RICH and victorious, now desired to efface the stain inflicted on his reputation by the sentence of 1431. He wanted to prove to the whole world that it was no witch who had conducted him to his coronation. He was now eager to appeal against the condemnation of the Maid. But this condemnation had been pronounced by the church, and the Pope alone could order it to be cancelled.

In the March of 1450, he proceeded to a preliminary inquiry and matters remained in that position until the arrival in France of Cardinal d'Estouteville, the legate of the Holy See. Cardinal d'Estouteville, who belonged to a Norman family, was just the man to discover the weak points in Jeanne's trial. In order to curry favour with Charles, he, as legate, set on foot a new inquiry at Rouen, with the assistance of Jean Bréhal, of the order of preaching friars, the Inquisitor of the Faith in the kingdom of France. But the Pope did not approve of the legate's intervention; and for three years the revision was not proceeded with. Nicolas V would not allow it to be thought that the sacred tribunal of the most holy Inquisition was fallible and had even once pronounced an unjust sentence. And there existed at Rome a stronger reason for not interfering with the trial of 1431: the French demanded revision; the English were opposed to it; and the Pope did not wish to annoy the English, for they were then just as good and even better Catholics than the French.

In order to relieve the Pope from embarrassment and set him at his ease, the government of Charles VII invented an expedient: the king was not to appear in the suit; his place was to be taken by the family of the Maid. Jeanne's mother, Isabelle Romée de Vouthon, who lived in retirement at Orléans, and her two sons, Pierre and Jean du Lys, demanded the revision. By this legal artifice the case was converted from a political into a private suit. At this juncture Nicolas V died, on the 24th of March, 1455. His successor, Calixtus III, a Borgia, an old man of 78, by a rescript dated the 11th of June, 1455, authorised the institution of proceedings. To this end he appointed Jean Jouvenel des Ursins, Archbishop of Reims, Guillaume Chartier, Bishop of Paris and Richard Olivier, Bishop of Coutances, who were to act conjointly with the Grand Inquisitor of France.

On the 7th of November, 1455, Isabelle Romée and her two sons, followed by a long procession of innumerable ecclesiastics, laymen and worthy women, approached the church of Notre Dame in Paris to demand justice from the prelates and papal commissioners.

Informers and accusers in the trial of the late Jeanne were summoned to appear at Rouen on the 12th of December. Not one came. The heirs of the late Messire Pierre Cauchon declined all liability for the deeds of their deceased kinsman, and touching the civil responsibility, they pleaded the amnesty granted by the king on the reconquest of Normandy. As had been expected, the proceedings went forward without any obstacle or even any discussion.

Care was taken not to summon the Lord Archbishop of Rouen, Messire Raoul Roussel, as a witness of the actual incidents of the trial, albeit he had sat in judgment on the Maid, side by side with my Lord of Beauvais. The most illustrious Thomas de Courcelles, who, after having been the most laborious and assiduous collaborator of the Bishop of Beauvais, recalled nothing when he came before the commissioners for the revision.

Among those who had been most zealous to procure Jeanne's condemnation were those who were now most eagerly labouring for her rehabilitation.

Huge piles of memoranda drawn up by doctors of high repute, canonists, theologians and jurists, both French and foreign, were furnished for the trial. Their chief object was to establish by scholastic reasoning that Jeanne had submitted her deeds and sayings to the judgment of the Church and of the Holy Father. These doctors proved that the judges of 1431 had been very subtle and Jeanne very simple. Doubtless, it was the best way to make out that she had submitted to the Church; but they over-reached themselves and made her too simple.

But there was another reason for making her appear as weak and imbecile as possible. Such a representation exalted the power of God, who through her had restored the King of France to his inheritance.

On the 16th of June, 1455, the sentence of 1431 was declared unjust, unfounded, iniquitous. It was nullified and pronounced invalid.

On Wednesday, the 22nd of July, 1461, covered with ulcers internal and external, believing himself poisoned and perhaps not without reason, Charles VII died, in the 59th year of his age.

On Thursday, the 6th of August, his body was borne to the Church of Saint-Denys in France and placed in a chapel hung with velvet; the nave was draped with black satin, the vault was covered with blue cloth embroidered with flowers-de-luce. During the ceremony, which took place on the following day, a funeral oration was delivered on Charles VII. The preacher was no less a personage than the most highly renowned professor at the University of Paris, the doctor, who according to the Princes of the Roman Church was ever aimable and modest, he who had been the stoutest defender of the liberties of the Gallican Church, the ecclesiastic who, having declined a Cardinal's hat, bore to the threshold of an illustrious old age none other title than that of Dean of the Canons of Notre Dame de Paris, Maître Thomas de Courcelles. Thus it befell that the assessor of Rouen, who had been the most bitterly bent on procuring Jeanne's cruel condemnation, celebrated the memory of the victorious king whom the Maid had conducted to his solemn coronation.

FLAME TREE PUBLISHING